Imperial Raider

Imperial Raider

Andrew Moriarty

ISBN 978-1-956556-26-1

This is a work of fiction.

Special thanks to my dedicated team of beta readers – A J, Adam G, Aleeta, Alex, Barbara M, Bryan, Christopher G, Daniel C, Danny H, Dave M#1, Dave W, David H, David M#2, Djuro D, Elizabeth S, Greg D, Haydn H, James A, Jim C, John E, John S, Jolayne W, Justin H, Keith C, Kent P, Lorna R, Mark H, Michael G, Michael R, Nathan T, Penny L, Peter B, Ralph J, Ryan P, Scott, Skip C, Susan G, Tigui, Vince, and to my editor Beth Lynne.

Chapter 1

"Emergence," Lieutenant Villa, the Pollux's Navigator, announced. "Target, planet Gandy, dead ahead. In position and on course."

Prefect Lionel lounged in the captain's chair. Twelve consoles formed a semi-circle between him and the main display. He used his own display to mirror the output of each. No red warnings. "Very well. Villa, any beacons?"

"Us and the planet so far sir."

"Our friends?"

"Not yet sir."

"Very well. Trevor. Take us in."

Trevor, the helmsman, nodded. "Understood." A blue-white marble filled the main screen as Trevor overlaid course plots on it. The *Pollux's* bridge was only half manned. Villa the Navigator and Trevor the Helmsman were doing double duty, covering the sensor and comm channels. Midshipman Rudnar, a competent, tanned brunette, mirrored navigation. Calroy, son of a countess, mirrored the helm. All other positions, except weapons, were empty.

"Acceleration, now." Trevor hammered his controls. Acceleration alarms bonged. The *Pollux* surged forward, racing to the planet. G forces pushed Lionel back into his chair, and locked his hands by his side. He swallowed his gorge. *But for once, it's regular accel, not stomach-emptying corkscrewing. Could be much, much worse.*

"Status change," Villa said. "Jump emergence. Beacon. Two beacons—multiple beacons."

"Whose?" Lionel asked.

Villa took five seconds to swap between sensor and comm settings. The shortage of experienced officers was already affecting combat efficiency. "Imperial beacons. *Valhalla*, *Hydrogen Queen*, *Moose Jaw*.*"

"Very well. Continue vector. Rudnar, you're supposed to observe and learn. Why do I see your hands moving?"

Midshipman Rudnar jerked her hands back from her board and laid them on the at-rest pads. "Yes sir. Sorry sir."

"We're all a little tense right now, so let's keep it to militarily necessary actions." Lionel frowned. "What were you doing anyway?"

"Calculating a course sir."

"A course? A course where?"

Rudnar grimaced at the video pickup on her board. At action stations, she kept herself strapped into her chair, in case the *Pollux* had to maneuver.

"To the jump limit sir."

"Why would we need a course to the jump limit?"

"If those beacons were hostile sir, and if there were three of them, doctrine is to flee. I've started a sub-routine to give us a course to the jump limit, avoiding weapons range of those potential hostiles."

"Those three friendly beacons?"

"We didn't know they were friendly when they arrived sir."

"You knew they were coming, those three ships. Bit of a waste of time, isn't it?"

"Lieutenant Villa had to challenge them sir. They're not friendly 'til they answer the challenge. And if they didn't answer the challenge, then we'd have a course that much sooner."

Lionel blinked. "Absolutely true. Cancel my last. Calculate whatever courses you think appropriate for the duration of this engagement. Carry on."

"Sir."

"Calroy." Lionel brought up a private channel. "What about you?"

"Me sir?"

"Yes, you sir. What do you have to say for yourself."

Calroy shook his head. "Nothing sir. I'm watching the helmsman maneuver."

Lionel waited for more. There wasn't any. More useless ignorant privileged children. *We should ban noble families from the Navy.* "Very well. Keep your hands where we can see them." He surveyed the bridge. The only other person on the bridge was Bosun McSanchez, sitting at the weapons console. Even the duty Marine that normally guarded the door was gone. "Bosun?"

"Prefect?"

"Comments?"

"That's the biggest storm I've ever seen sir." McSanchez pointed at the planetary display at the front of the compartment. "Covers the whole southern hemisphere, looks like. Computer says winds of two hundred kilometers per hour. And it's huge. It would bang a battleship sideways."

"Explains why nobody lives on those coasts."

"Dismal place."

Planet Gandy had a population in the low millions, centered around a land-locked sea on the northern continent. High solar output produced giant hurricanes that slammed into every ocean coast. An axial tilt of thirty-seven degrees steamed the tropics during the summer, and froze the northern latitudes in the winter.

Lionel brought up a screen and scanned it. Nothing of interest, but since this was the Imperial Navy, everything had to be done twice. At least twice. "Sensors, report."

"Sir," Villa said. "No ships other than the task force. No orbital stations. Three communication satellites in equatorial geosynchronous orbit. Two more in modified Molniya orbits over the northern habitation area. Standard Imperial D73 class colony orbital packages. Communication, navigation, weather, and planetary monitoring. No other space-based assets. No indications of any weapons."

"Helm, drop to one-G." The pile-of-rocks feeling on Lionel's chest disappeared. "Comm, release the task force. Rudnar, still have a course to the jump limit?"

Midshipman Rudnar nodded, then flicked her camera on and nodded again. "Yes sir."

"Load it up for the helm, then. Helm, follow Rudnar's course out to the jump limit then assume standard military orbit. Keep us outside of the jump limit in case we have to go, but close enough that we can provide orbital fire support to the landing. And keep us in comms with the *Valhalla* and the *Hydrogen Queen*."

"Yes sir." Trevor smiled. "Shall I calculate that orbit myself, Prefect?"

Lionel shook his head. "Rudnar will have one ready for you by the time you're there, won't you, Rudnar."

Rudnar's eyes widened, but she gave the only permissible answer. "Sir, yes sir!"

"Carry on everyone." Lionel leaned back and put the task force up on the screen. The tanker *Hydrogen Queen* and its escorting corvette loitered outside the jump limit, ready to retreat if threatened. The Marine assault carrier, the *Valhalla*, powered in and dove for the planet, passing behind and below the *Pollux*. Lionel worried they were going too fast to pull out of the orbit. *But if I call those boneheads and ask that, they'll go faster just to 'show those Navy pukes a thing or two'.* Lionel watched the assault carrier's course angle farther in, insanely farther. *Brave boneheads, though. The Empire is lucky to have them.*

"Sir?" Bosun McSanchez flashed a private channel request. Lionel brought up a link. "Yes, Bosun?"

"Sir, I'm just a simple bosun and all, not an officer and not with all your experience in space combat and that—"

"Didn't you take command of some destroyer when the forward weapons bay exploded and killed the command staff?"

"It was a very small destroyer sir, hardly worth the name."

"And brought it back safely?"

"Just a matter of letting the computers do the work sir."

"Two jumps and a gravity slingshot?"

"Short jumps sir. And not much of a slingshot." McSanchez coughed. "In any event sir, the task you've set young Midshipman Rudnar to—"

"Is impossible, I know. Stay outside the jump limit. Stay over the landing zone, and also act as a commo relay. Can do two of the three. Not all three. Let's see if she figures it out."

"Very good sir."

"Think you could make that work, Bosun?"

"Probably sir."

"How would you feel if you became an officer, McSanchez?"

"How would you feel if a disgruntled crew member shot you in the kneecap sir?"

Lionel laughed. "Bosun, are you threatening me?"

"You started it sir."

Lionel laughed harder, then brought the sensor screens up again. "Sensors?"

"No change. *Valhalla* is releasing her landing boats."

"Very well. Put the feed from the landing boats up on the screen."

"Unable, sir. *Valhalla* has embargoed her landing boat feeds, claiming tactical necessity."

"She has, has she? Get Brigadier Santana on the comm, then."

Brigadier Santana did not answer his comm, for the excellent reason that he was strapped into the *Valhalla's* fourth landing boat, separating and diving for the planet's surface.

"Maneuvering. Hang tight," the landing boat's pilot said over the intercom.

The landing boat pitched 180 degrees and shoved Santana onto his restraints. Then the main drive fired, dropping them slower and lower. Santana slammed back into his seat.

After forty-seven seconds, the engines stopped, and the boat pivoted back bow-forward. Bright yellow light streamed in from the rear viewport. The landing boat vibrated. The yellow changed to light orange.

"Magnetics," the pilot said on the intercom.

Santana tensed, gritted his teeth and opened his lips. He hated the magnetics. A thousand bees climbed over his arms as the fields loaded up. The walls thrummed and growled—the superheated air flashed to a plasma as the pilots used the magnetic fields to steer them in a series of S-turns. At this velocity, wings or canards would have melted off. Only the magnetic fields allowed them to retain control.

The thrumming got worse. The air heated and the smell of burning metal filled Santana's nostrils. The engineers said that no metal burned, that the smell was all in his head. Santana disagreed.

"Feet dry."

Santana punched up their course on his handheld comm, showing the four boats in staggered formation crossing the southern landmass. The position indicators blinked orange—only inertial measurements were possible. There was too much interference to correct via radio.

"Feet wet. Crossing the equator northbound. Terminator ahead."

The outer glow burned red now, and they continued to swoop side to side. Anybody watching below in the dark would have seen four fire-red streaks moving north across the sky. The outer red light lightened as they passed into the sunlight.

"Off magnetics in ten seconds." The pilot flashed the cabin warning lights. "Brace. Brace. Brace."

Santana pocketed his comm and grasped his seat arms as tightly as he could, and counted down. On one, the landing boat's engine engaged, then it slammed back as it rammed its own shockwave. The turbulence increased, the walls banged, and the outer lights dimmed to orange. They now skidded rather than turned. Santana waited two beats for the radios to synchronize, striving to not be slammed sideways. A bong rang in his ear.

"Santana. Status?"

"All boats nominal," his operations officer back on the *Valhalla* yelled. Even with the volume on high, if the Marines wanted to be heard over the landing noises, they needed to shout. "Navy says no opposition."

"You believe them?"

"Never."

Santana laughed.

"Feet dry. Two minutes to dirt," the pilot yelled.

Santana sat stolidly as the bucking lessened. The first boats would be nearly down now. His Marines were not going to let him land first. *Wonder what their excuse would be this time?* Previous attempts to join the first landing wave led to strange mechanical failures that somehow didn't impede the mission, but required all the others to ground ahead of him. He'd given up.

"Thirty seconds."

Green flashed outside the back port. Their landing zone was forest and grassland to the south of a mid-sized town. They'd be on the ground any—

WHAM

They skidded right, left, then crunched to a stop. The pilot quick-released the restraint belts, and the two side and one rear ramps flattened down. Or tried. The port one stuck a third of the way open. The lead Marine kicked it three times, then swore and yelled at his comrades. They raced to the other ramps.

Santana stood and joined the group debouching from the starboard side, and jogged down the ramp, two Marine escorts following. The heat of the re-entry flowed from the hull. He kept running across a field and stopped in a small copse of trees. For once, he wasn't an hour behind the lead groups—the other ships hadn't managed to hit more than twenty seconds ahead of him. Squads of Marines fanned out ahead of the four landing boats, chasing into the town ahead and running to a beach visible downslope.

Santana inspected the battle space. Other than some crushed trees and dead cows, the landing field was empty. *Those sneaky bastards are out there somewhere, but where?*

Seeing no threats, he moved to follow the lead Marines. His two escorts dashed ahead and assumed point.

"You don't have to wait for me, Wallams, Sigurd," Santana called. "Go join the others."

"Yes sir. Sorry sir. Gunnery sergeant said we were to stay with you."

"Don't you think I outrank the gunny, Sigurd?"

"Of course sir." Sigurd didn't bother arguing. He didn't leave either.

Santana caught a rust-red on the label of Sigurd's magazine. "Marine, do you have live rounds loaded?"

"Yes sir. Issued personal from the gunnery sergeant. He said your guards should be well-armed. Sir."

"I don't remember authorizing that."

"Yes sir. Have to ask the gunny sir. Only rounds I have now."

Santana shook his head and marched into the town. It was called Darfinkle, a port on the interior sea. The main port rail station lay downhill from the landing field.

Santana listened on his comm as his troops swept through the town. *No opposition. Strange.* His escort leading, he strode down the steep hill, crossed the tracks and headed into the seaport area.

The planet's only railway ran along the shore of a giant lake almost due north-south, connecting seven towns on the west side. Freighters and ferries served the eastern side. An Imperial Shuttle sat next to the ferry dock, above the high water-line. The charging Marines ignored it as they dashed into the town. Santana arrowed toward it.

He walked up to the shuttle, got directions from the crew, then climbed a stairway next to a sign advertising lake excursion ticket prices. At the northern end of the ticket building was a restaurant with a terrace overlooking the lake. Three-thousand-meter-high mountains stretched to the west and north, with a rocky peninsula shielding the bay to the northeast. Six metal-framed wooden covered piers jutted out into the bay. Rail lines ran onto four of them, and container cranes graced two of those.

A robed man drinking wine at the table with the best view waved him over.

"Outstanding view," Tribune Devin said. "Please be seated, Brigadier. Forgive me not rising, but I've just had the most incredible lunch and I'm feeling bigger than a Beefalo. Do you like seafood chowder?"

"Fresh seafood? Of course." Santana sat.

"You'll love the chowder, Santana. They use corn instead of potatoes."

"I've had corn chowder."

"Not like this." Devin waved a hovering waiter over. "Chowder for everyone, please. My friend and his companions. And wine as well. The white."

"Those Marines are working, Tribune."

"Very well. No wine for them. But bring us the bottle. We'll be here a while."

Santana held up a hand. "Serve them first. No food for me until they are fed. Troops eat first."

The waiter left. Devin raised his eyebrows. "Troops eat first?"

"And officers second. It's our way. I should really be waiting 'til the town is secure, but it seems like the exercise is going well. Suspiciously well, in fact. No casualties, and no opposition."

"No opposition? Hardly a fair test, then."

"I'm concerned about that. You promised to provide opposition."

"I did, didn't I."

The waiter dropped plates on the troopers table, then brought a white chowder for Santana, and a fresh wine bottle for Devin.

Santana took a spoonful. "It's sweet!"

Devin nodded. "It's a sweet corn, but they still make it creamy." He poured wine for both. "The contrast between the salty seafood and the sweet corn is magnificent. And the wine cuts the sweetness."

"It's an outstanding meal." Voices crackled over Santana's comm. He answered two questions, then returned to his plate. "Still no opposition, Tribune. And the sensor ghosts that we saw from orbit have disappeared. The jamming is off too."

"Outstanding. How did you accomplish that?"

"I'm guessing that the naval officers you assigned to the ground forces have been using naval class stealth drones hidden in town somewhere."

"Aha. That's why Imin wanted the bridge crew." Devin nodded. "Needed them to operate the drones."

"They could have abandoned them before the bombardment started."

Devin frowned. "You said that you could seize an inhabited town without a bombardment."

"No, I said I'd try my best, without spending the lives of my Marines."

"You understand my position?"

"Yes. We can't go destroying every Imperial planet that doesn't roll over for us. But..."

"I can't bombard inhabited targets."

"And I have a limited number of landing boats, and Marines, and the only way to protect them is to have a secure landing zone. That's why we have orbital bombardments."

Devin sipped his wine. "I want this test to succeed."

"I do too. But without opposition, without a red force, this isn't real. We're not learning anything. Your people should be shooting back."

"Yes, they should. I'm surprised that they haven't yet."

"Surprised? You're in charge of this."

Devin drank more wine. "I don't know everything. I assign good people, like yourself, and give them free rein. I don't know what's supposed to happen here any more than you do. I told my planning staff to arrange a way to defend the town and defeat the attackers, while minimizing damage. Think outside the box, all that."

"That's all you told them?"

"That and I expected a fantastic lunch while I was watching the exercise unfold. Which reminds me." Devin waved the waiter over again and ordered two of the 'special' steaks.

"Special?"

"Butchered this morning. Top notch local beef. And a pepper sauce! They grow pepper here. Costs a fortune, but there's enough for everybody. You, me, all the ground crew. And the planning staff."

"How big is the planning staff?"

"One."

"One person? There's one person on your planning staff?"

"One very good person."

"As the Tribune says." Santana shoved his empty chowder bowl to the side. The waiter removed it, then brought out new cutlery.

Devin's comm burped. He tapped received. "A communication for you, Brigadier."

Santana already had his comm in his hand. He paged through a screen then brought up a call. The heavy encryption garbled the voice on the far end, and he had to strain to hear what was being said. "Complete? Confirm all objectives? Yes. Very well. Continue." Santana sat the comm on the table and glared at Devin.

"Yes, Brigadier?" Devin poured them both wine. "You have a question?"

"My troops say they have achieved all their objectives. No casualties, no opposition. No problems. Easy peasy."

"Outstanding job, Brigadier. Your troops are to be congratulated." Devin rubbed his hands. "And here it is."

The waiter's platter overflowed with steaming, juicy steaks. He forked two apiece out for Devin and Santana, then withdrew.

Santana grasped his cutlery, then held up his knife. "This isn't a steak knife. It's not sharp enough."

"My steward Imin says that's all you'll need, a butter knife. The steak is so tender, you can cut it with anything, fork, knife, whatever. He arranged to have the steak tenderized before it was brought out."

"Smart man."

"It's one of his favorite sayings. 'Don't let the tools define the job, let the job define the tools.' I agree."

Santana took a bite. "This is amazing. Absolutely amazing."

"Yes, Imin showed them how to cook it earlier. To make sure they had it right."

"Where is Imin?"

Devin shrugged. "Don't know. In town somewhere."

Santana swallowed his bite. "In town? Doing what?"

"Defending it. He's the defense force. He was the planning force as well."

"Your steward is in sole charge of defending the entire planet against Marine occupation?"

"Well." Devin brandished his piece of steak. "Nobody expects me to do it. I'm just a rebel Tribune and dilettante fake naval officer, that's the rumor. Not suitable for defending a vineyard, according to my critics."

Santana cut another piece and chewed. "But the exercise is over. It was a success for the Marines."

"Is it over already?" Devin cut another piece of steak. "Ummmm." He swallowed. "What's the official end time?"

Santana finished chewing. "Well, when we return to the ship…"

Devin pushed the last of his steak into his mouth and swallowed. "Amazing. He's such an artiste. I wonder what's for dessert?"

Santana crossed his knife and fork on his plate. "Tribune, where did this steak come from?"

"Imin arranged it. He bought some cows and had them brought into town, then had them slaughtered for fresh meat."

"Slaughtered?"

"You know, killed? Then cooked."

Santana grabbed a napkin and stood, dabbing his mouth. "Killed? Cooked?"

"Yes. To be eaten."

"And then skinned?"

"I guess so. Perhaps. Why?"

"How many?"

"Lots. How would I know?"

Santana took in the quiet town, the hills, and his four landing boats, sitting in a line in the field above. He thumbed his comm. "Status? Nothing? No activity." He paused a beat. "Withdraw, now. Order the troops to—no, I'll do it."

"Something wrong with your victory, Brigadier?" Devin asked.

Santana set his comm unit on the table, swiped screens, and typed in a code. This was only the third time in his career he'd used an all-channel override. *It was probably too late already*. "All units, this is Santana. Immediate disengage all units. Retreat at optimal—no, strike that. Expedited retreat to the landing boats. All units, engage and destroy all cows you see. Kill the cows. Shoot up any cow carcasses you see. Get back to the boats. Go, Go, Go."

The Marines' table crashed over as they retrieved their weapons, and raced to the Tribune's table, taking guard positions.

"Submit you retreat with us, Brigadier," Wallams said.

"No." Santana slumped into a chair. He poured a giant glass of wine and gulped it down. "You go. I'll be staying here with the Tribune."

"Sir, with respect, we'll carry you to the boats if you don't come."

"Wallams, we won't be leaving on the boats unless you and Sigurd get out there and kill some cows. And carcasses."

"Sir! Yes sir! Except..."

"What is it, Marine?"

"Sir, this Marine doesn't know what a cow looks like, sir."

"What?" Santana gestured at his plate. "But you just ate a steak!"

"Sir, yes sir. This Marine knows what a steak is sir!"

"Steaks come from cows!"

"They do? I mean, yes. Steak comes from cows, yes sir. But... Sir! This Marine was raised on a station! Vat meat sir. I've never seen a real live cow before sir."

"You don't know what kind of animal a cow is?"

"Sir, no sir. I think it has fur sir."

"Cows do not have fur ."

"Sir, should I shoot all animals I see without fur sir? Birds sir?"

"No just cows. Live or dead. Immediately."

Wallams and Sigurd exchanged glances, then their eyes swiveled to the table. "Stand clear sir!"

"No, do not—"

Both Marines pointed their rifles at the table. Santana covered his eyes.

Devin guessed what was coming. He grasped the wine bottle in one hand, and a glass in the other and pushed off backwards from the table. He dropped the glass as his chair bounced, but managed to keep the hold of the bottle as he rolled clear.

On the *Pollux*, even Tribunes had to work out weekly in the gym.

The interfering senior officers out of the way, the two Marines fired a barrage of shots at the inoffensive steak platter, smashing the table, crockery, and juicy meat into burning bits.

Once the cloud of charred meat dissipated, Sigurd turned to Santana. "Cow destroyed sir."

Devin pushed himself up, bottle clutched in one hand. "Outstanding. Well done."

"Sir! Thank you sir," Sigurd said.

"Well, at least I saved some wine." Devin gestured the open-mouthed waiter over. "Sorry, misunderstanding. Add that to my bill. Please bring us another bottle, and four glasses. And another table. On duty or not, I think these two heroes have earned a drink."

The waiter ran back to the kitchen.

Santana wiped the splatter of corn chowder and pepper sauce from his face. "Thank you, Marines."

"Sir!"

Santana looked up at the hillside above him. Squads of Marines were streaming out of the town, leapfrogging in tactical advances. The four Marines assigned to guard the grounded landing boats had, correctly, formed an equal-spaced perimeter, facing away and outward from their charges.

The area between the landing boats and their guards was clear. An empty field, with only a few splintered trees.

And cow carcasses.

One of the cow carcasses twitched, then rolled aside. Imin, Devin's steward, rose from the mess. He wore a blood-stained coverall, dirt-covered mittens and boots. He dropped a stained face mask, then pulled out a revolver.

"What's he shooting?" Santana asked. He might as well ask, it was too late to change anything.

"He had a flare gun when he left this morning."

"And you didn't ask what for?"

"I don't ask questions I don't want the answers to."

Invisible behind the guarding Marines, Imin took a two-handed stance, and shot, taking deliberate aim each time. FOOMP. FOOMP. FOOMP. FOOMP. Four flares impacted harmlessly on the armored hulls of the landing boats—one foot to the right of the open hatches. Two feet to the left, and any sort of explosives round would have hit and destroyed the interior.

The shaking waiter arrived with a tray of glasses and an open bottle. Devin helped him set it on another table and sat. "One question I do want to know the answer to, though." Devin poured four glasses of wine, handed them around and took a sip. "Outstanding. Sweet with a hint of tartness. One thing I want to know is how the referees will score the exercise now?"

Santana grabbed his glass and drank it in a gulp. "Badly. We screwed the tabbo on this one."

"I agree." Devin sipped his wine. "And how in Jove's name are we going to fix it so we don't screw up the real thing?"

Chapter 2

"We should have brought more guns." Senior Centurion Anastasios rolled down the limousine window and squinted against the blue-white glare of Andaman's two suns. He sniffed the humid air. "I feel underdressed without a shotgun."

Dena, seated across from him, waved her hand in front of her face. "Do we have to have the window open, Old Man? It's hot out there. And dusty."

"Situational awareness. I need to check the sight lines."

"Situate my buttocks. If you're worried about sight lines, why did we spend so much on a car with tinted windows?" The limousine had leather seats, tinted glass, a built-in bar, and no useful defenses of any sort.

Ana continued to scan the scenery. "They wouldn't let me mount a rocket launcher on a truck, so I compromised and got the vehicle with the biggest engine that would fit all six of us. Besides. We can always smash the windows out if need be. Still, I'd be happier if we had some long guns."

"Where would I hide a long gun in this dress?"

"Didn't have to be that short."

"Did have to. This way, I can grab my slingshot." Dena hiked up her skirt, showing lots of thigh, a garter, and a holstered slingshot.

"I like the heat." Sandra Caroline Ruger-Gascoigne, aka Scruggs, sat next to Ana. Like Dena, she wore a little black dress and heels. "Makes me think of sitting on the patio with a cool drink. Reading. Relaxing."

"Boring." Dena shuddered. "If we have to sit on a patio, I want a group of sailors to flirt with. And alcohol. And a more expensive dress. The old man is better dressed than we are."

Ana wore full Imperial Planetary Auxiliary Army dress uniform—dark blue, almost black tunic, white Sam Browne belt, high, round collar and gold buttons down the front. His hat was white with a gold Imperial Starburst—the Polaris system. Dark blue pants with a gold strip tucked into highly polished black leather boots completed the outfit. He tapped his belt holster. "Just a regular uniform. Keep the window open. I smell smoke. I want some idea where it's coming from." *And who's making it. And why. And how well armed they are.*

"Cooking smoke?" Dena raised an eyebrow. "In this heat?"

"Not cooking smoke." Ana breathed in the smoke and licked his lips. He tasted plastic. "Somebody-blew-up-a-building type smoke. And there aren't enough people outside for this time of day, and not enough traffic." He held up his hand. "Listen."

The engine of the car hummed. The street was dead quiet, but a low rumble rang in the distance.

"That's either a riot or a jump ball game. Want to take bets which? Something is going on." Ana checked his revolver, then pulled a pill bottle from his pocket and shook out a pill.

"How many pills do you have left, Centurion?" Scruggs asked.

"Somewhere between none of your business and leave me alone." Ana dry-swallowed a pill and made a face.

Scruggs stared at him, unblinking.

Ana relented. "Twelve."

"I'll get more," Scruggs said. "First chance I get."

"You will not. They're too expensive."

"You don't tell your troopers how to spend their money." Scruggs climbed up on the seat to peer out the window. "If I want to buy pills, that's what I'll buy."

Two-story adobe brick buildings swept by as they headed for Empire House, the Imperial Governor's official residence and workplace. Wooden balconies extended from the second story to cover the sidewalks and store entrances, shading the arcades and patios that fronted the street. All were deserted.

Scruggs gazed into streets as they flashed past. "Nothing moving on the side streets, Centurion, and I don't see any on-coming traffic on the other side."

Dena fanned her face. "When the primary sets, people should be outside to take advantage of the cooler tempera-ture. Go people-watching." Dena was tall, fit, and sexy. She'd joined the crew after a botched revolution on her home planet of Rockhaul. During the botching, the planetary executive, her stepsister, had been thrown out of a starship to her death. Dena was responsible for the botching. And the throwing.

"Maybe it's not cool enough yet.," Scruggs said. If Dena had a guileless younger sister, it would be Scruggs. One who drank milkshakes instead of beer, and studied grammar for extra credit. The type who goes away to college in ribbons and saddle shoes, but comes back with a collection of tattoos and a five-vodkas-a-day habit.

"Maybe there was an accident that blocked the road," Dena said. "Maybe that's why the road is empty."

"Or maybe there was a riot," Ana said. "And the rioters scattered when the local constabulary started shooting them, except for an angry crew bent on revenge that are hiding under one of those balconies with their rocket launcher, waiting for some unsuspecting Imperial visitors from the Spaceport to drive cluelessly by before blasting their limo, then running out and bayoneting the survivors in the gizzard."

"How oddly specific," Dena said. "Old Man, you have the best fantasies. Blood, guts. Gizzards."

"Humans don't have gizzards, Centurion," Lee, their navigator and medic, said from the front seat. "No mammals do." Like most Jovians, Lee was tall and lean, whip smart, and fanatically loyal to the Empress. Why she was on a broken-down ship with a group of reprobates was her business.

"You sure?" Ana asked. "I'm sure I've stabbed somebody in the gizzard."

"We're not birds, Centurion." Lee pointed to white awning. "Even the ice cream shops are closed. In fact, all the stores are closed."

The entire next block was padlocked doors and mesh fences pulled across windows.

"Tell you what," Ana said. "I'll find somebody to stab, then cut out what I think is their gizzard and bring it to you. You can help me identify it."

"You're probably confusing it with the gallbladder or the spleen."

"No, I've cut out people's gallbladders and spleens before. Totally different organ. Different colors, for one thing."

"Anteaters have gizzards, Centurion," Scruggs said. "Did you stab an anteater, maybe?"

"You think I can't tell the difference between a person and an anteater, Private?"

"Oh no, Centurion." Scruggs's eyes were very wide. "I assumed that when you were fighting, you killed everything you saw. People, animals."

"And anteaters," Dena said. "Then when you went around cutting out spleens and suchlike, you got confused, mixed up your pile of pancreases with your stack of gizzards. Got them all stuck together. Easy to do."

Ana tilted his head. "That could be the case. There's always lots of blood and confusion. It's not like you label them when you pull them out."

"I'll get you a labeler for Saturnalia, Old Man," Dena patted his knee. "You can practice putting names on random rotting organs. Why were you cutting people's gallbladders out?"

"Some people pay big money for bear and wolf gallbladders."

"People aren't wolves."

"Same people can't tell the difference between different types of gallbladders," Ana said. "Give em a gallbladder, any gallbladder, and their money spends the same."

"Speaking of spending money." Lee tapped her comm. "After that incident renting the car, I've been doing some research." There had been a problem with their credit at the spaceport. "I'm still having problems accessing the Tribune's funds. The credit chips he gave us are coming up invalid."

"Trust that stupid Imperial anus," Ana said. "Gave us fake money."

Lee frowned. "Why do that? He didn't have to give us anything. And his money worked up to here, but now the chips aren't working."

"What makes a chip show as invalid?"

"Could be something wrong with the chips. Or the local bank could be having a problem."

"Or the issuing bank in the Core could have canceled the accounts," Scruggs said. "Taken the money away or closed them."

Everyone stared at her.

"This is the first Core-connected system we've been to. We're here to look at military courier routes. But can't military couriers carry banking updates?"

"Especially if ordered by the Navy, or the Imperial Home Office," Lee said.

"Focus, everyone." Dirk Friedel, former Imperial Naval officer and current fugitive, sat in the very back seat next to Dena. He was their pilot, their captain, and their leader. He was also such an insufferable snob, they mostly ignored him.

"As exciting as getting eye of newt and toe of frog and all that, we've got a party to go to."

"Not a party unless you have enough guns," Ana said.

"Newts aren't real either, Pilot," Lee said.

"Do frogs have toes?" Scruggs asked.

"The old man will cut some off for you if you ask nicely, Baby Marine." Dena giggled. "Or even if you don't ask nicely."

The car swung right to the main north-south highway paralleling the river. Oak trees lined both sides of the boulevard. The canopy where they met overhead shaded the road from the worst of Andaman's burning blue-white sun.

"Remember what we practiced," Dirk said. "This party is our chance. Nobody gets into Empire House except on official business. If we don't get in tonight, we'll have to invent reasons to get inside, or we'll have to wait six months for the next formal ball."

Dirk was a convicted felon, the so-called Butcher of New Madrid, cashiered Imperial officer and current pilot of the trader *Heart's Desire*. He and the crew had been sent to Andaman on the orders of Tribune Devin, the rebellious governor of the Verge sector. Devin wanted a look at the databases of the courier boats that passed through Andaman to figure out what warships were transiting the area so he could destroy them.

"Stick to the plan. We need to get close to the governor's office to get the radio frequencies so we can steal the courier boat files. I'm your employer. Degenerate son of a duchess, my cover name is Charles Garnier. Kicked out of the Imperial

Navy for insubordination. Told to leave home and never come back again. Paid to stay away. Dena, you're a party girl who wants a good time, and is not averse to some extra fun when the Duke isn't looking. Scruggs, you're my younger naive cousin Sandra who I'm ruining with a life of crime and debauchery. This is our first time in this system, and the first time we've been out of the Verge."

"When do we start acting?" Dena asked. "Kind of the truth so far. I'm looking forward to this party. I've never been to a governor's levée. I'm not sure about this dress, though. It's short enough but hides my shoulders. Might not be revealing enough."

"You can show shoulders or legs, not both." Scruggs said. "One makes you look sexy. Both make you look slutty."

"Men like both," Dena said. "Gives them options. Who told you that?"

"My mom."

"Your mom told you this? Before you ran away from your rich family and a boring coddled life of leisure to become a trained killer?"

"I'm not fully trained yet."

"To continue," Dirk said. He pointed to the front seat, where the sixth figure in the vehicle sat. "Gavin is our steady engineer. And he's got the scanners. We get him close enough to the administrative offices, we might get everything we need without going into the party. Lee is, of course, an Imperial Praetorian on a special mission. People don't question Praetorians."

Dena patted Dirk's arm. "Nothing new there."

"Ana is the voice of reason, our seasoned guard who's trying to keep me out of trouble and dealing with physical threats."

"I do that already," Ana said.

"And all of you are my honorable and loyal retainers. And you all love and respect me."

"Whoops, that was a shot too far," Ana said. "Took on more targets than you could hit."

"Yeah," Dena said. "Can't I just tell everyone I'm with you for your money?"

"That's what I'm going to say," Ana said.

"Me too." Gavin said from the driver's seat. "Lee?"

"I'll say it's a Praetorian thing."

"Well, I'm going to say it like I was told to." Scruggs patted Dirk's shoulder. "I'm going to say that you're the best Duke ever, and you've been gracious and kind, and that my family is poor, and in debt to you and that you've been very generous in offering to take me along, his younger cousin, for this trip, at your own expense, and asking nothing from me except companionship."

"Say it just like that, Baby Marine," Dena said. "Those exact words. Gracious. Kind. Generous."

Ana nodded. "Don't forget poor, in debt, companionship, and asking nothing."

"Just put the word 'yet' in there somewhere.' Dena winked.

The limo stopped in front of the security line at the entrance to the governor's residence. Other well-dressed groups were lined up ahead.

Ana climbed out first, then held out his hand to help Scruggs out of the car. "That's an outstanding outfit, Private. Makes you look sophisticated. Elegant."

Scruggs grinned. "Thank you, Centurion. You look dashing,"

"What about me, Old Man?" Dena waved off Ana's hand and awkwardly stumbled out. "Empire damned shoes. Do these heels need to be so high?"

"Heels are part of formal wear."

"So? What do you think?"

"They make you look slightly less feral than usual," Ana said.

There was a thump in the distance. A flow of air washed over everyone. The crowd noise dimmed, then recovered. The crew scanned the area for threats. Without realizing it, they formed a defensive circle, scanning all directions.

"What was that?" Lee asked.

"Not sure." Ana grunted. "Keep your eyes and ears open."

Dena pouted. "What did you mean by less feral?"

"Slightly less feral, I said. You look like you might use cutlery for a change."

"Bite me, Old Man."

"Like I said." Ana smiled. "Slightly."

Another boom sounded in the distance. The crowd stilled, looked around, then voices chattered.

Dena stretched upright, nearly tipping over. "There it is again. Sonic boom?"

"It could be a starship, Centurion," Scruggs said. "Heel and toe, Dena." Scruggs demonstrated how to walk with heels.

"Didn't list trans-sonic travel in the briefing," Ana said. That was heavy weapons firing in the distance. This is an Imperial Colony world. Who's shooting off artillery? And why?

The party was a major event. Well-dressed groups exited limos and private cars at the front of Empire House, and climbed steps to an inner courtyard where they lined up for entry. Dirk's attempt to push past the line with the two women on his arm failed.

"I am the Duke Charles Garnier. I do not need an invitation. Certainly not to this…place. Fetch me the governor, at once."

Two Imperial Marines in full uniform blocked the terrace door. Both were female, both were sweating, and both were unimpressed. "Need an invitation sir. Governor's orders," the shorter of the two said. Her nametape read Suprapto.

"Surely not for a visiting noble. I've travelled in from the space port. What a horrible drive. Does it have to be so far away?" The drive in had taken over two hours, even running the rental at full speed. "I shall present myself before seeking lodgings in the town." Dirk mopped his brow and gestured at the stairs inside the Imperial Administration building. Awnings overhung the exterior mezzanine. Where the awnings didn't cover, Andaman's burning suns faded the plasti-rock to pale red. "It will be but a moment to dash inside and greet him."

"No visitors without invitations sir."

"Keeping me in this heat is a huge social faux pas. The governor isn't even a mere baron. I should be demanding he meet with me at my leisure, not wasting my time at such a sweaty locale."

"Demand away, but through official channels."

"I am not accustomed to being made to wait."

"And we're not accustomed to allowing random individuals without documents into official areas."

"I told you that we suffered a database failure, thus our lack of documents."

Neither Marine bothered to answer.

Dirk snapped his fingers. "Enough of this. Fetch me the governor."

The Marine's eyes narrowed and she brought her rifle up to high port.

"Let me take care of this, your grace." Ana emerged from the gloom under the awning where he and the others had been sheltering.

"Be quick." Dirk snapped his fingers again.

Ana snatched Dirk's fist in his own, and crushed his palm over Dirk's fingers. "Ms. Scruggs?"

"Centurion?"

Ana held Dirk's hand like a vise. "Do you have a set of pliers handy?"

"No, Centurion. Sorry, Centurion. It's not part of planet side kit. And I'm not exactly..." She indicated her form-hugging dress.

"Very well."

"What do you need done, Centurion? Maybe something else can help?"

"I need something removed from a finger."

"A splinter, Centurion?"

"Kind of like a splinter." Ana waved his hand. "Medic Michaelson?"

"Yes?" Lee had followed Scruggs. "What do you need?"

"Can I use pliers to remove things stuck in fingers?"

"Somebody get a splinter?"

"Not splinters. Fingernails."

"Fingernails? You want to pull out fingernails?" Lee laughed. "Then they won't be able to use their fingers at all."

"That's the point," Ana gripped Dirk's hand. "Not using the fingers."

"Hey, Old Man!" Dena said. "We used to smash claws off animal carcasses with hammers."

"Hammers? That's creative. Outstanding idea." Ana smiled. "Does anybody have a hammer?"

"I am not a carcass," Dirk said.

"Yet." Ana nodded to the grinning guards. "Lance Corporal Suprapto? Are you senior?"

"I am." Suprapto, the darker-haired of the guards, said. "Is there a reason you're holding the Duke's hand, Senior Centurion?"

"He's really the youngest son of a Duke, not *the* Duke. And I promised his mother, the Duchess, that I'd keep him from getting hurt." Ana nodded at Dirk's hand. "Looks like he was about to get hurt, in my opinion."

"We wouldn't have hurt him, Centurion." Suprapto grinned. "Much."

"That's what I figured."

"Won't his mother be upset if you crush his hand?"

"She said not to let him get hurt. Didn't say anything about not hurting him myself. Lance Corporal, you two are working. I don't want to bother you. Could you call somebody with nothing worthwhile to do right now? The officer of the guard, maybe? Or somebody equally useless?"

"We could call the governor's social secretary."

"I'm sure she's useless enough."

"It's a he. And maybe not as useless as you think." Suprapto grabbed her comm. "I can ask."

"Outstanding. We'll wait for this overbred fop over there." Ana dragged Dirk fist-first to a table and chairs across the terrace. Dena followed. Suprapto spoke into her chest comm.

Dirk struggled. "Centurion, that hurts."

"It's supposed to." Ana released the hand. The group followed and collapsed in a sweaty heap on the chairs.

The Imperial Administration Building reminded Ana of every Imperial building everywhere. Square, massive, stone, and boring, it looked like three blocks of different sizes had been laid in a line. It was surrounded by a paved promenade, low stone walls and manicured lawns. The only concession to local conditions were teak pillars supporting fabric awnings covering the walkways.

Dena stood on tiptoe. "You can't see the river without standing. That stupid lawn and fence blocks the view. Why have these beautiful promenades and no views?"

Ana snorted. "Go to that stone wall and face the river. Kneel down and pretend you've got a rifle in your hands and you're shooting at a horde of drunken looters who've burned the town and are coming for the citizens. You'll find that having those walls there slows down attackers and makes them good targets."

Dena stepped to the stone wall. "This is a fortress, isn't it? Are we in a moat?"

Ana pointed at the two-foot external wall. "Dry moat. That's the counterscarp. A couple squads there can decimate anybody crossing the lawn. The wall behind us, what do you notice about the windows and doors?"

Dena peered into the gloom. "No windows on the ground floor."

"None. Nothing to smash. You'd have to force the doors. Good luck doing that with the Marines behind it. And those slots are loopholes to poke guns out of."

"Speaking of Marines." Dirk rubbed his fingers. "You made me look like an idiot."

"I did, didn't I?" Ana grinned. "But I can't take all the credit. I had great material to work with. Engineer, did you get what you need while we were doing our charade?"

Gavin Crewjacki, their engineer, lounged in the darkness down the hallway. He pushed a scanner back into the pocket of his coveralls. "Yes and no." He rubbed sweat from his face. "Even if you can't see that river, you can feel it. The humidity here is double what it was at the spaceport."

"Never mind the river. Yes and no? Explain?"

"To you? Do I have to? Be difficult. I'm not sure I know words that short."

"Gavin," Dena said. "Explain it like you'd explain it to somebody as dumb as me."

"Well, if you take two pieces of string, and some re-usable cups—"

"Jump to the end."

"Right. I scanned the frequencies. Standard Imperial equipment, current military codes. With the equipment Tribune Devin gave us back on the ship, we can listen in, once we've programmed the right settings. We're recording now so we can go over things later."

"So we can pull information from the courier database?" Andaman was on the edge of the Verge sector nearest to the first of the core components of the Empire. Stellar geography required courier ships outbound from the Core to jump in, then split up to follow three different routes to the nearby sectors. The courier service maintained real-time records of fleet and military movements for all the adjacent areas. Devin wanted those records.

"Once we get a valid ID, yes. Give me a few hours and I'll know the protocols. But it will take time to extract information from the database. Download speed is slow."

"We can get that at the party tonight," Ana said. "Provided Duke Useless here plays his part."

"Duke Useless, I like that," Scruggs said.

Ana snorted. "Private, you should not call our glorious leader Duke Useless. It's demeaning."

"He called me cute-but-crazy before. That's demeaning. Shouldn't I be able to do the same thing?"

"Your logic is compelling. But in the military, logic gets in the way of efficiency. We need efficiency."

"Don't worry, Baby Marine." Dena tapped Dirk on the head. "I'll call him Duke Useless for you."

"If you've all had your fun," Dirk said, "I remind you we're not going to survive in that party tonight without a real live aristocrat. That's me. You all need to show more respect."

"Well—" Ana said.

"Show more. I don't care what you think. Fake it. This is a military operation, and I'm in charge. Do as I say."

Ana turned to Lee. "Listen to Mr. Officer here. Are you going to help remove the stick up his butt when we're done?"

Lee shrugged. "I agree with the plan."

Gavin coughed. "Skipper is just trying to make sure everybody knows what their job is. That way, nobody messes up by accident, and nobody gets hurt. That's what good officers do."

"First time I've heard 'good officer' and 'Dirk' in the same sentence." Ana glared at Gavin. "And you've been doing a lot of sucking up to him lately. How come?"

"I'm just pointing out the obvious," Gavin said. "Tribune Devin gave the Skipper an important job, and he doesn't want to let him down. Neither do I."

"Really?" Ana crossed his arms. "On account of you're really a spy and you're worried about what the Tribune might do to you if you let him down. Something involving airlocks and no suits?" Gavin's past as a notorious spy was a sore point.

"That's not it."

"Sounds like it. Fine. Go ahead, Duke Useless. Impress your Tribune. Give us your plan. Your new best buddy Engineer-spy Gavin is waiting to assist. As for the rest of us." Ana uncrossed his arms. "Scruggs will follow your orders because she's a good Imperial Citizen. Dena's in it for fun and shooting, and we'll have lots of that, and Lee serves Tribune Devin, so she's onside too."

"I serve the Empress," Lee said. "Not Devin."

"I thought he was your priest?"

"He's still my priest. But my loyalty oath is to the Empress, not Devin."

"Interesting distinction," Ana said. "What happens if those two come into conflict?"

"She's his sister."

"And brothers and sisters always get along?"

"Why are you helping the pilot, then?" Lee asked. "We've got some money, we've got a ship. You could just buzz off. But you're still here. Why?"

Ana tilted his head. "Habit. I've served the Empire for years. I'm used to it. This is what I do."

"As do I," Gavin said.

"Now you do, you mean." Ana put two fingers to his eyes. "I'm watching you, Engineer-spy. And you, Medic. I'm watching you too."

"I am on the Empress's business."

"So you say."

The six exchanged baleful looks.

"Glad that we all agree I'm in charge, however reluctantly. Gavin, you never finished your briefing. What was the 'no' you mentioned?"

Gavin turned so the guards couldn't see the comm unit he pulled out. "There's a whole whack of other codes going around in there. In the governor's office looks like. Lots of traffic. Commercial codes."

"Can you break them?"

"We're a freighter, not a military communications ship with a code-breaking unit."

"Don't you have some special items your other employers provided for you?" During a sojourn with some pirates, the crew of the *Heart's Desire* had discovered that Gavin had been spying against both the Union of Nations and the Confederation of Planets. For the Empire. He was on the Empire's side.

Maybe.

Gavin waved the comm unit in his hands. "Nope. I might be able to figure out who is talking, but not what they're saying."

"Navy," Ana said. "I don't normally spend time in governors' offices. Is this commercial code thing normal?"

Dirk shook his head. "Imperial Marines use military codes exclusively, and they provide communications for the governor's staff as well. Even if the governor has some sort of private venture going on, talking about it in his office isn't likely. Official spaces are monitored and recorded."

"So why would that type of traffic be there?"

"No idea." Dirk shook his head again. "No idea."

"Really?" Dena said. "You have no idea why? None of you?"

Everyone shook their heads.

"None of you." Dena waved her hands. "None of you have any idea why an Imperial Governor would have private comms in their office?"

"Nature Girl," Ana said. "Why don't you tell us?"

"What type of private communications do you want to keep away from your military buddies?"

"Well, it would be embarrassing if you had to explain, for example, why you had to put a girl over your knee and spank her because she wouldn't explain things fast enough."

"First, spanking is not embarrassing, it's kind of fun." Dena snapped the rubber of her slingshot. "Second, not nearly as embarrassing as explaining why your arm is in a cast because some girl broke it with a rock, don't you think?"

"How is spanking fun?" Scruggs furrowed her brow.

The rest of the crew looked at her, then all eyes swiveled back to Dirk.

"What?"

"You're the skipper," Gavin said. "Crew education belongs to you."

Dirk closed his eyes. "I'll explain later. Or get Dena to."

"We can just wait 'til the party," Dena said. "I'm sure I can find somebody to demonstrate it to her. Actions speak louder than words, all that."

"I still don't get it," Scruggs said.

Dena laughed. "You will."

"Focus, people," Ana said. "Private comms. Nature Girl, why would there be so many private comms?"

"Girlfriend," Dena said.

Everyone, even Scruggs, nodded at that.

"Yeah, can't send that through official channels. Too embarrassing." Ana nodded again. "Well done, Nature Girl. I won't have to spank you."

"Spoilsport," Dena said.

"Lots of traffic, though," Gavin said. "Unless this guy has ten girlfriends…"

"It's been known to happen," Dena said. "Need to get a good look at him and see."

"Company, Centurion," Scruggs said. A figure was conferring with the two Marine guards at the door. Suprapto pointed at them, and the figure marched across the terrace.

Ana stood. "Show time, people. Remember, we're the crew of Duke Useless's ship, *Heavyweight Items*. Guards, engineers, mistresses and pilot. We need to get into the Imperial headquarters and plant some bugs, and this party is the way to do it. Follow Dirk's lead."

A black-haired man stepped out of the gloom. He overtopped everybody except Ana. His clothes were immaculate. Creased white linen pants, white tunic with gold buttons, polished black boots, with real leather belt. As he approached, he placed a white-peaked cap on his head. "My Lord Duke." He saluted Dirk. "I'm the governor's social secretary, Jack Boone."

"You're wearing a uniform," Dirk said.

"Can't fool the aristocracy's highly developed perception, can I, my lord?" Jack said, holding the salute.

"That's a naval uniform."

"Naval Reserve," Jack said, dropping his hand.

"You can't just wear an Imperial Naval Reserve uniform," Dirk said. "There are regulations."

"You can if you're in the Naval Reserve."

"How did you get into the Naval Reserve?"

"The usual way, my lord." Jack raised his eyebrows. "I joined the Navy, was discharged after ten years, and regulations require a further five in the reserve. Once I got this job, it seemed easier just to wear the uniform to work."

"This job." Dirk blinked. "You're the governor's social secretary?"

"Yes, my lord." Jack said. "The governor apologizes, but he had no advance warning of your arrival. But he would like you, and your entire party, to attend the monthly levée this evening, as his guest. Refreshments, entertainment, dancing if you wish."

"Mr. Jack." Dena smiled at him. "Do you dance?"

Jack smiled back. "Like a dream, madam. I love to dance."

"Well then, my lord." Dena took Dirk's arm. "It's settled. We'd love to meet the governor."

Jack grimaced. "I'm not sure that he'll be available, but I'll speak to the Marines on duty, and they'll get you in to mingle with the other citizens. If you don't mind joining the line..." He gestured at the groups that had formed while they waited.

"Mr. Boone," Ana said. "We keep hearing loud noises. Thumps."

"That's not unusual," Boone said. "Some type of mining equipment, as I understand."

"Mining equipment? Really," Ana said. "Sounded like artillery to me."

Boone stared Ana down. Ana stared back. After about ten seconds, Boone said, "Mining equipment, I'm sure. You'll have to excuse me, I have duties to attend to."

"Of course." Dirk waited until Jack left, then led the group to the line. "Centurion, how sure are you of this artillery?"

"I've heard lots of artillery in my time. Those noises, the lack of people on the streets. Something bad is going on here."

"Well, we can ask the governor, when we meet them," Dirk said. "Engineer, what happens now?"

"At worst, we need to get closer to those offices to get better quality intercepts. At best, we use the bugs we have, but they're only short-ranged…"

"Very well. We'll get inside, and figure out some way to get close to the governor's office, or the communication center, and set up our clandestine observations."

"Jove wept," Ana said. "Clandestine observations? You mean bugs?"

"Yes, I mean bugs. Shouldn't be hard."

"Um, Skipper." Gavin jerked his head. "Most everybody is looking at us. We're the new game in town. Hard for us to sneak away."

"Good point. Anybody have any suggestions?" Dirk asked.

"Jove wept even more," Ana said. "Trust the aristocracy. Brainless, helpless, useless. Private Scruggs?"

"Centurion?"

"Time for you to learn how to operate on your own. Create a diversion of some sort. Get us inside. Then we need you to cover the others while they plant bugs. I'll be your backup, but it's your call what happens."

"Understood, Centurion. When should I start?"

"Anytime."

"I don't have any weapons, Centurion."

"Girl." Dena nodded. "Those legs are weapons. Why not use those?"

"My legs?"

"What do you think all those men over by the door are looking at?" Dena gestured at a group near the head of the line. "Dirk's brooding manner? Or your calves? Use that."

"Fine." Scruggs furrowed her brow. Then her mouth made an 'O' and she glared at Dirk and raised her voice. "Pilot! You, you, you're a pig!"

Dirk jerked, then understood. He raised his voice. "I'm not. I haven't done anything."

Scruggs' voice rose. "Is that what people think? That you brought me here for, for that!"

"Scruggs, keep your voice down," Dirk hissed. "Everyone is watching!" He made sure he hissed loud enough for everyone to hear.

Scruggs slapped him. He stumbled back. Dena shoved her foot out and tripped him. He fell full length with a thud. Scruggs kicked him once, then stormed up to the front of the line and started arguing with the sentries. The crowd goggled. Gavin helped Dirk to his feet. Dirk fingered the red mark on his cheek and glared at the grinning crowd. "Well? What are you all looking at?"

The crowd muttered amongst themselves. Dirk stepped up to Ana. "Did you tell her to do that?"

"Nope. She came up with it by herself." Ana smiled. "Couldn't have gone better if I'd planned it. Now everyone will be watching her to see if there's more slaps. The others can sneak off. That was well done."

"She didn't have to hit so hard."

"No, she didn't." The guards motioned to Ana. He dragged Dirk to the entrance. "But she knew I'd enjoy that part. I'll thank her later."

Chapter 3

"Also missing is the entire collection of spare parts for the radars and radar receivers. If they break, we can't fix them in the dark. We'll be dead in space." Bronwin Hooper followed her scowling captain down the station corridor. "Maneuver drive efficiency is at sixty-eight percent. If it drops two more percent, we have to go in for a mandatory emergency maintenance period. And in addition, we have only one type of tray for rations, and since supply says they are short of everything and orders are backed up—"

"Bugger supply." Senior Lieutenant Franceska Monti stopped. The path they had been following dead-ended. "Tell them we've got orders to leave in seven days. Where is this conference room? I hate this station." *If I'd gotten on an earlier shuttle, they never would have caught me.*

"Everybody else also has orders to leave in seven days, Franky. And everyone else is much more senior than you are. Oh, and congrats on your promotion to acting commander. Pretty impressive for a senior lieutenant, especially a volunteer reserve one at that. Command must have finally recognized your leadership qualities."

"Command was appointing anybody they could grab who could navigate and had a heartbeat. And don't call me Franky on duty." Monti put her hands on her hips and glared at the wall. "Were those directions spinward, or anti—"

"Anti."

"You positive? I'm sure I heard spinward." Monti pushed her black hair away from her dark eyes. She was above average height for a woman, two inches taller than Hooper. Both were originally from the planet Melbourne, but hadn't met until assigned together in the naval academy. They were close enough in size and looks that they'd once swapped clothes and names on a lark and confused their respective dinner dates. "We should be going spinward."

"Go spinward, then." Hooper rubbed the bulkhead. "Feels like orbital-grade steel. Lightly rusted but still strong. I'll sit here and watch while you bang your head. Won't be the first time I've seen you bang your head against a wall."

"Like math at the academy, you mean?" Monti hadn't known Hooper was on station until she arrived on the corvette *Collingwood* two hours ago. They hadn't seen each other in over four years and were still catching up and trading old stories.

"You passed eventually."

"With your help."

"Like I'm helping you with directions now?"

Monti grunted, reversed, and strode back down the corridor. Hooper skipped to keep up with her. "In any event, I'm sure that early command will do nothing but improve your naval career—"

"I don't have a naval career, you wombat-lover. I did my time. The Navy wasn't supposed to re-activate me. I was quite happy with C&R Lines, thank you very much."

"Should have read those forms you signed."

"Four years in the academy, seven on active duty, and I was supposed to be done. I wish I'd made it off station. If I'd been off station…"

"And if wishes were wombats, we'd have a farm."

"I don't know why they appointed me. You're a much better navigator than me. You should have been…wait a minute." Monti glared at her friend. "You *are* a much better navigator than me."

"Am I?"

"Yes. I've seen you navigate. You're amazing."

"I am, aren't I?" Hooper twirled and ran her hands over her uniform. "And not just in navigation either!"

Monti glared more. "Why are you my first officer? Why don't you have a ship of your own?"

"Unlike you, Command has not seen to recognize my brilliance."

"You threw the test. Or you faked the records. What did you do?"

"I have no idea what you're talking about."

"You're such a good navigator, you knew exactly when you had the right answers. Once you knew you had enough for a pass, you blew the rest of the questions. What did you do? Turn in blank answers?"

"Blank answers are suspicious. But minor problems in transcription, well, that can happen to anybody."

"Which is why they picked me to command this stupid assignment rather than you. But you're here…"

"Well, you're not the only one who wished she'd been on a transport a day earlier." Hooper pointed ahead. A blond woman holding a comm stood at the end of the hall. "That's our conference room. And look who's here!"

"Leather jacket. Dark pants. Ankle boots. Superior attitude. Internal Security. Marvelous."

"Never mind the uniform. Look who's wearing it."

Monti looked, then cursed. "Shoot me out the thruster nozzles."

Agent Hernandez, Internal Security, watched the two naval officers approach the door to the conference room. *Not those two. Can this day get any worse?*

The two women stopped next to her. Monti, wearing the angled stripes of a senior lieutenant in the Imperial Naval Volunteer Reserve, as well as a ship commander insignia, glared at her. Hooper, same stripes but no command indicator, smiled.

"You're both late," Hernandez said. "They've started already."

"Hello, Hernandez," Monti said. "Haven't seen you since forever. What are you doing here?"

"Running herd on officers who can't read their orders."

"We only got these orders this morning, two hours ago, in fact. And we've spent the day reporting to the ship. What's going on?"

"They'll tell you inside. After they finish reaming you out for being late."

"Always a pleasure to see you, Hernandez."

"Why do I not believe you?"

Hooper grinned wider. "Because she's lying. She hates you. Hey, you usually partner with Weeks. Is he here too?"

Monti turned to her subordinate. "Not this again. Don't tell me Weeks is here?"

"I hope every dreamy bit of him."

"We don't have time for this."

"We always have time to irritate Agent H here." Hernandez's partner, Weeks, had been third year at the academy when Hooper and Monti were first years. Hooper had seduced Weeks. Or Weeks had seduced her. Or they had seduced each other? Opinions varied. Either way, they had enjoyed an on-again/off-again relationship for years. Hernandez had been partnered with Weeks for much of that time, and she barely tolerated his lovers in non-work situations.

Hernandez snarled, "You'd seduce him to irritate me?"

"Not just to irritate you, but as an added bonus, sure, why not? Irritating Internal Security is the responsibility of the officer corps, right?" Hooper gave the cross-chest salute. "I serve the Empire."

The other two women glared at Hooper. Hooper smiled.

"Never mind that. ID here." Hernandez thrust her comm forward. "Both of you."

The two officers thumbed the screens and answered questions, then Hernandez typed a message, and they waited.

"Well?" Monti said. They stood in silence. "You going to let us in?"

"Can't." Hernandez shook her head. "Security seal. Has to be authenticated, then somebody inside has to let us in."

"Lots of security for one corvette movement," Hooper said.

"It's not one corvette movement. It's four." Hernandez's comm bonged. She gestured the women to the door. "And a complete convoy and escort. Plus tankers, supply ships, two destroyers, a light cruiser, and a battleship."

"A battleship? Are you kidding me?"

"Yes. *Canopus*."

"*Canopus* is not a battleship."

"Yes it is."

"It was a battleship a hundred years ago. It's not much bigger than a modern cruiser, for Jove's sake."

"You'll have to take that up with the admiral." The door slid open, and she waved them inside. "In you go, ladies."

Monti and Hooper marched through the door. They turned left, faced the Imperial seal, and gave the formal cross-chest salute.

"The Wavy Navy's here!" a voice muttered from their right.

"The Curvy Navy, anyways," another muttered.

At the front of the room, a man in an admiral's uniform stood. They faced him and saluted again. "Lieutenants Monti and Hooper reporting for duty sir," Monti said.

The admiral returned their salute. Monti had no idea who he was. Not old. Not young. Tailored uniform. *Rich, then, probably a noble. But what noble would get this lousy assignment?*

"You're late."

"Yes sir. Sorry sir. We only received our orders this morning."

"What is that vile accent? Can't you speak Standard? Speak properly."

Monti and Hooper exchanged glances. "Sir?"

"You talk like drunken tabbos at the bottom of a well. Stop it."

The flag captain behind the admiral cleared his throat. "Pardon, Admiral. That's a Melbourne accent. The lieutenants are from Melbourne."

"Melbourne?"

The captain nodded. "Yes sir. They all speak like that there."

"They're not putting it on?"

"Ah, no sir. The whole planet speaks like that. Always has."

The admiral glared at the two junior officers. "Did you not learn how to speak properly at the academy?"

Monti shook her head. "The topic never came up sir."

"Surely they offer elocution lessons there."

"I don't think it's part of the curriculum sir. I..." Monti turned to the flag captain for support.

"The written language is the same sir," he said. "And the lieutenants would have had to pass all their exams in Standard, sir, so the academy deems it sufficient. That being said, sir. We have deadlines..."

The admiral snorted. "Very well. I suppose that punctuality and proper diction is too much to expect of the Wavy Navy. Be seated and we will continue."

Monti sat. Hooper flopped next to her. There were almost fifty people there, half in uniform, half not. Hooper scrutinized each face until she saw Weeks, Hernandez's partner, grinning back at her. She beamed a smile at him, and he winked back. She poked Monti in the side, and pointed him out, then settled with an audible sigh. Monti set her mouth in a flat line and glared at Weeks. He grinned at her and winked again. She grunted and turned to watch the briefing.

The Benwe-3 system was huge. Three suns. Thirty-one planets. Six habitable, all with significant water. Gas giants, mineral-rich asteroids. Hundreds of moons. Merchant ships roamed over the entire area. The only downside was its enormous jump-limit. With all those gravity wells around, ships had to travel for days and days to get clear.

The base wasn't large as fleet bases went. In fact, it was more of a flotilla base than a fleet base. But it could fix jump drives, and had a full complement of naval engineers and civilian repair crews. The main courier route passed through the system so commanders in the capital could harass the working officers on a regular basis.

Monti and Hooper weren't the most junior officers at the meeting. Two other lieutenants, the commanders of the corvettes *Trail* and *Moncton*, were the same rank but inferior in terms of service. The rest of the room was commanders and sub-commanders, except two full senior captains sitting in the front. They commanded the tankers *Hydrogen Pride* and *Hydrogen North*.

"Recognize either of them?" Monti whispered to Hooper.

"Nope. Reserve officers, though. Old reserve officers."

"They look very old-school." Both officers—one male, one female—had gray hair, well-lived-in uniforms and a complete indifference to the navigation instructions being offered by the admiral's aide in front of them. They gave the impression that they navigated a million-credit starship with a stopwatch and a pair of binoculars, the stopwatch being optional. "I think one is from the Avalon line. She's a senior captain ."

"And you were complaining that your salary was going down when you got called up. Imagine how much of a hit she's taking."

"They probably keep paying her while she's in the Navy." Monti's activation had put her new job and much higher salary on hold. "I hope we get this over quick. Why do we need such a big escort? Have the Confeds attacked?"

"I don't follow politics."

"War isn't politics."

"Politics by other means, as the man said. You should have paid more attention in class."

"I did pay attention. And took notes. And asked questions. And wrote papers, and I still barely passed. You, on the other hand, came in hung over and half asleep most of the time and you still came out nearly top of the class."

"I paid attention."

"Remember in tactics class end of third year? When they turned down the lights to show the battle of Sagamon, you passed out and drooled all over yourself. And you snored."

"Oh! I do remember that. Great party the night before."

"I hate you."

"Don't hate me because I'm smart." Hooper tilted her head. "Well, not just because I'm smart. I'm beautiful too."

"I wish I was back at work."

"I don't. This will be a great lark. A few months on naval service, meet old friends, impress my bosses here on Benwe with my dedication to the Empire. And I'll get veteran's preference when I get back. I can change to one of the faster shuttle routes. Get time in the seat, and a bonus."

"Why'd you take that shuttle driver job?"

"They were the first offer after graduation. Seemed good enough, so I took it."

"You're happy driving shuttles?"

"Why not? Do it for a few years, get seniority, move back to Melbourne, get a government job with astro control, home every weekend, on the beach during my time off. Sounds great."

"Sounds like boredom. I'm glad I'm away from Melbourne. Too... conventional. Too many rules. Too many social mores to be followed."

"Well, that's your thing, not mine. And, frankly, if you wanted to live a life of unbridled hedonism, the Navy's an odd choice."

"It was the most cost-effective choice to get off planet. Nine years and I got a skill and some money, and I can travel the galaxy. I've been to seventeen planets since I left."

"Seventeen? That's it?"

"That's more than my dad. More than my entire family combined."

"Well, good for you. Sorry about this war, though. It must be inconvenient for you. Then again, I'm sure you have detailed contingency plans for getting on after this is over."

"Not that detailed. I'm not sure this is a war. Are we fighting the Confeds? Or the Nats? Who's coming?"

"And whoever they are, how did they get this far toward the Core without us hearing about it? How many ring knockers do you count?"

Monti swept her eyes around the room. "*Canopus*, of course. One over there. The cruiser captain probably, by his age. The others are all reserve."

"And us third-class citizens here. I see another wavy strip over there." Her attention was drawn to the front. The admiral's aide put another display up on the screen. He claimed it was an improvement on the standard convoy escort positions. Even to the junior officer's eyes, it looked both over-complicated and ineffective.

"Up the volunteers." Monti tried to do a count. "Three regular officers? That's it."

"They're all supercilious twits. I won't miss them."

"But only three. Where's the regular Navy?"

Hooper shrugged. "Too busy drinking cocktails at gala soirees in the Core? Or at big game hunting parties in the barrens? Not a clue. Maybe Weeks will tell us." Both woman's' eyes drifted to the natty Internal Security officer. He saw the two women watching and winked again.

"Speaking of supercilious twits."

"I don't care about that. The question is, is he an informed supercilious twit?"

"I'll count on you to find out."

Hooper grinned. "Thanks."

"I hope you like what you hear from him."

The admiral's aide put up a jump schedule. It wouldn't work. He'd gotten the distance parameters wrong.

"I hope so too." Hooper wrote down the numbers on the screen. "Because I sure don't like what I see here."

Chapter 4

After Scruggs forged ahead, Jack spoke to the grinning guards to pass them through. The crowd gave them dirty looks. Dirk made a beeline for the bar down the tree-lined paths. The crew followed along behind.

The governor's residence abutted the Imperial administration center, Empire House. It occupied an entire block at the north end of the complex, fronted by gardens, a large round driveway for visitors to use, and public ballrooms. Every few months, the governor hosted a dance on the terrace, and the guests entered it through the surrounding park.

Dena dragged a hand on the bark of each tree as she passed. "Two different types of bark. One's smooth, the others have a grain. Are these palm trees?"

"What makes you say that?" Lee asked.

"Soil is too sandy for pines. But don't palm trees grow in sandy soil?"

"You can tell the soil in the dark?" Lee asked.

"My heels are digging in."

"It's palm," Ana said. "The smooth ones. The rest are teak."

"Didn't know you were a tree fancier." Lee ran her hand on the tree bark as she passed. "It is smooth. Might make nice furniture."

Ana tapped one. "Teak and palm are excellent woods to build field fortifications out of. Those species have high levels of silicate that will blunt explosions—they make great bunkers."

"So much for furniture." Gavin peered into the gloom. "It's dark already, but I'm still sweating. But there's no under-growth. This is the weirdest jungle I've ever been in."

"Dry season. Wait 'til we're in the wet season. You'll be glad for the sand."

Dirk had beat them to the bar and grabbed two drinks off a tray. The first had vanished by the time they arrived. He downed his second drink. "She nearly broke my jaw."

"I know." Ana sipped a glass of amber liquid. "I'll talk to her about it."

"Get her to stop next time?"

"Nope. Make sure she uses a closed fist. If she's going to hit somebody, I want you to go down hard. Dena, have you located your target?"

Dena stood beside the two, scanning the crowd. "Hunky social secretary? Not yet." She tasted her wine and made a face. "Is this wine spoiled?"

"It's Imperial wine, not local. Most likely spoiled in transit. Try the other glasses."

Dena gulped the rest of the wine, then picked up a lighter colored vintage. "If it's spoiled, why serve it?"

"You're at a governor's party. Nothing but the finest in Imperial products, no matter how bad they are. Listen up. While Scruggs keeps everyone's attention, get that secretary into the governor's office and get the bugs in there. Distract him so he doesn't know that you're doing it."

"Distract him? However shall I do that, Old Man?"

"He was in the Navy, like the pilot here. Show him your slingshot. Simple things like that keep naval officers occupied for hours."

"All these people are glaring at me." Dirk gestured with his drink. The crowd was giving him dirty looks. "They think I've been abusing Scruggs. Does everybody believe that?"

"We'd all believe it," Dena said. "No problem at all."

"Indeed. Well, here comes your hunk." Dirk gestured. "Your new friend Jack."

The governor's social secretary, Jack, shuffled across the room to them. "My Lord Duke, welcome to our party. The governor has been unavoidably detained by official business, but hopefully, he'll be able to carve out some time later. I'll update you when he can see you. Are you enjoying your visit so far?"

"Yes, thank you. This wine is superb. Is it a local vintage?" Dirk waved his glass.

"It is, your grace."

"Indeed. The ballroom is amazing." *Better butter him up.* Dirk gestured at the colonnades surrounding three sides. The inside was open, but tables, chairs, and stand-up bars extended outside. "Those carvings on the pillars, are they original?"

"First Exodus from old Earth sir. Andaman is an old, old colony."

"First Exodus?"

"Part of it is the first expansion sir. The entire residency is a work of art. Amazing wall paintings everywhere. The interior ceiling frescoes are spectacular."

"I'd love it if you could arrange a tour, for myself and my staff."

"I'll see what I can do, my lord. But it's a working complex. Even this late, some of the staff are slaving away, so I'm afraid there is little chance of getting back there. The governor has strict rules about bothering working staff."

"I remember that, working late hours in the Navy."

Jack sipped his drink. "You were in the Navy sir?"

"For a time, yes. Everyone in my family does it. Had to leave, unfortunately. Family business."

"Yes sir."

"Best years of our lives, don't you think, Jack?"

Jack pursed his lips. "There were some good times, my lord. But I'm happy to be out. Once my commitment was done, I moved on."

"Unfortunate that you moved on to this hades-hole," Dirk said. "Sweaty, stinking, bug-infested jungle of a planet. Whatever did you do that the foreign office felt the need to send you here?"

Jack stiffened. "I volunteered sir."

"Volunteered? For here?"

"Yes sir."

"But it's a furnace. A sweaty, stinking furnace."

"I don't mind the heat, Lord Duke. I grew up with frost. I don't miss it. I love it here. I rent an apartment by the river about a mile from here. Every morning at dawn, I get up and swim a half mile in the river. It's quiet, and it's warm. I don't even have to dry off."

Dena butted in. "I grew up swimming, but I never get the opportunity these days."

"You can swim anywhere in the river, Ms.... Dena, isn't it?"

"Dena, yes. What about animals? I hear there are some creepy-crawlies type things. Some icky fish."

"Icky?"

"Yah. I don't like icky."

"There are some fish, and a type of water snake that are best avoided, but it's easy to spot them if you know how."

"Maybe you could teach me? Show me those fish?"

"If you like, but you'd have to come by the river early in the morning."

"Oh, I'm sure I could arrange to be at your house first thing." Dena grabbed his arm. "I could stay over the night before, if necessary."

"Did you bring a bathing suit?"

Dena shook her head. "Nope. I don't wear them. Will that be a problem?"

"I'm sure we can find you something that works."

"I'm sure we can." Dena ran her hand down his arm. "Why don't you give us that tour that his Dukeship wants. He can look at the sculptures, and I'll look at the paintings."

"You like paintings, Ms. Dena?"

"I just love paintings." Dena grabbed his arm. "In fact, I spend a great deal of my time staring at those ceiling paintings wherever I go. Isn't that true, guys?"

"Completely ma'am ." Ana nodded. "Ms. Dena spends a great deal of her time on her back wherever we go."

Dirk coughed. Jack blinked, then blinked again as Dena hauled him in close to her side. "Let's go see those sculptures."

"I'm afraid I can't right now ma'am. Milord, the governor is extremely strict on who goes back to the working areas. I'm not allowed to bring guests on my own account. But he does want to meet you later, so perhaps he can take you on a tour." Jack pried Dena's hands off his arm.

"Will he show Ms. Dena the ceiling?" Ana asked.

Jack grinned. "He might at that. I'm sorry, but I have duties with other guests, ladies, my Lord Duke, sir."

The three watched as Jack hustled to the door to greet two late arrivals— two short women with curly black hair in their thirties.

"Something's not right with him," Ana said. "Too fancy for this place."

"I agree," Dirk said. "Too fancy for here, but too common for a governor's aide. And too friendly to those people. There. Did you see it?"

Ana nodded. "I did." One of the women had pressed something into Jack's hand, which he slipped into his pocket.

"The way to his heart is through his wallet."

"Looks like the offices are back there," Ana said. "I wonder who those two women are."

"Not Jack's guests, so they must be here to see the governor. And they're locals, not Imperials."

"How can you tell?"

"Clothes," Dirk said. "Imperial officials always look overdressed and sweaty."

"Too dumb to come into the air conditioning, are they?"

"Also." Dirk tilted his head at the bar. "The bar staff are all short, fair, but straight hair. Whatever the dominant ethnic group on Andaman was, they fill all the service roles. The waiters are short, but the people at the tables are taller and darker."

"Ruling class is a different ethnicity from the proles," Ana said.

"Dumb," Gavin said.

"Speaking of dumb," Dena said. "Spend all my time on my back? Really, Old Man?"

"How else are you going to see those frescoes?"

"Frescoes?"

"Paintings on plaster... never mind."

"You didn't have to paint me as such a complete immoral slut."

"If the painted-on outfit fits..."

"It helps us, though," Dirk said. "Now, when you fake-seduce that Jack fellow, he won't be suspicious."

"When I what?"

"Fake-seduce him. You know, pretend to seduce him and then don't follow through?"

Dena looked at Ana. Ana shrugged. Dirk's eyes flickered between his blank-faced crew. "Oh. Right."

Lee and Gavin had followed a steaming Scruggs to a different bar. She ordered a glass of white wine and stomped off to a corner, the two trailing discreetly behind. Lee counted four Imperial Marines in the hall—two front door guards and two at the entrance to the administrative wing. Four Marines was too many for the centurion to shoot, they were too professional for Dena to seduce, and too intelligent for Dirk to confuse. The crew would have to resort to sneakiness, not her strongest suit. *Is this what it's come to for me? A proud servant of the Empress reduced to helping criminals break into a building?*

"Lee," Gavin said. "I'm worried Scruggs is out of her depth here."

"She can pull it off." Lee wiped dust from her arms. "Jove willing. She just needs to pretend to be a sheltered young Imperial lady."

"Nobody is going to believe she's this stupid," Gavin said. "Or this naive, whatever."

"People can believe six impossible things before breakfast if it suits them. And she's not either. She thinks well of people. She's more upset that people keep disappointing her."

"We haven't disappointed her. Well, you haven't."

"And you have?"

"She didn't like working with a spy." In addition to being their engineer, Gavin had been a spy against the Confederation for the Union. Or against the Union for the Confederation. Or both.

"I think she feels that pilot has let her down."

"As far as the skipper's concerned, she should get used to disappointment. I know, I know–" Gavin held up his hand. "He's a good pilot. Exceptionally good, now that he's stopped drinking. And he does know how to run a ship Navy-style."

"So how has he let us down, then?"

Gavin scratched his nose. "You know, that's an interesting question. We kind of disdain him a lot, but he's doing his job, as well of the rest of us. He's just not…"

"Acting like an Imperial Duke should."

"Right." Gavin tilted his head. "I didn't get that before, but you're right. I wonder why we're like that?"

"No time right now." Lee waved. Two figures were approaching Scruggs. "The vultures are circling around Scruggs."

"Does she need help?"

"With what?" Lee shrugged. "She knows our job as well as anybody else. Get into those back rooms, get some bugs in there, get into those databases, and get out of here before we get caught."

"How's she going to do that?"

"She's a pretty girl, she'll think of something."

"Sandra." Scruggs took a slug of wine. "My friends call me Sandra."

"How nice to meet you." The young man, Scruggs's age, extended his hand. "I'm Cleon, and this is my twin sister, Clara."

Cleon and Clara were both dark-haired, dark-eyed, and dark-skinned. Cleon was an inch taller than Scruggs, Clara an inch less. Their expensive clothes stood out from the regular crowd's. "Pleased to meet you both."

"You caused quite a scene there earlier," Clara said. "What did the Duke say to you?"

"You know D—I mean, you know the Duke, Duke Charles?"

"Duke Garnier, but I suppose you call him Charles. Or Charlie," Cleon said.

"No, I call him Pilot," Scruggs said. "He's the pilot of our ship."

"Really?" Cleon cocked his head. "Interesting. The rumor is that he was thrown out of the Navy for incompetence."

"He's not incompetent. Well, maybe." Scruggs remembered Centurion muttering something to the guards as they entered, setting up part of the legend they were using to be able to sneak into the party. "I wouldn't know." She drained her glass. "Can I get another glass of wine?"

"Where are my manners," Cleon said. "Clara, take her to our table to meet everyone. I'll get her some wine."

Clara led Scruggs to a table in the corner of the reception terrace. Four men and four women, all her age or nearly, sat at the table. The clothes were loose, gauzy, and expensive. They all wore extensive jewelry. One poured a shot from an unmarked private bottle, then topped her glass off with green liquid from a jug, then added two spoonsful of a white powder.

"Everyone, this is Sandra, she's part of our visiting Duke's entourage. Sandra, everyone."

Everyone introduced themselves. Scruggs missed all the names except for one. Narla was the prettiest and had a ginormous blue sapphire pendant at her neck.

"So the rumor is that he was kicked out of the Navy," Narla said.

"Where did you hear that?" Scruggs asked.

"It's everywhere. Everyone's heard it." Her matching sapphire earrings flashed as she twisted her head. "Nice dress. Very... understated. Is that what they're wearing in the capital these days?"

Scruggs looked down at her little black dress, then up at the others. The women all wore bright gauzy sarong-style outfits, in pale greens, golds, and oranges. The men all wore light linen pants, thin belts, and orange or green shirts. The color patterns made Scruggs suspect family alliances.

"I don't know, I haven't ever been to the capital."

The group regarded her blankly. Clara coughed. "I thought you were, um... a noble relation to the Duke?"

Scruggs shook her head. "Distant cousin."

"How distant?"

Scruggs gave them the made-up story. Poor relation. Dirk's generosity. Asking nothing to take her around the galaxy. Midway through the talk, they started nodding. Scruggs blushed and stammered as they looked knowingly at her. *Does everyone think I'm one of Dirk's playthings?*

"So, I stick with them, help out where I can, on the ship."

"On the ship, what do you do?" the only man at the table dressed in a uniform asked. Scruggs thought he would be handsome if he didn't act so pompous. His uniform—green shirt, open to the waist, with matching sage-green pants—was spotless. His holster belt was tooled black leather. Black mid-calf boots and a sage-green side cap completed the outfit.

"I guard mostly. Watch the dock. Keep an eye on the hatches. Don't let anybody in."

A waiter arrived with a tray of red and green mixed drinks. Scruggs sampled the green. "Yuck. What is this?"

The table crew laughed and bantered in a language Scruggs didn't recognize. One of the men spat out a plant he'd been chewing and grinned at her.

Clara translated. "Lime juice, rum, and sugar. It's harsh if you're not used to it. Stick with wine. You guard the ship? That's your job?"

"One of them."

"I'm sure she has other jobs, Kel," one of the other women said. She fingered a ruby pendant. "Helping the Duke out when he needs something."

The whole table laughed. Scruggs flushed. This is not going the way I want. I need to help create a distraction.

Cleon returned with her wine. "There you go, Ms. Sandra. I see you're keeping everybody entertained."

"Ms. Sandra here was just telling us that she's a guard on the ship," Kel, the pompous one, said. "She watches the doors. Keeps an eye on things. Fights the vagrants off."

"Well, you would know about vagrants, Kel." Cleon laughed. "Being in the Planetary Guard and all."

"What's the Planetary Guard?" Scruggs asked.

"Like the Imperial Army Reserve, except planet-based," Kel said. "I'm an officer in the guard."

"Oh, good for you." Scruggs said. "I always wanted to join the Imperial Marines before, but I was too young. Maybe I can, now that I'm older."

The whole table laughed again.

"What?" Scruggs said.

Kel cleared his throat. "The Imperial Marines have demanding standards, Ms. Sandra. You have to fight, and fight hard in the Marines. They're tough."

"Kel tried to join the Marines," the woman with the diamond pendant said. "But they rejected him, even with his father's blessing. Isn't that true, Kel?"

"I was not rejected." Kel glared. "I withdrew during the initial application process because I thought I could better serve the Empire in the Planetary Guard."

"And you don't have to go camping in the jungle every weekend."

Clara interrupted. "Don't be mean to Kel. The Planetary Guard is important. My stepfather says so. And, Kel, you do look handsome in that uniform."

Kel preened, and all the women, except Scruggs, nodded and catcalled.

Scruggs looked more closely at Kel's belt. "Your sidearm? Is that an original M1911? Did they give it to you? The Planetary Militia?"

"My what?"

"Your sidearm."

"You mean my gun." Kel patted his holster. "It's a family heirloom. Old Empire. But they gave me special dispensation to wear it. It's still a functional gun."

"Don't call it a gun." Scruggs shuddered. "That's not proper. It's your weapon, or your sidearm. Never a gun. Centurion would punish me if he heard me calling it a gun."

"Centurion? The old decrepit guy who came in with you?"

"He's not—well, yes, he is old. But he's not decrepit. He's a dangerous man."

The table laughed again.

"Well, he is."

"I'm sure he is, I'm sure he is." Kel grinned. "To you. Not us. So, why don't you tell us about life on your starship. What you do for your Duke. Guarding him, all that."

Clara frowned at Kel. "Kel, there's no reason to make fun of the girl."

"It's okay, Ms. Clara," Scruggs said. "I'm proud of what I do."

"You are our guest," Clara said. "We should be entertaining you, not the other way around."

"I'll tell you what." Scruggs pointed at Kel's holster. "Let me look at your weapon, and I'll tell you all about life on our ship."

Kel was reluctant, but the others chided him. He pulled it out of his holster. "Don't break it. It's expensive."

"Your family has plenty of money, Kel," a woman with a ruby wrist bracelet said. "They can buy you another."

"It's worth more than one of our plantations are," Kel said.

"Plantation?" Scruggs extended her hand for the gun.

"Kel's people are in rice," Ruby Bracelet said. "They grow a lot of it."

"You're a farmer?" Scruggs said.

Ruby Bracelet giggled. "Sure, he's a farmer. And I'm a miner. My family anyways. What would that make you, Narla? A lumberjack?"

Narla's blue sapphire glittered as she laughed. "The whole family is lumberjacks, then." She grinned at Scruggs. "My family is in teak. That's a tree so that makes us lumberjacks." She pointed at Ruby Bracelet. "Taww's family mines rubies, as you can tell by her jewelry. Everybody else has something special." The others around the table introduced themselves. All were involved in resources. Gems. Teak. Rice. Lumber. One said they were a sailor.

"He means his family owns three dozen river freighters." Kel grabbed a napkin and covered his pistol before handing it to Scruggs. "So tell me, Ms. Sandra, what do you do as a ship guard for the Duke?"

Scruggs unfolded the napkin. "Wow. A real M1911. Time me, please."

"What?"

"Use your comm to start a timer. Say 'go' when I can start."

"Why would I—"

Cleon held up his hand. "I'll do it. But you have to tell us about living on a ship and traveling to other planets. How you get there. How you arrive. What you do."

"Sure."

"Okay. Ready?"

"Ready."

He stabbed his comm. "Go."

Scruggs released the magazine and placed it to her far right. She jerked the slide and checked the chamber. "Clear. Well, first, we come in for a landing."

"At the starport?" Narla asked. "Sounds boring. Like coming in on a plane."

"No, never the starport. We're usually, well, we, I mean the pilot, he says it's best to avoid starports, there are officials and customs and things, and we don't like them on the ship." Scruggs grabbed the bushing at the front of the barrel and rotated it counterclockwise. Nothing happened.

"Why don't you like them on your ship?"

"We have weapons. Revolvers. Rifles. Shotguns. Lots of times, there are questions, and rules and things."

"You have shotguns? Plural?"

"I have five myself." Scruggs rotated the bushing in the other direction. "Short ones for on ship. Big ones for on the planet. We have lots of guns. And drugs. The medic, she's also the navigator, she has special drugs for wounds and shock and injuries. Drugs only doctors should have, and we want to keep those too. Maybe I shouldn't talk about that." Scruggs fussed with the bushing. "Regardless, we try to stay away from the starport. That makes the landing much rougher."

"Rougher?"

"Well, starports are usually in flat places with lots of room. But if you land in the mountains or by a river or in the woods, it's much harder. The descent is steep, and Pilot has to fire the engines a lot. Aha." Scruggs continued the counter-rotation until it freed the recoil spring and the recoil tube. She laid them next to the magazine. "Pilot was a Navy shuttle pilot, so we don't glide in. One orbit, dive straight down, and it doesn't matter if the weather is thunderstorms or hail, we have to go through. And the landing zone isn't a big airport or a landing field. Sometimes it's a rock ledge above a clearing, or the top of a frozen plateau on a deserted planet. We landed on one plateau so small that it just fit our ship and the other we were going to meet."

"You met another ship on top of a frozen plateau?"

"Yeah, we had a container of things they wanted." Scruggs fiddled with the slide. It didn't come loose.

"What was in the container?"

"Never mind that," Kel said. "What are you doing to the gun?"

"Frozen fish," Scruggs said.

Cleon raised his eyebrows. "You met someone on a deserted planet to exchange containers of frozen food?"

"It wasn't deserted. There were dogs. That's where we got Rocky."

"Rocky?"

"Rocky. Our space whippet. Aha!" Scruggs found the slide release pin and pushed it. "He was part of a group of feral dogs that chased us through the snow and tried to eat us in the forest."

"Why were you in the forest? I thought you were on the plateau."

"The rest of the crew had to jump off and run into the storm, the other people shot at us and the ship had to fly away... maybe I shouldn't talk about that either. There."

Kel's eyes widened at the pile of parts. "You're breaking the gun."

"I'm field-stripping it. Don't you do that in the Planetary Guard?"

"Never mind that," Cleon said. "Tell us more about this landing."

Scruggs popped the slide loose and set it to her right, next to the spring. "So we land, away from everybody, and try not to attract notice. Then once we're on the ground, we refuel the ship or do repairs. And we have a sentry while we do that. I do that a lot."

"Be a sentry?"

"Yes. I take a shotgun and get up on the roof. Or a rifle if we think it's a long-distance threat. Or I wait at the ramp and point my shotgun at anybody who's trying to get on board." Scruggs removed the recoil spring guide and set it aside.

"Have you had to do that? Shoot at people trying to get into your ship?"

"Yes. Lots of times. People don't listen. Even when I point the shotgun in their face. How do I get this barrel off? There must be another piece..."

"When you're a sentry, you shoot people who are trying to get on your ship?"

"If they won't go away? Sure. I've done it before."

Kel held up his hand. "Wait, you expect us to believe that if we try to sneak onto your ship and you're there, you'll shoot us in the face with a shotgun?"

"Of course not," Scruggs said. "That would be silly. Maybe here." She rotated the bushing on the front counterclockwise.

"Right." Kel nodded. "Silly. So you don't shoot people in the face?"

"Centurion would be angry with me if I shot somebody in the face." Scruggs glanced back to where Ana lounged in the corner of the room. He nodded. *Good. They're getting ready. I need to keep their attention a bit longer.*

"The old man."

"Yes. He would be very, very unhappy. He taught me to always shoot for the center of mass. Got it!" Scruggs clicked the bushing over, the barrel released, and she set it aside. "There! Time!"

Cleon read the time out. Scruggs grinned. "Not bad for the first time. I'll do it faster now. Start again." She didn't wait for Cleon to start, but reversed the entire process, sliding the barrel back in, rotating the bushing, returning the spring and guide, reattaching the slide, pushing the slide release back in. "But no, never shoot people in the face. Always aim for the center of mass. Best way is to push the barrel into the stomach." Scruggs rotated the bushing, pushed in the spring and recoil tube, then locked the bushing. She brandished the pistol, shoved it into Kel's chest and dry-fired it. "Into the stomach, like I said. Then pull the trigger. Twice." She dry-fired again. "Just to make sure, you know."

Chapter 5

“Nature Girl, take a look at those women over there.” Ana took a sip of his brandy. “The ones behind Scruggs. They interest me.”

Dena glanced at two young women. One wore a light orange flowing sundress, the other a similar style but in light blue. “Cute dresses, but women don’t generally interest me. Men do. Second, they’re too young for you, unless you plan on paying them. And third, yuck.”

“Interest was the wrong word. They concern me. Something is off about them. They’re not fitting in here.”

“It’s a party for vapid Imperial twits. How could they not fit in?”

“You’re a vapid twit, and you fit in. Or seem to. They don’t.”

“Maybe they’re not vapid enough, Old Man.”

“See? I knew you understood. What’s wrong with them?”

“Nothing. Well, they are shorter than the ones seated. So they’re the local servant class, right? But this is the Empire. Everybody can get rich. Or so they tell me.”

"Look closer."

Dena gave the two women a once over. "Sundress, check. Tooled leather belt on sundress, check. Bored attitude, check. Haircut... huh."

"What about the haircut?"

"It's short. It would be easy to do your hair that way."

"Is that good?"

"Nooo." Dena twirled her long hair. "Party like this, you need to look your best. A few hours setting your hair up makes a big difference."

"Did you even wash your hair on that rockpit planet?"

"Sometimes we even showered. If we wanted to impress somebody. What drew your notice? Other than the see-through outfits?"

"They're not the only ones with see-through outfits here, not even the most revealing. They don't look like the people in front of them, and they watch everybody who walks up to the table. Like they're evaluating a threat."

"You think they've got a shotgun hidden in their cleavage? Going to go check, Old Man?"

"I think they've got a pistol in those over-sized handbags. And I would have said a knife in their spiked heels too, but look at their shoes."

"Flats." Dena looked them over again. "Practical, if you need to run away from an angry girlfriend. You're right. The outfits are off. They fit in, but they're not as nice or expensive as some of the others."

"What's not as nice or expensive?" Dirk joined them. He'd been cornered by an old couple who peppered him with questions about Core politics. Dirk had concocted appropriate lies.

Ana gestured. "Those women's outfits, over there. Look at them, and think like an Imperial Duke. What do you see?"

Dirk turned to wave at his departing friends. "Ta ta, Ms. Chen. Thank you for a fascinating discussion." His gaze swept over the two women in question. "If either of you want to learn all about teak plantations, I just got an education. Those two women you are looking at are guards or servants. Guards, I think."

"How do you get that?" Dena asked.

"Jewelry," Dirk said. "Not expensive enough. The couples seated at the table with Scruggs have diamonds, rubies, big ones. Those women have small gold chokers and stud earrings. What in the Emperor's name is she doing? Is that a revolver?"

"M1911 model pistol." Ana grinned. "The boy on the other side of the table was wearing it. She's field-stripping it."

"That's outrageous!"

"I agree. First time took her longer than five minutes. Should have been thirty seconds. I'm going to talk to her about that. She should be much, much faster."

"You can't go to a party and field-strip guns."

"As I've mentioned before, some would say it isn't a party unless there're guns involved. That jewelry thing is interesting."

"How do you know so much about jewelry, Dirk?" Dena asked. "Is this another area of expertise you've been hiding from us? Oh wait, that would mean that you have areas of expertise—other than incompetent seduction and crazed piloting.”

“No, Navy’s right,” Ana said. “Now that I know what to look for, I can see another dozen guards. The clothes all fit, and they’re all well-groomed, but it’s the accessories that don’t match.”

Dirk fingered Ana’s uniform. “Where’d you get this?”

“Don’t touch that again.” Ana jerked away. “Or at least wash your hands. This was custom made.”

“That’s my point. A good tailor and a pattern and you can make clothes for your retainers. Notice the colors. Some are orange-green, some are light blue. It probably designates particular families. But jewelry is supposed to be unique. One of a kind. It would cost a fortune to equip the guards with that. Only the very richest families can afford it.”

“I’m impressed, Dirk,” Dena said. “But there’s a hole in your logic. We don’t have anything expensive here. No jewels, nothing like that. And they think that we’re nobles. Or at least that you are, and we’re your faithful retainers.”

“It’s a problem,” Dirk said. “I don’t think they buy it. Our story that I—we—didn’t show up here in a yacht, with piles of credits, so all the local aristocracy is suspicious of us. Notice that the governor keeps fobbing us off. If they thought I was a duke, even if I’m not coming from the Core, they should have fallen over themselves to see me.”

“Kind of ironic that the first time you’re saying who you truly are, nobody believes you,” Ana said.

“I can live with it, Centurion. But it’s not helping us get the information we need, or to do what the Tribune wants.”

"My heart breaks for the Tribune." Ana looked at his glass. "In fact, I'm so broken that I might get another brandy to drown my sorrows."

"How much are those jewels worth?" Dena asked. "I know about diamonds from Rockhaul, but ours were small. What would that pendant be worth? The one the lady next to Scruggs has?"

Dirk sipped his drink. "The attractive lady with the pretty eyes next to the man she just threatened with that pistol?"

Ana shook his head. "She didn't threaten anyone. It's a dry-fire test, perfectly acceptable."

"And she's not that pretty. I'm prettier than her," Dena said.

Dirk gave Dena a look. "That pendant could be a sapphire. If it's real, and if I could sell it somewhere civilized in the Core, it might buy a starship. A small one."

"That much? Holy bison breath, these folks are wealthier than drunken rock miners after a gold strike," Dena said.

"We expected a planet of provincial Imperial twits," Ana said. "Not excessively rich provincial Imperial twits. What do we do now? Especially if they're not buying our act."

"I said they didn't buy it *completely*. But I'm confused, even if they thought I was semi-fake, I should have got some invites."

"Something is not right here," Ana said. "All those jewels."

"And the governor not wanting to meet us. And those commercial codes."

"Those explosion things."

"And the spaceport said weapons were prohibited, but there's a lot of them here."

Dena nodded. "Even worse, Jack hasn't tried to sleep with me right away."

The two men glared at Dena.

"What?" She shrugged. "I know weirdness when I see it. He's acting strange, for a social secretary. What happens now?"

Ana touched a stud on his comm. "Send Lee to talk to Scruggs, maybe they can work something out."

There was soft thump and a push of air. The lights flickered twice, then came back on. The crowd stilled, then voices picked up again as the lights came on.

"Speaking of weirdness," Ana said.

Scruggs pushed the slide onto the top of the pistol. "Sounded like an explosion to me. And why did the lights flicker then?"

"Ignore it," Cleon said. "Tell us more about this tank."

"It wasn't a tank, it was a wheeled, casemated self-propelled tank-destroyer, but it still looked impressive. And we hit it first shot. I got hurt, though."

"Hurt?"

"Shot up bad. I don't like to talk about it." Several planets back, she and the centurion had been badly wounded destroying a tank while allowing the *Heart's Desire* to lift and escape an Imperial Corvette chasing them.

She clicked the trigger. "Done. Time?"

Clara examined her comm. "Forty-one seconds." Cleo and Clara had shooed others from the table. They'd pushed half empty glasses of wine and plates of partially eaten snacks away to give her room to work.

Scruggs sat in the middle. The twins sat to her right and left, timing her as she stripped the pistol. Narla, the teak lady, Kel, the pompous one, and three bejeweled women crowded the far side. Scruggs thought of them as Ruby, Diamond, and Emerald.

"Have to get it faster. Below forty for sure. Hello, Lee."

"Hello, Sister Scruggs." Lee stood to her right. "What was that explosion?"

"Nothing to worry about, I'm told," Scruggs said. Gavin stood behind Lee. "And this is our Engineer, Gavin."

Lee gestured. "The Duke is asking for your assistance."

"He is?"

"Yes. With that matter discussed earlier."

"Did you get your tour? See the rest of the building?"

"No, the governor has been too busy. Perhaps later, after dinner."

Scruggs stood, stretched, and looked across the room. Dirk, Dena and Ana were watching her. She locked eyes with the centurion. He shrugged and tilted his head. She nodded back. "Everyone. This is my friend Lee. She taught me zero-G fighting."

"Wait." Cleon held up his hand. "You're a Praetorian, aren't you."

"I am."

"I've never seen one up close before."

"Now you have."

"What are you doing here on Andaman?"

"I came with the Duke."

"The Duke Garnier? You travel around with him? For fun?"

Lee glared at him. "I am on the Empress's business."

"The Empress sent you to travel with the Duke? Why?"

"I am sure that if she wants you to know why, she will tell you."

Kel, the pompous one, stirred across the table. "We don't normally let Praetorians eat with us. Imperial murderers, the lot of them."

"Kel." Clara glared at him. "These people are our guests."

"The Duke is your father's guest. His playthings and servants aren't."

Scruggs leaned on the table, pushing. It moved a fraction of an inch. *Not too heavy. Time for her act.* Her right hand covered a steak knife. "What did you call me?"

"Plaything. Servant. Both." Kel laughed. "You think because you can take a gun apart you're a real warrior? You and your mongrel friend?"

Scruggs lifted her left hand to play with her hair, using the motion to cover palming the steak knife with her right. "Don't talk to Lee like that. She's my friend."

"Your friend the mongrel."

"You think because you make fun of people that makes you brave?"

"I don't have to take this from a little girl. No matter how exotic her tricks."

"I'm not a little girl." Scruggs glared.

"Fine, you're a woman." Kel balanced on the rear chair legs and raised his hands. "A woman."

"Better."

"One of many that Duke Garnier keeps around. I'm sure he likes your tricks, when you're in bed. Does he call you—"

Scruggs shoved the table. Drinks flew in all directions. Scruggs kept lifting and pushing, knocking Diamond Girl to the side. Ruby Girl fell next. The rolling table slammed right into Kel, knocking him back and tipping his chair. Scruggs ducked as his red wine splashed over her hair and dress. Narla the teak lady dropped on her back as the table landed on her.

Pandemonium ensued. Everyone skittered away. Guards rushed from behind nearby pillars, brandishing weapons and dragging their principals away.

Scruggs leaped over the table and kicked Kel's ribs. He yelped and scrabbled backwards, pulling his pistol. She stomped on his hand, then kicked the pistol clear. His guard lunged to grab her. She ducked under his grasp, grabbed his outstretched arms, and drove her right elbow into his stomach. When he grunted to a stop, she pivoted and rammed his head into a pillar.

Gavin tackled a guard moving in from the right. They smashed into a warming pan, showering them both with green fish sauce. Lee hip-checked another, getting a half shirt-full of red sauce in the process. The rest splashed on Scruggs.

Scruggs dropped a knee on Kel's chest. He woofed his breath out. Scruggs leaned in and pointed the knife tip at Kel's eye. Red wine dripped from her chin and dropped on his face.

"Calls me what?" She jerked her knee. "Calls. Me. What."

Ana and Dirk caught the start of the fracas.

"What's going on?" Dirk asked.

"No idea. Nature Girl, put that away." Dena had produced a small metal slingshot from her décolletage and was stringing it.

"We need to help Scruggs."

Ana produced a burnished aluminum box from his pocket. "Nope. This is her play. She can handle herself, and I'll go help. The guards are distracted. Get into the back offices and plant these bugs."

"Me?"

"And Navy. Make like you're hunting for a bedroom or something. You've got maybe five minutes before people notice you're gone. Don't waste it. Go."

The door to the administration wing was unguarded and unnoticed. The crowd focused on the ongoing confrontation in the corner. Dena grabbed the box and hustled to the door as fast as her heels would allow. Dirk followed, taking her arm as they cleared the entrance.

The crowd formed a circle and gawked. All the tables adjacent were empty—everyone moved in close to get a better view. Ana shoved to the inside of the viewing circle. Dozens of well-dressed guests surrounded the fight. Scruggs knelt on a man's chest on the far side of an upturned table, pointing a steak knife at his eye, and dripping red wine everywhere. A guard type rolled on the ground next to them. Well-dressed women were being shielded by pistol-packing guards, male and female. One female guard waved her pistol at Scruggs. Lee waved her pistol back. Another guard covered Lee. Gavin had stepped next to Lee. His revolver pointed at the ceiling.

The two Marines from the door had pushed through the crowd and un-shouldered their gauss rifles. One tracked Scruggs. The other spoke into a wrist comm.

"Attention," Ana yelled. His command voice stilled the room. "Scruggs, are you going to stab that man?"

"Maybe, Centurion."

"Maybe?"

"I haven't decided yet."

"Well, stab him or don't stab him. It's getting late. And do you see those Marines to your right?"

"I do." Scruggs wiped wine from her face. "I ruined the dress."

"Never mind the dress. Those are automatic gauss rifles they're pointing at you. You know what happens if they shoot at you?"

"Cut me into little pieces, Centurion."

"Exactly."

"But the projectiles that chew me up also kill this dirtbag here, his guard, and those three ladies at the end of the table."

Ana tilted his head a measured the angle of fire. "Most probably."

Diamond, Ruby and Emerald jerked back.

"And perhaps hit that bar over there. And that nice picture behind the bar."

"Picture behind the bar?"

Scruggs pointed. Her dress flopped, and she had to catch a strap. "The green one. I think it's a tree."

Ana peered into the gloom. "Looks more like a drunken lizard, I think."

"Definitely a tree, Centurion." She grabbed her dress strap. "Centurion, do you have any safety pins?"

"I do not. It's a lizard."

"Tree."

Kel whimpered. "Stop talking about trees and get this crazy lady off me."

"Scruggs," Ana asked. "Why, exactly, are you going to stab this man?"

"He called me a bad name, Centurion."

"A bad name?"

"Yeah, he said I was D—the Duke's plaything. And some other bad names."

"What were these bad names?"

Kel whimpered again. "I did not. I didn't I didn't I didn't."

Ana crossed his arms. "He said he didn't."

"Well." Scruggs bit her lip. "He didn't actually say everything. He didn't get around to saying it. But he was going to."

"He didn't say it?"

"Not completely, no."

Ana glanced over his shoulder toward the Marines, but looking beyond. The door to the admin section was empty. Dirk and Dena were nowhere in sight. "So you're going to stab a man in the eye because of something he might say?"

Scruggs's eyes followed Ana's. *Dirk and Dena got through. They'll need more time.* "Well, yes. But he was going to say it."

"If he hasn't said it, then why stab him in the eye?"

"You told me that was the best place to stab him, Centurion. Go right for the eye, you said. Maximum psychological threat, you said. Did I hear wrong?"

"No, it's true. Stabbing him in the eye or threatening him with a stabbing there is very effective."

The Marines joined the conversation. "Great way for a woman to control a larger man too," Suprapto, herself a small woman, said.

Scruggs nodded. "Us girls have to stick together, don't we, Lance Corporal?"

"We do," Suprapto agreed. "I have a safety pin back in my kit ma'am. When we're done here, I'll help you with your dress."

"Thanks." Scruggs grimaced. In addition to the broken strap, the leg slit had ripped up an embarrassing amount. "I think I ruined it."

"Just needs a little TLC. But I'm sorry ma'am, you'll have to release Lord Kel, there."

"If I don't?"

"We'll have to shoot you ma'am. Governor's orders, no murders before dinner."

"I haven't murdered him. And if you shoot me, you'll catch all these others."

"No orders regarding others ma'am." Suprapto hefted her rifle. "But I do have to shoot you if you murder him."

"I haven't murdered him yet, have I?"

"No ma'am. But it does look kind of trending that way."

"But not yet?"

"No."

"So, I'm safe for now. You can't shoot me until I murder him, right? You've got to wait until I try?"

Suprapto shrugged. "It's a conundrum ma'am. Not sure how this is going to play out."

Cleon, at the end of the table, coughed. "Excuse me, Ms. Sandra?"

"Call me Scruggs. Everyone does."

"Miss Scruggs, is it absolutely necessary to stab Kel? Or have anybody shot?"

"Not absolutely, no." Scruggs locked eyes with Ana. He glanced at the admin section door, then nodded.

Scruggs flipped her eyes back down at Kel and grinned an evil grin. "It would be kind of fun, though. But don't worry, Mr. Cleon, nobody is going to shoot anybody tonight."

The Marines snorted. "You seem sure of that."

"Lance Corporal, you have your safety catch engaged. And you haven't powered the coils yet."

Suprapto rotated her rifle vertically. She clicked a stud, then pushed a button. A red light flashed on the stock and the rifle hummed. Her companion Marine did the same. Both kept their rifles pointed at the ceiling.

"What about now, Ms. Scruggs?"

"Now." Scruggs nodded. "Now you can shoot me. So I guess I'll put my knife away." Scruggs sat up, flipped the knife in her hand and stuffed it into the top of her hair braid. Then she pinched Kel's cheek. "Don't worry, Mr. Kel. I was just having some fun. Flirting, you understand."

Scruggs stood and stepped back. Kel's friends swarmed over him. She flexed her arms and smiled. "Mr. Cleon?"

"Yes?"

"I'm sorry I knocked your table over. I'll pay for the damage."

"I wouldn't worry about it. We have lots of tables."

Kel stumbled to his feet. "She's a crazy lady. Arrest her. Arrest her. She tried to kill me."

"Did not," Scruggs said. "Just some fun. A bit of wrestling. Wasn't serious at all."

Kel turned to the Marines. "You saw it. She was threatening me. She tried to stab me. Arrest her! Arrest her."

The two Marines exchanged glances. "Well ma'am. Threating to stab somebody with a knife is a problem."

"I never threatened him," Scruggs said. "I just asked him a question. I wanted to know what names somebody called me."

"With a knife pointed at his eye?"

"Best place to point a knife, right?"

"We already covered that..."

Ana intervened. "Excuse me. Lance Corporal?"

"Centurion?" Suprapto said.

"Senior Centurion. The uniform that boy there is wearing, what is that?" He pointed to Kel's loose green shirt, light green pants and holster belt.

"Planetary Guard, Senior Centurion."

"Is that an Imperial formation?"

"No, Senior Centurion."

"An Imperial Auxiliary formation?"

Suprapto shook her head. "No, Senior Centurion."

Kel waved his hands. "Why are we talking about my uniform? Arrest this crazy person."

Ana glowered at Kel. "Be. Quiet. Do. Not. Speak." He turned back to Suprapto. "I don't understand. Not in Imperial service at all?"

"Ah, well, Senior Centurion, it's a planetary unit. Defense of Andaman, and all that. But only here. They can't be compelled to operate off planet."

"Defending Andaman? Against who? Lizards and high humidity?"

"Above my pay grade, Senior Centurion."

"Who's in charge?"

"Colonel Kel sir. Planetary Guard, not Imperial."

Ana pointed at Kel. "This boy is a colonel?"

"My father." Kel glared at Scruggs. "I'm Kel junior, he's Kel senior."

"Right." Ana put his hands on his hips and surveyed the room. Dirk and Dena were still not visible. Lee and Gavin watched him for a signal, weapons at the ready. *I'll give that useless Navy puke another two minutes.* "Well, be that as it may. I'm assuming that any sort of conflict with... military units is going to be under the purview of the governor, correct?"

"Well, that would be—"

"And I'm sure that an officer of the Planetary Guard, or whatever you call it, would be a trained fighter."

"There might be some dispute about how effective their training—"

Ana rode right over the disclaimer. "So, of course, there is no way that a trained officer of the Planetary Guard could be attacked, surprised, disarmed, his guard knocked out by accident? Especially by a tiny girl only half his size. Must have been a game that got out of hand. Isn't that true, Lance Corporal?"

Suprapto safed her gauss rifle and shouldered it. "Maybe it's as you say, Senior Centurion. Lord Kel, is that the case? Were the two of you playing?"

Kel's jaw dropped. "She tried to stab me. She almost killed me."

"Is that how you want it to read in my report, Lord Kel? The young lady here attacked you, disarmed you, dropped you and controlled you. This—" Suprapto gave Scruggs a once over. "This maybe a hundred-pound woman. This tiny little girl?"

Scruggs made a fist. "I'm not—"

"Scruggs," Ana said.

Scruggs released her fist and looked at Ana. He shook his head. She crossed one ankle in front of the other, dropped her chin, and used her free hand to toss her hair. "I'm not going to talk about my weight." She gave a fake wink at Suprapto. "Girls never do, right, Lance Corporal? It was just a game. Otherwise, a little girl like me could never hurt such a big, strong, brave man."

The crowd sucked in a breath, then a tall man in the back row barked a laugh. The woman next to him snorted, then the whole crowd burst out laughing. Kel's face burned bright red.

Cleon pushed past the others and whispered into Kel's ear. Kel shook his head no, then no again, then grimaced. Cleon came front, grabbed his shoulder and spoke, his words drowned out by the laughter. Kel gritted his teeth and nodded once, and Cleon slapped his shoulder and stepped back. Cleon faced the crowd and held up both hands. The crowd quieted. "Just a game, everyone. Just a game that got out of hand. Right, Kel?"

"Yes, Cleon."

"There you go. Everything fine with you, Ms. Sandra?"

"Call me Scruggs. And yes, I'm fine. Could I have another drink?"

"I think that would be a good idea. Clara?"

Cleon's sister grabbed Scruggs's arm and led her toward the bar. Staff came and righted the table and set the chairs back up. Cleon drifted over to Ana. "Hello. I'm Cleon. Senior Centurion...?"

"Anastasios," Ana said. "But Centurion is fine. Or Ana, for you nonmilitary people."

"I will call you Senior Centurion," Cleon said. "Quite the lady, your Ms. Scruggs."

"She's a very capable young woman."

"Is all that true, about her shooting things and guarding the ship and blowing up tanks?"

"You'll have to ask her," Ana said. "But she's never lied to me."

"Your Duke and his friends have certainly livened things up. By the way, where is he?"

Ana shrugged. "He and Ms. Dena went off alone earlier. The gardens, I think. They do that from time to time."

"You're not worried about his safety, alone with Ms. Dena?"

"She won't kill him. She might kill anybody who bothers her while she's.... busy."

"Yes, I suppose given how formidable Ms. Scruggs seems, Ms. Dena would be the same."

"You'll have to ask her that yourself."

"Seems like I have a lot of questions to ask."

"Careful you don't get answers you don't want. Speaking of questions and answers, where is the governor tonight?"

"My stepfather was called away earlier. Affairs of state."

"Stepfather? You're not his son?"

"Adopted. My sister and I. Twin sister, if you haven't guessed."

"And your mother..."

"Dead these last five years. Just after our biological father died. He was in the Navy. Training accident. Mother re-married to a diplomat, the current governor, so we've followed them here."

"Are you following in the family business, so to speak?"

"Soon as I can get out of here, I will. I've applied to the naval academy. I've been stuck here an extra two years. Age restrictions, available slots, paperwork, all sorts of things. But I should be out of here within a few months, Jove and the Emperor willing."

"Well, congratulations. I'm sure you'll enjoy the academy."

"I hope so. Your Ms. Scruggs, is she seeing anybody? Does she have a boyfriend?"

"You'll have to ask her that too."

"I think she's cute."

"Quite a few men think that. That's part of her nickname."

"Cute? Cutie? Something like that?"

"Almost. Cute." Ana took a drink. "Cute but Crazy."

"Why do they call her that?"

"You'll find out." Ana laughed. "Oh yes, you will."

Chapter 6

"I do not think that test was realistic." Brigadier Santana took the glass of wine from Devin. After lifting from Gandy, Devin's troops and sailors had spent shifts practicing landings on airless moons, combat refueling, and ship-to-ship boardings. At the end of the maneuvers, Santana, Devin, and Lionel had returned to the orbiting *Pollux*. They were sampling small smoked sausages Imin had brought from the planet.

"I agree." Lionel sipped his wine. "All of your Marines should be counted as dead if it was realistic, not eighty percent." *As they all would be if they assault a defended planetary position.*

"One man with personal weapons is not likely to damage an armored shuttle craft."

Lionel took his own glass from Devin. "But at some point, you have to open the doors, and no more armor."

"We would have detected a weapons system of sufficient killing power to destroy the interior of the shuttle."

"If he's sufficiently close, you don't need 'killing power.' You can't detect a man with grenades standing next to where you want to land. Hide close to a likely landing zone and you can heave a whole cow carcass into your Marines."

"Landing zones are random. The defenders are unlikely to consistently pick the one we come in on. And they are not normally outfitted with multiple cow carcasses."

"They don't have to pick the one you come in on. They only need to defend the ones closest to the objective, which means either you land close and get hit by a bucket of beef guts, or you walk." Lionel set his glass down. "Imin!"

Devin's steward, Imin, stuck his head in from the pantry. "Prefect?"

"How did you decide which field, or site, or whatever to…"

"Garrison?"

"I was going to say defend, but yes. Garrison."

Imin glanced at Devin. Devin had limited himself to sipping his wine and scowling. "Fill them in, Imin."

"Standard Imperial doctrine, sir. Deploy the warships in the fleet to destroy orbital or space-based weapons systems. Ships and stations have more or less the same limitations on power and range, so it's an even fight. Ground defenses are a different story. Can't win a fight against massed missile batteries, so they have to go. Evaluate up to three potential landing zones. Use long-distance orbital bombardment, destroy known short-ranged weapons that might target them. If it's possible to destroy all the weapons targeted on a particular landing zone, do so, and that becomes the primary landing point. If you can't guarantee total suppression of defensive fire, pick the zone with the weakest defenses after bombardment that is closest to the objectives, then send in the boats. Swarm 'em like a rampaging herd of tabbos."

"Excellent tactical summary, Imin." Santana raised his glass. "Almost sounds like you went to staff school."

"Six months sir."

"You went to staff school? But it's only for fleet officers…"

"I didn't attend the classes sir. I was a cook there. Needed a low-stress job while I recovered from some wounds after some… activities I performed."

"You learned this while cooking?"

"Lots of the lectures had snacks sir. I'd set them up and stand at the back and listen."

"I never got snacks when I went to staff college," Lionel said.

"Of course not, Prefect," Imin said. "You attended by correspondence."

"I did—wait, how did you know that? That part of my service record is sealed."

"Must have heard it around somewhere, Prefect."

"I've never mentioned it." Lionel glared at Imin.

Imin extended a wine bottle. "More wine?"

Santana snapped his fingers. "We couldn't bombard anything. The software. That's how you knew, isn't it, Imin?"

"Knew what?" Lionel sipped more wine. "What are you talking about?"

"The battle-planning software. It takes all sorts of inputs. Sensors. Intel. Guesses. Intentions. We told our battle-planning software that we wouldn't be bombarding, and we had limited knowledge of the defenses. So the software zeroed those factors out in the decision process, and it would default to the closest landing zone. You knew we'd be landing close, so you threw some dead cows around and waited."

Imin nodded. "Imperial doctrine and software is complicated, Brigadier. But finite."

Devin emptied his glass. "More wine, please, Imin. That's finite as well. Fine. We know what happened. How do we fix it?"

"If you won't let us bombard the targets?" Lionel asked.

"Are you asking for permission, Prefect?" Devin cocked his head. "Because you don't have it. I'm not ready to kill thousands of Imperial Citizens for the sin of disagreeing with me."

"Fine." Lionel said. "*Pollux* and I will close the target sub-orbital, and deploy as battlefield fire-support for the Marines."

"And get blown out of the sky by any sort of anti-starship defense because you can't maneuver worth a damn in a close orbit, and ground stations can have near unlimited power sources." Santana shook his head. "Unacceptable naval casualties."

"How would you Marines fix it, then?" Lionel asked.

"We'll drop the boats farther from the target's closest landing zones. Somewhere safe to get down, and then we'll tactically advance to our objective."

"And get slaughtered on a field or a road en route by any sort of local defense forces. If they have any armor or any air support, they'll blast at you from a distance until you melt.

Nope." Lionel shook his head. "Unacceptable Marine casualties."

"Are you saying we're too... shy to do this?"

"Are you saying I am?"

"What I want to know," Devin put his glass down, "is where will I be during this slaughter-fest. On the starship being destroyed in the sky by missiles, or with the Marines getting blown up by tanks."

"The Tribune is far too valuable to accompany the troops—"

"*Pollux* will be unsafe while conducting these operations. Command will have to devolve to another fleet unit, perhaps the *Hydrogen Queen*—"

"I will not command an attack from a tanker." Devin waved off another drink. "Nor will I allow Imperial Marines to liberate a town without my presence. I will accompany one or the other of you."

"Sir," Santana said. "I protest."

"I agree with the Marine. Huh." Lionel cocked an eyebrow. "There's a sentence I never thought I'd say. But he's right. You should take our advice, Tribune."

"So far, gentlemen, your advice is an argument over which of you will be allowed to die gloriously for the Emperor, while in the process destroying critical fleet elements or Marine units."

"Tribune." Lionel sat his wine glass down. "If this is a real rebellion, somebody is going to get killed. That's what rebellions are. Either you kill the people in the way, or you sacrifice troops on our side. Us, or the Marines and Navy personnel."

"Unacceptable." Devin shook his head. "Find another solution."

Lionel grimaced, drank his wine, and held his glass out for a refill.

"Besides," Devin said. "The purpose of a war is not to give your life for your country, it's to convince some other poor bastard to give his life for his country."

"Never should have given you those books," Lionel muttered.

"What's that, Prefect?"

"Nothing sir. Wondering what's for lunch, is all."

"Imin?"

Imin appeared from the pantry. "Prefect?"

"What's for lunch?"

"Creamed corn, followed by fried oysters from the planet, with that local white."

"Never had fried oysters."

"You either love 'em or you hate 'em sir. Won't know until you try."

"Indeed. Then?"

"A spicy beef ragout with a local red."

"Sounds amazing. But why a ragout? Why not steaks like we had for lunch?"

"Something different this time sir. Plus, we had plenty of beef."

"How is the beef?"

"Bit over tenderized."

"That's not like you, Imin. You seasoned it too much?"

"No sir. Somebody parked an assault shuttle on top of it."

"Right. Sorry." Devin led the way to his personal dining room and sat. The corn smelled like a fresh field, the oysters smelt like an ocean, and the beef smelt like heaven. "Gentlemen, we need a better solution. Something that doesn't get us all killed, and doesn't get the troops killed, and doesn't destroy every landing ground we want. Thank you, Imin."

"Tribune. Try the paprika on the corn."

"I will do. Imin, you went to staff college. What's the best way to attack the fortified portion of a planet?"

"The best way?" Imin ladled out more creamed corn. "Don't attack the fortified part at all."

"Don't attack the fortified part?"

"No sir." Imin dropped the ladle in the bowl. "That's why it's fortified. Attack somewhere else."

"Where?"

Imin smiled. "Well sir, I have some ideas. You know what the key to winning a war against the Chancellor is?"

"What?"

"Snacks." Imin held up a cracker. "Snacks will win the war."

After the lunch was cleared, Devin put up a map of all the worlds in the sector on the briefing screen. Then he had the computer update it to show trade routes, starports, Marine bases, naval depots, local militias, system defense forces, and armed corporate stations.

And after that fiasco produced a color salad of inexplicable confusion, he blanked the whole thing and started over.

"Right. Gentlemen, what can we not attack?" Devin asked.

Lionel highlighted several planetary systems. "Any naval base of any sort, if it has defensive patrol craft. These bases all have non-jump-capable craft assigned. Cutters, some as big as corvette-sized."

"How accurate is this information?" Santana asked.

"It's a combination of our database here," Devin said. "And I've got Dirk and his crew collecting intelligence data from databases on the planet Andaman."

"What data, how's he getting it, and how will it help my Marines?" When it came to his troops, Santana wasn't shy about demanding answers.

"We won't know 'til he returns, but we'll have the latest fleet and troop dispositions, along with any orders in the pipeline." Devin looked at his comm. "When they get back with it, that is. For now, we're working with the data I've received here on *Pollux*. One key point is that outside of ourselves, the biggest ships in the verge are corvettes."

"We can defeat corvettes," Devin said. "We have corvettes of our own. And larger ships."

"Yes, but why bother?" Lionel highlighted a few systems. "We come in outside of the jump limit, and we capture inbound merchant ships. No supplies get through. They eventually surrender."

"Not true," Santana said. "They can go months without new supplies. They'll have the resources of an entire system to call upon."

"They're not going to run out of food or water," Lionel said. "Not with any sort of planet nearby. But any sort of military consumables—weapons, ammunition, parts—those come from the Core. Air filters. Replacements. Reinforcements. And fuel. We jump into a system, chase the cargo ships away, double luck if we can chase a tanker or two away, or grab a gas giant refueling base. They need hydrogen."

"You can get hydrogen from water," Santana said. "Or gas giants. Even us Marines know that."

"You can get it from water if you're designed to land on a planet, like a freighter or a shuttle is. Not if you're a system patrol boat. And if you can't leave the planet you're defending to go hide in a gas giant, what do you do? At a certain point, you have to go ballistic to conserve resources. And these ships are small. They have limited endurance. We force them to patrol for two months, their combat effectiveness will be in the toilet. Morale will be worse than a fleet officer seconded to the Marines."

"So we steal their supplies," Santana said. "We still have to attack and defeat them at some point. They can hoard their ammunition until then."

"These are not first line troops, Brigadier," Lionel said. "This is the Verge. The people who got sent out here don't want to be here, and the ones who volunteered are not your fast burners. They want a quiet life, do their thirty years, enjoy the dental benefits then a pension and a seaside condo spending those Imperial credits. Who would be willing to die defending the Imperial 'sector propulsion rebuild factory and spare parts depot'? None of them. Imin's right. We wait them out."

"Where do my Marines come in, then?"

"They occupy the key bases, the ones that have some special resource or are at an important nexus for supplies. Your Marines will do that. Remember, we're inside the Empire already. We don't need to attack fortified border posts. We can pick the most vulnerable locations and occupy them. Then make a sweep with the naval units and collect whatever we can in terms of warships."

"They'll fight."

"If it was the Nats or the Confeds coming after them, sure. Fight, and probably fight hard. But what if, rather than fighting, you sat in a hole in a moon for two months, and didn't know what was going on? Then we bring out our secret weapon."

"I'll bite," Santana said. "What's our secret weapon?"

"I give you," Lionel waved at Devin, "the Mad Dog of the Verge! That crazed lunatic who has declared war on the entire Empire to save his sister's rule. Truth! Justice! Cheap wine!"

Devin shook his head. "Not cheap wine. Never that. Prefect, this sounds good, but I will admit, in the privacy of this meeting, that we cannot defeat the entire Empire, not with the forces at our disposal."

"Agreed," Lionel said. "But we don't have to defeat the entire Empire all at once. Or even parts of it at once. Imin had it right. Small bites. Snacks. First, a bold move, disrupt everything. Capture one or two key points with critical supply lines, garrison them, and make it difficult for reinforcements to reach here. Then phase two, go back along the supply routes and speak to the folks in question. It's all in how you frame things. Brigadier, what would your Marines say if I asked for volunteers for a suicidal mission against the Union to defend Imperial territory?"

"They'd all volunteer. You'd need a lottery to decide who gets to go."

"Good. Now, take those same Marines, put them in their suits on an airless moon for six weeks defending a single container unloading dock at a zinc mine, and ask for volunteers to die in a distraction to keep the enemy occupied while the others destroy the mine."

"They'd do it. Probably." Santana shook his head. "No, the truth is, it would depend. They'd follow me if I led them. Once. I couldn't guarantee twice."

"Do you think the officers on these planets will be of equal stature to you?"

"No."

Devin laughed. "Nothing like a touch of arrogance to get you through the day. You think you're that good, Brigadier?"

"Yes. You have to believe that, if you want to be a Marine." He shrugged. "I'm not saying it's true, but you have to believe it."

"Given a choice between dying gloriously in a battle that nobody will remember for nothing important, or taking the orders of an Imperial Tribune and Sector Governor, which way do you think it would go?"

Devin highlighted several points on the screen. "It won't be that easy everywhere."

"Nope," Lionel said. "But it will minimize casualties. And, as a side effect, save the Empire from the Chancellor." He examined the screen. "It's a good plan. It should work. We'll meet our goals. Keep casualties down but keep going forward."

Devin nodded once. "Low casualties. And save the Empire."

Santana grinned and saluted. "Currant ad bellum."

"Twice today I've agreed with a Marine." Lionel saluted as well. "March to the sound of the guns—Currant ad bellum."

Chapter 7

"If your hand goes any lower," Dena said, "you're going to lose it."

Dirk jerked his hand off her hips. "It's customary for a gentleman to hold a woman's waist when walking with her, especially if said man is a member of the nobility."

"That wasn't my waist. My waist is higher. Whose custom?"

"General custom."

"Is it customary for members of the nobility to have only one hand because the other was cut off? Because that's what's going to happen if you grab my butt."

Dirk and Dena strolled arm in arm down the hallway to the Imperial Government Headquarters. Dena draped one arm over Dirk's shoulder and clasped a bug-stuffed purse in the other.

The two Marines guarding the connection to the party terrace had rushed to deal with Scruggs's table toss, and Dirk and Dena had beat feet to get down the hallway.

"I'm committing to our role here. If somebody sees us, I want them to see a duke and his sleazy glamor girl. We need to act in character, follow our instincts."

"Fair. Okay, go ahead." Dena leaned into his shoulder. "Act in character. Follow your instincts."

"What? Really?"

"Sure."

"There's got to be a catch."

Dena dragged Dirk by the hand. "You know there is. Where's the governor's office?"

"It will be farther down. We go to the central courtyard, climb to the third story, and the governor's office will be down the major hallway."

"You've seen plans? Or have you been here before?"

"Everything is to a pattern. This is a Class 7 Imperial capitol building. Four stories, stone. Governor's office and administrative spaces are on the third floor. Always. Class 6, and it would be on the second floor?"

"What's on the fourth floor?"

"Governor's private quarters, VIP guest quarters, like a visiting admiral or tribune. Duck in close, walk faster, and eyes right. That hallway leads to the side entrance." Dirk pulled her shoulders in tight and hugged her as they strode past a hallway.

"Why did you do that?"

"They have cameras covering the doors. My instinct says central security is watching the fracas on the terrace right now. If they see somebody flash by the door cameras, they'll ignore them. They'll assume since we're inside the perimeter that we're authorized and ignore us."

"And how do you know this?"

"I'm a naval officer. We took courses on security, courtesy, how to comport ourselves in a strange planet. This place isn't that strange to me. I can trust my instincts."

"You said you are a naval officer, not that you were."

I did, didn't I? Damn you, Devin, and your Imperial honor. "Here, I can trust my instincts."

"Good instincts. You should follow them."

Dirk pointed at the bust of an ancient emperor occupying an alcove as they scooted by. "What if my instincts say drag you into that alcove there and kiss you on your lips?"

"Gotta follow them, then."

"Really?"

"Sure. Go ahead. Do what comes naturally."

Dirk zigged left past stairs leading to the basement. "There's got to be a catch."

"There always is."

"If my instincts say give you a kiss, what would your instincts say in return?"

"Stab you in your liver."

"Knew there was a catch."

"I told you there was. Wow. Was there a sale on carved pillars?" Dena trailed to a halt. "Badly carved pillars." An atrium opened in front of them. Twin marble stairs climbed, then split ninety degrees to the second floor. A line of carved white stone columns connected the second to third floor. The carvings were crisp, detailed, and made Dena nauseous.

"Imperial architecture, colonnades. Standard in Class 7 buildings. The carvings will be by local artists, specially commissioned when the building was upgraded."

"They look... hideous." Dena pointed. "Is that a turtle? Or an alligator."

"I believe that it's the last sector Duchess's great-grandfather."

"Her grandfather was an alligator?"

"Or a turtle. You said you can't be sure."

Dena nodded. "Right. We need to get up to the third floor. How? Up the stairs?"

"Then turn left, the second- to third-floor stairs will be directly above us."

"Confusing."

"Tactical security through architecture, they call it. The centurion would love it here. Nobody can rush the building all the way up the stairs. If there is a Marine guard in front of the third floor offices, they have a clear field of fire at anyone trying to climb up across from them, and we can't shoot back."

"How do we sneak up?"

"We don't, that's the point. We climb up those stairs like we belong here, head for the governor's office, and in we go."

"And what about those Marines you promised?"

"Then you'll have to follow your instincts," Dirk said.

Dena leaned into Dirk, and they ambled across the courtyard to the stairs.

"Any Marines?" Dena whispered into Dirk's ear.

Dirk nuzzled her neck. "Can't tell without turning. Not a good idea."

"Are you enjoying that?"

"I am."

"Good. I feel everyone's last moment on earth should be a happy one." She poked his side. "Liver is there, right?"

Dirk disengaged as they reached the second-floor balcony. She lagged behind and giggled.

"Don't slow down."

"I can see up top. Two people."

"Marines?"

"Uniforms. Don't look like Marine uniforms. Not the same."

"How not the same?"

"Different color. Light green. Sage-green, in fact. Like juvenile pine trees in the spring."

"Now you're an expert on colors?"

"Forest colors, I know. Different times of the year in the forest, you need different colored camouflage."

Feet clattered on the stairs ahead of them. Two uniformed men raced down the stairs, pausing as they saw Dena and Dirk.

"Nice uniform, soldier," Dena said. "But you forgot to button your shirt up."

The two men had the same uniform as Kel had worn. Sage-green shirts, open to the waist, with matching sage-green pants. Black mid-calf boots and a sage-green side cap completed the outfit. Both carried sidearms in elaborate tooled holsters.

The first man's name tag said 'Ferks.' "Member of the Governor's Own are permitted unbuttoned shirts, Ms. What are you doing here?"

"Where's the nearest bedroom?"

"What?"

"Bedroom." Dena pulled on Dirk. "Room with a bed. Guest room, sort of thing."

"You can't be here."

"That's not what the governor said." Dena nodded. "My friend here is bringing me to the governor."

"You're going to see—"

The other man—his name tape said Seshamon—said, "Governor isn't here right now, Ms. You'll have to go."

"What's the Governor's Own?" Dirk asked. *And why are there so many of you?*

"You don't know about the Andaman Governor's Own?" Ferks straightened. "Only the most famous military unit in this sector."

"Never heard of it," Dirk said.

Dena leaned into Dirk's shoulder. "Me neither. Is it like the Imperial Marines?"

"We're much better than the Marines," Ferks said.

Dirk and Dena exchanged glances. If they said that to a Marine, the least they could hope for was a broken nose. Because the Marine would snap their arm off and beat them about the face with it.

Seshamon rolled his eyes. "Ferks."

"Well, we are. We protect the Governor of Andaman personally."

Seshamon rolled his eyes again. "Never mind. You two can't be back here."

"The governor said he wanted to meet me."

"He doesn't meet all his guests."

"He was most insistent."

"Yes sir, I'm sure he did, but he's busy right now, and—"

"He particularly wanted to meet Ms. Dena here. Said I should bring her."

Dena did her best hip cock. Seshamon and Ferks gave Dena a once over. "Well, Ms.," Seshamon said, "we—" A comm on his belt squawked and a testy voice asked where in the Empire's name they were.

Seshamon pointed up. "Office waiting room directly above us. Wait there. We'll contact the governor, and he'll send somebody." The two guards clattered down the stairs.

Dirk leaned over the balustrade, then looked up the stairs. "It can't be this easy."

Dena grabbed his hands. "Don't look a gift moose in the antlers. Let's go."

It was that easy. They climbed the stairs to the third-floor balcony. There wasn't a soul visible. On the wall was a map with different offices labeled. Wooden doors opened to balconies on the east and west sides, fronting dual staircases to the fourth floor. A corridor with attached offices ran south into the government sector. The northern side opened to a reception area with pictures of the Emperor, the Empress, and various planetary dignitaries.

"But why would somebody give you a horse?" Dena hustled to the reception area. Dirk had tried to correct Dena's metaphor.

"Because they have troops hidden in it."

"A gift horse? Don't be ridiculous, horses are too small. You can't fit a person in there, unless it's you. You're saying you can hide in a horse's ass. Is that an Imperial Navy thing?"

"I'm not saying I did. The Greeks did."

"Greeks. You mean like Anastasios?" Dena asked. "That does make sense. He's kind of a horse's ass. I could see him doing that. But mine makes more sense. Somebody gives you a moose they killed for free, you don't complain about how big the antlers are. That's where the expression comes from."

"It comes from the Greeks. From the Trojan war."

"Never heard of it. Where's Trojan?"

"Troy. The war was in Troy."

"You said it was the Trojan war."

"Yes."

"The Trojan war was in Troy?"

"Yes."

"Why not call it the Troy war, then?" Dena shook her head. "The more time I spend in the regular Empire, the weirder it seems. I thought Rockhaul was strange, but I had no idea."

"Never mind. Where is everybody? Shouldn't there be more people working?"

"Biggest party of the week, and you expect people to be in their offices. What sort of a loser are you?"

"Not big enough, apparently. And unskilled with moose identification."

"Snazzy." Dena ran her hands along the wall. "Feels rough. Real wood. But kind of... rustic? Exposed wood. Polished stone floors. I'd expect glass and plastic, all sorts of spacey type stuff."

"It's all fake," Dirk said.

"What?"

The two ducked through from the foyer to the entrance room, passing through open double doors.

"Look how big this door is. Check out the top." Dirk gestured up at the door frame. "At least a foot thick. That's steel and concrete in the middle. See there." A six-inch hole was inset into the roof. "That's the locking cylinder. There will be four, one per side. Lock the door and those come down, freezing it shut."

"This an office or a bank vault?"

"The floors are all reinforced concrete, those wooden doors will be steel cored. The polished stone is a veneer. All Imperial buildings are built like fortresses."

Dena stopped in the foyer. Two desks sat against the far wall, flanking a door. Carved wooden chairs lined this side of the room. She reached into her purse for a bug. "Well, we need to bug this fortress and get out of here."

A red light flashed in the corner. "Kiss me," Dirk said.

"What?"

Dirk dragged her close and nuzzled her neck. "Camera." He sniffed. She smelled as good as he remembered. *You don't do that anymore, Dirk. You're an officer again. Not a bandit.*

Dena leaned into him. "Didn't think of that."

"Me neither. I'm new to this spy thing. We can't bug things with them watching us."

"How do we know they're watching?"

"We don't, but we know they're recording. If somebody catches us, they'll check."

"So what do we do now, big Navy guy?" Dena asked. "We're all the way in here. We need to bug things so we can get the courier database."

"I saw something on that sign. Come on, follow my lead." Dirk grabbed her hand and hauled her out into the corridor, and down one door. He fumbled with the handle. "Get a bug ready. We're only going in for thirty seconds." Dirk opened the door and stepped into the darkened room beyond.

"We need lights." Dena followed, palming a bug from her bag.

"Nope." Dirk moved ahead in the gloom. "Coffee machine. Put one here, right above it."

Dena attached one of the micro bugs Ana had given her. Smaller than a fingernail, it had recording, storage, and a radio receiver that could be queried remotely.

"Everybody comes in for a coffee, and they always talk. We'll learn more here than we will elsewhere. Put one under that chair over there."

Dena obligingly stuffed one under the cheap metal chair, and allowed herself to be led out. "If they find those bugs, they'll know—"

"Nothing." Dirk dragged her along. "Every single person in the building will be in that office sometime or other, and they'll have no idea who did it. And they won't check there either. Nor will they check here."

Dirk dragged her outside, down the hall, and shoved her through a second labeled 'Planetary Guard Operations.'

"What's Planetary Guard Operations?"

"No idea, but I'll bet it's the one area that the Marine counter-intelligence group won't be welcome in. The chances of it getting scanned for bugs are minimal. Even if they found it, our bugs are Imperial Navy style. It will look like the Marines were snooping those idiots."

Dena stuffed a bug under a chair, and another behind a whiteboard. "Our story won't hold up hitting all these different offices. We're supposed to be waiting for the governor."

Dirk gestured. "No beds. We're still in search of one. We've had lots to drink, and we're trying to open doors. No beds, we don't stay. Let's go."

"We don't have an unlimited supply of bugs." Dena dug in her purse. "And we're supposed to put these repeater things up, and at least one by a window."

"Bugs first. Then the repeaters once we know where they have to go."

They hit two other offices before returning to the balcony. Dirk bypassed the courier department. "None of these are high-security," Dena said.

"I know. But the whole place is odd. Those explosions earlier. All those gems. This Planetary Guard thing. Why does the governor need his own troops? Something unusual is going on, so we have to be careful."

"Gavin will figure it out. He's the professional spy," Dena said.

"I forget that," Dirk said. "Right, let's get out of here—"

Voices called from below. Dena leaned out over the balcony. "Company." A squad of eight men in sage-green uniforms raced up the main stairs from the first floor.

"Marines?"

"Nope. Those weird Planetary Guard guys."

"I have a feeling I don't want to be interrogated by them."

"Me neither." Dena grabbed Dirk's arm. "Come with me."

"Where are we going?"

"For that sexual tryst that we've been faking all night."

"Much as I find you attractive, I think that—oh, out there. Great idea."

Dena dragged him out onto the balcony. "Only three stories. We can do it."

Dirk leaned over the edge. "Can you climb in heels?"

Dena climbed over the railing and stood on the ledge. "We'll find out."

Chapter 8

"**N**o, I am not kicking them off, I like these heels." Dena stretched. "They make my legs look great."

"You shouldn't be wearing heels when you're trying to burglarize an Imperial Planetary headquarters." To hide from the searching soldiers, Dirk had led them onto the balcony and pulled the door shut. He leaned over the rail. "Long way down."

The three stories of the residence below them were a sheer wall, unbroken by windows. Ground-floor awnings hid them from the party's view. Only trees and half a duck pond were visible below.

"I was *told* that we were going to a party," Dena said. "Not a burglary. These are party shoes. If I'd been told I had to climb up walls or swing from tree-to-tree, I would have worn something different. I'm not like Scruggs. I have more than one pair of shoes." Dena leaned over next to Dirk. "It is a long way down. This is the third floor. We shouldn't be more than thirty feet up. This looks double."

"Reinforced concrete floors and high ceilings," Dirk said.

"Well, I'll take the rope out of my backpack that I always carry and drop it. Oh wait, I don't have any rope. Or a backpack." She held up her purse. "Just the bugs Ana gave me."

"Scruggs would have had rope."

"You've already been slapped once tonight. Want to go for a second?"

Dirk climbed up on the railing. "That's probably all the action I'll get tonight."

"She'd lower you halfway down and then wish you good luck on the rest of your journey. We didn't put in any of those repeater things."

"No time. We need to get out of here. Try to get over there." Dirk pointed. Six feet away was a window with a planter outside. Foot-tall rails enclosed the plant boxes. They were filled with dirt and flowering hibiscus. "You can step out there if you try. Look down." A line of windows lay below. "Then we can climb down from one to the other."

Dena climbed the railing and lowered herself down until she hung from her hands. Then she swung her leg and tried to hook her feet into the planter. "Do you know how much these shoes cost?"

"I'll buy you new ones." Dirk crouched in the corner of the balcony, out of sight from the inside. He rubbed sweat from his hands. *Must be humidity. Not from worry about getting caught.*

"Liar, you've said that before." Dena swung her feet again. "Don't worry about the tear, Dena, I'll buy you another dress when we're done, Dena. It's only a T-shirt, Dena, don't worry, we can get a new one. I promise not to leave you alone in bed naked and sneak out the window in the middle of the night when we're done without saying goodbye, Dena."

"Sneak out in the middle of the night? I've never done that."

Dena swung farther. "Yes you have." Her shoes brushed the next balcony but didn't catch. Her and Dirk's balcony had nothing under it except a three-story drop to the yard. But five feet away and six feet lower was the planter box. There was enough room for two people to stand on that ledge. If they could get there.

"Never. Not even once."

Dena swung again and stabbed her heels into the planter. Her right heel stuck. "You sure?"

"Positive. Did you ever sneak out on a man in the middle of the night without saying bye?"

"Sometimes I had to get up early in the morning." Dena wiggled her foot. "I'm stuck."

"You're projecting. You're the one who ran out in the middle of the night."

"I did not run out. I left early. Are you going to help me?" Dena hung at a forty-five-degree angle between the main balcony and the line of planters.

"I told you to kick the shoes off."

"No. They stay on. And... I can't move."

"Stay there, then, for all I care. Claiming that I'm not a gentleman. Threatening to stab me in the liver. Next time I do a break-in, I'm taking Scruggs."

"Speaking about getting stabbed in the liver. You try to fake-kiss her, she'll cut it out and dice it into pieces, and then feed it to Rocky for breakfast."

Dirk found himself momentarily envying the ship's dog, who was probably right now lounging on Dirk's bed or defecating in Dirk's shoes.

"But she likes me."

"She'll feel sorry afterward. Very sorry. Dirk, are you going to help me?"

"In a minute. I want you to suffer a little longer."

Shouts echoed from inside. An officer's voice ordered troops out onto the balconies. Dena laughed. "I'm not going to be the only one suffering if you don't help me out. Time for you to do the right thing and get me out of this."

"I hate doing the right thing." Dirk climbed over the balcony rail.

"Yeah, but sometimes circumstances force you to. Don't worry, I'll lie about how you didn't do it."

Dirk climbed over and faced away from the railing. He wiped the sweat off his hands, then crouched down and grasped Dena's hands. "I'm going to push you up and over, you should be able to get your other foot onto that rail. Ready."

"Go."

Dirk grabbed her hands and shoved her out and away. Dena's hand skittered across the featureless stone wall, she slid down, then she got her hands around the windowpane. "Almost—Crap."

Dena's left foot stabbed down. She missed the plant box, and momentum tilted her out, leaning back. She grabbed at the window pane, but it was smooth aluminum and she had no purchase. "Dirk—"

Dirk jumped. He landed in the middle of the planter box, knocking a shower of dirt and hibiscus blossoms loose. His left hand grabbed Dena, arresting her tilt. He braced his feet against the far side of the wooden planter and pushed his back into the wall. Dena drooped lower. He grabbed both her arms.

"Well, isn't this nice," Dena said, hanging back. "Now we're like the kids back home hanging out of the tree, holding each other from falling."

"Quiet, they'll be on the balcony any second."

The door slammed open and lights flooded the upper balcony. The lights flickered as at least two soldiers came out. Dirk shoved his back into the window, holding tight.

"Clear here," a voice said.

"Check the other balconies," a different voice ordered. "Check all the windows too. They have to be somewhere."

The balcony door above them slammed shut, and the light dimmed.

Dirk's breath whooshed out. "Close."

"Still close. We need to get down."

"I'm going to lower you, slowly. If I keep my back straight and my legs braced, I can drop you down about four feet. You should be able to stand on the next ledge down."

"Yes, except my feet are stuck in this stupid plant pot, and I'm edged out over the abyss here."

"It's hardly an abyss," Dirk said. "We're on the second story."

"Fine, you drop first. Count out loud for me, let me know how long it takes you to turn into red mush."

"Lean into me, I'll pull you back, you can step up at me, and your feet will be free."

They pushed and pulled, but every time Dena tried to step up, she unbalanced, and Dirk had to yank her back. The searchers' noises got closer.

"Dirk, they're coming. Faster."

"Be quiet. They'll pass by. And even if we get caught, I can explain things."

"How?"

"Okay, I can't explain things, but it's still better than getting thrown off the roof into the yard."

"Quiet, they're right here."

Voices called out behind him, beyond the window, inside the building.

"Dirk," Dena whispered.

"Quiet," Dirk hissed.

"This window, can they see out of it?"

Dirk glanced left and right. No light either side. "It's blacked out. Probably covered inside."

"Does it open up or out?"

"Shsssss." Voices were right behind him. A handle screeched, and the window pushed out.

"This one's stuck sir," one of the soldiers said.

"Oh no," Dirk whispered.

"Dirk? What?"

"Push," the second voice said.

"Can't sir." The soldier again. "It won't move."

"Dena." Dirk pushed back against the growing pressure. "I'm sorry about this."

"What are you sorry about now?"

"This window. The one I have my back to." The pressure relaxed. Dirk let out a breath.

"What about this window?"

"It opens out. If they get behind it and give it a shove, we're going to—"

The soldier's friends arrived. The window slammed forward, unbalancing Dirk and sending Dena and him rocketing out and into the dark.

"Mr. Cleon. Again, I'm sorry for threatening to stab Mr. Kel." Ana's head shook and Scruggs changed her answer. "I mean, pretending to stab Mr. Kel. Just in fun, you know."

"Felt pretty real to me," Kel said, mopping red wine off his head.

Ana coughed and glared.

"But of course it was fake. No need to report to my colonel."

Ana smiled and nodded.

"But she did break Jaas's wrist and knocked him out."

Kel's guard, Jaas, stood stolidly. A medic in the Planetary Guard uniform was wrapping a bandage around his wrist. "Sorry sir."

"Beaten up by a little girl," Kel said. "We'll talk later, Jaas."

Jaas grimaced.

"I'm sorry about your wrist, Mr. Jaas." Scruggs wiped red wine from her hair. "Those were big glasses of wine. But you shouldn't have extended so far, made you vulnerable."

"Extended?" Jaas said.

"Sure." Scruggs pointed. "You pushed your weapon hand too far forward, so I was able to get inside your reach and disarm you. Um, would you like me to show you?"

Jaas held his bandaged arm up. "Maybe later, Ms."

"Right, sorry."

One of the other female guards—part of the group with Ruby and Sapphire—held up her hand. "Can you show me? You were moving too fast to see."

"Sure. I need a volunteer."

"Maybe Mr. Kel will volunteer."

The crowd laughed.

"Um, perhaps not..." Scruggs looked around.

"I'll do it." Cleon held out his arm and mimicked a gun. "Bang. Bang. What happens next."

"Thank you, Mr. Cleon."

Cleon smiled at her. "Just Cleon, Ms. Scruggs."

"Just Scruggs, then." She smiled back.

Scruggs walked them through the disarm sequence, showing the moves and answering questions. The questions ranged from professionally respectful from the attending local guards, polite corrections from the grinning Marines, and seriously appalled from some of the more squeamish guests.

"Then you turn him like this." Scruggs pushed Cleon's arms back. "You can break his wrist then, or slam his face into the wall." She swung his arm up behind his back and arrowed him forward and pushed him gently into a wall, leaning in until her chin pressed on his shoulder. "That way, you can keep him where you want him, even if he struggles."

One of the younger men at the table laughed. "Oh, he's not going to struggle at all."

Scruggs sniffed. *He smells really nice.* Cologne. Very masculine. She held him a beat longer, realized that she was leaning into him too closely, and stepped back. "I mean, if you need to—"

BANG. Scruggs backed into a waiter who had picked up a tray of broken and near empty glasses. The tray went flying, and again, glass and wine slopped everywhere.

"Oh no!" Scruggs grabbed her face. "I'm so sorry. Again." She looked around. "Sorry. Sorry. I'm never going to get invited to a party here again, am I."

"Are you kidding?" Clara said. "This is most exciting party we've had in years."

"It is?"

"Yes. We're at the ass-end of the Empire. Nothing ever happens here."

CRACK. Voices screamed from outside, behind Ana. They pivoted to peer outside. A shower of small objects pattered over the awnings, and two heavy forms ripped through it.

Dirk had forgotten that the windows were armored glass and darkened against laser fire. The guards inside couldn't see him leaning against it, and assumed his back pressure was the reinforced frame resisting. When the windows stuck, they put their shoulders to it and heaved.

He shoved into Dena, knocking her backwards. Both of them rolled out in a shower of dirt, plants, and busted wood boxes. Dirk flailed his arms and rotated, grabbing Dena and dropping below her. *How long does it take to fall sixty feet? She wanted me to count. One-thousand-one-*

BANG.

He landed back first on the awning covering the garden. The awning ripped, he jack-knifed through and dropped the last ten feet. The rip widened as Dena followed. Both splashed into the duck pond in the center of the courtyard. Dirk missed the stone steps by a foot. Dena missed being impaled on an outdoor light stanchion by less.

A wave of water surged out of the pond, splashing over the curb and onto the steps, then back, submerging them. Dirk kicked with his feet. His heels slammed into the ground, and he opened his mouth to gasp in air. One big gasp before he sank, choking on a surge of green, slimy water. He pushed himself up. Dena was floundering next to him. He grabbed her arm and yanked.

Dena spat, gasped, and spat again. She leaned into Dirk as they stumbled out of the pond and up the steps to the courtyard. Dena's dress was destroyed, ripped in a dozen places. She had magically kept one shoe on. Green slime draped her hair, and her purse was nowhere to be seen.

Dirk had kept his shoes. But the fall had split his jacket down the back, and it hung in two separate pieces draped over his arms, like half of a straitjacket. He stumbled up the stairs, holding Dena and wheezing.

Clara had jumped up at the first noises. She dashed outside with the first crash and made it down the flagstones, and stopped at the top of the stairs. Ana jogged out behind her.

Dirk and Dena swayed as they stumbled out, then halted as Clara approached them.

"My Lord Duke!" Ana yelled from behind her.

All three turned.

"My Lord Duke." Ana marched up. "This is Ms. Clara. The governor's daughter. Ms. Clara. The Duke Garnier."

Dirk swayed. He was bleeding and covered with green slime. His hair was hidden behind a shredded hibiscus that had survived the fall. Dirt streaked on his arms. His coat hung in two pieces, his pants were torn, and he smelled like slime. He extended his arm and grasped hers. "Ms. Clara. Charmed. A great pleasure to meet you."

He bent down and kissed her hand, and thrust it back. Then he stood, smiled, turned to his right, and puked his guts out. "Sorry, old war injury."

Jack, the social secretary, pushed his way through the crowd. "Duke Garnier?"

"Yes?"

Jack surveyed the group. "Is this your whole party?"

Dirk wiped blood and green slime off his face. Dena tried to hide rips in her dress. Scruggs's straps were drooping, and her entire outfit was covered with red wine. Lee had fish sauce on both arms. Gavin's coveralls were stained red. Only Ana appeared clean.

"All of them, yes. Why?"

Jack looked from face to face. "Follow me, please." He smiled. "The governor will see you now."

Chapter 9

"**I** submit, Admiral, that I have no enthusiasm for this plan." Mahony, the captain of the *Hydrogen Pride*, had been the first to raise her hand when the admiral's aide called for questions. "It simply won't work. The numbers don't allow it." Muttered exclamations filled the room, and the admiral's face burned bright red. Admiral Bracebridge did *not* like being contradicted.

Monti shook her head. She, Hooper, and the convoy captains had been assembled, again, to hear the staff's latest plan. Freighters were slogging across Benwe-3's crowded space lanes to form up. It was the third conference in two days.

The admiral glared. "You have no enthusiasm, do you, Captain…"

"Captain Tara Mahony, Imperial Naval Reserve sir." The gray-haired woman at the front stood. "Master, sorry, commander, I meant to say, of the *Hydrogen Pride*." She turned sideways so that she half-faced the crowd. More senior officers jammed the front row, with the juniors piled into the back rows, and the most junior lining the walls. "Given the variety of ship classes and capabilities present here, my colleague Captain Llewling—" she pointed to the thin gray-haired man seated next to her—" and I don't believe you have allocated enough time for operations."

"Not enough time? Based on what?"

"Based on the fueling capacities of the ships here."

"We haven't discussed their fueling capacities."

"No need, we know them. They've all identified themselves, and their ships, after all." Hooper grimaced, but to herself. The admiral's aide had required them to introduce themselves. How everyone introduced themselves was educational. The senior officers, ring-knockers all, gave rank, date of rank, and year of academy graduation. The reserve officers always gave their name, then ship name. The Imperial Naval Volunteer Reserve officers, like Monti and Hooper, gave just name and rank. The admiral had introduced himself with only his title.

Monti shifted in her seat. *Pompous wombat-loving twit.*

"Captain Mahony, then you must find enthusiasm. With the right attitude, all that is listed here can be accomplished. I know that sort of thing is difficult for you reservists to understand. But when you are in the Imperial Navy, you are expected to make do with what you have, and envision the proper attitude when carrying out your duties."

"It's not a question of attitude, Lord Bracebridge." Mahony pointed to the display. "It's a question of math. Merchant ships expect to refuel every jump. If our tankers have to do the refueling, it will take forever. And when we run out of fuel, we won't be able to refuel the fleet at all until we've skimmed some ourselves."

"We have taken these estimates directly from fleet manuals. Are you saying that you expect that these fine people here can't meet our requirements?"

Mahony shook her head. "I can't. Not with a new ship. Not right away." The crowd gasped.

The admiral's aide sputtered, "Captain, are you saying your ship is not up to standards?

"I've commanded over a dozen ships in my career." Mahony shrugged. "Not a single one was up to standards when I first took over. New crews take time to gel. This one is no different."

"Captain, I think your crew could stand some proper discipline. Now you have a regular forces ship to act as an example." Monti stared over his shoulder and tried to not make eye contact. "Many of these ships, particularly the INVR ships, could stand an example or two.

Does he mean good example or bad example? Monti thought.

"Well, Admiral. I won't argue with that. It would be nice to have an example. For once. Since we haven't seen much in the way of regular fleet officers here in years. Any idea why things are that way?" Mahony cocked her head but didn't get an answer. She grunted. "I see. But even if I pretend that my ship is special, it still won't work. You've used the wrong numbers for pumping."

"These numbers come from your specifications! You provided them."

"Yes, but..." Mahony left her chair and walked up to the front and started pointing at numbers and charts.

Hooper had been ducking down and not making eye contact as the aide laid out his disastrous plan. Monti rubbed her forehead and leaned over to her. "This will be a disaster. I don't think that lieutenant has ever served on board a ship on active duty."

Hooper leaned closer. "I don't think that admiral has ever served on board a ship, period."

"I'm glad that reserve captain jumped in."

"She must not care about getting promoted."

"I think she cares about floating around in the black with no fuel and freezing to death more, and I agree with her."

"Admiral doesn't look happy." Captain Mahony had forced them to go back to earlier parts of the presentation and was arguing more numbers. The aide argued back, but the admiral frowned. The other reserve captain had joined his colleague, pointing at more questionable assumptions.

Monti paged through the reports on her comm. "This is a huge convoy. Two transports with ground force equipment. Navy small craft on a carrier. Lots of freighters. Big ones. Look at the cargo lists. Electronics. Computers. Power supplies. Navigation equipment. Ship parts. Jump drive parts. Wow. Jump drive parts. Must be a Navy freighter. This is like six months' worth of supplies for every military unit in the Verge."

"Why do we need a convoy at all? Let them head out when they're ready. Who's the suspected opposition?"

"Not sure, but if we do meet somebody, the Imperial Corvette ISS *Collingwood* won't do much against a modern warship."

"That's what the *Canopus* is for."

"It won't do much against a modern warship either."

A hiss to Monti's right drew her attention. Weeks, the Internal Security Hunk, tilted his head at the front of the room. The four senior officers had stopped talking and were staring at her.

Monti stood, braced to attention and saluted. "Lieutenant Monti. Beg pardon sirs. My first officer and I were reviewing the convoy list with the intention of optimizing our patrol pattern. Could you repeat the question, please?"

"Lieutenant," Lord Bracebridge said, "I expect my officers—"

"To know their ships' capabilities." Mahony pointed at the display. "How big is your fueling port, and how many tons per hour fuel can you take?"

"I—"

Hooper stood, saluted. "Lieutenant Hooper sirs. Ten centimeters. Two hundred tons per hour."

"Very well." Mahony sketched a schedule on the screen. "Four corvettes at two hundred tons an hour. Well within our pumping capacity, but they'll take up all four of our transfer stations, and the timing to move them around is problematic. They don't magically appear and disappear as they are fueled up. Let's put up a list of the potential ships by pipe diameter and fuel requirements..."

Mahony gave a brief class in orbital-fueling 101, leaving the admiral looking more confused than before. Mahony's companion, the other Naval Reserve officer, poked her, and the two of them convinced the admiral to step into an adjacent briefing room. The flag captain told the remaining officers to stand easy, but wait in the room. He hustled after the admiral. The remaining officers relaxed, stood, and formed chatty groups.

Hooper beelined across the room. "Hiiiii, Weeks. How are you, big guy?" Hernandez and Weeks had slipped out of all the other meetings early, and this was her first chance to schmooze.

Weeks leaned in and gave her a big hug. "Great times. Great to see you, Bron. It's been so long. And you too, Monti." He opened his arms wide.

Monti crossed her arms. "No hugging. What's going on? Why this convoy? What's happening?"

"You don't know?" Weeks grinned. "You didn't hear? Where have you been, hiding behind some asteroid grinding ore?"

"I was en route to my new job with C&R lines."

"C&R Lines? A passenger liner?"

"Best in the Core."

"Impressive." Weeks turned to Hooper. "I hear you're working for a short-haul shipping company."

"Yep. Regular routes. Deliveries. Goods, or an entire ship. If you lease a ship, somebody has to deliver it to you. That's me."

"A taxi driver?"

"A taxi driver who worked with the very latest in drive and communication technology, got non-stop piloting time, and all the docking and undocking I wanted."

"Well, good for you. But that will have to wait. The Empire calls."

"I noticed. The recall papers were specific. Answer the Empire's call or go to jail. Decision to be made forthwith. What are we called on to do?"

"Escort this convoy to the Verge."

"Why? The Verge is Imperial territory. It doesn't need a convoy."

"There has been an increase in pirate activity in recent months—"

Monti held up two fingers. "Which means we should have a corvette, or two, with a group of five freighters. There's not a pirate out there that can't be shot up by two corvettes. We don't need all these hulls. The *Canopus*, for Jove's sake. It's so slow, it couldn't catch a drop shuttle even if was attached."

"It's a shield," Hooper said. "The *Canopus* is a shield."

"What?" Monti furrowed her brow. "What shield?"

"It's big and heavily armored. The guns aren't that long ranged compared to a modern warship, but plenty long range for pirates. And there's lots of them and they're powerful. Put it in the middle of a convoy. As long as the convoy goes slow and clusters around it, nothing can come in close enough to attack. Not and live. One shot from *Canopus* and any would-be pirate is so much space dust."

"It's half the speed of modern warships."

"And most freighters are still slower. They can all lumber along right next to it and nothing can touch them."

"But the pirates—"

"This isn't for pirates in up-gunned freighters." Hooper shook her head. "They're worried about something bigger. Regular Navy."

"Wow! Beautiful and smart!" Weeks grinned at Hooper. "So many talents."

"Oh, Weeks." Hooper smiled back. "You have no idea how talented I am."

"I just threw up in my mouth," Monti said. "Fine. Big, slow battleship keeps other ships away. What are the rest of us here for?"

"Pursuit," Weeks said. "Battleship stays with the convoy and protects it. Corvettes can chase any pirates. Destroyers too."

"Destroyers are a bit of overkill for a pirate ship," Monti said. "And what's the cruiser for, then? You've already got a battleship, well, what was once a battleship. Hold that thought. Look who's here."

Hernandez had sauntered up. "Weeks, didn't I tell you not to feed the lieutenants? They're like stray cats. Feed them once and they'll show up every time."

"You never said not to feed them. You said not to play on their gullibility."

"That too."

"Feed the lieutenants?" Hooper grinned and tapped Weeks' shoulder. "Great idea. Maybe after I'll follow you home."

"Can I keep you?"

"Depends what you feed me."

Monti rubbed her head. "Please shut up, both of you. I can't stand much more of this."

"Me neither," Hernandez said. "Odd to be agreeing with you. Did you get your briefing?"

"Only that we're supposed to miss dinner while those reserve captains argue with the admiral." Monti crossed her arms. Again. "Why do we need a convoy? Why to the Verge? Why this escort?"

"Because of Hernandez's boyfriend," Weeks said.

The two Navy lieutenants exchanged glances, then looked at the two Internal Security officers. Hooper rubbed her ears. "Must be getting old. My hearing is going. Did you hear 'Hernandez's boyfriend'?"

"I did." Monti rubbed her own ears. "I must be getting old too."

"This convoy's real reason, if the admiral ever gets around to announcing it, is to convey Lord Bracebridge to the Verge to become the new governor. The current governor, Devin, Lord Lyon—"

"Also known as The Mad Dog of the Verge," Hooper said. "I've heard of what he's doing. Pretty dashing type."

Hernandez ignored her, "Anyway, Lord Lyon—"

Weeks interrupted. "Hernandez's new boyfriend."

"What?" Hooper said. "You're *dating* him!"

"We're not dating. We just, we just had diner together—"

"A sumptuous dinner. Alone on his flagship. They practiced wrestling in the gym. He was teaching her to use his sword—"

"Shut up," Hernandez said. "Devin, I mean, the Lord Lyon—"

"It's Devin now, is it?" Now Hooper crossed her arms. "Dinner alone. Sword practice. Wrestling. Do tell."

"It's not like that." Hernandez glared. "He's what, twenty years older than me?"

"He looks good for his age." Weeks said.

"He's handsome," Monti admitted. "I've seen pictures. Quite striking."

"And really, really wealthy," Hooper said. "Fabulously wealthy."

"That's not. It isn't..." Uncharacteristically, Hernandez seemed flustered.

"Tell them about dinner," Weeks said.

"Yeah." Hooper nodded. "Tell us about dinner. And afterwards."

"It was incredible." Hernandez launched into a discussion of the food, the wine, all the courses, what a great meal it was. The others listened in silence.

"And finally, his steward brought us this dessert—"

"He has a steward?"

"Imin. He's amazing. An amazing cook. And a little scary."

Monti raised her eyebrows. "What do you mean, scary?"

"Scary. Dangerous. Violent."

"You think Lord Lyon's steward is dangerous?"

Weeks interjected, "I've met him. Imin, that is. He scares me."

Hernandez nodded. "He scares me too."

"Well, bite me." Monti frowned. *Say what you like about Hernandez, she doesn't scare easily.* She scanned the room. The participants had broken into groups by service class. Regular Imperial Navy, the smallest, mostly from the *Canopus*, lounged in one corner. The two dozen Imperial Navy Reserve officers sat and chatted in groups. Other than Monti and Hooper, the only Imperial Navy Volunteer Reserve were the lieutenants commanding the other two corvettes, who were hiding in the corner hoping not to be noticed.

"So this gathering of the finest naval officers, at least the finest available at short notice at Benwe-3, is doing what?"

Hernandez looked around the room, and then back at Weeks. He shrugged. "What do you think of Devin, the Lord Lyon?"

Both Monti and Hooper shrugged back. "Imperial noble," Monti said. "Brother to the Empress. I heard him talk once. Gave a great speech. Duty, Honor, Empire. Very old school. Standard stuff. He made it seem real. I left the room wanting to go fight for the Empire."

"Fight who?"

"Didn't matter. Whoever the Emperor wants, I guess."

"I hear he won't have any luxury on his ship that the crew can't share. Clothes, food, that sort of thing. And I've heard that he cuts people's heads off."

"He does that," Hernandez said. "And the food thing is true." She recounted how Devin used his private stores to feed his troops and pay for anything the ship needed. "And he leads from the front. He's always in the thick of things. If there's some danger, he wants to be as close as possible. Very admirable really. An honest man. Dedicated."

"Wow." Hooper rolled her eyes. "She's got it bad. Did you and this honest, dedicated man—"

"He's rebelling," Hernandez said.

"What? No way. Devin? The Lord Lyon? That Devin?"

"Had declared himself in rebellion, according to the secret intelligence briefings I've seen. There's a secret Imperial warrant out on him. Bring him to the Core to face the Emperor's justice. But it's all sealed, no public announcement yet."

"Wow." Monti shook her head. "What's the Empress say about this?"

"Nothing in public."

"She must say something. And what about the Emperor? His wife's brother is a traitor. He must have something to say about that."

"You watch the news."

"Sure."

"You hear any public statements about this? For that matter, when was the last time you saw a picture of the Emperor or the Empress in public, saying anything in any event?"

"I don't really follow—"

"Think hard."

Monti and Hooper exchanged glances. "Well, he gave a speech at the academy..."

"Which was how many years ago?"

"We don't keep track of him like you do."

"I'm telling you he hasn't been seen in public in over a year—almost two. And the Empress either."

"Okaaaaay." Hooper cocked her head. "But he's still the Emperor. She's still the Empress. We still follow orders, even if we thought we'd got out from underneath it. What are we doing here, then?"

"The very regal and formidable, the Lord Bracebridge, is promoted Imperial Tribune, and is replacing Devin, the Lord Lyon, as the governor of the Verge."

"Bracebridge is replacing Lord Devin?"

"Yes."

"But Lord Devin is a famously competent, not to mention loyal, fleet officer. I've been reading the reports on his fights out on the Verge. He can fight. He has fought. And Lord Bracebridge is..." Monti turned to Hooper. "What is Lord Bracebridge?"

"Something at court. Money person. Lots of credits." Hooper nodded. "And a friend of the Chancellor, isn't he?"

"He is."

Monti's eyes swiveled up to regard the ceiling. "That's why the *Canopus*. An admiral needs a battleship. He needs enough force to overawe Devin into quitting—"

"But not enough to think of taking action on his own once he's away from the Core."

"Only a madman would take on the Core fleets with a few squadrons from the Verge, even if he has a battleship."

"Well, I'll tell you that Devin disagrees. He's declared war on the Chancellor and demanded he produce his sister and his nephew for discussions. And he's apparently on his way core-ward with what forces he can gather to enforce his demand."

"He's a crazy man," Monti said. "He can't take on massed Imperial fleets by himself."

Hernandez shrugged. "They don't call him the Mad Dog of the Verge for no reason. I'm sure he has a plan."

"What are you doing here?" Monti asked.

"I had some messages to deliver coreward. Then I got some replies that confused me, so I aborted my journey, and I'm heading back out to the Verge. I need to talk to Devin."

"Talk to him? Aren't we going to fight him?"

"That's the plan."

A scowling admiral, a blank-faced flag captain, and two disgusted-looking reserve captains re-appeared from the adjacent conference room.

"Well," Weeks said. "It appears Admiral Bracebridge has solved his fuel problem."

They all sat.

Monti leaned over to Hernandez. "How are you going to get a message to Devin if we're supposed to fight him?"

"I have my ways."

"What if he's killed in the fighting? We've got battleships and cruisers, and a convoy of supplies and replacement parts. He's got one frigate and some random ships."

Hernandez gestured to the display, where the flag captain was presenting a different course path and fueling schedule, one that they might possibly be able to follow. "That's true. And if it comes down to fighting, who do you think will win? The Mad Dog of the Verge? Or this guy?"

Monti looked at the fuel estimates on the screen. "Jove save me."

Chapter 10

"His excellency said now, he meant now." Jack marched down the hall to the central courtyard. He'd collected the dripping group from the pool and escorted them into the administration wing. The grinning Marines sauntered behind.

"We're not exactly ready for an audience." Dirk waved at the group. His jacket was shredded. Dena had kicked off her remaining shoe and was barefoot. Green pond scum dripped from them both. She clutched a dripping purse that she had dug out of the duck pond. Scruggs's shoulder was bruised from slamming the guards, and her dress was drenched with red wine—and held together by safety pins. Lee and Gavin smelt like the fish sauce smearing their arms. Only Ana was unscathed. "We need a moment to fix our clothing, collect ourselves, get in the right mind for meeting such an important person as a planetary governor." *And dump the purse full of spy-evidence that Dena's carrying.*

Jack led them to an elevator, pushed the button to open the doors, and stepped back and crossed his arms. "Not necessary. Or possible."

"Surely you could give us—"

Jack pointed at the two trailing Marines. "Do I need to call for more Marines?"

Ana shoved Dirk into the elevator. "Nope. Everyone in now." The rest crowded inside after him and the doors closed.

"Centurion." Dirk shook his shoulder free. "Those Marines didn't want to shoot me."

"They did not," Ana agreed. "But from the looks on their faces, they did want to shoot that Jack guy, and we'd be a convenient excuse. And in the line of fire."

"Why won't the governor show his face at his own party?" Scruggs asked.

"Why do the Marines want to shoot the social secretary?" Lee asked.

"And more importantly, what's with this bunker?" Dena pointed to the elevator display, which showed them dropping deeper and deeper. "Is this a part of a Class 7 Imperial building that you didn't know about, Dirk?"

Upon arrival at the bottom end of the elevator journey, they were thoroughly and professionally searched by more Marines. The Marines were polite but insistent. The noncom in charge said that 'the barefoot girl could keep her purse, and the electronics in it' before leading them down a concrete hallway lined with electrical conduits. At the end was an armored door. He tapped a code into the door control, faced a camera, then gestured them in as hydraulics opened the door. "All the way through into the inner office," he said. "And I suggest washing up." He wrinkled his nose. "You smell like burned fish."

Dirk led the group through a small anteroom. To their right was a counter with built-in comm station, to the left, a dozen plain wooden chairs. Ahead was another door, already open. They stepped through into the dim light and found a sitting room. Three couches faced a small table, sideboard with bar, and a display covering an entire wall. A fleshy face filled the screen. "Welcome, Duke Charles Garnier, master of the fishpond. Or should I say Duke Dirk Friedel, the Butcher of New Madrid?"

Dirk froze in the doorway. He stared at the screen then laughed. "Marvelous, the people you meet in the Verge." He flopped onto a couch. "Hello, RC, long time. Haven't seen you since after academy graduation."

"Probably that," the screen face agreed.

"I hear you got kicked out of the Navy, your gambling finally caught up with you."

"I hear you got kicked out of the Navy, you killed a few thousand people and started a war."

"Still better than not paying your gambling debts."

"Should we ask all those dead people on New Madrid whether they agree?"

Dirk looked around. "Somebody get me a drink. Dena, see what's on that sideboard."

"See what's there yourself, I'm not your waitress." Dena nodded to the screen. "Hello. You the governor?"

"I am. Stafford Rafe-Cardigan. RC to my friends, or former classmates. Your name is Dena, I'm told. And you don't have an Imperial warrant on you, as far as I can tell. Interesting."

"And that's interesting why?"

"Other than to make me curious why you were bugging my headquarters? Because there was one on Dirk, and it was canceled, and also on some of the others. Some canceled, some not. All sorts of interesting things about you folks in the files. That fellow in the back—Gavin, he calls himself. The word is, there's some organizations, not Imperial organizations, interested in talking to him. They'll pay well for the privilege. And the young lady there, she's got a price on her head, but no details. And several people want to speak to the Jovian. They've offered some incentives as well."

Dirk was digging through the bottles on the sideboard. "Your intelligence is good as usual, RC."

"I try to keep up."

Dirk held up a bottle. "What's this?"

"Local rum. Palatable, especially when mixed with the local fruit juice."

"I hate rum. What are you going to do? Cash us all in to pay for your gambling debts?"

"The thought had occurred to me," RC said. "Any reason I shouldn't?"

"Lee works for the Empress. Is this whiskey? Real whiskey?"

"Real enough. Why should I care who a Jovian works for? The Empress is a long way from here."

"But she has a long memory, and she won't like anything happening to her people."

"So I leave the Jovian and turn you in. By the way, the Empress wants you dead."

"Could be, but if she does, she wants to do it herself." Dirk sipped. "This could be real whiskey. Centurion, there's brandy over there."

Ana drifted over to the sideboard. "Looks like something of the kind. Say, Mr. Governor, how come you won't meet with us in person? Some people would think that was rude."

"I'm naturally shy," RC said. "And fearful."

"Fearful?"

"Of that remaining weapon you have in your boot. Some sort of pistol. Guards didn't get it, but there's a scanner built into the door."

"I could leave it outside."

"Only if you leave that young redhead lady outside too. She nearly killed a half dozen private guards with a dinner table and a steak knife. Jove alone knows what she'd do to me if she got her hands on one of the office chairs. No, it's safer for everybody if I'm here, and you're there."

"Where is here?"

"Nowhere you need to know," RC said. "I watch all the arrivals at my parties on camera. Lo and behold, who should show up tonight but my old classmate Dirk. Accompanied by one of the Empress's Jovians, a wanted heiress, and a suspected spy, plus two others that I can't identify. One looks like a washed-up soldier, the other a barefoot peasant girl who's the world's worst secret agent. Bugs on the water cooler? Didn't you know we'd have cameras everywhere?"

"First time bugging an Imperial building," Dena said. "Wasn't part of my peasant education. I'm still learning the ropes."

"A colonial, by the accent. Even better," RC said.

"No need to lock us up like this," Dirk said.

"No, but I sense money," RC said. "I should be able to cash in on one or two of you, now that I know who you all are. I'd like you to stay as my guests for a while until I sort this out."

"Not great quarters," Dirk said.

"You've got booze, some ration bars in one of the closets, there's a bathroom, and the humidity is much nicer than outside."

"And I'll bet there's some sort of knockout gas in the fixtures or something."

"Knockout, lethal, not sure." RC smiled. "I haven't tested it recently. Want to help me update my security procedures?"

Dirk downed his glass. *RC was never this crude before. He doesn't want our money, or to kill us. He wants something else. Time to call his bluff.* "Well, this has been a fun talk. But, RC, you're not going to hurt us. You're going to help us get what we want. Then you're going to give us a full tank of H at the starport, and wish us on our merry way. We'll be out of sight and out of mind."

"Why would I do something that strange?" RC asked.

"Because of our new employer," Dirk said.

"And who is your new employer?"

"Devin, the Lord Lyon." Dirk smiled. "Remember him?"

RC's face stilled. Dirk had knocked him off stride. "Imperial Tribune Devin?"

"The very one." Dirk went to get another drink. "Do you still owe him money? I think you almost paid him off after you lost last time. Mortgaged some property, as I recall. Your mommy wasn't happy about that. Said it wasn't worthy of a nobleman."

"That was a long time ago. He'll have forgotten that by now."

"Know what he's calling himself these days? Mad Dog of the Verge. He's putting together a little fleet, not too far away. We're working for him."

"Wait," Ana said. "This worm knows the Tribune guy?"

"Indeed." Dirk sipped. "They used to play poker together."

"How'd that work out?"

"Devin won. RC didn't pay in time. Devin threatened to cut off various parts of his anatomy with that sword he carried. RC mortgaged most of the family estate and paid off...about half maybe. RC's mother kicked him loose, went to Devin and offered the rest of the estate in payment. Devin declined—he's the last Imperial gentleman—and said he'd take care of it at some point in the future. Mommy kicked her little poker-losing wuss out of the house, RC swiped some heirlooms and boarded the fastest spaceship he could find to get as far away from Devin, his mother, and society in general."

"And now he's here." Ana looked at the screen. "I met your stepchildren earlier this evening. Seemed like fine kids."

"That's because they're step-kids, not natural ones,' Dirk said. "If they were his kids, they'd be slobbering deadbeats."

RC scowled through the screen. "I can push a button up here and gas you all to oblivion."

"Why don't you, then?" Ana asked.

"I don't respond well to threats," RC said.

"It's not a threat. It's a question. Why aren't we dead already, then?" Ana tapped his chin. "Ran away with the family jewels, hiding out here in the Verge. New family." Ana turned to the screen. "New family. Was she rich?"

"My monetary affairs are none of your—"

"She had to be rich," Dirk said. "RC had a type. Tall. Busty. Stupid."

"I've always hated you, Dirk, did you know that?" RC said.

Dirk raised an eyebrow. "Really? I always quite liked you. Witty. Fun at a party. You had some good jokes. That one about the mules was outrageous. And as for convincing stupid women to sleep with you, who holds that against a man?" Dirk's eyes tracked the group for a moment.

Dena glared at him. "Careful what you say, lover boy. I'm right here, and I'll bet I could get you before that gas does."

"I didn't mean you. You're actually...intelligent."

Dena shook her head. "Too slow. Have to say that faster."

"She's smarter than you, not that it's that difficult to be smarter than Navy here." Ana nodded. "Let me guess. This woman you married. She wanted the title, but she wasn't as stupid as you think. She tied the money up in a trust or something for the kids, didn't she? Even though she's dead, you can't get at it. The kids turn of age soon, and when they head off to the Core for school, the money goes with them. And you've been holding it all high and mighty over the locals, probably on the strength of what you can get from the kids. Now the payment is coming due. That's why you haven't gassed us yet. You want something."

"I don't need anything from you. I could gas you right now."

Dirk grinned at the screen. "No you couldn't. The centurion is right. If you could, you would have done it by now. The Marines would be angry, but they wouldn't challenge a sitting governor. Wait, how did you get that sorted out? How did a reprobate like you become governor?"

Lee spoke from the back. "I'll bet he bought it. I heard rumors about that, that if you knew the right person in the Chancellor's office, you could buy an appointment. Nothing important, nothing directly under the Emperor or Empress's purview, but fringe planets."

"Unimportant planets," Dirk said.

"This planet," Ana said. "Aha. The artillery. The locals paying off that Jack guy. You bought your way into respectability here, and you've been robbing the planet blind since you got here. The locals have had enough. They're shooting things up. You want to get off this planet ahead of la revolution."

"This is my assigned post. I will not be leaving," RC said.

"Of course you will. You want out and we have something to do with it."

"I don't like your tone. Remember, I can gas you anytime I want."

"Devin knows we're here." Dirk said. "If we disappear, he'll track you down eventually. He'll think it's a matter of honor. And you know how relentless he is about his honor." *And I know he scares you. He scares me.*

RC rubbed his forehead. "Is it true, then? He's started a rebellion? We've had a problem getting news out here. The chancellor's people seem... overactive recently."

"He's responding to certain activities in the Core, but yes, I suppose you could call it a rebellion. But he knows we're here. In fact, he sent us, and he's expecting us back shortly. And one thing about him. Compared even to the Empress, he has no sense of humor at all. Imagine what he'll do to you if you get in his way."

"What does he want?"

Dirk smiled. *RC wants something. He'd trade the database for whatever it is.* As long as it wasn't too expensive, Dirk could give him what he wanted.

"Just some items from your local courier database. Something well within the gift of a sitting Imperial Governor. You can do that. And in return, you want...what?"

RC nodded. "The rest of you, grab some drinks and head into the other room. Dirk, sit down. I have a proposition for you."

Chapter 11

"**B**leagh." Dirk rolled down a window and spat. "I'm still tasting frog pond slime."

Dena licked her lips. "The governor should have at least fed us, or given us a nicer car. How long were we down there anyway?"

"Long enough for him to put as many bugs onto this car as he wanted. Gavin?"

Gavin looked up from the scanner on his lap and nodded. He held up three fingers, pointed to the ceiling, the driver's console, and the built-in bar in the back. Everyone shut up for the rest of the drive.

RC's Marines had brought them out to the driveway, returned their weapons, and shoved them into their limo. Then he told them to beat feet out of town. The roads were 'generally unsafe after dark due to local bandit activity.' Ana popped on a pair of heavy sunglasses that doubled as low light enhancement goggles and took over the driving, with Scruggs as shotgun. The others crowded the back and tried to ignore how badly they smelled. The sun was setting as they arrived at the starport and parked the car on the deserted tarmac.

After tramping on board, they all played with Rocky, had showers, then headed for the lounge. Scruggs brought out a plate of local fruit, mostly melons, and started pouring them drinks of juice.

"What's this?" Dena poked at her fruit. "Is it good?"

"I don't know. I thought because they were so expensive…"

"Enough discussions about food," Dirk said. "Everybody listen to me."

The crew obediently turned to him. "Well, this is weird," Dirk said.

"What's weird, Pilot?" Lee asked.

"Everybody is paying attention. That's a first." *And it probably won't last long.*

Ana snorted. "We've gotten used to listening to you spout your latest plan, Navy. That Tribune guy more or less hired us and put you in charge, so it's always worthwhile to listen to you."

"Because I make good plans?"

"Because I'll get bored if I have nothing to do but eat melon. And I enjoy a good laugh from time to time. Tell us about your amazing plan to get the data we need."

"Right, I was talking to RC. He has this strange thing—"

BOOM. The ship's hatch was open to vent their stench, and the low-pitched boom came from the distance.

Ana held up a hand. They sat quietly. Ana shook his head. "That's another one. The tempo is increasing?"

"I've heard it more often tonight," Gavin said.

"Outstanding. Well, Navy. You were talking to RC about this strange—"

Scruggs raised her hand.

"Private?"

"Cleon said he'd call me later."

"And he didn't do it. Yes, men do that. They lie. You'll have to get used to it. But we're talking about explosions and plans here."

"No, I mean, yes, I know. But he said it would be in a couple of days. He said his unit had been activated today and they were going on operations, and he'd be back later this week."

Ana thought for a moment. "Dena, did your boy-toy set up to call you this week?"

Dena shook her head. "Nope."

"Does that surprise you?"

"Yes. I expected to be skinny dipping in a river by now."

"Seems like we've arrived at a time when the operations tempo is increasing. Interesting. Navy, how come the Marines haven't scragged this governor guy?"

"Hasn't done anything disloyal. Marines protect the Empire, not enforce laws. Now, about RC—"

"He's stealing the place blind. Enough that the locals have raised an army against him."

"As long as they don't attack Empire House." Dirk snapped his fingers. "That explains this Planetary Guard thing. Governor is in charge of local irregular forces. He's created his own private army to put the squeeze on the locals."

"And they're getting ready to fight back. Outstanding."

"One other thing, Centurion," Scruggs said. "As we left, there were more... poor people in town."

"Poor people?"

"There were some groups of badly dressed men and women wandering the market. They weren't buying anything."

"How badly dressed? Like ripped clothes?"

"No, just disheveled, like they had been hiking for a long time."

"Interesting." Ana stared off into space for a moment. "Let me just enumerate our successes so far." He ticked off his hands. "On the downside. One, everybody knows who we are, so we can't hide or sneak around. Two, they think Navy is a twit and possibly not a real duke, Dena's a complete airhead, Scruggs is a psychotic killer, and Gavin and Lee are trigger-happy guards."

"Not a completely inaccurate assessment, Centurion," Lee said.

Dirk gave up and sipped his drink. *I'll get back to RC in a minute.* "Gavin does look trigger happy."

"And you don't look like a duke." Gavin raised his eyebrows. "What about you, Old Man?"

Ana drummed his fingers on the desk. "They think I'm a mean old man who likes to shoot people in the head."

"Now," Dena said. "That's not very fair to you."

"It isn't," Ana agreed. "Wait. You're defending me?"

"Of course. Even I know you're not like that." Dena took a drink. "This mango thing is good. I could get used to it. No, Old Man, everybody knows you're not like that."

"Well, thanks, I guess."

"Sure. We all know you'd rather shoot somebody in the stomach."

"Better target," Scruggs said.

"More painful," Dena agreed.

"Takes longer to die," Gavin said.

Ana spun his cup in a circle. "I don't know whether to be embarrassed or proud."

"You choose." Dirk drained his cup. "You said those were the downsides. What's our upsides?"

"You tell me." Ana nodded. "What did your old friend RC say?"

"He has a proposal." Dirk sipped his basic. "He'll give us a database dump of the last six months of messages from the Core. That includes fleet and merchant movements. Imperial Naval traffic, operations plans. Everything that's passed through his office."

"Gotta love the loyalty of the officers the Empire's picking these days," Ana said.

"I'm a commissioned naval officer with a formal request from a sector governor for a copy of backup information. There's a request form for it. We spent most of our talk filling it out and getting my signature on things. Given that Devin is still a governor, it might be legal."

"Isn't he under arrest?"

"The Subprefect—no, he's a Prefect now—he was ordered to arrest Devin but hasn't done it yet. So anything Devin does 'til then is legal."

"That's it, he's just going to do it? I smell a rat. What if he doesn't give us the information?"

"I told him I'd want one of our people there while he did it to watch, and take random samples of the information. He's giving it to us on portable datapaks. It's a lot of information."

"You can do that? Check the validity?"

"No, I can't. Maybe Gavin..."

"Skipper." Gavin looked embarrassed. "I can break some codes and things, but I'm not sure—"

"I'll do it," Lee said. "I'm familiar with Imperial databases and codes. And I can look for some routine but necessary updates that should be there that he won't think of hiding. Things like astro updates, some Jovian deployment notices. If those are there and the code-hashes match, I'll know we have the whole database."

"Huh." Ana nodded. "Well, for once, having a Jovian onboard turns out to be a good thing."

"Every time we plot a course it's a good thing, Centurion," Dirk said.

"Or shoot it out with a tank," Scruggs said.

"Or do any sort of cargo operations," Lee said.

They all turned to Dena. "What?" Dena shrugged. "I like her too, but I don't understand what she does. It's important, right?"

"I stand corrected." Ana stood and bowed. "Praetorian. Glad you're onboard. So we drive in tomorrow, you oversee the downloading of this database, and we drive away. What's the hitch?"

"Not much of a hitch," Dirk said. "We have to take some cargo out for him. Not even far, delivery to the next major world on the courier route."

"Special cargo? Things he's stolen?"

"I'm sure. Private special cargo. A dozen crates, one big one—two meters cubed—and the rest all less than a meter."

"Two meters." Gavin stretched. "Six feet more or less. Individual crates, not a container stuffed with them?"

"No containers. Crates. And they must be stored in atmosphere."

Gavin nodded. "We'll put them in the hold, inside the cages. How heavy?"

"Heavy. Smaller ones are hundred kilos. Larger one about five hundred."

"If we bring them up the ramp, I'll need to set up skids and check the interior crane." The *Heart's Desire* had drag winches to load cargo, and an internal rack and chain system to shift cargo in the hold.

"What's to stop us from saying no after we get our database download?" Ana asked.

"He says he'll encrypt it on the datapak. Our contact at the next planet will have a decryption key that will let us sort it out."

"You believe him?" Ana asked. "Can we trust him?"

"No, and absolutely not," Dirk said. "But I told him that if we got to the destination, we'd decrypt the data first. If it didn't decrypt, we'd dump all his precious crates out the airlock. He didn't like that."

"We'd open them first," Ana said. "Find anything good in them."

"Like what? Gold? Gems?"

"I was thinking field artillery or lasers."

"It might be wood," Dena said.

"Wood? He's smuggling wood?" Ana laughed. "You think that?"

"Yup. Did you get a look at how fine-grained some of those tables were? Made of teak. Carpenters love that sort of stuff. And from what you said, it's near bulletproof. I can see some Imperial alpha-bear getting this desk or table set that's unique in the universe. It also stops lasers and rifle shots, 'cause it's so heavy."

"Wow. That's actually smart." Ana finished his glass. "Who are you and where did you hide the real Nature Girl? Or is this tree thing something that everybody on Rockdirt knows about?"

"Common sense. Which you don't know a thing about. And I had to work in planet side trade for a while," Dena said. "I paid attention. Nature products are great cargos for starships. Things like special woods and plants and food can't be duplicated easily elsewhere. Big payoff in the luxury market."

Ana laughed. "It's a special day. Nature Girl taught me something new."

Another boom floated in from the hills. Dirk jerked. "More of those booms. Ana, are you sure they're artillery?"

"Yes. Big ones. But they've been re-chambered for a different caliber and lost some muzzle velocity."

"Whatever that means," Dena said. "Can we keep it simple?"

Ana slapped his chest. "Big boom go bang. Big bang. Bang different. Simple enough?"

Dena stuck her tongue out at him. It was stained orange from the melon. "Are we worried about these explosions?"

"I don't understand them. I don't like surprises." Ana grimaced. "It's not important. Probably not important. How soon can we get off this stinking pile of jungle?"

"We can't just leave." Lee waved around the ship. "We promised the Tribune we'd get those records. One way or another."

"Let's try one thing, then," Dirk said. "Then another."

Chapter 12

"We're convoy Core-Verge number thirteen," Lieutenant Hooper told Lieutenant Monti. "CV-13 for short. Fleet numbering scheme."

"And they decided to start with thirteen? Because it's lucky? Jove save us. Are we ready?"

Monti gestured at the bridge of the corvette ISS *Collingwood*. They had returned to the ship after finally getting orders to assist in the convoy formation. "We've got exactly two petty officers, other than us, who are watch standing qualified. We don't have an engineer, just a chief petty officer who's familiar with the systems. We have exactly eight people on the crew who have been in the Navy longer than four years."

"Does that eight include us?"

Hooper lowered her voice. "Correction. There are six people on board, other than us, who have been in the Navy longer than four years."

"Jove save us. Are we ready to undock at least?" After the fiasco of the briefing meeting, the admiral had ordered them to depart, overriding the complaints.

"As ready as we'll ever be."

"That's a no." Monti adjusted her command chair down. The bridge ceiling was so low, she'd bang her head if she stood. So many extra control boards were jammed in, there was a real danger that if she stretched, she'd hit something important, like the master airlock override or the slug thrower eject button. *Have to remember to keep my hands on my lap when I'm talking.*

Her chair was to port, Hooper's to starboard. Ratings occupied three of the four stations in front of them. A screen covered the front bulkhead, the bottom half obscured by the control stations. Weapons control was the port side, then a combined sensors and comm station, then a combined navigation and helm. On the starboard sat an empty engineering station. One of the overhead lights was burnt out, and the comm console had a six-inch dent on the top. The whole place stank like old socks.

Monti pointed to the engineering station. "No engineering ratings?"

"None to spare for the bridge. They need them in the back."

"Right." Monti took a breath, then whispered, "At action stations, I'll take helm, navigation, and engineering. You take weapons and sensors. I'll tell you where we're going, get us there and avoid any return fire. Use the sensors to find what's out there and shoot it if necessary."

"Engineering?"

"We'll hope the engines keep working. If they don't, there's nothing we can do, got it?"

"Right. What about comms?"

Monti pointed at the three ratings, heads together, debating the meaning of a display screen. "Surely between the three of them, they can figure out how to make comms work."

The leftmost rating stabbed at the screen. All the cabin lights went out, and music played over the main system until he managed to slap it off. He blushed and turned to the captain. She waved him off, then closed her eyes and sighed. "How can this get any worse?"

"Got good news for you, then. Hernandez and Weeks are coming with us."

Having the two Internal Security officers on board turned out to be a good thing, to Monti's surprise.

"Yes, we can both stand watches," Hernandez said when they caucused in Monti's quarters. "We're both watch qualified."

"You can fly a starship?" Monti asked.

"Fly? Nope. Not pilot. Not this class. But we can both navigate, and we're engineering and weapons watch qualified. Both of us can read a board and decipher warning messages. You can get some sleep while we're here. If it's important, we'll wake you up. If it's not, you can sleep. And we can tell the difference between when to wake you and when to let you sleep."

"Right, now, in the matter of seniority—"

"You're in command. We'll do as you say. No complaints."

"I'm surprised."

"You've had a lot more ship time." Hernandez shrugged. "Weeks and I have been doing other things since the academy. You're more current. Underway, you're the boss."

"Well, that's... good. Thank you." Monti frowned. "Why are you here?"

"To serve the Emperor."

"Yes, but why are you serving the Emperor on this particular ship. Why not the *Canopus*?"

"For starters, having a corvette that can zip between ships will help us with some of our communication duties. We have packages and things to deliver."

"Packages to deliver?"

"Intelligence briefings. It's in your orders—all approved by the admiral. He didn't ask for any details—he's as fond of Internal Security as you are."

"Are you here as Internal Security, or Naval Intelligence?"

"Both, but we're operating under Internal Security orders right now."

"Jove save us. Fine. What do you need from me?" *Please don't ask me to do any secret Internal Security things. It's bad enough to have an idiot admiral, but add in supposedly secret maneuvers...*

"While we're meandering along, we'll need to visit a few ships. Pick some things up, drop some things off. Speak to some people."

Crapdoodle. "And I don't want to know who these people are?"

"You will at some point."

"And when will this point come?"

"You'll know. If you're not sure, we'll help you out."

"I don't like this. What's really going on?"

"You'll find out. Look, the flag captain is calling. Better answer that."

Monti took the call, said 'yes sir' several times, and signed off. "Hooper, prepare new patrol routes for three corvettes, rather than four, and send it off to the convoy escort commander."

"Who is the convoy escort commander?"

"That would be me."

"Not the destroyers?"

"The admiral insists that the 'properly crewed ships' remain close as his escorts, and the 'reserve ships' take on convoy protection duties."

"I thought one of the other corvettes was senior."

"Nope. Me."

"Why are we short a ship?"

"Complete jump drive failure. Dockyard job."

Hooper pulled up her comm. "We could barely do a competent screen with four ships. With three, there's always going to be holes."

"I already told the flag captain that."

"What did he say?"

"Said we needed to show the proper attitude."

"Jove save us."

Seven days later, the convoy departed Benwe-3. More than eighty ships traveled together to a half dozen destinations in the Verge. The admiral had issued a plan to have the *Canopus* and the cruiser, flanked by the two destroyers, lead as they departed. The remainder of the ships formed a hexagonal pattern—a ship at each point of the hexagon, and another ship in the center. Then extend this back for ten to twelve ships in column. The three corvettes and two smaller mine removal vessels scooted along outside in loose formation.

"Never seen a convoy form up like this before," Hernandez said. She and Weeks were stuffed into the back of the bridge, watching the ship movements on the main screen. "Not even in the stranger simulations."

"That's because, tactically, this is a disaster in the making," Hooper said. "From the front, *Canopus* and the cruiser can't protect anything—they'll have to fire through the convoy if somebody comes up behind or even the side quadrants. Raiders will get free shots at the rest of the ships before they come into range. And keeping the destroyers in concert destroys their tactical flexibility."

"For a Wavy Navy type, you talk a lot of military words."

"Unlike you, I paid attention in tactics class."

"I didn't." Hernandez shrugged. "I thought Naval Intelligence would be more fun. I was right. So, our formation is not tactically flexible. That sounds bad."

"It is bad. But never mind tactical flexibility. Station keeping will be impossible. Check this out." Hooper highlighted one of the ships in the center of the hexagonal ring. "This is an attack transport. Its Auto-ID is squawking a capability of four-G acceleration."

"So it's fast."

"Yes, faster than the ships outside of it."

Hernandez shrugged again. "So? What does that mean?"

Hooper shook her head from the captain's chair. "Wait for the first turn."

Forming up was only a minor disaster.

"I don't care what your admiral says, you can tell him to shove his course corrections up his Imperial behind," the master of the *Sweet Campari* said. Lord Bracebridge had ordered *Collingwood* to chase down wayward freighters who refused to drop into formation. "I'm not getting any closer to that ore carrier. He'll run me down."

"Captain..." Monti checked the convoy book. "Captain Rihari, you must return to your sailing station, two-eight." Sailing stations IDs were one of the seven columns followed by the position in the column. "The admiral expects you to be in your assigned position before we maneuver to reach the jump limit."

"My assigned position has another ship in it."

"I understand that the ship behind you in the column, *Alatiri*, hasn't allowed the proper interval between them and the next ship, but I'll be speaking to its captain—"

"Jim Carrington is *Alatiri's* captain. And if he isn't drunk by this time of day, it's a special day. Every skipper in this system knows that's why he was kicked off the intra-system shuttle run, for being too soused to steer. And the shuttle companies aren't known for enforcing drinking regs, so if you get fired from them, you're a menace to yourself and others."

"I'll convey your concerns to the admiral, but convoy regulations dictate that—"

"Screw you. Screw your convoy regulations. Screw your admiral, and screw sailing station two-eight. You like it so much, you fly there. I'm staying out here where I can see who comes running at me, where I'm safe. Rihari out."

Monti's screen blanked. "Damn all freighter captains!"

"Don't you want to be a freighter captain?" Hooper asked.

"Passenger liner captain. Totally different thing."

"Doesn't sound like it. What now?"

"Can we hit him with the main laser?"

"Blast him out of the sky? Ballsy, even for you." Hooper brought up a screen. "He's in range."

"Not at full power. Put it at one percent."

"Even one percent will seriously annoy him."

"How will that be worse compared to how annoyed he is now?"

"Good point." Hooper turned back to her screen. "Let me set up the targeting."

"Fine." Monti raised her voice. "Silaski, mirror Lieutenant Hooper's screen so you can see what she—Jove. Are you sick again?"

Silaski, the heavyset woman at the weapons console, pulled the bag away from her mouth. "Yes, Captain. Sorry, Captain."

"This is the third time. Do you always get space sick?"

"Every time, Captain. Any sort of maneuvering in zero-G, and I puke."

"Why did you join the Navy, for Jove's sake?"

"Naval Volunteer Reserve ma'am."

"Why did you join the reserves, then?"

"Why? Eighty-six credits a month, and two weeks a year at fifty credits a day."

"But you knew you'd have to go into space."

Silaski shook her head. "In the volunteer reserves? Never had to before. This is my first time on a ship. Never fired any of the weapons before."

"But you're weapons rated. How is that possible?"

Silaski looked sheepish. "Well, you see sir, since there was no chance of ever getting on a ship, the usual way, if you're interested..."

"Very much so. Interested. Concerned." *And possibly terrified.*

"The usual way was to take the computer test, then have your petty officer certify you as 'examined,' then you get the qualification."

"Why would you do that?"

Hernandez coughed from beside Monti. Monti half turned. "What?"

"Money. Qualifications mean raises."

Hernandez turned back to Silaski. "You paid for your rating?"

Silaski nodded. "Everybody does it."

"Well, I'm going to put a stop to that. It's unethical and dangerous. Consider yourself on report."

Silaski nodded, then grabbed her puke bag and retched again.

Hernandez shook her head and looked over her shoulder. "Are you going to put her chief on report as well?"

"What? Why?"

"Because the chief took a kickback of her first three months' pay raise as payment for certifying her."

"That can't be true." Monti turned to Hooper. "Is this true?"

"You always were a bit on the straitlaced side, Franky."

"Well, if the chiefs are taking bribes, then I'll contact their officers—" Monti's eyes widened. "No. Are the officers in on it too?"

"Franky." Hooper typed on her screen and sighed. "Did you ever wonder why the regular force and the regular reserve hate the volunteer reserve people and don't trust them? It's because most of them are incompetent. And crooks to boot."

"But I'm not incompetent. Neither are you."

"We went to the academy. We got proper training from people we couldn't bribe even if we wanted to. Well, not with money. And most people who go to the academy sign up for regular service. You and me, we were almost the only ones who took the early out with Imperial Space Navy Volunteer Reserve ratings rather than regular forces."

"I wasn't going to be in the Navy for ten years!"

"Neither was I. But we're the exception. Remember, most ISNVR types are like Silaski here. Barely trained. Not qualified for their ranks. No actual time in the job. No practical skills. And that's the ratings. The officers are even worse."

Hernandez nodded. "And some of them are even convicts. Half a dozen of the engine room ratings were brigged dirtside for some sort of offense. They're in the Navy now!"

"But we've got a ship full of them. How are we going to survive?"

"We gotta find something that they can do. Silaski!"

"Ma'am?" Silaski sat up straight.

"What can you do—no. What have you done? What skills are you competent at doing?"

"I'm a pretty fair carpenter ma'am."

"Space skills. Starship skills."

"Ummm. I can work a comm board, I think. I've done that before."

I've got a ship full of untrained idiots, but Bron and I can't do everything by ourselves. Get them to do what they can. "Outstanding. Well, you're senior comm rating now. You'll handle communications."

"Yes ma'am. Thank you ma'am. But.."

"But what?"

Silaski opened her mouth to reply, gulped once, then grabbed her bag. She spewed the remaining contents of her stomach into it. Bits of vomit missed and sapped into the console, and the sweet smell of stomach acid floated around the bridge.

She wiped her wrist across her mouth. "Thank you ma'am. I'll do my best. Happy to help." Her eyes widened and sweat broke out on her forehead. She shoved her mouth back into the bag, and took four rapid breaths, slowing down. Then she removed the bag and stared at the bridge officers. "Happy to. But I think you should wait 'til I get my space legs."

Chapter 13

"Everyone into the car," Dirk said. "Lock up the ship and set the security systems."

Because RC was going to provide a truck, Lee had rented a different limousine the next day to bring them into town. Dirk didn't want to deal with finding all the bugs and not being sure that they missed one.

"It'll be safe here." Dirk watched the ramp lift behind them. "The Marines always defend the starport."

"Because they want to protect Imperial equipment?" Dena asked.

"Because that's their way off planet if things go sideways. They always protect their line of retreat. If things go sideways, we'll be able to get away with them," Dirk said. *As long as we get back here in time, of course.* "Let's roll."

"I feel like I've seen this spaceport before," Dena said.

The spaceport had six pads surrounded by berms. Each berm had a road that opened into the center area where the passenger terminal building was.

"Class 7 terminal. Matches Empire House," Dirk said as their car rolled past the terminal and onto the access road. "Hangars for maintenance, fire station, Imperial Customs office, operations, that type of thing."

"And the most overpriced rental cars I've ever seen," Lee said.

Today's limousine was more truck than car. Heavy electric motor up front, batteries in the floor. Shiny black finish and snazzy blue and green hubcaps completed the setup. Gavin and Ana sat up front on a bench seat wide enough for four. Dirk and the women sat facing each other on two bench seats in the back.

Dirk had them dress up like they were going to an afternoon party. Gavin and Lee both wore clean ship coveralls, and they were already sweating. Since they'd destroyed their party clothes previously, Scruggs and Dena wore brand new brightly colored sundresses that Gavin had bought at the starport market. They didn't fit perfectly. Scruggs thought they were too revealing, Dena not enough. But both wore heavy boots with the dresses rather than heels.

"The boots ruin the outfit," Dena said. "But at least I can walk. And if I had heels, I couldn't stand on this." She thumped the four-foot metal box that Gavin and Ana had jammed onto the back seat floor.

"They only ruin it if you're embarrassed about it," Dirk said. "Tell everyone that it's the new style coming out from the capital. You'll start a trend." He himself wore a loose shirt tied at the neck and wrists, and loose linen pants.

Only Ana looked partially formal. His uniform was almost the same as he had worn at the disastrous governor's levée before.

Gavin made sure they were all belted in and accelerated past the terminal and out past the boundary fence. Rocky sat in the back between the two women and wagged his tail. The pack was moving! Adventure!

"Any particular reason you've insisted on being overdressed, Centurion?" Dirk asked. "Why not wear coveralls like the others?"

"Because we might need to talk to the Marines again, and I can't wear decorations on coveralls."

"Why would the Marines care?"

"They probably don't." Ana looked out the window. "I don't. But I don't trust that RC guy."

"Because he's a duplicitous political type?" Dirk asked.

"Because he's a friend of yours. Did he tell the Marines who we were?"

"He said no. Part of the deal is we keep it a secret. I commed him this morning to tell him we're on our way in to pick up his shipment, and he stressed the secrecy part. But if we keep our word, he'll keep his word."

"He's a weasel. Why would he keep his word? He'll double-cross us at the first opportunity."

"He needs something from us. He'll support us as long as we can get what he wants. We can trust him 'til then."

"Really?"

"Yes. Until then. But after, he'll double-cross us."

"Good to have a schedule." Ana grimaced.

Gavin stood on the brakes as they rounded a corner. Just short of a crossroads, a truck with a green diamond on it—the logo of the Planetary Guard—blocked the exit from the starport. Incoming and outgoing traffic was forced off the road on either side, where rifle-toting troops stood. Those coming into the starport were being questioned, those leaving waved through.

"That's new," Gavin said. "Marines searching people entering the starport."

"Not quite," Ana said. "Those aren't Marines, they are those Planetary Guard types. See, they're chewing and spitting something. Watch."

One of the guards turned his head, spat out a partially masticated ball of blue-green leaves, then shoved another into his cheek.

"Any sergeant caught his Marines doing that, they'd do ten thousand push-ups on the spot. And they weren't on the starport reservation. That's not stopping people entering the starport, that's stopping people leaving the planet. Subtle difference, but important."

Dirk looked out the window. "What are they chewing?"

"Some sort of local narcotic plant."

"Speaking of subtle." Gavin leaned to get a view of Ana's chest, then snorted. "Good camouflage, Centurion, those awards, that'll impress them."

"I figured it would," Ana said.

"What will you tell them if they ask for details on how you got all those awards?"

"I'll tell them." Ana looked out the window. "Everybody keep your eyes peeled. Something's off."

Their limo zoomed along the road in silence. It was a good road, concrete, two lanes, clear area on either side. The starport was eighty kilometers outside the city up in the foothills—riverbeds and muddy flood plains are not good places to park heavy starships. The road ran along a hillside overlooking a meandering stream. The stream was dammed at intervals to produce fish ponds and irrigate crops.

"Smoke, Centurion." Scruggs pointed out the side windows. "Back there, in the hills. Something is burning."

Dirk twisted in his seat to look. "Could be forest clearing."

"Or a vehicle," Ana said.

There was another of those soft 'bumps' that they had been hearing for days, and smoke blossomed from a hill in the distance behind them.

"That's the turnoff that we passed, where that Planetary Guard was."

"Where did that road go? The crossroad?"

"That's the one with the teak plantations," Dirk said.

"If it is," Lee said, "then that makes that other smoke the road up into the mountains where the mines are."

Scruggs tapped her comm. "My comm is down. I can't raise the ship."

"Mine too," Dirk said. "They brought the network down. Whoever they are."

"Outstanding," Ana said. "Navy, we've switched from one thing to another. Scruggs, get that box open."

Dena removed her booted feet and popped a latch. Scruggs did the same. The box was an arsenal, and they handed out the weapons to the crew. Scruggs and Dena got shotguns, Ana, a rifle. Gavin got a spare shotgun, and Dirk and Lee revolvers.

Ana checked his rifle and cursed.

"Problem with the rifle, Centurion?" Scruggs asked.

"Yes. Not enough of them. I've forgotten that we're in the field, and not on a ship or in a building. Wrong mix." He pointed. "One rifle. Three shotguns. You girls are fine in a close fight, but we need more long-range firepower." Ana turned to Gavin. "Can you hit anything at a distance?"

Gavin kept his eyes on the road. "Nobody can hit anything at a distance with a shotgun."

"Outstanding. And two handguns."

Lee and Dirk strapped on holsters.

"Listen up everybody," Ana said. "Something bad is going on. It's not our bad, but we're here and have things to do, so we might get caught in the back blast."

"Should I turn around?" Gavin asked. "Road is clear now."

"We've got definite fighting behind us." Ana waved at the smoke behind them. "And nothing in front. We can't stay here. Move on."

"We're not part of their fight, Centurion," Scruggs said. "Why would they attack us?"

"They won't attack us—" Ana said.

"That's good."

"I wasn't finished. They won't attack us if they know who we are," Ana growled. "Which they don't. Which means on this road, right now, we're target number one."

Chapter 14

"Centurion. Something is not right." Gavin gently steered the car through the next turn. The fields on either side had disappeared, replaced by woods. The few farms and houses were well back in the trees, nearly invisible.

"I know." Ana checked his rifle.

"What is it? I know something's different, my hackles are rising. But I don't know why."

"You see any farmers or workers in those fields, Engineer? Or in those buildings."

Gavin set the auto cruise and craned his neck for a better view. He and Dena were the two best ground vehicle drivers. Dena was unused to electronic systems, so usually, Gavin drove the higher tech vehicles. He drove them past a driveway that led into a cluster of buildings. Two garages, a barn, and a house. Not a soul was visible. "Nope."

Dena knelt on her seat. "It's the middle of the work day. If they're not working, we should see cooking fires or groups drinking water or lying in the shade. And I don't see cars or horses or even bicycles. Where is everybody?"

Rocky growled. He was strapped in, like he always was, but he picked up on the tension.

"They got the word. Somebody came by yesterday or this morning and told them to call in sick, or be late, or head out into the bush. Something is going down. Today. Now." Ana wound down his window. "Windows down everyone."

"Won't they give us protection?" Dena played with the buttons on the door.

"It's only glass. All they can do is blind us with splinters and interfere with shooting. Everybody gun up and be ready."

"Can't we call for help?" Dena asked.

"Even if our comms were working, help for what? Nothing's happened yet. And we're miles out of town. What do we do while we're waiting? Sit by the side of the road and collect frogs?"

"We could go back to the starport..."

"If they'll let us in. Those Planetary Guard people were there."

"But they're the governor's troops, aren't they?" Dena asked.

"They were. Who knows who they answer to now?"

Scruggs watched the back road. "Centurion, there's a car back there."

Ana stretched to look. "So much for that option. How long has it been there?"

"It came from that farmstead we passed."

"That's the rear element," Ana said. "There will be a forward element ahead, blocking the road. Something will force us to stop, and we'll be caught between the forward element and the pursuing one. If we can fight through, we're fine." *Provided there isn't a fire element overlooking the ambush with heavy weapons. Or another forward element to catch runners.*

All the windows came down. Scruggs and Dena gripped shotguns. Ana had his rifle across his lap.

Gavin cut the auto-cruise then swerved around a pothole. "I haven't seen any traffic from the direction of the city since we left the starport."

"Scruggs," Ana said. "Load the shotgun for the engineer here. Dena, keep that slingshot handy. You two, strap in. Dena, on the right, covering out the right window. Scruggs, strap in on the left and watch our back. Pilot, middle of the back seat so Dena and Scruggs can fire past you if needed, but put the navigator in the center on the floor and shield her."

"Thanks for your concern, Centurion." Lee brandished her pistol. "But I can shoot."

"I know you can." Ana's eyes never left the road. "But none of us can medic. Not as well as you. Everyone, here's the drill. We are not leaving this vehicle unless it explodes or is on fire. Our best bet is to power through anything in our way. Engineer, do not stop for any reason unless the car does. Understood?"

"Understood, Centurion."·

"Navigator, or should I say medic. Keep your pistol. If we crash, or roll, your job is to get the wounded into cover. Behind the car. Out. Wherever. Even one at a time. Got that?"

"Get them out and take them where?"

"The opposite direction from where we're taking fire."

Lee was no fool. "And if we don't know or it's coming from more than one direction?"

"Nearest woods," Ana said. "Hide the wounded. Everyone else. If—when—we are ambushed, we attack it as fast and as hard as we can, with whatever we've got. But only if the car stops. If the car stops, skids, dies, whatever, exit and charge the nearest fire source. Right away. All at once."

"Be still, boy." Scruggs stroked Rocky's shoulder. "But be ready, we might need you."

Rocky bared his teeth and growled but sat still. The pack masters were talking, and the pack was going into battle. He'd be ready when called.

"Isn't that kind of risky?" Dena asked. "Charging? Shouldn't we shoot from cover?"

"You're good with that slingshot, aren't you?"

"Sure. Better than you are with your pistol."

Ana ignored that. "How far away can you hit somebody with it?"

"I hit a hundred-yard target once, in a competition."

"This isn't a competition. They won't be standing still, they'll be firing back, and your hands will shake from adrenaline."

Dena scrunched up her face. "Fifty feet."

"With a weapon that's customized for you, which you trained with for years. How far away do you think we'll be able to hit something with one of those shotguns? Or those handguns."

"Not fifty feet. So we have to get in close, which means charging."

"Remember." Ana gestured. "Those folks out there, unless they're trained and experienced, they'll be nervous too. So if we go after them, we'll rattle them. In these close-ranged battles, whoever fires first usually wins. If they mess it up, the more trained and experienced group usually takes the field."

"That's us," Dirk said.

"Us? What? Who us? Which us?" Ana said.

"Centurion." Dirk waved at the group. "This isn't my first gunfight. It's not even my first gunfight with you. And the rest of your lady-killers here, you've been training them for this."

"Lady-killer?" Scruggs asked. "I like that."

"Doesn't mean what you think," Dena said. "But never mind. Dirk's right. Our best bet is do what we're good at."

"Which is what?" Lee said.

"Mayhem," Dena said.

They all laughed. "Some days, you're all right, Nature Girl," Ana said.

"You too, Old Man."

"Heads up." Gavin depressed the brakes as they crested a hill. "Traffic on the road. Decision time."

The limo crested the hill, giving them a view down into the valley. The river snaked in from the left. The road followed the shore above the river, on a shallow bank nearly six feet tall. On the right, a series of rolling hills stretched from the woods to the road. Rather than climbing up and over the hills, the Imperial engineers had blasted through. They kept straight on and shored up the low escarpments with brown granite masonry.

A battered gray car had slid onto its side past one of the retaining walls. There was no visible damage or fire, but it blocked the left lane, almost touching the river. Flares lined the road starting a hundred feet short of the accident, and directed traffic off the road to the right, past a tow truck parked behind the wreck. The tow truck had a line attached to the car, and a man fiddling with the controls. The protruding hill blocked the view next to the truck. A casual observer would see a flipped car being towed upright, and traffic rerouted.

"Behind that hill to the right, that's where they'll be," Ana said. "Another vehicle blocking that path, or a squad with rifles. If we go past on that side or stop for the block, somebody sticks a rifle in our ear."

"I'm going to run it," Gavin said.

"Don't. Drive down slow, slow down even more as you approach 'til you're coasting. At the last minute, turn left, toward the river and floor it."

"Not right?"

"There will be something hidden around the corner blocking the path. Spikes. Tires. Barrels. Something to stop us. Instead, make like you're going to the left and parking. Then gun it."

"Not enough room to the left... we'll drop into the river."

"There's enough room. You'll have to skid around the car."

"I'll try." Gavin increased speed.

"When do we start shooting, Centurion?" Scruggs asked.

Dirk laughed. "Bloody-minded girl now, aren't you."

"Better them than me," Scruggs said.

"Keep the guns on your lap, and in your hands." Ana fiddled with his rifle. "Make sure you're belted in. The engineer will have to move fast. Pilot, scan left. Dena, scan right. Scruggs, watch behind."

The limo rolled down the hill. Gavin took his foot off the accelerator, but didn't touch the brake—just what a confused driver would do. A worker in a reflective vest waved them right, away from the river.

"Slow more," Ana said. Gavin touched the brakes.

"Contact rear, Centurion," Scruggs said. "The same car from before. It just crested the hill. It's closing."

"Right side in the hills. There's somebody up on that ridge," Dena said. "Two somebodies. They stood up to get a better view."

"Weapons?" Ana asked.

"Can't see anything special," Dena said. "But you know they have something."

"Pilot?"

"All I see is the river, Centurion." Dirk stretched. "Can't see behind that rolled car. But I don't think there's enough space to get by it on the river side."

"I agree," Gavin said. "Centurion, it's too tight."

"Don't care, we're doing it anyways." Ana's eyes flickered back and forth across the front. "Get ready—when I say go, give yourself as much power as you can, and hit that vehicle two feet back from the front. Hit with your right bumper. That'll pivot it out of the way, then cut back sharp right to stay on the road."

"The Empire!" Dirk said. But his voice cracked.

Ana's eyes tracked left. The flipped car had been a four-door sedan. It was dented but looked otherwise sound. The frame didn't appear bent, all the doors closed, and the windows were intact. A skinny kid in a florescent blouse waved them right with a flag. He had no visible weapons. *Picked the youngest and most useless of the squad, took his rifle, and hung him out to dry.*

"Centurion." Dena leaned over the front seat and spoke into his ear. "Those two on the right, at the top of the hill. They've got one of those machine gun things I've seen in the vids. I can see a barrel."

Ana twisted. "Light machine gun. Low tech but effective. Wonder where they got that?"

"Somebody snuck it in on a starship. Somebody like us," Dirk said.

Dena shook her head. "I'm not going to charge one of those."

"Going to have to," Ana said. "It can shoot through this car. And its range is a couple of kilometers. Don't know how fast you can run, but if they target you, your only choice is whether you'll get shot in the front or the back. I choose the front. Scruggs?"

"Rear vehicle still closing, Centurion. It will be up to us in maybe thirty seconds or less.

"Scruggs, do not fire on them until they fire. Clear the window with your first shot." Ana's eyes flickered forward. "Engineer, get ready. Spin, accelerate, and ram two feet from the front. I've got the kid in the vest. Ladies, anybody else with a weapon, open up on them. Understood?"

"Ready." Dena turned and strapped herself back in.

Scruggs gripped her shotgun. "Ready."

Lee gripped her medical kit and looked over Ana's shoulder. "Centurion, that flagman looks awful young."

"Do I need to shoot you first?"

"Nope, just reminding you." Lee stroked Rocky. "Sorry we brought you, Rocky. This could get awkward."

Rocky leaned up and licked Dirk's face, once. Dirk rubbed the spit away. "Now he likes me?"

"He's reminding you that we're all on the same side," Dena said. "Don't get used to it. He can go back to hating you after the battle."

The flagman redoubled his waving.

"Rear car is stopping," Scruggs said.

Gavin wiped sweat with his forearm. "Now, Centurion?"

"Stand by."

Gavin slowed even more. "Gonna stop completely soon."

"Stand by. Stand by," Ana chanted.

"Centurion." Scruggs racked her shotgun. "Doors are open back there. I see long guns."

"Movement left. Uniforms. Gun. Gun." Dirk shifted to the left and pointed his gun out the window. Scruggs's shotgun came up.

"Stand by. Stand by. Stand by. LEFT. GO. NOW. NOW."

Gavin stomped on the accelerator and swung the car. The flagman dropped his red warning stick and, incredibly, drew a pistol and pointed it at the car. Ana brought up his rifle and aimed at the center of mass of the flagman. Then he cursed all pansy-assed Jovian pukes and their wussy fighting skills and changed his aim down and to the right. His first blast hit the ground next to the flagman, peppering his leg with ricochets and bounced pellets and gravel blasted from the road. The flagman's leg gave way, and he dropped. The wound would be painful, bloody, and debilitating, but not fatal or permanent.

"Jove save me from young idiots," Ana muttered. "That one's for you, Praetorian."

Gavin rammed the blocking car. As Ana had expected, it pivoted enough that they shoved it aside. Their limo pushed past the damaged car, the rear wheels skidding over the ditch. Momentum kept them moving.

What they hadn't expected was a second blue compact car parked behind the blocking car. Smaller and lighter than the other, it still stopped them as Gavin slammed into it. A squad with rifles stood behind it. They had been hiding there on the river side of the car, not the hill, as Ana had foreseen.

"Weapons free!" Ana sighted across the parked car at one of the soldiers. *He's in Planetary Guard uniform. Are they revolting? No time to find out.* He blasted away.

The soldier dropped. Ana tracked right, skipping two gaping soldiers until he saw the tabs of a lieutenant. He didn't look like much of a lieutenant, but Ana shot him anyway.

Dirk had rolled left as the car banged around and dropped on Lee to cover her. Dena fired out the right side of the car, and missed everybody. But the shots ranged over the two soldiers who had been hit as the block car pivoted. The scrape of the car, the noise and gun fire left the two squad members gaping.

The rear wheels couldn't grip. They spun. One of them grabbed wet grass and pushed the car up the bank, shoving the crashed blue car forward.

Their rear window shattered. Somebody up at the machine gun had panicked and started firing, walking shots left to right. Bullets smashed the rear of the limo, blasting more glass free, then started shredding the blocking car.

Scruggs stuck her shotgun out the rear window and fired at the trailing car. She hit nothing, but all the troops dropped into cover.

The machine gunner kept shooting, blasting the blocking car to bits and sending stray shots beyond. Two of them hit the blue compact, blowing a quarter panel off and smashing windows. The squad of soldiers, under fire for the first time and with their officer down, melted. Half dropped their rifles and ran. One on the ground rolled over and skittered toward the hills. Another dropped and covered his ears with his hands.

Dena and Ana fired out to the right, not hitting anything. Dena was having problems aiming the shotgun in the close confines of the car. Ana shot above the squad. He figured they'd run if he panicked them.

The machine gun now tracked back from right to left. Bullets buzzed down the road, through the blocking car, into the blue compact, and past the rifle troopers. The firing sloped high, then the gunner corrected, bringing it down and striking the rear of the limo.

The rest of the ambush squad turned and ran.

Gavin's dashboard controls died, and the wheel froze as control lines were cut.

"I've got no steering," Gavin yelled. "Aaagrh." His left shoulder jerked. "I'm hit."

Their limo ground along shuddering, then stalled. The machine gun kept buzzing and the car kept shaking. They were stuck, and the machine gun kept blasting.

Dirk looked out the window and yelled, "What color are our hubcaps?"

Lee yanked him down. "You want to go car shopping now?"

"There's a blue and green wheel bouncing into the river. It's ours. Centurion, rear wheels are gone. We're stuck."

"Everybody out." Ana yanked his door out and rolled onto the road. "Get behind that blocking car. Stand by to assault that machine gun."

"I told you, I'm not charging into a hail of gunfire," Dena yelled, but she rolled out behind him.

"Won't have to." Ana crawled behind their stuck limo, putting both the blocking car and the limo between him and the fire. "They've been on full rock and roll since this started. That barrel will overheat shortly. Bad things happen then. It either jams or warps. And they don't have unlimited ammunition either."

"What now, Centurion?" Scruggs slid in next to him.

"Reload!" Ana yelled. "When he stops, we go."

Dirk and Lee had hauled Gavin out and were fussing over him.

"Just a gouge," Lee said. "Must have been a ricochet. You're lucky."

"Don't feel lucky," Gavin said.

Dirk helped settle Gavin, then ducked back into the limo and released Rocky. Rocky jumped out and huddled back behind the car with the rest. This was fun! The pack was running in the woods! Maybe there would be treats.

The machine gun had kept firing, shredding the back of their vehicle, because it was the only thing the gunner could see to shoot at.

The ripping sound stopped. Ana didn't wait even a second, but skittered around their limo, and then peeked past the blocking car. Two figures up in the hills were waving their arms.

"They're jammed." Ana stood. "Up the hill, follow me." He ducked around the car and ran.

Chapter 15

"I've never robbed a bank before." Devin watched the jump countdown on the main screen.

"Sure you have," Lionel said. They sat on the *Pollux's* bridge waiting for jump emergence. Lionel reviewed reports while Devin fretted.

"I have? When did I do that? And, by the way, this is the shortest time I've ever spent in jump space. What went wrong?"

"Nothing. Gotta stop thinking like you're in the Verge, Tribune. Closer we get to the Core, the denser the stars are. That's why we re-tuned the drives." The *Pollux* and her escorts, the *Valhalla* and the *Hydrogen Queen*, had executed a micro-jump. After the latest re-tuning and software upgrade, they could jump eight times farther than a freighter of the same mass could in the same time, or they could jump shorter distances ten times faster.

"Yay for Imperial technology. What's our safety margin with these jumps?"

"Nothing."

"I meant, how much fuel do we have when we come out of jump?"

"None." Lionel shrugged his shoulders. "Well, enough to maneuver and fight, but not enough to jump out."

"What if we face a superior force upon emergence? We won't be able to retreat."

"Not without refueling from the tanker."

Devin raised his eyebrows. "Which will be impossible under combat conditions."

"I'm counting on our in-house superior strategist to keep us out of that position. That's you, in case you're confused."

"What if I'm wrong?"

Lionel shrugged again. "You're in the same ship as we are. Don't be wrong. You won't like it."

"You have a lot of trust in me." *Do I deserve it?*

"My job is to move the ship and fight it. Tactics and Operations. Yours is strategy. Where to jump. Why. Which banks to rob. That sort of thing."

"I told you I don't remember robbing any banks."

"Haven't you heard of taxes? That's robbing people."

"Taxes are payments from citizens to governments for services that only the government can provide."

"What services is the Empire currently providing in the Verge?" Lionel brought up a channel. "Trevor, what's this yellow in the status report?"

"Main drive is falling out of alignment, Prefect," Trevor, the helmsman, said. "Still within tolerance, but it's a warning to schedule a re-tuning."

Lionel put the status report in question on the main screen, and displayed it for the whole bridge crew. "Which we need a full naval depot or a major starport for. Where's the nearest starport that can fix this?"

"Not anywhere in the Verge, Prefect," Trevor said. "You'd have to go coreward to get it fixed."

"Outstanding. Tribune, you didn't answer my questions. What services is the Empire providing in the Verge again?"

Devin waved his arms. "Defense. Protection of Trade. Enforcing the peace between systems. Capturing pirates."

"That's all you've got?"

"Maintaining Imperial authority. Communication networks. Enforcing... I don't know, enforcing measurement standards."

"We barely fought off an incursion by Confed forces. You do recall destroying that Confed cruiser, the *Kazan*?"

"There was a battle of some sort, wasn't there?"

Lionel glared. They'd lost propulsion and almost drifted into a sun before Dirk and his hijacked fleet support ship had towed them back out. "And you recall the engagement with that Nat commerce raider, the *Pinguin*?"

"A common trader, no more."

"Who seized a few dozen of the merchantmen we were supposed to be protecting."

"He didn't do the bulk of the seizing, that was the *Castor*."

"Ah yes, the Imperial Starship *Castor*—an Imperial frigate gone rogue, pirating ships and killing their crews. Good thing we had that going for us. Let me see. So far, we haven't been able to stop war, invasion, commerce raiding, or piracy. Not really doing our job."

"We have other jobs. I listed some of them."

"Trevor!"

"Sir?"

"What's the definition of a meter?"

"A meter?"

"Yes." Lionel held out his hands. "Meter. About this big."

"A measured meter sir? Um, it's one two hundred ninety-nine million, seven hundred ninety-two thousand, four hundred fifty-eighths of the distance light travels in a second."

"There you go, Tribune. Trevor knows the definition of a meter."

"I'm glad he knows the definition. Also surprised at his precision."

"We strive to be precise in the Navy."

Devin shook his head. "What's your point, Prefect?"

"Trevor?" Lionel put Trevor's face up on the main screen.

"Sir?"

"Did you have to call anybody in the Empire to figure out what a meter was?"

"No sir."

"So a meter is a meter is a meter, whether the Empire is around or not."

"Uh, I guess so sir."

Lionel glared at Devin. "Trevor says that he doesn't need no stinking Empire to know what a meter is. So your last service provided by the Empire, standardization of measurement, isn't necessary either. So, when we meet these banker types, and you ask for taxes, and they ask what do they get for them, what are you going to say?"

Devin bit his lip. "Give us money or we'll blow you up?"

"Perhaps we could start with something other than naked threats?"

Devin shook his head. "We need the money, Prefect."

"Yes, Tribune," Lionel said. "Of course, Tribune. As you say, Tribune."

Devin glared. "Well? What do you suggest, then?"

"Yes, we need the money. But there are ways…"

"Have you dance as a joy-boy and see who pays?"

Lionel flexed a bicep. "Body like this? I might get more than you think. Tribune, we can't start with threats. Why not ask for the money first? Ask for a loan."

"A loan? Borrow money?"

"Yes. From a bank. Ask them for money to pay for expenses, salaries, that sort of thing."

"I've never borrowed money."

"Which surprises nobody."

"We should have access to Imperial funds immediately."

"Sure we should. We won't. They won't give them to you."

"And why not?"

"Because, Tribune." Lionel dropped his voice. "Because we might not win."

Devin looked down at his screen. "You don't believe that we'll be able to defeat the Chancellor?"

"We don't even know if we have to defeat the Chancellor. All we know is part of the Navy has orders to arrest you and your friends. Not even sure why. Could be a misunderstanding."

"It isn't a misunderstanding."

"Nope, it's not. But we need to act like it is, at the start. Then we need to take action to defend ourselves. Everyone likes a strong man who stands up for justice and what is right. Nobody likes an ungrateful rebel trying to enrich themselves."

"I'm not making any money out of this."

"Which is why you ask for a loan first. No demands. You're sure that our cause is just. With the Empress's help, you'll be able to fix things, that the Navy isn't an issue. You need some short-term liquidity help."

"Our cause is just? That's your line?"

"And our hearts are pure and our spirit flies free with the best of the Empire in mind. We only need a little working capital to smooth things through. Why, we've already got all the fleet units in the sector on our side, plus the Marines, and all the bases."

"We don't have the bases."

"All the important ones. Some of them. At least one. Well, soon we will. Just need the money for some...unexpected administrative expenses. Organizing things. Dealing with the disruption in communications. Minor deal."

"So." Devin sat up straight. "You see, Ms. Banker, we're not really in rebellion. We're legitimate Imperial units who have received conflicting information. We need a short-term loan to handle some unforeseen administrative expenses while we re-establish the status quo."

"Re-establish the status quo." Lionel grinned. "I like that. Banks like the status quo."

"Indeed. I understand now." Devin sat quietly and monitored his screens.

"Lionel?"

"Yes, Devin?"

"What if they won't give the loan? The money. The banks. What do we do then?"

"What do you think?"

"We blast them to little bits."

"Outstanding, Tribune. You're getting the hang of this Empire thing already." Lionel checked his timer. "Emergence in two minutes. Sound the emergence warning."

Pollux made a standard emergence at the standard distance from the standard planet Pekak. It wasn't much of a planet—or colony, rather. It wasn't even self-governing, and didn't even have its own legislature.

Gravity lighter than standard. Temperature colder than standard. Less water than normal. Food possible but hard to grow. The lowlands were bogs, and the highlands were scrub hills. In between were pine trees. The only field crops were rye or other cold-adapted wheat, potatoes and turnips, and the occasional apple.

And berries. The marshes and wet lowlands were berry factories. Blueberries. Cranberries. Huckleberries. Bearberries. Gooseberries. Black currants.

"What's a bearberry?" Devin wanted to know.

"Cross between a cranberry and black currant, Tribune." Imin buckled Devin's sword belt outside of his robes.

"Doesn't help. What's a currant?"

Imin adjusted Devin's toga. "It's a deciduous shrub that is grown for its edible berries."

"What? A shrub?"

"We make liquor from it, Tribune." Imin checked that the sword belt didn't impede Devin's ability to walk. "That black liqueur that you drink with champagne for pre-dinner drinks?"

"Kir-Royale?'"

"That's the one, Tribune."

"Haven't had it for a while."

"Out of creme de cassis, Tribune. I'm going to try to get some on the surface. Do some shopping maybe, while you're at your meeting. Or after. I might go and visit one of the berry swamps."

"Berry swamps?"

"Most of these berries grow in swamps, Tribune. Lots of farms that cultivate the berries. I want to go right to the source. I have a lot of recipes that call for cranberries especially. Want to get some fresh ones."

"That's why you're coming down with me?" Devin cocked his head. "Imin, you're wearing a weapon."

"Yes sir."

"To defend yourself from the bog monsters?"

"I'm not going to bogs, Tribune. I'm going to swamps. Bogs are standing water, swamps are slow moving running water, or regular inundations."

"I stand corrected. I don't think you need a weapon."

Lionel waited by the door. "He doesn't if you let me send the Marines with you."

"No Marines."

"Four with you on the shuttle. Then they act as guards."

"They stay on the shuttle."

"Then Imin is armed."

Devin slapped his belt. "You don't think my sword will be enough?"

"Nope. Why are you wearing that?"

"It symbolizes Imperial power and my Imperium."

"I thought we were agreed that we're rebelling against the current government, which is why you are going down there for a meeting. To beg for money."

"You said ask for a loan."

"I dressed it up."

"Fine." Devin shook Imin loose. "It's fine, Imin. Dress this up, Prefect. I'm going down there as Tribune Devin, the Lord Lyon, Sector Governor. Whether I'm in rebellion or not, I'm currently all those things. Deny me a favor, deny the Empire a favor."

"What if they know that you're a rebel? Or they've been told that you're a rebel. By now, there's a price on your head."

"The communication blackout with the Core works both ways. We don't know what's going on there, but they don't have good intelligence of what's happening out here either. I'll bet they don't know, or they'll pretend to not know. And you're right about one thing, Prefect. They won't want to get me mad at them."

"You get mad at me all the time. Doesn't bother me at all."

"I should have said they don't want to oppose me."

"Why not?"

Devin put his hand on his sword hilt. "Because we might win."

They'd contacted two local banks from orbit and arranged a meeting for 'discussions critical to the future of the Empire.' The banks' chief executives waited in a local office tower, and the banks had sent a luxurious ground car to the starport. Their shuttle had dropped onto one of the pads, and two Marines stood guard outside. *Pollux* remained in orbit.

Four heavily armed cutters orbited the planet and protected its space infrastructure. Plenty of firepower, especially since they weren't jump capable, so had double the weapons load, armor and fuel normal for that size. But *Pollux* could take them.

"This planet is busier than I expected, Tribune," Imin said. He sat across from Devin in his number one uniform, a black leather briefcase on the seat next to him. "Quite the transportation infrastructure. This road looks brand new. That's a monorail up there. And heavy lift trains as well."

The split in the middle of the road had four tracks. Two were elevated monorails, two ground side. Devin tapped a button, and the driver answered over a speaker.

"Sir?"

"What's the population of this planet?"

"Nine million people sir."

"Big city for a planet with only nine million."

"Everybody lives in the city, Tribune. Ninety percent of the population."

"Why?"

"Winter. It's cold and damp. Or freezing. Or foggy. No fun at all. The planet's mostly woods or bogs. Nothing to see outside of the towns."

"What's your business here? What's the economy?"

"Break bulk sir. We're the end of a trade route from the Core. The bigger transport ships come out here, offload to smaller ships. We handle insurance, finance, warehousing, that sort of thing. There's enough planet here that we can grow food to feed the orbitals, but nothing special about the planet. Nothing major in the way of minerals in the belt."

"You're the jumping off point for the Verge."

"One of them sir. This is your stop." The driver pointed. "That's your escort. They'll see you upstairs."

The escort wore a business suit and was bland and uninformative, mouthing platitudes and escorting Devin and Imin up to the top floor of a twenty-floor office building. They almost didn't make it—Imin set off every security alarm and weapons scanner they had. He refused to give up anything, only Devin's explicit threat to drive right back to his shuttle got them through. After, that is, Imin gave up a hidden pistol and knife.

"Imin, what's the meaning of this?" Devin followed their escort to the elevator. "We're among friends here."

"Begging the Tribune's pardon, but we're not. Not you, Ms." Imin blocked their escort from entering. "Just send us to the right floor and warn them that we're coming. We can take it from here."

Their escort shrugged and pushed the elevator close button.

Imin watched the floors go by. "The Prefect was most explicit on that."

"I do wish my staff would stop trying to save me from myself."

"Best we do it. You won't."

Devin glared.

"Sorry, Tribune. Slipped out."

"You and the Prefect think you're so smart." Devin shook his head. "All that sound and fury signifying nothing, all that bad feeling, and we didn't get any weapons by them."

"Begging the Tribune's pardon again, but in the midst of all that sound and fury, they forgot you have a two-foot-long sword on your hip. And I've still got a solid steel briefcase plated with laser reflecting armor." Imin held up his briefcase. "Crush strength of this is ten tons. I jam it in a bank vault, and you'll never get it closed. And the inside is plated with a sodium-potassium compound. Scrape the plating off and add water and bad things will happen." Imin swung the suitcase. "Or I can beat people with it. I figure that signifies something. Tribune."

Devin patted his hip. "Forgot about that. Huh. You're right. What would I do without you, Imin?"

"Probably lose some weight sir, on account of you'd have to cook for yourself."

The elevator slid open at the top. Another nameless escort gestured them past a reception desk, and down a hallway with oil painted portraits. Devin examined them as they passed. *By their expressions, they've eaten something bad for lunch.*

The guide knocked once, then pushed open two double doors, and gestured Devin and Imin in. She closed it behind them.

A blond woman in a brown suit greeted him from next to a polished pine conference table. "Aki Seele. Merchants Consumer Lending."

Her companion continued the blond/brown duality, except it was her hair that was brown and the suit blond. "Zeda Navara. Reserve Mortgage."

"Devin, the Lord Lyon. My steward, Imin. Nice view." Devin pointed to the wall high windows.

"Really?" Aki looked out the window. "If you like trees, I guess."

"I'm surprised at the development here," Devin said.

"We are too sometimes," Zeda said. "But there it is."

"Well, it seems like a very pleasant planet," Devin said.

The two women exchanged glances. Aki shook her head. "Just another colonial world. Nothing special."

Do they hate everything everywhere, or is it just this planet? "I understand you have nice berries."

"They're nice." Zeda shrugged. "Are you a berry fan, Tribune?"

"My steward is. But, I have limited time. Perhaps rather than berries, we can talk about investments."

"That's what we do. Fire away."

Imin settled down in a corner, Devin put on his most sincere smile, and started to talk.

It took him a good half hour to outline what he wanted. Loans. Expenses. Special drawing rights for traveling warships. Loan guarantees. Fuel accounts. Shipments. Services. Free postage. The woman made noncommittal grunts and nods, and waited until he was finished.

"...which means, in conclusion, we will be able to pass through this period of small confusion with minimal disruption to Imperial efforts." Devin nodded. "What questions do you have?"

"No," Aki said.

"No what? No questions?"

"No, we won't be loaning you any money. At least, Merchants Consumer Lending won't. And I don't think Reserve Mortgage will either." Aki looked to Zeda.

Zeda nodded. "No."

"No money?"

"Right."

"No questions either."

"I don't understand." Devin tilted his head. "I expected questions."

"I don't have questions," Aki said. "It's not something that we're interested in getting involved with. Too risky."

"Surely there should be some discussions about, well, interest rates, or fees." *Lionel told me to stress the fee parts. They all like fees.*

"Nope, we're fine, thanks. Not interested. Zeda?"

"Thanks, Aki, we're fine. I don't like the risk profile either."

Devin looked at Imin. Imin was looking at his comm. "Well, if this isn't something you're interested in, I'm sure your associates, or perhaps your competitors would be interested."

"They might. You can always try. But I warn you, we're the two biggest banks on the planet, in this part of the sector, and we have strong commercial links to other banks in this sector. They'll follow our lead."

Devin raised his eyebrows. "You're not willing to help out the Empire? This was not what I expected."

Aki shrugged. "We're not responsible for your expectations, Tribune."

The door behind Devin kicked open. He jumped up, his hand dropping to his sword. A short chubby, redhead woman waltzed through. "Don't get up, don't get up. Sorry I'm late."

Aki and Zeda exchanged glances. "What are you doing here, Raka?"

The woman walked to Devin and extended her hand. "Raka Flintheart. Verge Development. You would be the Lord Lyon."

Devin shook. "I am."

Raka spun around. "You're Imin, right?"

Imin nodded.

"Well, the gang's all here."

Devin sat. "I don't recall you on the invite list, Ms. Flintheart."

Aki scowled. "That's because she wasn't. She's not a real banker."

Devin raised his eyebrows. "Really?"

"That's true." Raka nodded. "No charter. These fine folks here—" she pointed to Aki and Zeda "—they represent Imperial Banks with Empire-wide charters. They can bank anywhere, do anything. We're more of a limited organization. Operating in the Verge only."

"Thus your name, Verge Development?" Devin asked.

Raka grinned. "They said you were smart. Yes."

"Well, thank you. But that depends on who 'they' are."

"Some local folks. Ship owners, shipping companies. Some industrial concerns. Nothing large by Empire standards, but big enough out here. They're quite pleased with the way you've been handling the pirates, and incursions, and those sorts of things. Put yourself in harm's way to protect them and theirs."

"That's the purpose of Imperial Government," Devin said. "To provide law and order. Administration. To govern."

"Couldn't have said it better myself, Tribune. Now, let's discuss your financial needs."

"They are considerable, but these ladies here—"

"I'll bet they told you that the risk profile was too high, or something mushy like that."

"Something like that. Are you going to say the same thing?"

"We're not the same type of organization. Our business is much different from theirs. For example, Aki here, she makes most of her profit off of abandoned accounts they seize."

"Abandoned accounts? I don't understand."

"Well, people, miners mostly, they come out here to work. We get a lot of young people out from the Core—trying their luck as belters. Within two parsecs, there are six systems with big asteroid belts. Lots of good metals out there. And we're talking big, system-wide belts. Some of these belters make fortunes if they get a good strike. You know Francis Rail?"

Devin nodded. "F R Enterprises?"

"That's the one. He made his first strike two systems over. Didn't tell anybody, just came back and ordered the equipment he needed to prove it on the next shipment from the Core. Nearly lost his claim. The local bank held up the order and he almost missed the deadline."

"The local bank." Devin's eyes swiveled to the Aki and Zeda. "What was the name of the local bank?"

Raka pointed at Aki. "Our good friend here. Merchants Consumers Lending. She wouldn't let him have his money. She thought he was dead."

"I don't understand," Devin said. "Why would his bankers think he was dead if he was in front of them?"

"Thing is, Tribune, here in the Verge, that's a good way to make money, if you're a bank. Have people deposit their working capital with you while they go out and prospect. Lots of prospectors die. So the rules here are different than the Core. A bank has no activity on an account for a year, they assume you're dead and keep your money. They're usually right. Aki specializes in that."

Aki glared. "This is libel."

"Since I'm talking, not writing, it's slander." Raka grinned. "And this information is public record, so I'm fine. But, yes, Tribune, Merchants Consumer Lending makes most of their money on abandoned deposits. Our other good friend, Zeda, she deals in insurance. Like insurance on ships. You need a ship to prospect. She'll sell you the most beat up, dented, piece of junk you've ever seen. Great rates, though. But there is one catch."

Devin folded his arms. "There would be. Tell me the catch."

"She insures it. And keeps the payout herself. You find ore, she gets a cut. You don't find ore, she gets the mortgage payments. You vanish without a trace..."

"She gets the insurance." Devin nodded. "I understand, but what does that have to do with me?"

"Well, Tribune. I represent a group of local investors—that is, local, Verge-based investors, not Core-world transplants who come out here for a few years to fleece the peasants and retire back to their estates. We've got friends all over the banking and financial fields, which is how we knew you were here. We invest in speculative ventures, and we're not afraid of risk. Francis Rail is one of our principals."

"Again, what does that have to do with me?"

"You're starting a rebellion. That's a risky venture. You need money."

"I do. And?"

"Well, Tribune." Raka grinned. "Have we got a deal for you!"

Chapter 16

"Put your hand here. Now hold." Lee pushed Dirk's hand down onto the bandage. "Gavin, I'm going to give you a shot."

"Hurts like I got smacked with a spanner," Gavin said. Dirk had dragged him out of the battered limousine and shielded him from the stuttering machine gun.

Dirk pressed hard. "Spanner. You mean a wrench?"

"Yeah, wrench." Gavin gritted his teeth. "Hit with a wrench. This hurts."

"Lee will fix you up." Dirk pushed down. "Lee, the blood isn't stopping."

"We need—"

BRRRRRAAAP. Machine gun bullets tore overhead and splintered the limousine roof. Dirk ducked onto Gavin. Powdered glass and paint dust floated down.

"WHAT?" Dirk yelled over the crew's return fire.

"We need to sew it together."

Gavin shuddered. "Will that hurt?"

"Oh yes," Lee said. "Lots and lots."

Gavin cursed in a low voice. Lee plunged a needle into his other shoulder. "That will hit you soon. You'll feel woozy."

"Woozy is better than now." Gavin shifted. "Feeling a little dizzy."

"Blood loss. Move." Lee shoved Dirk aside and checked the wound. "Need to staple this. Put your fingers here, Dirk, and squeeze the flesh together."

Dirk placed his fingers where he was told and squeezed. "Will he—" Dirk yelled, then dropped his voice. The machine gun had stopped firing, and Ana was yelling instructions in the quiet.

Snick. Snick. Snick. Lee stapled Gavin's shoulder together. He grunted at each click, but held still.

"He should be okay," Lee said. "It's not as bad as it looks. I don't see any arteries, and the bones don't look broken. Won't be able to use it for a while, though."

"Navy! You too. Let's go," Ana yelled as he sprinted around the cars. Dena and Scruggs followed. Rocky barked once and dashed after them.

Dirk dropped Gavin's arm. "Lee, can you manage?"

"Yes. I've got to get some more drugs into him. Go help Ana and the others."

Dirk stood, drew his revolver and raced to the far side of their limo.

Their limo was a wreck. One rear wheel was shredded bits, the other was gone. Fluid pooled under the car, smoking lightly. It didn't smell like gasoline, and Dirk remembered that the limo was electric. *Acid—the batteries must be shot, though.*

He ran between the block car and the river. A jeep blocked the road behind them. A figure crouched behind the passenger door, firing. Dirk saw the muzzle flash but didn't hear the shot or see where it went. The flagman in the florescent vest crawled to the side of the road. Scruggs and Ana ran past him. Rocky ran up and snarled at him. He dragged faster.

Scruggs passed Ana and vaulted the ditch at the side of the road and ran along the retaining wall. Two men crouched over the machine gun on the hilltop. One swung a hammer, striking it.

The other had dropped his pants and was peeing on the barrel.

Scruggs passed the end of the wall and climbed the hill, holding the shotgun at port arms. Ana was several steps behind her. He raced to the wall and braced his rifle. He took a measured aim at the machine gun, and fired once. Dust spurted above.

Dena yelled, and Dirk's attention snapped back front to her. BOOM. CLICK. The jeep's passenger door window exploded. Dena waved her shotgun. "Get on the driver's side, I've got this one."

Dirk ducked to his right, as far as he could without falling into the river. He jogged up the road. Movement. Another soldier had rolled out from the back of the car and aimed a rifle. Dirk stopped, gripped his revolver with both hands, and fired three spaced shots. Two went nowhere that he could see. The third kicked up dust in front of the soldier. The soldier ran.

Dena outpaced Dirk. She fired again at the passenger side door. A figure stood and rapid-fired five rounds from the rifle in Dena's general direction, then ducked and scrambled away.

Dirk and Dena raced up to the jeep. It was empty, still running, the only damage a dented passenger door and a broken window. The other doors stood open. Two shooters were running into the woods on the land side of the road. Dirk hadn't seen when the other passengers had left, or where they'd gone.

Dena stopped, breath heaving. "Okay, we have a car. The others?"

Up the hill, Scruggs was ten feet below the machine gun and still climbing. The hammer man was nowhere to be seen. The other stumbled back into the woods, pulling his pants up. Rocky raced by Scruggs, barking, and chased after the man. Scruggs ran up to the machine gun, pointed her gun down and fired twice.

Dirk looked at Dena. "You okay?"

"Yes. Where is everybody?"

Dirk did his own circle. The road was empty except for the shot-up cars and the crew of the *Heart's Desire*. Even the flagman dragging a leg had disappeared into the woods. "No idea. Scrugggggggs!" Dirk yelled and waved when Scruggs turned. She waved back, then bent over and disappeared. Seconds later, she stood up and hit the gun with a hammer three times. Then she walked up to the tree line, yelling for Rocky.

"Let's check with Lee." Dirk stepped up to the running jeep and pressed the button to stop the engine, removed the keys, then followed Dena back to Lee.

"That was awesome!" Dena skipped along. "That was way more fun than I expected. I know why the centurion gets so up on this. Better than hunting neo-moose. Better even than hunting the neo-bears. I could run a mile right now."

"The Imperial Marines will have a new recruit soon, sounds like. We may have to go after Scruggs... no, there she is." Scruggs had re-appeared over the hill, a panting Rocky with her. "I'm surprised at that dog."

"Where we go, he goes."

"But the noise and all that..."

"We're his pack. You fight with your pack." Dena twirled the shotgun. "Woo hoo."

"Please don't do that," Dirk said. "Or at least put the safety on." Dirk stepped past the broken cars and found Lee putting a final bandage on a snoozing Gavin. "He passed out?"

"Sleeping." Lee pulled a knot tight on a sling. "Drugs knocked him out. He'll sleep for a couple hours and be woozy afterward. Anybody else hurt?"

Dena and Dirk shook their heads no. Scruggs jogged across the road to check the jeep, then jogged back along the river, Rocky bouncing along. "That car looks like it will still work. Can we start it?"

"It does work. I have the keys." Dirk held them up.

"Let's get out of here. That machine gun is wrecked. After Centurion shot the gunner, I used the hammer to pound a metal rod thing into the breech. But all these others will be coming back at some point."

Dirk eyed the debris littering the road. "We can collect the rifles and count them."

"Which will tell us how many rifles are here, not how many are in the woods with their rifles," Dena said. "Let's make like a river otter and get swimming."

"Sound advice. Scruggs, help me get Gavin to that jeep. Dena, whatever we can take out of that limo, take it."

Dirk and Scruggs dragged Gavin to the jeep and put him in the back between the seats. It would be a tight fit, but the two in the back could hold him. Lee collected all her medical equipment, and Dena grabbed two bags with extra weapons and ammunition.

"Right," Dirk said. "I'm sorry to say this, but, Dena, you're a better driver than me, so you take the wheel. Scruggs is a better shot, so she can go in the front. Ana will—"

All four looked at each other.

"I thought he came back to be with you," Scruggs said. "Where did he go?"

"He was following you up the hill," Dirk said. "I thought he chased those soldiers into the woods."

"Nope, I haven't seen him since before I charged up there."

"Spread out. Check the tree line, the ditches, all in the direction Scruggs ran."

They moved. Less than a minute later, they found Ana, lying in the ditch at the side of the road, right below the stone wall he'd used to shoot the machine gunner. He had a hole in his right side, between the ribs, and bloody air was frothing in and out.

Chapter 17

"I said if you do fall out, I'm not coming back for you," Dena yelled. The wind whipped into the jeep through the broken passenger window.

"I'm not going to fall out. He keeps pushing me." Scruggs shoved Gavin's lolling head. "It's hitting my rifle."

"And you're supposed to be a super soldier, so keep your rifle ready."

"How long 'til the city?"

"Don't know."

"I'll try the comm again." Scruggs fiddled with her unit.

"For Jove's sakes, Scruggs. Hold on to something." Dena kept the jeep rolling at top speed. She, Scruggs and a snoozing Gavin were jammed in the front seat. Gavin was belted in, and Scruggs was half on top of him, hanging partway out the broken window.

Lee and Dirk were working on the centurion. Lee had him draped across their laps. Rocky had curled up under their legs. "Drive smoother!"

Dena slowed. "Smoother means longer to a town, to a hospital. That what you want?"

"We're working back here," Lee said. "I need stability."

Dena slowed more. "This good enough?"

"No." Dirk shook his head. "Dena, speed up. Fast as possible to town."

Dena sped up.

Lee cursed and dropped the needle in her hand. "I can't fix him if we're rocking all over the place."

Dirk grabbed her hand. "You can't fix him even if we're not rocking. He needs a hospital and a med pod, not first aid."

"He has a punctured lung," Lee said. "At least that, and other internal damage."

"Which you can't fix without hospital equipment. You've done your best. Now we need a med bay."

"I can help him."

"Stabilize and transport," Dirk said. "That's what I was taught. Get him to a med pod or a human surgeon. The governor's office will have med pods. They'll take care of him. Faster we get there, the better. They'll fix him up there." *I hope*.

Lee cursed some more, then pulled out a pack of saline. "He'll die before we get there. He needs blood. Fluid volume at least."

"Dena," Dirk yelled. "Lee needs to put a needle in his vein. Find a safe, hidden space and come to a stop for thirty seconds."

They crested a hill. The river still ran to their left, the hills to their right.

"Hang on." Dena roared down the hill. The country to their right opened up and the hills retreated. She measured the distance, stamped on the brakes, then swerved off to the left, onto a grassy patch by the river. They skidded to a stop. "Clock's ticking. We're too far from the trees for anybody to get a good shot at us, but if they start moving now, they can sneak up on us."

Lee prodded and poked. Dirk held Ana still. *Not really necessary. He's not moving.*

"Scruggs," Dena yelled, "if you won't point that rifle at the trees, give it to Dirk."

Scruggs tore her eyes away from Ana. She was supposed to be on guard. "Understood."

"Got it." Lee held up the saline pack. "This will help. Go."

Dena rocketed back onto the road.

Rocky poked his head up and sniffed once, then licked Ana's face. Something was wrong. The big man was sick.

Lee stopped them twice more to add another saline bag from her kit. Dirk helped, but there was nothing to do. They kept rolling into town. They heard three more booms. Fires dotted the landscape in the distance.

"Dena, how much gas do we have?"

"It's another of those electric jobs. Still have twenty percent."

"We should be there by now. I don't remember the road being this long."

"It was an hour drive in before, we're doing it faster."

"With time off for ambushes." Dirk peered out the right side. "Scruggs, Dena. Lots of smoke ahead. Could be on the road."

"It is on the road. I got a glimpse earlier. What's our play?"

"Fast as we can," Dirk said. "They won't expect anybody coming from this direction, they'll figure their buddies got us. Back-to-back ambushes. Standard insurgency tactics."

Dena spared a glance over her shoulder. "That's a very intelligent observation. Very specific. If I was the centurion, I'd ask where a Navy officer learned all that."

"If you were the centurion, I'd tell you to suck vacuum. Since you're not, I was in an insurgency once. As an observer, not as a participant. The Navy sent me to report on some Navy things."

"You were in an insurgency. I'll bet you use that to get girls."

"I tried. But they're less interested in it than you'd think."

"How'd it go? The insurgency."

Dirk looked at Ana lying across Lee's bloody lap. "Everybody died."

They hit the ambush without warning. Dena climbed three switchbacks, came around a corner and there it was. Three cars littered the road, one was burning. Groups of soldiers and civilians milled on the road. It wasn't clear who was ambusher and who was ambushee, given that there were uniformed and non-uniformed bodies on the road.

"Hang on." Dena weaved the car back and forth.

"Scruggs. Shoot whatever you have." Dirk fumbled on the floor for his revolver.

Dena swerved again, rocking them left.

Scruggs wrapped the sling of the centurion's rifle around her arm and lay down on the broken door panel. As Dena swung them back and forth, she aimed at any uniform visible and pulled the trigger.

Dena swung past a sedan stuck on a spike belt, past two carts missing their horses, and back onto the road.

Dirk found his revolver and stuck it out the window. He fired twice before the hammer clicked on an empty cylinder. *Forgot to reload. How do these ground types remember in the noise? Glad I joined the Navy.* Ana gurgled next to him and hocked blood out of his mouth. *Very glad I joined the Navy.*

"This is not doing Ana any good," Lee yelled.

The rear window shattered. Somebody behind had gotten a shot off.

"That wouldn't do any of us any good," Dirk yelled back.

Scruggs's rifle clicked empty. "Pilot, do you have any reloads?"

"Why would I have reloads for that?"

"Didn't you take them off the centurion?"

"What?"

"His belt. He'll have a fresh magazine."

Dirk ran his hands along the belt. "Here? Or here?"

Dena swung left, around a truck. A woman was running to a truck. As they passed, she yanked the door open and vaulted into the rear compartment.

"Too late. We're clear."

Dena floored the accelerator. The jeep's wheels thrummed as they passed from the concrete road to a metal bridge. The woods disappeared and the land fell away on either side as the road crossed a ravine. A mountain stream thundered below them, flowing to the river to their left.

"What was that woman doing?" Dena asked.

"She disappeared inside that truck behind us," Scruggs said. "It's got antennas and a scanning dish."

"Radio truck? How do you know—"

CRUMP. The jeep jerked up, then rolled off the bridge onto the highway. The whirr of wheels on concrete replaced the thrum of wheels on steel, and a blast of air rolled over them.

"The bridge!" Scruggs yelled. "They blew the bridge."

Dirk jerked around and saw fire and smoke behind them. Metal beams spun in the air, and the smoke boiled.

Dena swung right and the trees blocked the view. Smoke roiled in the air behind them.

"Glad we weren't on that," Scruggs said.

"And now we know what those bangs we've been hearing for the last week were," Dirk said.

There was no more traffic until they got to the city. Dena hung a right off the ring road onto the main boulevard leading to the governor's office. They passed empty streets, closed shops, and shuttered windows.

"Everybody got the word here too." Dena slowed at an intersection and checked both ways, but kept moving.

Scruggs had switched back to her shotgun. She held it upright between her legs, one hand on the shotgun, one hand on the door. "Nobody told us."

"Because we're the outsiders, from the Empire." Dirk waved to the side. "Even the boats are gone." The road paralleled the river. Earlier, there had been speedboats ferrying people and freight up and down the river, small paddle boats, a few fishing craft. Now the docks were empty, locked up. They passed three barges. Two stacked high with cut timber, and one that was half unloaded at a mill, a tugboat tucked in behind it. No crew were visible.

"Should I go direct to the hospital?" Dena asked. "Wherever that is. Anybody know?"

"No." Dirk shook his head. "Empire House. The governor's Marines will have a medical unit attached, and they'll have med pods and real people medics. They can fix Ana up."

"Won't the hospital have better equipment?"

"It might have more equipment, but not better. Empire outposts get the best technology. And the hospital will be crowded with other casualties. And those folks we tangled with might want to finish the job. We'll be safer in the government center."

"Will they let us in?"

"We're Imperial Citizens, they have to let us in."

"I'm not." Dena slowed for an intersection, checked both ways, then sped through. "I don't think Ana is, never asked. Gavin's not."

"I'm an Imperial Duke."

"But not the Duke they think you are."

"Right, I'm a different Duke, but I'm a Duke." Dirk shook his head. "Shut up and drive. We'll figure it out at Empire House."

The first burned-out cars appeared at the next cross street. They passed four more before the burning buildings showed up. Every block had at least one, some a half dozen. And it looked more like they had been bombed or shot at. The fire had been a secondary effect.

"That must be one faction's," Scruggs said. "The green and cream, or whatever. Wasn't that the ruby lady at the party?"

"Don't know. I should have read the briefing notes," Dirk said.

"Briefing notes?"

"The report Devin gave me. Talked about the tension here. Never mind. Too late now."

"You knew something was going to happen? And you didn't tell us?" Dena said.

"Well, it was secret, and you're not an Imperial Citizen."

"Scruggs is. Did you tell her?"

Scruggs shook her head and continued scanning the streets. "Didn't."

"Well, need to know, and all that—"

"Pilot." Lee was checking Ana's vitals. "Tell us now."

"We're almost there," Dirk said. "I'll explain later."

The park fronting Empire House appeared ahead. "Dena, slow down. We don't want to seem hostile. There will be Marines, and they'll probably shoot."

"Slowing down." Dena stepped on the brakes. "Maybe stop?"

"Pull over the block before. Lee, can we carry this old oaf two blocks without killing him?"

"Probably."

"Can you give me better than that?"

"Nope."

Dena pulled the car over. Everybody piled out and organized themselves. Lee, Dirk, Dena and Scruggs grabbed Ana.

Scruggs grabbed her shotgun. Dirk shook his head. "Leave it. No long guns. Gavin, can you walk?"

"Sure. I can walk. Sing. Dance." He did a two-step. "Lee, what type of drugs did you give me?"

"Good ones. Lift on three. One, two, three." They hoisted Ana up and marched down the street.

The Marines wouldn't let them in. "Just drop him right there," one called from behind the barrier. "One of you walk forward slowly, hands up."

Dirk elected himself and approached, hands high. "We're Imperial Citizens. We've been attacked."

"Everybody's been attacked today sir."

"He's injured. We need medical assistance."

"Is he an Imperial Citizen?"

"Yes," Dirk lied.

"Who is he?"

Dirk looked at the female guard. "You're Suprapto, aren't you? You met him. It's the centurion, Ana."

"The senior centurion?" Suprapto nodded. "I remember him. Impressive guy. But he's not an Imperial Citizen. He was Imperial Auxiliary Legion."

"How in Jove's name did you know that?" Dirk asked.

"The Marines know. We know a lot of things. For example, we've figured out that you're not really the Duke Charles Garnier, because there is no such person. We'd have some questions for you later, but we're kinda busy right now."

"Dirk!" Lee yelled. "Speed it up. He's not doing well."

"Give me a minute!" Dirk yelled back. "Look, can you take him in, then, not us?"

"Nope. Only Imperial Citizens. Real ones."

"Fine." Dirk dropped his hands. *Time to step up.* "I'm not the Duke Charles Garnier. I'm Dirk Friedel, the Butcher of New Madrid. There's a warrant out for my arrest. My companion, the Jovian, is on the Empress's Staff. The goofy-looking engineer guy was our major spy in the Union of Nations. They have a death sentence on him. Oh, and the freckled redhead is heir to a vast fortune in the Core. Sandra Caroline Ruger-Gascoigne. There's a warrant out for her too."

The Marines laughed. "Duke Dirk Friedel. Of course you are," Suprapto said. "A big warrant?"

"One hundred thousand credits."

"Of course, of course. And what about this furry fellow?" Rocky had followed Dirk. He rubbed himself against the Marines, wagging his tail. "Is he some sort of killer attack dog?"

"He chased away some of the soldiers at the roadblock," Dirk said. "And he kills poisonous snakes. Shakes them to death."

"This twenty-pound mutt chased soldiers away?"

"Yes."

"And I'll bet that other girl, the one with all the skin showing, she's some sort of super-secret marksman warrior?

Climbs trees and kills people with a garrote—something like that?"

"Um. She kills people with a slingshot, yes."

The Marines howled. "Great stories, I'll give you that. Killer dogs. Secret spies. The Butcher of New Madrid."

"Dirk," Lee yelled. "I need help, more plasma."

The Marine squad medic had been hovering in the background. Now he locked eyes with Suprapto, and through some Marine eye-speak, got permission and jogged out to help.

"You've got to help us," Dirk said.

"No, I do not gotta. I gotta protect the governor, Imperial Citizens, and Imperial Property, in that order. Nothing to do with fake dukes, no matter how good a story they put out."

"If you let us in, you'll be rewarded."

"If I let you in, I'll be put up against the wall and shot."

Dirk wavered. "What would they charge you with?"

"Being a dumbass. Secret dukes. Empress's staff. Great story."

Rocky barked.

"Sorry, furry buddy. You're the most believable. I'll bet you could kill a snake."

The medic reached Lee and pulled a plasma unit out of his bag. Lee was speaking to him urgently, but the medic shook his head. They clipped the plasma unit onto the tube Lee had snaking down, and he held it upright. Then he reached down and pulled Ana's shirt back and did a double take. "Lance Corporal, come here, please."

"What do you want, Lwazi?"

"You need to see this."

"See what."

"Come here and double-check me."

Suprapto glared. The medic nodded twice and did the Marine eye-flick thing. Suprapto issued some orders to his squad. They stood to, weapons pointing out to cover Dirk.

"You, Secret Duke. Stay here." Suprapto climbed the wall onto the grass yard and jogged to Ana and the others. The medic pointed down at Ana's chest and made urgent motions.

Suprapto stood. "Duke whatever your name is, come over here."

Dirk looked at the nearest soldier who wasn't quite pointing a gun at him. "Well?"

"Lance Corporal says go. You go."

Dirk walked back. Suprapto was talking to the Marine medic. The Marine medic kept shaking his head.

"...within the hour without help, for sure, Lance Corporal."

Dirk arrived and looked down. If Lee hadn't been there holding his head, Dirk would have assumed Ana was dead. He was as pale as the dust in the road, and his chest didn't move, but red blood rasped out of his wound.

"What is it, Suprapto?"

Suprapto pointed down at Ana's chest. "Is that real?"

Dirk twisted his head. Lee had cut Ana's shirt away on one side, but not had time to remove it in the jeep. "His shirt? What do you mean?"

"Not his shirt." Suprapto tapped Ana's chest. Ana had worn his number two uniform, along with decorations, planning on impressing the locals. "This decoration."

Dirk stared. Ana wore only three small medals. "I assume so. I never asked."

"You never asked?"

"What is it? Some Marine thing?"

"Some Marine thing." Suprapto raised her rifle—it was a gauss rifle, standard Imperial issue—possibly to shoot Dirk, but then thought better of it. "Yes, it's some Marine thing. Where did he get it?"

"How would I know? I told you I never asked."

Suprapto and the medic exchanged glances.

Scruggs had followed Dirk. She leaned down and tapped Ana's chest. "This one here? Light blue stripes?"

"Yes."

"He got it from the Empress, he said. Private session. He was proud of it."

"How do you know he was proud of it?"

"He has dozens of medals. Only wears the ones he did something useful for."

"What did he do for this one?"

"He said he killed somebody the Empress wanted killed."

Suprapto wavered. "It could be fake, like the rest of you."

"Lance Corporal," Scruggs said. "You met the centurion. Do you think he's the type of soldier to wear an award he's not authorized?"

That did it. Suprapto picked up her comm and ordered a medical squad out to collect the centurion and his 'party,' as he called them, and deliver them to the infirmary.

"We'll cover you 'til they get here," Suprapto said.

Dena stuck her head in to look at Ana's chest. "Glad we can go in. But what is it? What type of medal?"

"That is the Marine star," Suprapto said.

"Wow! A Marine star!" Dena shrugged. "And I have no idea what that is. Like a famous Marine?"

"It's a medal for bravery. You get it for saving Marines."

"Not for shooting random people for no reason? 'Cause that's more likely with this guy. He hates Marines. Or so he says."

"His chest says otherwise."

"You sure about this?"

"I think so. I've only ever seen pictures before, never a real one."

"So pretty rare, then."

"Yes."

"What did he do to get it?" Dena asked.

"I want to know that too," Suprapto said. "He didn't get it the normal way, that's for sure."

"How do you know that?"

"Well, normally." Suprapto looked at Dena. "Normally, to get it, you have to die."

Chapter 18

"**S**ignal from the flagship." Lieutenant Franceska Monti looked up from her fuel calculations as her intercom burped. "Unscheduled drill. Convoy to execute zigzag Bravo-Sierra-3 in five minutes."

Monti stood and stretched. She'd retired to her room for her first rest in sixteen hours. She'd wanted to sleep, but the *Collingwood* consumed six percent more fuel than predicted by the computer, and she needed to find out why. Either the computer model was off, or the systems were not reporting properly, or something was seriously broken in the pumps. *Or with my luck, all three at the same time.*

"Sync the timer," Monti said. "I'll be up." She stretched some more, adjusted her uniform so it looked less wrinkled, and pulled herself up to the bridge.

Hernandez, as promised, had taken a watch. She vacated the command chair for Monti. Silaski, their spacesick helmsman, typed frantically on her board. She'd cleaned herself up after her vomit incident, but the smell lingered. "Hack on the screen."

The screen displayed an expensively dressed blond woman with long legs perched on a stool, addressing two men in ties. Her name, flashed on the bottom of the screen, was 'Susy the Newsy.'

"Sorry," Silaski said. "I was watching the news download—I mean, playing the news download for the crew. Here you go, Captain."

Susy and friends disappeared. Now the screen showed a description of the maneuver and a timer. "There's no frequency for acknowledgment there, helm."

Silaski typed, then shook her head. "No frequency ma'am. No request for acknowledgment with the original message."

"Play me the original message," Monti said.

"It's text only." More frantic typing and Silaski put the message on the bridge channel. The message was from the admiral's aide. He had sent a time hack, the maneuvering orders, and that was it. Nothing else.

Hernandez settled into the second officer's chair. "Commander, I don't have all your freighter hauling experience—"

"Passenger liner." Monti grimaced. *She's been respectful, but she still gets her digs in.*

"Passenger liner, fine. But shouldn't there be some sort of ack requirement?"

"Ack sequences are not necessary when ships are under pilot ship maneuvering control, station local maneuvering control, or military flagship operating control. Imperial Regulations for the prevention of collisions, 1943.5. Or Colregs 1943, if you prefer."

"I'll remember that if I want an A on my test. But I don't see a pilot ship around here, or a station. And I have to admit, I don't know how to tell if we're under flagship control."

"The flagship," Monti said, "has not requested centralized control. Not of us. Not of anybody. Where's Weeks and Hooper?"

"Hooper is off watch, sleeping. Weeks is on the hull helping track down why the laser targeting is three degrees off center."

"He can do that?"

"At least as well as your so very talented engineering staff can. With the added incentive that he's been outside in the black before and won't go floating off like that guy in first shift. "

Monti shook her head to clear it. "Jove bless us. Get them back in. Sound general quarters. Get Hooper up here."

Weeks raised her eyebrows, but only for a second. She didn't have the instinctive obedience a regular bridge officer did, but she caught the tone of Monti's worry and didn't argue. The general quarters alarm bonged throughout the ship.

Monti brought up the local space display, including all the ships in the convoy. She plotted a course on the screen, then adjusted it to reflect the future maneuvers. Then she started adding instructions for the other two corvettes.

Hooper rolled in, looking woozy and adjusting the cuffs of her skinsuit. "What was that, five minutes asleep? What new disaster has overtaken us?"

"The admiral has ordered a convoy-wide twenty-five plus X, fourteen-degree minus Z course correction in—" Weeks checked the screen. "Three minutes and twenty-five seconds."

"You woke me for a course correction? Fine. Did you already ack?"

"No ack required."

"No ack required? With this many ships." Monti looked at the screen. "This many ships and no acks? Holy Imperial smash-up."

"I'm setting us up to maneuver away from the screen. Take the helm. Bring up the radars. Get ready to get us out of here."

Hooper shooed Silaski from her seat. "Messages coming in. Looks like the olds are already arguing."

The text crawl on the main screen had a smattering of responses to the maneuvering orders. Prominent was Captain Mahony's from the *Hydrogen Pride*. It started with 'respectfully submit' but the gist of it was 'are you out of your mind, you raving lunatic?'

Hernandez waved. "Weeks has cleared the others off the hull. He's waiting for them to cycle through. He'll be inside in two minutes."

The screen on the front counted two minutes fifteen seconds.

"Tell him to lock down in the airlock as soon as he's inside. In fact—" Monti pressed the all-ship intercom. "All stations. Lock in place. I say again. Lock in place. Prepare for extremely violent maneuvering. Seal all compartments. Seal all suits. Crew not at their station lock into nearest restraints, do not attempt to move. You have thirty seconds until full lock-down."

"What in the name of Hades is going on?" Hernandez said. "It's just a course change. Only twenty-five degrees."

"You think all those freighters can do a course change of twenty-five degrees at the same rate? You think they have helmsmen on station to do that? You think they're even monitoring their comms? Half of them are probably asleep and they're not going to wake up from some comm alert."

"But the military transport ships—"

"Will make the turn at high G. Some of the freighters will at low G. Some won't. When things start breaking up, we're about to be in the middle of a giant maneuvering free-for-all."

"We're kilometers apart. No way we're going to hit each other. That's ridiculous. Spaceships don't hit each other in deep space."

"It's extremely, extremely rare. But it's happened. I hope you're right, but if you're not, what's going to happen to us if a freighter a hundred times our size hits us a glancing blow?"

Hernadez adjusted all the buckles on her seat, and slapped her helmet down.

"All stations. Lockdown, now." Monti typed her own controls. Flashing red lights turned solid.

The timer counted down on the screen. Hooper fiddled with her board. "*Trail* and *Moncton* confirm orders. They will execute least-time maneuver at time hack, but not correct their attitude and keep their engines ready."

"What does that mean?" Hernandez asked.

Monti fiddled with her board again. "There are an infinite number of ways to change from one vector to another. Fire at ten-G for one minute or one-G for ten minutes. Sounds like the same thing. They're not. Imperial warships make the vector change as fast as possible, then pivot back to pointing down their course line. Merchant ships are more concerned about fuel, so they'll do the most fuel-efficient course change, which takes longer but gets them pointing in the same direction. All the Navy or Navy Auxiliary vessels will interpret this one way—the same way. But the freighters? Who knows. We'll all be running each other down in thirty-two seconds."

"I'm set," Hooper said. "Your course is laid in. I've got the radars up and pinging, and computer override set up if there's less than a second left before we hit."

"Computer override should avoid a collision, right?" Hernandez asked.

Monti pulled her straps tight. "Our computer and their computer might choose different avoidance courses. Or we might choose one that makes it worse. Or some other ship might react to what they see and manually change the situation. Stand by for pivot."

The *Collingwood* yawed starboard and pitched down to come onto the new vector, but didn't light its main engines. The timer ticked to zero, and the main drive fired, pushing them into their seats for thirty seconds.

Their position had been at the rear quadrant. They turned starboard and down. If the convoy had maneuvered properly, it would have turned away as well, and now be drawing away from them.

The flagship and its escorting destroyers made a ponderous turn at the head of the convoy. The Auxiliary Navy ships in the central pillar—the army transports, the tankers, and the weapons colliers—turned in reasonable unison and fired their engines at full force. Two fired at only one-G and dropped behind, but at least they turned.

Perhaps a third of the freighters missed the turn entirely and kept serenely sailing on their previous course. A small group of freighters took the turn at speed. The bulk carriers were simply too massive to switch vectors quickly. They had giant engines, but even when you double engine thrust, if you quadruple mass, you maneuver like a rock in a mudpit.

BONG. BONG. The collision alarm sounded.

"We're overhauling those guys in the back," Hooper said.

"Climb over them. Plus Z as much as you need," Monti said.

The ship pivoted again, and they climbed 'up' over the convoy. Hooper firewalled the engines. It was more than needed, but now they had an excuse for radical maneuvers, and the faster they got far away from the convoy, the better.

"Traffic on all the comm channels," Silaski said. "*Trail* and *Moncton* are both calling on the escort channel."

"Tell them to steer clear of the convoy, then release them to independent maneuvers." Monti grimaced. She wasn't supposed to do that, and she wasn't clear she had the authority. *But after this cluster-f, nobody will care.*

"Right, we're heading out to deep space. Nothing can catch us," Hooper said.

"Keep us out here."

"Flagship is signaling," Silaski said. "General signal. Emergency signal. Um. It's a maneuver code. I don't know it."

"The system should tell you. Look it up—no, put it on the screen." Monti pointed.

Hooper's console bonged. "Something fishy up front. Radar says the flagship is acting weird. Like their main drive is offline."

Hernandez brought up a sensor screen on the main board. Monti hadn't known she knew how to do that with sensors. *I don't trust her at all.* We need to talk to her some more.

"You're right." Hernandez pointed. "*Canopus's* main drive looks to be offline."

"Main drive offline? Silaski, where is that message?"

"Here ma'am." Silaski swiped a message on the screen. "I can't find this in the military code database—"

"It's not a military code. It's a generic merchant code. Means 'unable to maneuver'."

Hernandez was playing back some sensor readings. "*Canopus's* main drive fired, then there was a burp, then it went offline."

"A burp?"

"Something blew. Because it's not firing now. Big problems if they don't move."

Monti gulped air, then forced a deep breath. *This could get ugly.* Why didn't I get on that shuttle a day earlier? Focus. "Bron, status?"

"We're clear, Franky." Hooper cut the engines, and they floated. "We're way high. Nothing can catch us now."

"Jove bless us. Keep this course while I check the others." Hooper called the other corvettes. They were intact, under command, and seething.

"Captain," Hernandez said. "I think you should watch this ma'am."

"Ma'am?" Monti looked up. Ma'am? Hernandez had been respectful, but not overly so. "There's no need—oh no."

Hernandez had zoomed in on the front, or what used to be the front, of the convoy. Ships were now heading out in every direction. The military line in the center of the hexagon had executed a time-on-target maneuver, at least in comparison to the freighters. One freighter was a possible danger, at least to them, and they'd taken early action to avoid it.

Monti's corvettes had been outside the convoy proper to start with, and were now farther outside, but going in a safe direction.

Freighters are massive ships, slow and ponderous to move. Freighter captains learned early to make slow, clearly signaled, easy-to-understand maneuvers and keep making them. Let the other small and more maneuverable ships get out of their way.

Unfortunately, battleships are almost as big as freighters, almost as massive, and if their main drives are down, even slower to change vector. The *Canopus* had started her maneuver, then her drive had failed. But her velocity had changed enough that the ships in the following columns, at least those that were awake, had to maneuver to avoid her.

The front of the convoy split like a bucket of water with a rock dropped into it. Ships splashed in all directions. *Colling-*

wood's computer couldn't keep up with showing all the intersecting vector changes, and portions of the display locked. The extended dotted lines that showed a ship's future course disappeared. The sensors weren't reporting enough data to make predictions, so only current position showed.

"Some of the freighters are crossing over the ones behind," Hernandez said. "What idiot does that?"

"They're just taking the easiest avoidance of what's in front of them. Fire your main drives and thrusters at once and scoot around what's in front of you. Let the people behind you worry about your new course."

The dots representing freighters scattered as freighters that had maneuvered to avoid the *Canopus* now maneuvered to avoid those avoiding the *Canopus*. And so on.

"They'll be okay," Hooper said. "Hernandez is right. Even in the tighter part of the convoy, they still have kilometers of separation."

"Had." Monti pointed at the screen. "Those two bulk carriers, the *Sigmund* and that green one, are closing."

The bridge was quiet. The dots representing the two bulk carriers, the *Sigmund* and the *Brothers Wessup*, merged on the screen. Then they passed through each other. Both blinked yellow as they separated.

"Did they hit?" Hernandez asked.

Hooper shook her head. "Nope, but some sort of damage. Drive plume burned off sensors, high-powered radar fried something too close. That yellow comes from them. They're signaling damage. We can't tell what type at this distance."

"Thank Jove for separation. Even this big of a screw-up nobody got hurt." Monti's breath whooshed out. "And that, children, is why there are minimal separation requirements in convoys."

"Glad nobody got hurt."

"You're right, Hernandez, they look closer together than they are, but bad things can happen when lots of ships are moving in close proximity."

"Flagship back under control," Silaski said. "Reports executing emergency vector change."

Hooper's and Monti's eyes flashed back to the screen. "No. No. No. The destroyers—" Monti said.

"What?" Hernandez said. "You just talked about this big separation between ships—"

"Freighters," Monti said. "Not escorts. They'll be tucked in as close to the flagship as possible to provide support and minimize comm delay. If they don't get the word—"

An update flashed across the screen as the computer calculated trajectories and digested sensor data. The real-time display was replaced with a countdown for next update.

The main display showed three green dots ahead of the convoy. The screen froze and the status line across the top changed to 'updating.' Five seconds later, a single red dot replaced the three green. The status changed to updating again. Five seconds after that, the red dot disappeared. Two dots remained. One green, and one brighter red.

Of the third dot, there was no sign.

Chapter 19

“**Y**ou should have gotten this man into a pod soonest.” Once inside the Empire House, Ana had been placed on a gurney. He was so pale, it was hard to tell where the sheet ended and his face started. “I can’t believe you waited this long. This wound happened hours ago.”

“Well, Marine—” Lee ducked to look at his name tag. “Marine Lwazi, we didn’t have any choice. This happened midway between the city and the starport. Took us a long time to get here.”

“Not in the city? Wasn’t this from the fighting near the river—earlier this morning?”

“No.” Lee helped push the gurney onto an elevator. The others waited in the hall for the next one. “We were ambushed on the road in from the starport after we left.”

“You drove in from the starport? The captain will want to talk to you. We’re in radio contact with the detachment there. They say that Planetary Guard troops have surrounded the airport and aren’t letting anybody in.”

"What's going on? Where did this fighting come from?" *And what's the governor's part in it?*

Lwazi watched the lights flash on the control panel. "Planetary Guard is fighting themselves. We're locked in here."

"Revolting? Throwing out the Empire?"

"Nope. It's more like a gang war between different factions. There have been some explosions up in the hills. Industrial sites, that sort of thing. This morning, a couple hundred of troops rolled into town. They shot up a bunch of buildings and sank some boats. Some of the others fought back. Planetary Guard on both sides. One side won."

"What did the governor do?"

"Nothing." The elevator ground to a halt. Lights flashed on the control panel. They were so deep, Lee couldn't hear the surface noises, only fans. Lwazi thumbed a sensor and typed a code, and the elevator moved again.

"Nothing? The governor did nothing?"

"Start of this whole thing, the Marines on duty had notes hand-delivered to them by random kids. Said there was going to be some shooting, but it was 'an internal Planetary Guard matter' and 'no Imperial Citizens or property would be attacked.' That's what happened too."

"They didn't attack Empire House?"

"Or the starport. They surrounded it, but didn't move in. And once they shot up the opposition or whatever here, they stopped. City is quiet. No shooting in hours."

"What's the governor going to do?"

"Nothing."

"Nothing? There's a revolt going on."

"Doesn't look like they're revolting against the Empire. It's something else."

"It's your job to defend the Empire!"

"I am defending the Empire. I support the Empire. I work for the Empire." The elevator door opened, and he pushed Ana's gurney out. The wheels squeaked as they rolled down another corridor. "I don't work for some spit backward jungle planet. They can fight their own wars."

Lwazi led Lee into a small but well-equipped infirmary, and Lee helped lift Ana into a med pod and connect sensors and monitors, and cut his clothes off. The doctor arrived and Lwazi shooed Lee out but let her take the bloody outfit.

"Is he going to be okay?" Scruggs asked. The others had arrived on the next elevator after harassing one of the Marines to bring them down. Dena pushed Gavin to a chair, and he collapsed on it. The rest clustered around the infirmary door.

"Doctor will know." Lee nodded to Dirk. "There's a revolt going on. Did you hear?"

Dirk nodded. "The Marines were talking about it."

Scruggs walked up to the infirmary door and peered through the window. "Maybe I should go in and help."

Dirk grabbed Scruggs's arm. "Dena, help me out here."

Dena took Scruggs's shotgun, which the Marines had ignored after seeing Ana's medals. She handed it to Lee and helped Dirk pull Scruggs away from the door. "Let the doctors deal with it. Sit here."

"I have to do something."

"Well." Dena grimaced. "Why not go upstairs and go with the Marines and shoot some random person. The old man would like that."

"He wouldn't want me to shoot some random person!"

"True. Being who he is, he'd want you to shoot a whole platoon of random people, and then cut their thumbs off and wear them like a necklace or something. But that seems gross. Maybe shoot two or three but keep one thumb."

"He's not like that!"

"Baby Marine, in my experience, he's exactly like that."

"I don't know what to do. I have to do something."

Dirk shook his head. "No you don't. Sometimes you just have to wait." Dirk stretched. "That was hard for me to learn when I was young."

"The centurion would—"

"The centurion can't help you right now. You have to decide for yourself what to do. But he would tell you to analyze the situation, decide on your goal, and make a plan to achieve that. How about we do that?" Dirk nodded at the door. "Situation, goal, plan?"

Scruggs swallowed. "The centurion is hurt. The goal is to fix him up. The plan was to get him to medical help."

"Mission successful," Dirk said. "Now you have to wait for others to do their job."

"That's hard."

"Yup. But that's what you have to do."

Scruggs swallowed again, then slumped into a chair. "I'll wait."

"Good for you." Dirk smiled. "We'll make an officer of you yet."

Dena laughed. "Look at you, Mr. Let's-teach-the-recruit how to be a soldier. You sound more and more like an Imperial officer."

Dirk shrugged. "I'm remembering."

The door swung open and Lwazi stuck his head out. "Doctor says he wants to know what drugs this guy is taking for his cancer. The names of all of them?"

"Cancer?" Dirk said. "I knew he was sick, but..."

"Four types," Scruggs said. She named them. All had lots of syllables. She repeated them, then spelled them for Lwazi before he went back to see the doctor.

Dirk waited for the door to shut, before glaring at Scruggs. "How do you know the names of all those drugs?"

"I buy them for him. He can't afford them. Whenever we're at a civilized planet, I go to the hospitals and buy him a big supply."

"He can't afford them? We're swimming in money from the Tribune."

"Well, now. Before, we weren't."

"Right," Dirk said. "You buy his drugs for him, outstanding. I knew he was sick, but I didn't realize how bad. How long 'til these drugs cure his cancer?"

"Never," Scruggs said. "The cancer will kill him, but it's in abeyance with the drugs. Slows it down."

"How much longer does he have?"

"He's already passed the normal limit."

"So, that means—"

"Means I don't want to talk about it." Scruggs took her revolver out of her pocket and started to field-strip it.

"Cancer. Marine medals. And a revolt. Lee, the Marines said that they haven't been shot at, not once."

"That's what I heard as well. Weird sort of revolt."

"Especially with Planetary Guard on both sides."

"Wow! Did you see this medal?" Dena sat next to Scruggs and showed her a screen. "Check it out, Baby Marine. The old man's a hero, if it's real."

"Most conspicuous gallantry and pre-eminent act of valor," Scruggs read.

"Conspicuous? Doesn't sound like the old man."

"Extreme devotion to duty in the presence of the enemy."

"Okay, that could be him." Dena nodded. "He wouldn't let a little thing like getting shot at stop him from doing anything."

"I can't see the centurion wearing a decoration he wasn't entitled to."

Dirk nodded. "Say what you like, that's not one of his sins."

"No wonder the Marines brought us in." Dena flipped through the pages. "He gets an annual pension and his own flag."

Gavin sat up. "He probably blew his pension on brandy." He wiped spit off his face. "Speaking of brandy, anybody have any?"

"You're back!" Lee stooped to look at him. "How do you feel?"

"Hungry. I could eat a tabbo. Two tabbos. Did I see the doctor?"

"Doctor's busy with the centurion right now. No news yet—wait."

The door to the infirmary swung open and Lwazi came out. "Your man is going into surgery. The doc has called in his surgery crew. They'll be here in half an hour and start."

"You mean," Lee said, "that they'll be here in half an hour to watch the med-pod surgery robot do its thing."

"Nope. He's got a bullet in one lung, cancer in the other, his immune system is all messed up from the drugs, he's missing a kidney, and his liver isn't in great shape either. The auto-surgeon is great, but it can only do so many things at once. Doc says he'll have to get in there and poke around before he decides what to take out."

"He's missing a kidney?" Lee turned to Scruggs. "Did you know he was missing a kidney?"

"Don't look at me, I didn't take it," Scruggs said.

Dirk snorted first, then Dena, then Scruggs smiled, and shortly, they were all giggling and laughing. Rocky barked and wagged his tail. Everyone was happy again!

"I didn't take it either." Dirk smiled. "Outstanding. Trooper Lwazi, what can we do?"

"Come along with me while we wait."

"We can stay here, out of the doc's way."

"I know you will, but I got a call. Somebody wants to see you."

"Who?"

"Governor demands your presence, right away."

"Outstanding." Dirk said. "Let's see what RC has to say."

Lwazi led them through some corridors, past a guard post. Dirk quizzed him about the tunnels, and seemed surprised by the extent.

Dena tapped the concrete wall. "Why do we care about the tunnels?"

"There's too many. This is a Class 7 building up above, but this is more like a Class 11 set of tunnels."

"There are standard tunnels as well?"

"It's a big empire. Everything is standard. Beacons. Satellite constellations, ships, docking bays, weapons. There's a rule and a regulation for everything. Even tunnels."

"Anyone ever tell you that you Imperials are all weird, anal-retentive weirdos?"

"Not anybody who had to run more than one planet, no." Dirk stopped as Lwazi knocked on a door, then stepped through, closing it behind him.

"Trusting sort," Dena said. "Where are we, exactly?"

Dirk pointed at a wall panel. "This is a main communications room. There will be an executive suite inside. Governor might be there, handling things himself."

The door swung open and Lwazi stuck his head out. "You're wanted. Follow me."

The five crew members crowded through the door. The first room was square, forty feet by forty feet. A giant display table filled the center—rectangular, twelve by twenty-four feet.

Right now, it displayed a view of the capital and surrounding region from space. High ridges and rolling hills formed a backbone that ran down the east side of the map. The widest river, the Pagoda river, ran from the northwest to the center of the map. The capital sat at the confluence of the Sao and the Pagoda. From the capital, the reinforced Pagoda snaked back and forth over the lowlands, heading south. Near the ocean, the Than River, nearly as big as the Pagoda, dropped out of the hills and joined up in the valley, forming a twenty-mile-long shallow lake.

At the end of the lake, the Thu River joined from the west. The newly invigorated Pagoda River roamed south, forming a giant mile-wide expanse of water, until it broke up into channels as it ran out to the sea. The ocean showed at the bottom, with the spaceport nearby on a hill overlooking the river delta.

"Great map," Dirk said. "Colorful. You missing some people?" There were six consoles on both side walls. Three were empty. Three were manned by harassed-looking Marines.

"Not your concern."

Dirk crossed his arms. "Where is everybody?"

"Only a hundred Marines on planet in total," Lwazi said. "Including the medical unit, the dental unit, air traffic control, and a special unit to secure the courier databases. We're a little short." He turned to the door. "Captain, they're here!"

A Marine captain entered from the interior room and looked them over. "You Duke Dirk Friedel?"

"For my sins. Who are you?"

"Rybus. Friedel? That's not the name you gave at the party."

"True." Dirk put his hands in his pockets. "It's not."

Rybus thought about that for a moment, then turned and stalked back into the office. The others exchanged glances, then Rybus returned and handed Dirk a plastic case. "DNA locked to Dirk Friedel. If you're him, you should be able to open it."

"If he's not?" Dena asked. "What then?"

"Explosive charge will destroy the contents."

"And also my hand," Dirk said. He thumbed the case and flipped it open. He removed a message chip, pushed it in his comm, then began to read.

"Any questions?" Rybus asked.

"Lots," Dirk said. "I need to look at your map."

Dirk explained their task. RC had loaded a truck with the crates he needed moved. It was parked in the basement of Empire House. Dirk was to drive the truck to the starport and load it onto the *Heart's Desire*. Captain Rybus had a datapak ready for them to inspect.

"I'm supposed to let one of you sample three points on it," the captain said. "Once you do the third search, it auto encrypts. I've got a key here." He held up an encryption chip. "Who's up?"

"Me," Lee said. She followed Rybus into the next room. Dirk started quizzing the Marines in the room about different paths to the starport.

"You sure the bridge here is blown?" One pointed to the map. "We don't have any reports on that."

"We were nearly killed by broken concrete chunks," Dirk said. "It's blown."

"If you're lying, I'll know in the morning when the weather satellite goes over. It's not a spy satellite, but the camera has good enough resolution to see a missing bridge."

"It's gone," Dirk said. "We're very, very sure."

"Well, then you're very, very out of luck. The next bridge is a good two hundred kilometers upriver. And it's not on a direct route. And driving a truck, and with all the reports we're getting about fighting, it won't be great fun to go up there. You could get into trouble."

"We can handle trouble," Dirk said.

"Sometimes," Lee said, returning from checking the datapaks. "Except the centurion is in surgery, and Gavin's kind of shot up. We can't go anywhere without them."

"We're not leaving the centurion," Scruggs said.

"No, we're not. Lee, what's his prognosis?"

"Depends on how the surgery goes. He was shot, but the med pods understand those things. They'll sew him up tight, and provided the surgeons put the other parts together, that should stabilize him. But he'll need to be stuck in the med pod for a few days. Gavin could use a day as well."

"I'm fine, Skipper." Gavin flexed his left arm and grimaced. "I can't drive, though. Or shoot. Not well anyways."

Dirk nodded. "We could stay here a week and see how things go. Things could get better."

"Or, Pilot, they could get worse,' Lee said. "Those datapak cases checked out, but they have timers on them. Wait too long and the data self-destructs. This one is two weeks."

"We can't wait." Dirk said. He turned to Rybus. "I need to talk to the governor."

"Governor isn't taking calls today."

"He'll take mine."

"No, I mean, his comm isn't answering."

"Well, send somebody to his quarters."

Rybus lowered his voice. "Won't help sir."

"Why are you calling me sir?" Dirk asked.

"You're kind of in charge now sir."

"I am not. The governor—ah, Imperial ankles." *RC had run away, leaving them holding the bag. Or the datapaks.* "Where did he run to?"

"Keep your voice down," Rybus hissed. "We don't know. He's not here, in Empire House. We haven't been able to find him since this morning. He authorized this shipment thing, and then he went off air, and he's not here now."

"But where did he go? Who's in charge?"

"His social secretary ranks us sir. He says not to worry. But that DNA box proves you're Dirk Friedel, the naval officer, in fact, the senior naval officer on station, so..."

"So I'm in charge." Dirk glared around the office. "Outstanding."

Chapter 20

"We need to defend Empire House, and the starport. We also need to transport those crates, and keep the Marines from getting overrun," Dirk said. He'd gathered his crew, Captain Rybus and Lance Corporal Suprapto in the office adjacent to the communication center. He sniffed the room's dry air. *It would be nice to stay here. Less humid. Quieter. No decisions.*

"It would be beneficial to find the governor too," Lee said. "See where he went."

All heads turned to Captain Rybus. He shrugged. "Nobody left the building since this morning."

"Check the cameras," Dirk said.

"We did. Nobody came in or out, not since those messages were delivered this morning."

"We need to get these datapaks off planet, and soon," Lee said. "And we need the governor's crates with us, or we'll have... difficulties with his contact."

"We can't go anywhere without the centurion," Scruggs said. "We can't leave him behind."

"Starport is far away," Gavin said. "Lots of fighting between here and there. And no easy bridges."

"Can we get the ship here to take all of us off?" Dena asked.

"First, we would have to get to the ship," Dirk said. "Which, given the available choice of roads, is going to be a problem. Even assuming we got the ship here, where do we land and how do we load up? Engineer, can we land in the city close to Empire House?"

Gavin shook his head. "Not without blasting down a bunch of buildings. Not enough room. We could try down by the river, land on the water."

"How do we get those crates into the ship on the water?" Dirk said. "They'd have to come to us. We're not a boat. We can land, but we can't taxi across some lake."

"And the centurion?" Scruggs asked.

"We've got a med pod on board," Lee said. "We move him off this one and onto ours. Or we could even winch it on board. They're designed to be transportable. Gavin, could we hover or something and winch it up?"

"Sure. Not a problem for a med pod. A single med pod. But those crates—there's what, twelve of them? We've only got one winch, and we'd need to rig nets, and we'd have to hover while we were doing it. And if somebody takes a shot at us while we're hovering..."

"Takes a big gun to shoot down a starship," Rybus said.

"Almost as big as it takes to blow up a concrete bridge, and they did that," Dirk said.

"These rebel people said they wouldn't attack Imperial facilities or personnel."

"That's what they said, yes." Dirk nodded. "But accidents happen, communications get confused, things go sideways, and people change their minds. We can't sit over a town for an hour and wait 'til they haul in their Howitzer or whatever they're using. We need to get in and out."

"Have to load at the starport, then," Gavin said. "Cargo ramps, equipment, all there."

"Can we drive the truck up the ship's ramp?" Dirk asked.

"Won't fit. And trucks won't drive over water," Gavin said.

Dirk cursed. "We may end up staying after all, and asking the governor to give us another copy of the data. If we find him. Or can you do that, Captain?"

"No sir." Captain Rybus shook his head. "Tied to the governor's ID, and I don't have that level of access. He set all this up."

Dirk cursed some more. "Right, we need to get some heavy things from here." He pointed out the city on the map. "To there." He pointed to the starport. "But not on these roads. How can we do that?"

"We can't fly," Lee said. "Might get shot down by accident."

Dena poked her head in between the two men. "How do I bring up a legend on this map?"

Rybus tapped a command and legend popped up in the corner. "This what you want?"

"Right." Dena traced a line. "We need to go from here to here, but we can't take the direct route."

"I think I just said that," Dirk said. "Any new ideas?"

"Sure." Dena traced a roundabout path that started at the city, twisted in loops a few times, made a few long sweeping curves, and came up right next to a road that ran into the starport. "Anyone fancy a river cruise?"

They checked as much as they could by asking the Marines. There was a river port only three kilometers upriver from Empire House. Electric barges that ran bulk cargos up and down the rivers docked there. It even had a loading dock, condition unknown. The starport end had a wharf only a few kilometers from the starport. The river was used to move bulk goods like lumber or rice. It went through the bush. It went the wrong direction through the bush for the first two hundred kilometers, but then it turned back. It would work. In theory.

"We board here." Dirk pointed. "First light tomorrow morning. Take the truck and that jeep, we should be able to rig something so that we can drive right onto that barge thing. You agree, Engineer?"

Gavin shrugged. "We'll know when we see it, but given that the riverbank is pretty low here, we can dig something out. There should be plenty of planks and suchlike nearby with all this lumbering. We should be able to get the truck on board. Should."

"How's your arm?"

"Getting better."

"Good enough. The centurion stays here in the med pod. He needs a few days anyways. We should be able to drive off the far end."

"Not to dump on your plan, Skipper," Gavin said. "But how do you know this?"

"If they use this to export wood, they must have a way to move heavy objects on and off at the starport. There will be something there. A crane at least. You four go with the shipment to keep an eye on things."

"Us four?" Dena looked at Dirk. "Us five, you mean."

"Nope. You four," Dirk said.

"And where will you be?" Dena asked.

"Well, there's a hitch," Dirk said.

"I cannot believe that you agreed to stay behind, Dirk." Dena held up a tool box. "Gavin, where does this go?"

Gavin pointed to the large panel truck. "Put the tools in the back with the crates. Scruggs, help me get the food and water into the car." There were no supplies at the river port, so they were loading up two weeks' worth of food and water. Scruggs had helped the Marines move their seized jeep down to the underground garage and load it up. Everybody had changed to more reasonable clothes for the journey.

"No, I won't help you. I'll do it myself." Scruggs lifted a box of water jugs and teetered to the open trunk. "You're not lifting anything with that shoulder. Where's your sling?"

Gavin muttered but obediently pulled out a sling and wrapped his arm.

Dena needed both hands to haul the toolbox to the truck. "Dirk, you Imperial dweeb, you could at least open the door."

"Sorry." Dirk yanked the door lever and opened the rear doors. "In it goes. That's a lot of crates." The back of the truck was littered with crates. A single large crate was shoved into the back and held in place by straps. "There's only one big crate. Governor said there would be two."

"That's all we've got." Lee stepped up behind Dirk. "Captain says the truck was loaded last night under the governor's supervision. He said this is what was going."

"I hope that whoever is on the far end only expects one big crate, otherwise, we'll be in trouble," Dirk said.

"We're in trouble now. Why are you staying here? Really why?"

Dirk tapped his uniform. The Marines had found him a regular uniform without rank tabs. "I'm an Imperial officer. The senior Imperial officer here, which makes me the commander. In the absence of the governor, I have a duty to stay. Commanders don't leave."

"Imperial bull," Dena said. "You're on some sort of self-loathing suicidal kick because you're ashamed of what's happened before and you want to wipe it out by doing something stupid to prove that you're brave."

Dirk regarded Dena. "What if I am? What's it to you?"

Scruggs marched up. "You're our pilot. We need you. You have responsibilities with us too. You can't go running away to play with the Marines."

"First," Dirk said. "I think that's exactly what you did, Dena. Run away. Or wanted to. Second, Devin's put a lot of trust in me. He's treating me like a real officer. I'd forgotten what that's like. He reminded me. Imperial officers, especially ones that work for Tribune Devin, don't run away from their responsibilities."

"You've got responsibilities with us," Scruggs said.

"I do. And that includes the centurion. If I go, who looks out for him right now? Rocky?"

"Rocky will guard him if I ask, won't you, boy?" Scruggs said.

Rocky's tail wagged assent. He was already sleeping next to Ana's med pod. He knew what med pods were. When the pack got hurt, they went inside and slept. His job was to guard them while they did that.

"I agree Rocky will keep any individual from hurting Ana, but he can't help organize the defense of the building that Ana's in, can he."

Scruggs shut up.

Dena didn't. "Who's going to fly the ship?"

"Lee. She's an excellent in-atmo pilot. And a better navigator than me."

"Who's going to navigate while she flies?" *Please don't say me. Please.*

"You and Scruggs. You've both been taking lessons. You can find your way from the spaceport to here no problem. Follow the river if you have to."

"I don't know—"

"Too bad." Dirk shook his head. "I'm taking charge because I have to, Scruggs is going to fill in for the centurion on security, and you're going to be responsible for navigation. You can do it. And we need you to do it."

Dirk's voice had risen during his tirade. The crew stopped and waited.

Dena took a deep breath. "Who's going to help Gavin run engineering, then? He can't do everything with just one arm."

"We will." The crew turned. Rocky wagged his tail and barked.

Cleon and Clara had walked up while they were arguing. Both wore the green-hued Planetary Guard uniform, including sidearms. And both stomped to attention in front of Dirk and saluted. By instinct, Dirk returned it, but he used the cross chest Imperial salute.

"Commander Friedel, at the governor's orders, we're your escort, reporting for duty."

"You talked to the governor?"

"Nope. But we have orders to report to your command."

"I don't believe you. He hasn't been seen around to give orders."

"Paperwork says he did." Cleon handed a chip over.

"So it does." Dirk read the chip. "But you screwed up. The issue time is an hour ago—after he went missing. You faked them somehow. But, hypothetically, if I accepted this as legitimate, would you tell me how you got these orders cut, and why you bothered? Why now?"

Cleon squirmed. Clara came to his rescue. "Theoretically, as family, we have access to his desk and codes in his office. And theoretically, now that our former classmates are shooting at each other, it's best we not be here. We're going to have to support one side or the other, and what if we choose wrong? Whatever happens with the Planetary Guard and Andaman, we're leaving eventually. Word is you are leaving town, and then the planet. We'll help you, if you help us get away from all this."

Dirk asked a few pro-forma questions, and then huddled with the crew.

"It's not true. They talked to him They're the governor's spies," Dena said.

"So?" Lee said. "We've got the governor's goods here, so it's not surprising that he wants somebody to keep an eye on things."

"His kids?" Dena said. "His step-kids? They're more likely to steal it for themselves than make sure it gets to the right place. Or they would be if we were on Rockhaul."

"They seem like fine young people," Dirk said. "And why would they steal this stuff?"

"Money," Dena said.

"They have their own money, or so I've been told. And they're familiar with the planet, with these river ports, and the roads. We need some local cover right now."

"They're spoiled rich kids. They want some excitement. Or this is some nefarious plan to get a title—"

"Nefarious?"

"Sorry, I've been reading some books Scruggs loaned me. They talk strange. Somehow this is going to benefit them, and not us. If their dad is dead, they're nobles. Or will be."

"They have that too already. If not now, when RC dies, they get it. If anything, rather than stealing the governor's stuff, it would make more sense to shoot him dead. Then they'd inherit what he stole, legally. "

"That's what I'd do," Dena said. "Shoot the old dork and be done with it. Take his stuff. Good point. They can come."

"I wasn't aware that I was asking you," Dirk said. "But thanks."

"Besides," Dena said. "If they cause a problem, we hit em over the head with a shovel and bury them in the woods. That's what I'd do if they were my step-kids."

"You play pretty rough on Rockhaul, don't you?" Dirk said.

"Family are the worst." Dena glared at the new arrivals. "The very worst. I'll keep a close eye on them. You help me out with this, Baby Marine."

"Sure." Scruggs squinted at the two of them. "I'll keep an eye on Cleon. You watch Clara."

All eyes turned to her.

"You're going to be keeping a close watch on that young man?" Dena asked. "That handsome, single, dashing young man? Thanks very much, Scruggs. We knew we could count on you. Out of curiosity, why did you pick him for you and her for me?"

"No reason." Scruggs tracked Cleon with her eyes. "Just best to have things, you know, assigned ahead of time."

"What if I decide that I'm going to keep a close watch on Cleon, and you watch Clara?" Dena wondered.

Scruggs rounded on her and glared. Her hands drifted to her sides and her fingers flexed. "I've got my responsibilities. You've got yours. I don't like it when people try to take over my job."

"Your job? Is that what you call it?"

Scruggs pushed forward into Dena's space and leaned into her face. "Yes. I'll do my job. You are saying I won't?"

The crew exchanged bemused glances. Dirk raised his eyebrows.

"She won't." Dirk cocked his head. "We've got enough other problems to take care of. " He laughed. "But maybe I'm safer here at Empire House."

21

Chapter 21

"What in Jove's name is a special purpose investment unit?" Lionel met the shuttle at the airlock. "What have you done? And what's all this?"

Devin exited the lock and handed a red cardboard box to Lionel. "Cranberries."

"What am I supposed to do with this?"

Imin followed Devin out of the lock. "They need to be dried, Prefect, then crushed. You can mix them with meat to make a nice paste for crackers. They make a good tea too."

"See?" Devin put his hand on his sword and headed for the bridge. "You can make tea. Everybody likes tea."

"I don't like tea."

"You don't like tea? But everyone likes—"

"I don't. Tribune, never mind the tea. What have you done?"

"I got money. Lots of it."

"So I've heard. That local company—Verge Development—they've been on the comm. Supplies, fuel, whatever we need."

"Good news."

"They're shuttling it up as we speak."

"Even better news."

"We don't even have to pay. Just sign for them."

"Indeed?" Devin kept walking. "Everything we need."

"Why am I suspicious? Imin. What's in your box?"

Imin hefted the box in his hand. "Blueberries, Prefect. Fresh. I'm going to serve them with some creme for lunch."

"Blueberries?" Lionel licked his lips. "I've had those. They were great."

"I'll make them up for lunch sir." Imin hesitated. "I couldn't get enough for the whole crew."

Devin stopped. "How many?"

"Maybe half sir. Full crew if I use some of the other berries."

Lionel stopped as well. "None for me, then. Tribune—"

"None for either of us. Imin, distribute them amongst the crew. Do a lottery if you need to. Enlisted, then the petty officers. Choose one of the officers. Not either of us. Imin, see to it. Prefect, my office."

Lionel was silent until he and Devin were alone in the office.

"Blueberries," Lionel said. "I love those. Next time, I go down to the planet surface."

"Next time, you will." Devin hesitated. "How is the crew?"

"Cheerful but tired."

"Any word from Dirk and his special group?"

"Nope. But there shouldn't be. First thing we'll know is when they arrive with more information."

"Or news of their capture and execution arrives."

"They won't be executed."

Lionel picked up his cup. "What is this?"

Devin sniffed his. "Tea, I think."

Lionel drank it down.

"I thought you didn't like tea?" Devin asked.

"I lied. For morale. What happened on the planet?"

"I lied. For money."

"I didn't understand your message. What's going on?"

"We've got money. Or access to money for now, and more coming."

"Enough?"

"Maybe."

"How?"

"Those Verge Development people. They have some of their own, they loaned it to us. And they... encouraged..."

"You mean extorted?"

"I wasn't in the room when that discussion happened. So who knows. But they got money from the other locals, from the banks, even the two that weren't going to give us any."

"So it's a loan. How do we pay it back?"

"We don't. We have to win. We win, then they get paid back. This one other thing..."

"Yes?"

"Taxes?"

"We pay them from taxes?"

"No. We don't take taxes from them."

"I don't understand?"

"Any of the investors in this company thing, when we win, they get a hundred-year tax holiday. Them, their descendants, families, heirs. For a hundred years."

Lionel got up and poured himself another cup of tea. "The cranberries do taste good. So you mortgaged the future of the Empire for a pittance?"

"A pittance that we need now. Now they're involved. Unlike a loan, they only get their money if we win. So they're going to support us."

"What's to say that they haven't made the same deal with the Chancellor?"

"Nothing."

"What is this special purpose investment thing?"

"They had to have some way of tracking who is on our good side and gave us money, so it's like a company or something. People buy shares. The more shares they buy, the more taxes are remitted. Some people only get five percent off, some twenty. It depends on how many shares. I don't know how exactly it will work."

"Who will figure it out?"

"There's a board of directors. They'll appoint people."

"Which people? When?"

"Already done. I'm on the board. So were some of those banker types. We appointed people to work it out."

"I'm glad that's done."

"Don't be. You're one of them."

"Thank you so much."

"We made you vice president in charge of compliance."

Lionel rubbed his forehead. "Jove save me."

The door whizzed open and Imin came in. "One bowl left, Tribune. The crew voted it for you."

"That's not really fair, Imin."

Imin extended the bowl. Devin grabbed bowls from the sideboard, and split it in three, then shoved the other two bowls at Lionel and Imin. The three slurped in silence for a moment.

"Outstanding, as always, Imin," Devin said. "You had a productive morning. Attending meetings. Making tea. Mixing creme."

"Yes sir. I'm sure that the Tribune did as well sir."

"You know what I did today, Imin?"

"No sir."

"I sold the rebellion, Imin. Sold it for money."

"Yes sir." Imin licked his spoon. "Did you get a good price?"

Devin licked his own spoon. "Yes, I did."

"Well." Imin set his bowl down. "That's the important thing, isn't it?"

Chapter 22

"We're ready, Pilot." Scruggs leaned out the window of the truck. "All packed up." The first light of dawn glinted through armored windows high on the garage wall.

Dirk waved at the Marine to raise the garage door. "Good luck. Report in every six hours until you're on the ship."

The three-car convoy drove out of Empire House, the primary sun hot on the horizon. Cleon drove the lead car, a shiny blue four-door town car, with Scruggs sitting next to him. It was one of the governor's personal vehicles, all leather and chrome inside, sleek lines outside. It was fast, armored against small arms fire, and had a radio tied into the Marines' network. Scruggs had both a shotgun and the centurion's rifle. She'd begged reloads from the Marine's arsenal, and changed into her usual ship coveralls and holster over skinsuits. She'd also begged a belt with ammo pouches, and stuffed them with the contents of a box of shotgun shells. Her belt now gave her fifty more chances to share shotgun love if need be.

Gavin and Clara were in the truck with the crates. Clara drove, being both familiar with the Andaman trucks and knowing the directions. Both had revolvers.

Lee and Dena were in the shot-up jeep in the back. They'd also donned ship gear over skinsuits.

Dena snapped her slingshot. "I still think I should be there with that girl. Scruggs is too young."

Lee accelerated to follow the truck. Humid air drifted in through the blasted windows. "Scruggs is a good shot, she doesn't panic under fire, and she's keeping a close watch on that truck load of goods."

"And a close watch on the governor's son."

"Not such a bad thing," Lee said. "Both of those kids are in front of us, with one of our people watching each of them. They can't try anything while they're driving. Gavin and Sister Scruggs will shoot them, they understand that. If something happens to either vehicle, we've got another vehicle who knows where they're going to follow. And we can pick up anybody who has to dive out of those vehicles."

"If it's Cleon or Clara, I vote we leave them there. You can pick them up if you want, but I'm not going to help you."

The convoy turned right outside of the driveway, then right again to pick up the main river boulevard. "The other reason to put Scruggs in that vehicle is that she takes direction. I can count on her to do what she's told. You, I have to keep an eye on."

Dena stuck her tongue out. "Pffft to you." She glanced behind them. "They've already got that door closed. Say. If somebody shoots us up, who's going to pick us up? There's nobody behind us."

Lee grimaced as she turned to avoid a smoking car wreck in the road. "Who do you think?"

"Nobody?"

"Yep." Lee swerved around a tire lying in the road. "You're only just now figuring that out?"

The boulevard widened to two lanes on both sides separated by a median. They passed from the arcaded stone and glass commercial area into a residential apartment section. Two- and three-story concrete block buildings lined both sides, set back with concrete sidewalks.

"I've had my eyes on other things," Dena said.

"I saw." Lee counted to four, then slowed the car.

"Why are you dawdling? Get behind them."

"No." Lee slowed even more, further increasing the distance between the vehicles. "Keep four seconds' drive time between each vehicle. That way, any explosion that knocks one vehicle out and stops it, we still have enough braking space to avoid hitting the wreck. Then we still have options."

Dena scanned out the windows. "The centurion would love to hear you talk about this. So why's our most junior person in the truck?"

"Good driver, good shooter. Most robust vehicle."

"I shoot better than her!"

Lee turned her head. "You think so? Have you compared yourself to her recently?"

Dena growled. "She's just a kid."

"Not anymore. She still acts like a kid, but she isn't."

"I can take her."

"I'll look forward to that contest."

"You do that. Why not put the truck first? It's the most important vehicle, right?"

"Yes, but that's why that semi-armored car is first. It's not exactly life's winners manning these roadblocks. Chances are if they see a car coming, they'll fire at it. That car is the most survivable, so if someone panics and starts shooting, the truck can divert and so can we."

The lead vehicle braked hard and turned into an alley to the right. Lee followed and the jeep bucked as it road up the eight-inch curve.

"Hang on," Lee said. "This is bumpy."

"Why are we going right?" Dena pointed. "River's off to the left."

"The landing is outside of town, and the river road is the direct and logical route. Which is where they would have set the ambush if somebody is calling ahead. Now they don't know where we're going. We'll cut across town, take a secondary road, and rejoin the river road short of the port."

"Dirk thought this out. I didn't think he had it in him."

"Me neither. Hang on." Lee turned right and rocked up over the curve. The alley walls pressed on either side. The walls were concrete with metal doors. The walls were stained green and brown with mold, but all the doors were a bright, blazing red.

"What's with the doors? Is it a law they all have to be red?'

"Probably somebody offloaded a starship full of red metal doors, cheap. Surplus from the Core. That's what they've got, that's what everybody uses. I've been to frontier towns where all the houses are pink or neon green or some such color, because that's the only color paint that got shipped in on a starship."

"Outstanding, as the old man would say." The truck blocked all vision past it. It bounced up on its shocks, then broke out into the light. Lee followed, counting quietly. Then they bounced onto a paved crossroad, lined on both sides with broken concrete sidewalks and battered shops. The truck disappeared into an alley, Lee followed.

"Where did you learn all this driving stuff?"

"It's in the Jovian manuals. In case you're assigned personal protections detail. I looked it up."

"You have a manual for anti-hijacking driving on frontier planets?"

"Jovians have a manual for everything. Anything we might have to do in the service of the Emperor, we have rules. Lots of practical information."

"Lee," Dena said. "Why are you out here?"

"I'm driving to the river. This is the best route—"

"No. I'm running away from home to make something of myself. So's Scruggs, just make something different and a different place. The old man is running on inertia, shooting things is what he does. Dirk's an officer who got screwed up, but he's fixing that now. Gavin's still a mystery. But you, Imperial Praetorian, navigator, medic, doctor. A pilot. You can do all these spacy things. You can shoot. What are you doing on a decrepit cargo ship on the Verge?"

"I lost my faith." A metal object bounced over the truck, banged off a wall and landed in the dirt. Lee stood on the brakes. "What was that?"

Dena gripped her slingshot. "Metal, shiny. It's a mirror. The truck mirror. Did it hit the wall?"

Lee sped up again. "These alleys are narrower than I thought."

Dena leaned sideways to get a better view. "Yep. Their passenger mirror is gone now."

"Cleon said these alleys were wide enough to drive in, but he must have been thinking of a car, not a truck. I should have checked."

"Too late now." Dena shrugged. "You said you lost your faith. Your faith in what?"

"Everything. The Empire. Jove. Jovians. All of it. What's it all about?"

"But I thought you worked for the Empress."

"I did. I do. I still do. The Empress and Devin. He was my priest, sort of. I needed to talk to somebody about Jove and work and duty. I found some people cheating, Jovians. I lost my faith in my people, my clan, a whole bunch of things. I went to talk to him. He told me that I needed to get perspective. Go out and see the universe for what it is. See the Empire for what it was. Go on a journey to find things out for myself."

"Have you?"

"Not yet."

"How will you know when you're done?"

"Devin said when I've had ten new lovers."

"That shouldn't take long. A week or two."

Lee laughed. The truck pulled out of another alley and turned left. She followed. "Maybe for you."

They were now traveling parallel to the main boulevard, but five streets away on a two-lane dirt road. Gated yards with brick walls topped with barbed wire lined the sides. Two-story houses were barely visible behind the gates. "Lee, why aren't we coordinating this on the radio? Or with our comms?"

"We don't have a radio on the Marine band, and neither does the truck. We could hook our comms in, of course, but Dirk was worried that somebody in the Planetary Guard would be able to read Marine traffic. Maybe stolen or bought a Marine comm unit. If they don't have a person directly watching Empire House, they might have missed our departure."

"Huh. So you're trying to find yourself in the Verge. What have you learned?"

Lee counted to four again, then sped up to close the truck. "The Empire is corrupt. The Chancellor is corrupt. The nobles are conspiring against each other for personal gain at the expense of the citizens. You can't trust the bureaucracy. The Navy and Marines are full of career layabouts and incompetent political appointees. Most Jovians got their positions by cheating or bribing somebody. The regular workers, the ship captains, the spacers believe in a fantasy empire that defends the rule of law, truth, justice, all of that. Instead, the Empire is a venal, corrupt, incompetent beast that stomps through the known worlds and imposes its will by crushing anybody who disagrees."

"Wow," Dena said. "That's bad."

"Yes. And you know what's worse?"

"What?"

"Devin told me all this when he sent me out on this journey. He fixed it with his sister, the Empress. She gave me a few tasks to complete, made it all official. But he knew all this before I started. He agrees with me."

"So if he told you all this already, and he agrees with it, and you knew it, why are you out here?"

The truck turned left into another alley. Lee slowed then followed. "Why am I out here? Well, Devin wanted me to learn the rest of it. After dealing with the Confeds, and the Nats, and the pirates and the various planetary governments, I finally understand what he meant."

"Well? Don't leave me in suspense," Dena said.

"The Imperial System, the Empire, the Emperor and the Empress is the worst, the absolute worst system to govern the known worlds that there is. The worst system, the absolute worst system." Lee swerved around a trash can. "The absolute worst system. Except..."

"Except what?"

"Except for all the others. This stinking mess of a government is still the best option we have. We have to save the Empire. Oh, Jove's toenails."

Metal screeched as the truck's bumper struck the wall, bounced slightly, then screeched again as the far bumper hit. They stuck, slowed down and the screeching got louder. SNAP. The other mirror popped off. The truck ground to a halt, nearly stuck between the walls.

"Too tight." Lee stopped and pressed reverse. "We need to get out of here before one of those rebel groups decides we're their next target."

Chapter 23

"Stop. They're not behind us." Scruggs watched the rear camera on the dash. "The truck didn't make the turn. Something's gone wrong."

Cleon checked his mirror. "They could be slow."

"They could be in trouble."

"We'll stop and wait."

"No." Scruggs shook her head. "Keep moving. Do a U-turn and bring us by that alley, but keep mobile. Sitting targets are easy targets, the centurion says." Scruggs checked her shotgun. Six loaded, and one in the chamber.

Cleon obediently spun an easy circle at the next intersection, turning back the way they came. The vehicle hummed quietly, and the armored glass and body panels dampened the exterior sounds. There was no sense of motion.

Cleon slowed as they passed the alley. "There they are. Why aren't they moving?"

The radio clicked. One of the Marines from Empire House spoke. "Car 13. Relay from your friends. They say, 'Too narrow. Stuck. Backing up. Meet at destination.'"

Scruggs clicked the radio. "Understood."

"Stuck. Oh." Cleon screwed up his face. "Stupid. They're much wider than us."

"Is there another way to the landing that doesn't involve alleys?"

"Yes, but we were avoiding it…"

"Can't be helped. Get us back to that other street."

Cleon slowed down.

"What are you doing?" Scruggs said.

"Going back to follow them up the alley—"

"No. Take us by the main streets or a different alley. Can we speed down to the next major intersection and double back?"

"Well, I suppose…"

"Do it. Take us up there." Scruggs pointed at a main street visible in the distance. "Then swing us back onto their road. We can talk then. Do it now."

Cleon glanced at her. "Did anybody ever tell you that you're bossy?"

Scruggs glared at him. "Better bossy than dead." *Centurion would want me to take charge.*

"You know that I'm the governor's son and this is his car?"

"I'm not one of your simpering fancy girls who titter when you make jokes because of who your father is. I've been shot at enough on this planet, I want to avoid it happening again. Get us in front of that convoy. Now that we can't sneak around, the engineer will take the most direct route to the landing. We need to get in front of them."

"Safer if we go there directly."

"Safer for us, not them. And I'm in tactical command. Do as I say."

"Yes, Ms. Scruggs." Cleon smiled. "I'll do it. Let me turn around first, there's a better street ahead of them."

"Fine."

"What would you do if I didn't?"

Scruggs cocked the shotgun and turned to Cleon. "I've driven a car before. I can do it again. I don't need your help. If you won't drive safely, you're a threat to my friends' safety. Are you going to drive or not?"

Cleon pulled them in a fast U-turn and headed toward the big intersection.

"Yes ma'am." He wasn't smiling anymore.

Lee backed the jeep up. Dena gave her useless instructions as she scraped from side to side, banging the alley walls until she bumbled over the sidewalk.

"Nothing coming on the road." Dena turned back. "And nothing behind us."

Lee spun the wheel, and the jeep slid left onto the street. She kept backing up at speed as they cleared the road for the truck. "We can't take alleys. It will have to be straight on from here."

"Lee, up on the balcony there." Two women in pale orange slit skirts and flowing yellow tops leaned out of a third-floor balcony above the junction. "They might be calling in some of these rebel people."

"They might be locals seeing what's going on." And I might quit this job to sell flower vases to tourists on Melcifive.

"One has a comm. The other is pointing binoculars at us."

"Jove bless us." Lee backed up. "Watch for the truck. I can't back up forever."

"It's coming out now." Ahead, the truck backed onto the street and smashed into a post. It stopped, drove forward then reversed out straight.

Lee stood on the brakes, then slammed into first gear and pulled up behind the to-and-fro-ing truck.

"Where's your four seconds now?" Dena asked.

"Can you see Scruggs?"

"Some car pulled out onto the road ahead and is closing. Could be Scruggs."

"Might not be. Keep an eye on it." The truck finally straightened and sped off. Lee followed, drifting farther behind.

"More people up there." Dena pointed at other balconies. "Orange and yellow outfits. Who do those belong to?"

"No idea. What's Scruggs doing? Is it Scruggs?"

"It's her." Dena leaned out the side window to see past the truck. "They're stopping. Going to reverse."

"Don't do a three-point turn. Back in and do a two-point turn." Scruggs gripped her shotgun. "I can't hear anything. How do we get these windows open?"

"Two-point? I'll just drive in—"

"Don't drive in. Takes longer. Back in, then drive out. Saves a turn. Pass that alley, then use it to back in there." Scruggs fiddled with the window. "How do I... Hah!" The window slid down.

Cleon backed into the alley. "You're right. Two turns, faster."

"Of course I'm right. Centurion trained me." Scruggs poked her shotgun out the window.

"That old guy? He's just some washed-up soldier." Cleon spun the wheel. "Now where?"

Scruggs snarled. "We don't have time to talk about the centurion now. But I'll have a few points later. Drive us the fastest most direct route to this river port."

"Can do. Should have done that from the start." Cleon sped up.

"Don't go so fast you lose the truck." Scruggs leaned out the window. "You see that woman in orange and yellow ahead?"

"Yes. She's got a comm in her hand. What's she doing?"

A whistle sounded in the distance. "That." Scruggs pointed. "Up there, I think. Four, three—"

"What are you—YIKES!"

A billboard on top of the three-story wooden building to their left exploded. Given the teeth and lips displayed, it must have contained a dentist's office. The billboard toppled and fell into the street. A giant picture of gleaming teeth blocked the road.

"Over. To the right." Scruggs racked her shotgun. "Speed up, but not too much."

Cleon pushed the pedal to the floor. "Why are they shooting at us?"

"No idea. Keep this speed. Get ready to stop."

"Stop? You want me to stop?"

"Not yet." Scruggs watched the woman lean out of the balcony and track the convoy. "A little farther ma'am. Make your call." The woman's mouth moved. Scruggs brought the shotgun up and waited until the women's eyes tracked to her.

Scruggs braced and fired. Then, "Stop. Stop. Stop now."

The woman disappeared behind the balcony.

Cleon slammed on the brakes, and the car skidded left until the auto-braking corrected.

"Did you hit her?"

"At this distance? With a shotgun. Of course not. Never make that shot."

"Why'd you shoot, then?"

"She doesn't know that I can't hit her, so she ducked. Now she can't see the road, so her count is off."

The road ahead exploded in a burst of dirt and smoke. "Good correction, right on target, but they assumed we'd speed up. Floor it."

Cleon obliged and they bumped into the hole and sped through the cloud of dust.

Lee cursed as the second shell exploded on the road. "Where did they get all these mortars?"

"People like us, probably," Dena said. "Independent traders. Smugglers."

"There aren't that many like us."

"Probably are now. The criminals are the first to know when things are going bad. Say, I'll bet that was why we stopped getting traders back on Rockhaul. The weapons."

"What does economic contraction on a nearly abandoned Verge mining planet have to do with weapons smuggling to a near-Core sector courier junction?"

"Huh?"

Lee twisted the wheel to skip a pothole. "Where's the money?"

"What's more profitable? Delivering cheap clothes and basic electronics to Dena the rancher on Rockhaul at her back country ranch? Or trading weapons to Dena the revolutionary gem-dealer on Andaman? I know which I'd take."

"Everything falls apart, the center cannot hold," Lee said.

"What?"

"Old quote. Scruggs is past that spot. She's shooting at something up there. Can you see it?"

"Don't see anything. Just that balcony."

"Go slow." Scruggs faced back and fired again. "Need to keep the spotter's head down."

A bullet pinged off the armored windshield. "They're firing at us, Ms. Scruggs," Cleon said.

"They are. Did you see where it came from?"

"No."

Scruggs looked forward and back. "An interesting tactical problem, like the one the centurion gave me. Proceed forward and find the shooter or stay here and suppress the observer."

Cleon wiped sweat from his brow. "How can you be so calm?"

"I told you, the centurion trained me. Slow down. No, stop." I'm not calm, I only sound that way. Centurion said it was more important to sound calm than be calm.

"Now?"

"Now. I have to keep that observer down."

Cleon's breath came in spurts. "Okay. Okay. We're okay." They jerked to a stop. Scruggs leaned out and fired back at the balcony. Another shot whistled overhead, smashing in the windows of the hardware store across the street from the dentist, and blowing lawn chairs onto the street. Scruggs fired, counted to ten, fired again.

The following truck swerved to the left around the craters and burning furniture, dodged the teeth sign, and swung into the center of the road.

Dena and Lee watched the truck swerve.

"Follow that truck," Dena said.

"What do you think I'm doing?"

A figure popped onto the balcony overlooking the crossroads. Dena leaned out the window. "Orange lady is back."

"Confuse her."

Dena fired her shotgun out the window. The jeep jolted her aim, and she missed. She fired again.

"Hitting anything?"

"No. That lady is still there. She's got a comm in her hand. How did Scruggs hit her?"

"Scruggs didn't, she scared her. Now she knows we can't hit her."

"Those explosions—"

"Speed up or slow down?"

Dena racked her shotgun. "Speed up."

Lee pressed the accelerator, and the jeep surged forward. "I have to swing wide."

"Are those lawn chairs?" Dena coughed as smoke and dust flew in.

"Now is not the time for garden work." Lee pulled to the left. "Almost by. Hang on."

"I'm hanging—WATCH OUT!"

Another shell whistled down and struck the building, sending splinters everywhere. Lee ducked and swung the jeep farther left as the smoke billowed up. The jeep rocked once, then a giant white figure gleamed ahead.

WHAP. The jeep struck the downed sign and smacked the remaining frame of the destroyed billboard. The wood snapped off and the canvas cover slapped over the jeep. Lee drove in the dark as the smoke billowed around. Two long seconds, and they pulled out of the smoke.

The windows were blocked with a vision of a giant gleaming white set of teeth.

"Slow down, slow down."

"No." Lee hauled the wheel right. "There will be another shot right behind that. If we stay here, they'll slam us. I'll stay in the middle of the road. Clear that junk."

Dena dropped the shotgun and leaned out the window. She pulled bunches of the flapping canvas into the car and shoving it aside. "This thing goes on forever."

"Pull, pull. I need to see where we're going."

Dena pulled some more. And more, stuffing loose canvas to the side and in front of Lee. "How big is this? Are giant clean teeth some planetary obsession?"

"I can almost see." Lee leaned left as the jeep pulled out of the smoke. "Incoming!"

The jeep smashed into the truck, stopped in the middle of the road in front of them.

Scruggs saw the collision. "Go back. Turn us around and go back."

"Turn us around?" The whites of Cleon's eyes were showing. "Go back? We just got out of there."

"They hit the truck. Turn around."

"I don't-- "

"Do it now." Scruggs waited as they spun. *At least, this time, he's doing a proper two-point turn.* "Faster. Faster."

The car smacked as it backed into something. "Hang on. Tight fit."

Scruggs shoved the door open. "Back and get me. I'll help the others." She raced down the street. She stumbled as she hit a pothole. *Don't fall. Don't fall. The centurion would be upset if I fell.* Scruggs grimaced. She didn't have time to think about the centurion right now. She pushed the thoughts away and ran harder. Her breath came in spurts. She was glad the centurion made her work out every day. Even gasping for breath, her legs ate up the distance between the vehicles in a few seconds.

The truck had stopped, and Gavin was awkwardly climbing out of the passenger side.

"I've got them, I've got them. Back inside. Watch her." Meaning Clara.

Gavin nodded and climbed back inside.

Scruggs ran by the truck. The jeep had slammed in hard enough that the right front hood had pancaked under the truck bumper. The billboard display jammed into the passenger window. The passenger door hung loosely on a single hinge. The front of the jeep was crushed, and the engine was smoking. The windows were blown out. Lee staggered out of the far side. "Help Dena."

Scruggs fought the canvas and grabbed for the door. She couldn't make it, and instead pulled out a pile of canvas. Lee dashed to help her, and the two of them yanked at the pile.

The truck moved. The jeep, jammed under the bumper, dragged with it. Clara didn't have mirrors, so she'd have no idea what was slowing her.

Scruggs and Lee raced to keep up with the accelerating truck. They lost contact with the door and ran behind.

"Can't keep up," Scruggs yelled.

"Grab the sign. And hold on." Lee snatched at the edge of a puffy red lip and held it.

Scruggs grabbed for a giant bicuspid, then fell, dragging the canvas with her. Her weight pulled the rest of the picture free, and the jeep's door snapped off, pulling the remaining picture out the side. A cursing Dena dove out on top of a giant toothbrush and rolled in the dust. The three of them lay in the middle of the road, surrounded by dust, smoke, and a charred dental advertisement.

Dena sat up. "Huh. If you didn't hate dentists enough already. Where's our transport?"

Both Scruggs and Lee pointed down the road. The truck disappeared in the distance, and the governor's car turned to follow.

"Outstanding, as the old man would say." Dena stood. "Anyone want to race?"

Chapter 24

Lieutenant Hooper and Agent Hernandez waited at the *Collingwood's* airlock, watching the external display. The flagship's cutter came to a zero-zero halt about ten meters away. A skin-suited figure pushed out from the airlock and jetted across. The commander of a mere corvette was too lowly for the admiral's coxswain to waste time docking. A cross jump was sufficient.

Two minutes later, the inner airlock door opened and Monti stepped through, helmet in her hands. Her skinsuit was clean and shiny, and her mag-boots were buffed silvery white. Her skin glowed and her hair was washed

"Well?" Hooper asked. She sniffed. "I smell lilacs."

"*Canopus's* captain let me use his shower. He had a full water ration."

"How convenient. And he had special lilac soap for his female guests?"

"It was either that or something called citrus-verte."

"Two soaps? That's taking it too far. What's the word?"

"It was the *Sable*. Aft section disintegrated, everyone died. Bow section bounced off and kept going."

"Survivors?"

"Thirty-seven."

"Thirty-seven." Hooper put her hand to her mouth. "Out of, what, four hundred?"

"Four hundred and thirteen. The admiral's aide is under arrest. And the flag's helmsman too."

"What? What are the charges?"

"The aide is charged with willful disregard for orders, and knowingly issuing false orders in the name of a superior."

"They're saying the aide made the orders up?"

"That's what the admiral said. The aide denies it, of course."

Hernandez interrupted. "What are they getting the helmsman for?"

"Lack of promptness in executing a direct order."

"Whose?"

"The admiral's. The flag captain of the *Canopus* figured out what was going to happen when the drive came online. He countermanded the helm's order and canceled the turn. The admiral countermanded that, and the helmsman got confused. The bridge was madness for a few minutes. With both the admiral and the captain yelling at him, he corrected per the admiral's orders, which ran down the *Sable*."

"So he's being charged with attempting to avoid a collision, until the admiral screwed everything up and caused the collision."

"It will all come out in the court martial."

"If there is one."

"What do you mean?"

"Lord Bracebridge? He won't want this to be discussed in open court. I'll bet you credits to food trays that his aide suffers an 'excess of conscience' and shoots himself or dives out an airlock."

"Dives out an airlock?" Hooper said. "How do you do that?"

"Take off your suit, climb into an airlock, disengage the safeties, then blow the hatch and yourself out into the dark."

"That's impossible! Too many cameras, too many safeties. No way to do that."

"Tell that to me again…" Hernandez checked her comm. "After our next jump. I'll bet you that aide is so ashamed that they do this before the fleet goes into jump. No time to check for a body, and no way to get any investigative team over there to find out what happened 'til after the jump, at which point it's been seven days. A lot can happen in seven days."

Monti racked her helmet. "You sound like you know all about this sort of thing."

"Never done it myself." Hernandez closed her comm and put it in the thigh pocket on her uniform pants. "Investigated a couple after the fact, in my early days in Naval Intelligence. I tried to find out what happened, 'til one old chief pulled me aside and said it was best I checked that all the paperwork was in place, and not ask too many questions. Long as it was between officers, or nobles, don't spend too much time on it."

"That's ridiculous. The fleet's not like that. This is the Imperial Navy. We have standards. We have honor. We have our duty." Monti glared at Hernandez.

"We did." Hernandez shrugged. "In the past, we did. Not now."

"The Empire is not like that."

"Look, Ms. Upright Colonial Melbourne girl. You've spent all your service in small ships. Destroyers at best. Colonial service only, no time in the Core. Ever been assigned to Capital Fleet?"

"No."

"Well, the closer you get to the center, the stinkier it gets. A tabbo rots from the head, remember that."

"I can't believe that." I don't want to believe it.

"Then tell me why the admiral brought armed Marines to the captain's meeting. And why he threatened that reserve captain, Mahony, with charges, her and her reserve friends. For interference with published orders. "

"Marines! Jove's knees." Hooper turned. "Franky, is she for real?"

"Don't call me Franky on duty, Bron." Monti turned to Hernandez. "How did you know that? This was a private captains' meeting."

"I've got friends in the fleet same as you. Not everybody is happy that the baking soda salesman is in charge of the fleet."

"Baking soda?"

"Didn't you know? That's Lord Bracebridge's thing. Bulk food products. Baking soda. Salt. Brown sugar. Baking powder. His family is the biggest bulk food processing company in the Core."

"He's not an admiral?" Hooper asked.

"By Imperial decree he is. Bought his commission last year from the Chancellor. Some time in the Naval Reserve years ago, or something like that. But either way, they'd rather a real officer was in charge. Some of them. Some of them aren't too happy with our mission."

"Who's unhappy about escorting a convoy?"

"Nobody. Some people are unhappy with replacing Devin, the Lord Lyon, with a baking ingredients salesman."

"He's not that. He's, well. He's an admiral."

"He sells baking powder."

Hooper frowned. "You said he sells baking soda."

"Baking powder, baking soda. What's the difference?"

"One has an acid salt to combine with a base to make the dough rise, one doesn't," Monti said. The other two women looked at her blankly. "What? Naval officers can't bake?"

Hernandez glared. "We'll ask the admiral, then. Maybe he knows that. Because he sure doesn't know anything about maneuvering a fleet. He's already gotten hundreds killed accidentally. What happens when he's trying to hurt people on purpose? How do you think he'll do in combat?"

"What are you saying, Hernandez?" Hooper asked.

"Look, Monti. Keep an eye out. This admiral is already a disaster. You're not the only one who noticed. Some serious people out here are unhappy with what's going on, at many, many levels. Don't be surprised if something happens."

"Something. Like what?"

"Something bad."

The convoy proceeded in formation to the jump limit. The reserve captain Mahony was leading the center column. She asked permission to maneuver the faster ships outside of the convoy to practice ship maneuvers. Permission was summarily denied.

Hooper was called to the comm at least once a shift for a tongue-lashing from the flagship concerning her inability to bring the freighters into better formation. For safety, the freighter captains had universally adopted the practice of maneuvering out of formation. *Collingwood* and the other corvettes spent all their time closing on ships and threatening dire consequences unless they complied.

Lieutenant Monti smacked her hand on her comm, shutting off the display. "I hate all merchant captains. Too stupid to follow orders."

Hernandez was in the helm position, taking a watch. "And yet, the commander of the *Sable*, whoever he or she was, did follow orders, and look at where it got them."

"What are you suggesting? That they're justified in not taking the correct maneuvering position?"

Hernandez rolled her eyes. "No, because I'm a career naval officer, and I would never disobey a direct order, certainly not one from an admiral, regardless of what type of food products he sold."

"That's treason!"

"What part? I said I'm all about obeying orders."

"It's the way you said it. This." Monti mimicked the eye roll.

"Good thing a transcript of the bridge won't catch that, then." Hernandez's board lit up. "Flagship for you, again."

Monti smoothed her hair, settled her cap, and took the call.

Twenty minutes later, Monti clicked the channel off and took a deep breath. The bridge crew hadn't heard the other side of the conversation, but Monti's side had been limited to 'Yes,' 'No,' and 'Tell the admiral I apologize.' Or variations of that.

She rubbed her eyes and clicked on another line. A sleepy Hooper answered. "Yes, Captain?"

"Can you come up to the control room, please. I need to leave the ship."

"Whoa! Don't do that. Coming right up."

Less than a minute later, a disheveled Hooper rocketed into the bridge. "You can't leave the ship."

"These merchant officers aren't responding. I need to go over and talk to them."

"Fire a shot at them."

"They know I'm not going to hit them."

"No, they don't."

"They do, because that idiot flag-lieutenant—"

"I thought the flag-lieutenant was in jail?"

"It's a new one. He's denying permission to fire on them. On the admiral's behalf."

"Why?"

"Because he's scared to death to do anything. So he's denying everything."

"You could go directly to the admiral."

Monti stared at her subordinate.

"Okay." Hooper shook her head. "Bad idea, I understand that. Flagship is not a safe place to be. But you can't leave the ship. I'll go. I can talk them around."

"I can't let you go. I need you on watch, and taking care of the ship while I, while I…"

"Take care of the admiral."

"Right." Hooper bit her lip. "You can't go either."

Hernandez spoke up. "Send me!"

"What? Who's going to listen to you?" Hooper asked. "You're just a lieutenant."

"So are you two."

"Yeah, but she's a captain lieutenant."

"That's not a rank."

"But you're just, just—help me out here, Captain."

"Look," Hernandez said. "Weeks and I think we're doing a good job helping out, you needed extra officers, and we filled a gap."

"You want me to thank you for all your hard work?" Monti crossed her arms. "Give you a pat on your head?"

"Captain," Hooper interrupted. "That's not fair. They've both been working full steam. Hernandez has been taking watch and watch with me. And Weeks has barely left the engine room since we lifted."

"I thought he was taking his turn in the rotation." Four hours on, four hours off. No wonder Hernandez and Hooper looked beat.

"We tried that, but there were some…almost incidents in engineering. We three thought it best to have him there keeping an eye on the engineering crew while Hernandez and I watched the ship."

Meaning the engineering crew had nearly blown them up a couple times. And Hooper needed her to be fresh for the admiral's comm calls and yelling at the freighter captains.

"Weeks has been in engineering this whole time?"

"He sleeps in one of the accel couches there," Hernandez said. "I've just been watching the boards so that you two can get some sleep. But you two must be on the bridge for maneuvering, and we're doing that all the time now, so I'm superfluous. Send me across to talk to these freighter captains."

"Why will they listen to you and not me?"

"Because I was in Internal Security. I know how to talk to these people."

"Talk? What kind of talk?"

"By talk, I mean threaten. I know how to threaten them. And not their ship. Them personally. No captain wants to get on the wrong side of Internal Security. A note in the database and they'll be boarded and searched ten times from Jupiter every time they try to clear into a civilized planet. And trust me, they all have something they're hiding."

"I don't like the idea of siccing IS on some random captain," Hooper said. "Seems mean."

"You want to stay awake for the next forty-eight hours giving helm commands?" Monti asked.

"Not really." Hooper shook her head. "And there could be a good outcome from this."

"Which is what?"

"Hernandez is so annoying, I'm sure that at least one of these freighter skippers will get so angry with her, he'll shoot her out his thrusters. But don't worry." Hooper grinned at Hernandez. "We'll revenge your horrid and hopefully time-consuming death. And, I'm sure Weeks will need consoling after the death of his longtime partner, and I'm just the girl to do it."

"You cannot sleep with Weeks while you're on the same ship." Monti shook her head.

"Captain! The needs of the service—"

"Are unrelated to your personal biological urges. Hernandez, how do we get you there? To the freighters, I mean. We can try to dock, but none of these ships will stand still for that. Can you do a combat jump? Like the Marines do?" *Collingwood* didn't rate any small craft. And maneuvering to dock with a freighter that didn't want to be docked with was a recipe for disaster. Monti was really asking if Hernandez could leap from the surface of one ship to another as they sped by. It was a risky way to cross and required practice and nerves of steel. Monti didn't doubt Hernandez's nerves, but the practice was an open question.

"Don't need to," Hernandez said. "*Hydrogen Pride* has a pinnace. We can use that."

Monti blinked. "That older reserve captain—"

"Tara Mahony."

"You know her name? Is she a friend or something?"

"Never met her. Heard of her, though. She's Naval Reserve. A solid professional through and through."

"How do you know that?"

"Doesn't matter. Let's call her."

"You want me, a junior lieutenant recalled to active duty, commanding her first ship, to hit up a senior reserve captain with decades of experience for the loan of her small craft?"

"We're not stealing it. We'll just be using it to visit some of these freighters and lay down the law."

Monti stared at Hernandez for a long time, then turned to Hooper, who was trying to comb snarls out of her hair. "What am I missing here? What am I not seeing?"

"I don't get it either." Hooper shook her head. "Something sneaky is going on. And this one here," she gestured at Hernandez, "is the queen of sneak. But it does seem like a reasonable suggestion. Which is why I'm worried."

Hernandez's board bonged. She read the incoming. "Flag is calling for you again."

"I can't keep this up," Monti said. "I'll call her after this."

"Cut me into the call when you do," Hernandez said.

Monti and Hooper exchanged glances. "Why?" Monti asked.

"Because. Cut me into the call."

"Again, why?"

Hernandez just shrugged.

It took an hour for the call to come through. One did not call the captain of a cruiser-sized ship and expect to be connected instantly. Hooper had gone back to bed. Monti slumped in the pilot's chair, hoping that some of the freighters she'd commed would at least attempt to rejoin formation before the admiral called her again. The channel bonged again.

Hernandez checked the ID, then flashed it up on the main screen and answered. "*Collingwood*."

An unidentified woman's face appeared. She glanced down at her own screens and said, "Captain Mahony for Captain Monti. Are you Captain Monti?"

"Stand by." Hernandez cut Monti into the circuit.

Monti sat up straight and patted her hair down. "I'm Captain Monti."

The woman didn't say anything else. The channel went to hold for seven seconds—Monti counted them to herself, then cleared to show the older Naval Reserve captain from the fleet meeting. Monti couldn't help but notice how calm and well-groomed she looked.

"I'm Captain Tara Mahony, *Hydrogen Pride*. You're Lieutenant Monti of the *Collingwood*?"

Uh oh. No courtesy captain title. Just rank and ship. "I am ma'am."

"What can I do for you, Lieutenant?"

"Well ma'am." Monti explained her request. The pinnace. Docking with the freighters. Sending Hernandez to talk to them. Mahony's expression didn't change the whole time she talked to her.

"So there you have it ma'am."

"You think that sending an officer onboard the freighters will make them see reason."

"Yes ma'am."

"And you want to use my pinnace and crew to do that?"

"Yes ma'am."

"Sounds like you haven't been sufficiently forceful, Lieutenant."

"That's true ma'am. But I'm just a voice on the radio. A personal visit will make a difference. Lieutenant Hernandez can be quite persuasive."

Mahony laughed. "You think your friend here will scare these captains?"

"I do ma'am." This was going horribly. She was going to be court-martialed for being a dumbass. Could reserve captains prefer charges? She'd have to read up on that.

"She doesn't look very scary to me."

"I can be very scary ma'am," Hernandez cut in. "I learned from the best, someone who'd scare even you."

"And who is it who'd scare me?" Mahony grinned. "You're Naval Intelligence, probably Internal Security. And Naval Intelligence can't, and IS doesn't, bother me at all."

"Well, that's neither here nor there. But I learned a few things from Tribune Devin when I worked for him."

Monti's mouth gaped open. What in Jove's name? Why was she bringing up the traitor?

Mahony's face was blank. "You worked for the traitor, Devin?"

"The Lord Lyon, the alleged traitor. I did. Handled a number of sensitive things for him. That was before his alleged treason, of course."

"Alleged treason, yes, that's true." Mahony nodded once, then sat still.

Monti wondered if they'd even bother to arrest her, or just toss her out of an airlock for consorting with traitors.

Well, alleged traitors. "Ma'am, I'm sorry, Lieutenant Hernandez talked out of turn. I see now that this idea—"

Mahony held up a hand. "A moment, Captain Monti. Let me check something." The screen blanked.

Monti held her breath. *Now it's Captain Monti?*

The screen refreshed. Mahony nodded once. "Stand by to receive my pinnace. The crew is loading and will drop as soon as ready. They'll dock with you. Captain Monti, please just keep a straight course. They're quite skilled at ship-to-ship dockings, and they have their own magnets and grapples. Understood?"

"Ma'am." Monti nodded.

"These freighter captains need to be brought into line. I agree Lieutenant Hernandez is the person to do it. I can't give you orders, of course, because you're not under my direct command. But I know these freighter captains either personally, or by reputation. If Lieutenant Hernandez could come by *Hydrogen Pride* first, then I can give her a briefing before she speaks to these other captains. Would that be satisfactory, Captain Monti?"

"I can hardly give orders to your pinnace crew ma'am."

Mahony nodded. "No, you cannot. They'll see you shortly."

"Thank you ma'am. Um, how long will Lieutenant Hernandez have the use of your pinnace for this activity?"

"Until it's finished." Mahony grinned. "Or at least until I decide it's finished. They'll be there in twenty-seven minutes. Carry on, Captain."

Chapter 25

Clara leaned on the horn as the truck left the city behind. The flock of chickens blocking the road scattered. She passed a faded sign that read '17' then turned left and bumped off the paved road and onto a rutted dirt track.

"You sure this is the right way?"

"Do most of the people you know who've lived somewhere for years not know their way around?"

"Some people don't pay attention."

"Some people aren't me. What are you looking at?"

Gavin had leaned out the window. "To see if they make the turn."

The truck spun downhill over the red dirt roadbed, bumping over big rocks. Ferns and knee-high grass crowded in from each side. Piles of rotting leaves separated the trees, and hanging vines obscured the spaces between them. The canopy met thirty feet overhead. Sharp white shafts of sunshine shot through the gloom illuminating spots.

"Cleon knows this road as well as I do. RC would take us down here all the time to see his barges going downstream. It was kinda fun. Sometimes we got to ride on them or help load them up. And the captains might let us pretend to drive them. Both Cleon and I got to take trips downriver when school was out, all the way to the spaceport."

"His barges?"

"Sure. He owned a bunch of barges that shipped things downriver and off planet. Rice mostly."

"Isn't it illegal for an Imperial Governor to own ships in the shipping industry on a planet they're in charge of?"

"Is it?" Clara shrugged. "I don't know. Nobody said anything."

"Think they would, to the governor?"

"Mom never complained."

"Your dad sounds kind of crooked."

"He's not our dad. He's just a diprock Mom married when we were younger."

"Diprock? You don't like him much."

"He brought us here, to Andaman. What do you think of our beloved home planet?"

"It's nice enough." It's a sweaty hellhole. Glad I don't live here.

"Really? Thinking of immigrating, then?"

"Look, I'm sorry your dad—"

"Stepdad."

"Stepdad wasn't the greatest parent. But at least he let you do fun things like ride boats and travel."

"Well, it's true that he didn't want to pay for babysitters, yes. And it was easier for him to carry on all his affairs with his girlfriends when we weren't in town."

"Wow. I thought I was cynical." Gavin bounced in his seat again. "Do you have to hit every bump?"

"No, and I'm not. I'm missing most of them."

Gavin stuck his head out the window. "There they are. They turned in."

"I hope they have everybody."

"They do. Scruggs will have made sure to pick them all up."

"Cleon was driving. He might have a different opinion."

"Not for long. Scruggs would disabuse him of it."

"Disabuse?"

"She'd shoot him if he didn't stop for them."

"You people are kind of casually violent."

"We're reactive, not proactive. Don't hurt us, we won't hurt you."

"Hang on." Clara slowed. "It's soft ahead. We have to bang through." She floored the truck, and they raced along the road. The undergrowth to their right thickened, becoming denser and darker. Head-high ferns replaced the trees, interspersed with creepers and vines. Blinding sunlight streamed in from the left, darkness on the right.

The road forked and Clara sped right. "Hang on. Stream crosses here. Need speed." The road dipped downhill again, and the surface changed from packed rock to speckled red earth to black mud ruts, full of greasy water. Clara floored the truck, and they skidded into the muck. The mud sucked the truck in, and they skidded to the side as the rear wheel raced. Clara steered into the skid, and they corrected, slipped sideways, then they were through and sped up. She dropped the power and brought them down to a crawl.

"Why'd we slow?"

Clara slid the wheel a quarter turn. "Too slippery. We try to take these turns at speed and we'll skid into the ferns."

The road zigzagged right and Gavin lost vision behind him. "I can't see them. Can't you make a straight road on this planet?"

"Not on the flood plain. We have to follow the heights." They turned gently to the right, avoiding a section where the ferns floated on a green pool. "Floods every spring, displaces the dirt. A permanent road would wash away. We have to bulldoze a new one every year after high water. The barges will be up ahead."

Gavin leaned out of the passenger window. "Never work with a spaceport."

"Well, Mr. Snooty Space Guy. That's why the spaceport is up on top of a hill, so it doesn't get flooded. And that's why all the barges are down here. Rivers flood every spring, nothing we can do to fix that. All the port facilities float. They bob up and down in high water. All we need to do is bulldoze a road across a mudflat. Can you think of a faster way?"

"Nope." Blue paint flashed above the ferns behind them. "I see them."

"Get ready. Port's coming up. Anybody behind us?"

"The car. I see blue."

"Anybody way behind us? Look up the hill."

"Okay." Gavin stretched to get a better angle up the hill. He could see the highlands behind him, and the red dirt road snaking down to the riverbed. "I see dust clouds up the hill. Fresh ones. Somebody coming down."

"Friends of yours?"

"Doubtful. How long to get onto a barge and get it out of here?"

"Depends on the barge. We don't know which ones are here 'til we get there."

"Wait, you don't know what's there?"

"Barges are boats. Boats float. Sometimes they float away." Clara glanced at him. "Are all spacepeople as clueless as you?"

"I work at it." Gavin pointed at a gap in the grass. "Is that the port up there? Those boats?"

"Yes."

"Why are they all leaving?"

The governor's car powered over the bumpy road. With the windows closed, they couldn't hear anything other than a soft hum. Cleon had collected the chasing trio and now followed the truck.

"Shiny. Good quality leather." Dena ran her hand over the seat. She and Lee had climbed in the back of the governor's car.

"Nothing but the finest for RC," Cleon said.

"Your dad?"

"Stepdad. He likes nice things. Part of the reason that Clara and I wanted to get off planet as soon as we could."

"You don't like nice things?"

"I'm fine with them. But I want to go to the academy, and maybe so does Clara, so we wanted to go while we still had money."

"You don't have any money?"

"RC has expensive tastes. They've gotten worse the last few years. We need to get control of our trust funds away from him. Best place to do that is the Core."

"Who do you know in the Core?"

"Friends of the family. Teachers. Random strangers. All of them have our interests more than he does."

"You're pretty down on him."

"Mom made a mistake marrying him. Dad died when we were sixteen, and she decided to remarry. She called RC her rebound mistake. She put up with him, for our sakes."

"For your sakes?"

"You're looking at the honorable Cleon, brother of Lady Clara. We'll inherit the title and Mom's dowry when RC dies, but there's some legal issues. We don't get our own money until we're twenty-five. Dad set it up that way. But we get it earlier if we enroll in an Imperial accredited institution. I wanted to get away and get enrolled before the trust runs out of money."

"So no love lost between you and um... RC, then."

"Nope."

"Why are you still here, then?"

"Ever tried to get off an Imperial planet when you're underage?"

"I have." Scruggs reloaded her shotgun in the front seat. "It's harder than most people think. The Empire takes a lazy interpretation of some cargo rules, but if you're traveling on a starship in Imperial space, you better have ID, you better be of age, and you better be able to pass a scan. It's difficult to do."

Dena slapped Scruggs's shoulder. "Baby Marine here knows how. She ran away from home. Found herself a ship and got trained as a soulless mercenary. She can tell you all about it."

"Really?" Cleon glanced sideways. "You ran away from home?"

"There's a hundred-thousand-credit reward on her," Dena said.

Cleon's eyes widened. "And nobody has tried to collect it?"

As one, Lee and Dena pulled out revolvers and cocked them. The car grew quiet. Dena tapped Scruggs on the shoulder. "Some people have, yes. Didn't succeed."

Lee held her revolver upright. "The truck is turning up ahead. Best slow down for the turn. By the way..."

"Yes?"

"All of us know how to drive. Any one of the three of us can do it. Just so you know."

They lost track of the truck through the greenery as they dropped onto the floodplain. The heavy car skidded around corners and dug in as it whined up the muddy ridges.

"This is the wrong vehicle for this mud," Lee said. "Does it have lower gears?"

Cleon slapped the control. "It's all computer-controlled. Traction, drive train, all of that."

The rear of the car fishtailed through another corner, and the wheels chewed into a bush, before righting and sliding back onto the muddy track.

The radio crackled. "Car-13. Empire House. Satellite view shows many barges departing loading dock at this time."

Cleon pushed a button on the wheel. "What was that?"

Scruggs slapped the button and glared at Cleon. "Keep your eyes on the road." She slapped the button again. "Empire House, car-13. Say again, over."

"Car-13, all barges are preparing to leave the loading dock. Two already headed downstream, two others maneuvering and raising steam. Convoy of armed vehicles has left city in pursuit of you."

"Understood, Empire House. How long until all the barges are gone?"

Long pause. "Minutes."

"Understood. How long 'til that convoy reaches us?"

Now the pause was longer. Finally, the voice said, "Sooner. Suggest you expedite."

"Car-13 out." Scruggs looked at the sea of green stretching on either side of the road. "Floor it."

Two tugs churned away from the makeshift dock into the middle of the river as Clara and Gavin crested the last hill. The barges were flat, square, with high parapets on each side. One carried stacks of timber, the other bags of rice. Both ends of the barges were square, with two-foot-wide metal teeth sticking out. The teeth were offset so that those in front would mate with those on the rear, like rail cars connecting together. A chain of barges could be coupled together and locked together as a single unit. The tugs pushing had their own set of collars, allowing them to maneuver the barges.

"Why are they all running away?" Clara asked.

"Probably they don't want to get involved in your little civil war here. But it doesn't matter," Gavin said. "We need to get on one of them. What about those two there?"

"It's not a civil war. I'll drive down and talk to the captain." Clara shoved the truck into gear and ground down the hill.

"If it's not a civil war, what is it?"

"Commercial dispute. Didn't my stepfather tell you?"

"He didn't tell me anything. He talked about rebels, or traitors, or insurrections, things like that."

"I'll tell you later. We need to talk to that crew."

The truck waddled through a flat spot, mud sticking to the tires. It struggled through the muck, then climbed up to a parking area in front of the floating docks.

There were two tug trains left. Both barges were flat, inches above the waterline. The front barge hung low, piled with stacks of timber. The second one was nearly awash. Piles of teak lined the front and side. As they approached, two men and a woman stepped off the front train and ran along the dock. They paused only long enough to lift mooring lines off bollards, then climbed up onto the deck. The tug in the rear swung into the current, dragging the barge along the dock. Metal screeched, and pieces of wood snapped off, and it backed out into the water, drifting downstream.

"So much for talking to the crew," Gavin said. "Isn't there supposed to be a crane here?"

"Barges carry their own cranes."

"This one doesn't."

"Crane would probably sink it. Well, we can unload the truck manually, I guess. That will take time. What's all that piled behind the tug?"

"Wood. Oh no."

"What?"

"That's one of the original tugs. First group we built. It's a sidewheeler."

"So? That's okay on a river, right? Doesn't break like a propeller, easier to fix."

"It's not the propulsion, it's the fuel."

"Electric motors turn paddle wheels as well as screws."

"It's not an electric motor. It's steam powered."

"Steam powered?"

"Yup. A steam boiler. And that raft of wood behind it?"

"Yes?"

"That's the fuel. We're going to have to put this truck on a wood-burning barge to escape."

26

Chapter 26

"We've got minutes," Scruggs said. "So let's not waste them. When we get there, pile onto the boat. We'll drive this car on."

"It's not exactly a car ferry port," Cleon said. "Only a dock to pick up supplies and swap out crew." He was right. Heavy loading was done at the plantation source, or upstream at the starport. "And we can't drive on. "

"Then how do we get all those crates out of the truck onto these boats?"

"Barges. Have to hand load them."

"We can't load them. All your friends are chasing us. Your friends who have been shooting at us, before. Didn't you think of that?"

"Um no." Cleon shrugged. "This is my first major theft. And they're not friends."

Dena patted his shoulder. "Don't worry, big guy. First one is always the hardest. Why, Scruggs had to hijack spaceships two or three times before she got it right, isn't that right, Baby Marine?"

Scruggs balled a fist, noticeably suppressed an attempt to rip Dena's hand off Cleon's arm, then relaxed. "Yes. I'm much better now. How can we get on board?"

"Give me a minute." Cleon spun around the turn, and the port came into view.

It shouldn't have been called a port. It was a landing, and a basic one at that. A wooden pier ran out from the shore, through the shallow water and onto a T-junction. There were no cranes or loading facilities visible, just tire-churned dirt, two old shipping containers, and lots of jungle grass reclaiming the parking lot.

Cleon paused the car at the top of a small hill. "If you're picking up people, or small packages, you drive through the parking lot, up that dirt ramp and onto the piers. Load and unload there, then reverse back along the dock to the shore."

"Pretty narrow there," Lee said.

"Narrow like new saplings," Dena said. "Will that truck fit?"

"It better, otherwise, we've got problems."

The radio crackled. "Car-13. Empire House. Convoy inbound your position. Five minutes. We've identified at least twenty armed men. Do you copy?"

Scruggs looked down at the stalled truck, the muddy lot, the narrow pier, and the nearly awash docks. She checked the loads in her shotgun. "Copy that."

Gavin hopped out of the truck and acted as cargo master. "Right, Clara, drive that truck out onto the pier. Dena, you and Lee get into the wheelhouse of that tug and make sure the engines are started and ready to go. Fire up the boilers, load some wood. Scruggs, Cleon, help me move some of those planks. We'll try to make a ramp from the dock down onto the barge."

"How do I start the engines?" Dena said. "It's coal-burning or something. I don't know anything about it."

"Figure it out," Gavin said. "That's your specialty—low tech stuff."

"It's not my specialty," Dena said. "We had technology on Rockhaul. Just because we didn't have the latest Imperial stuff doesn't mean that we spent all our time hunting with bows and arrows and making clothes out of hides."

"Your weapon of choice is a slingshot, which is kinda like a bow and arrow. And you wear leather clothes all the time. Leather is animal hides, right? In fact, you prefer leather clothes, the tighter the better, you said."

"But... but... I came here on a starship."

An engine roared in the distance.

"Problem," Scruggs said. "Marines say a convoy with twenty armed men are on their way here. We either need to get away, fight, or negotiate."

"I vote get away," Lee said. "Come on, Dena. We'll figure it out. There's smoke coming out of that stack up there. How complicated can it be?"

"That's the spirit." Gavin said. "Scruggs, you're security."

"Understood." Scruggs hefted her shotgun. *What would the centurion do? Improvise, adapt, overcome.* "We taking the town car?"

Gavin looked at the barge. "There's room for the truck if we get it on board. Not sure about the car."

"Right, I'll grab the ammo and supplies from it and dump them on board, just in case."

"Do it. Clara, drive the truck. Cleon, with me."

The crew split up and ran in all directions. Dena and Lee scrambled on board the tug. Scruggs retreated to the battered town car and reloaded her shotgun and rifle, then draped them over her shoulder. She popped the trunk and dug out a crate of ammunition. After tossing another box of shotgun shells into the car, she grasped the crate and waddled down the pier with it.

Clara returned to the truck, reversed into the parking lot, then lined up on the pier and edged up to the dirt ramp.

The ramp led to the pier's land side. Every ten feet, it rested on a stacked blocks. The water deepened to six feet at the last pile, sixty feet away, at the T-junction.

Clara stopped and hopped down. She checked the water level, then jumped back up into the truck, leaving the door open. She followed the ramp then the pier edge, keeping the door open to see to keep her wheels aligned with the dock edge.

Gavin and Cleon ran out and jumped down six inches onto the barge. "Over there." Gavin pointed at a line of cut wood posts. They dragged them across the dock and onto the barge to form a ramp.

Scruggs set her rifle and the box of ammunition onto the barge deck, then ran back for more. She had to edge sideways around the truck—the dock was only two feet wider than the vehicle.

Gavin and Cleon draped more posts between the dock and the barge. They put five in a row down, and waved Clara to a halt. "Drive up to them, but don't drive on them yet. We need to size them."

Clara eased the truck over the edge of the pier and onto the floating dock. The extra weight of the truck sank the dock lower, and it now dipped down to only inches above the barge deck. The water rippled, the dock flexed as the waves bounced around.

Gavin and Cleon maneuvered the posts around two line ties and adjusted them to match the wheel distance.

"Right, just have to drive on now," Gavin said. "Not too fast. Don't tip the posts over."

Clara leaned out of the truck and looked down at the rocking dock, and the rocking barge. "Sure. Easy as pulling a tabbo's tail."

"You should hurry up," Gavin said. "We don't have much time."

"How much?"

BOOM. CLICKITY BOOM. A shotgun fired on shore.

"None at all," Gavin said. "None at all."

"This is insane," Dena said, clambering past piles of ropes. "What do we know about tugboats. Or steam engines."

"Steam engines are basic physics. I studied them in school. Didn't you?"

"We *had* steam engines on the ships on Rockhaul, but I don't remember exactly how they work. We burn something, it boils water. The water pushes a metal thing and that turns a wheel."

"The water turns to steam, the steam pushes a cylinder, the cylinder turns a wheel."

"There's got to be more to it than that. What do we turn on first?"

"Not exactly sure," Lee said. "But it's kind of like a spaceship."

"This is like a spaceship?" Dena asked. "Are you out of your mind? We're on a river, not in space."

"Well." Lee looked at the lines that tied them to the dock. *Think logically, Lee. Run the freighter checklist.* "First, we're tied to a dock with ropes, like we use chains at a space station. If we want to move, we'll have to undock." She pointed to the lines that tied the barge train to the docks. "Those four ropes, they tie us onto the dock. When we're ready to leave, we untie them, and we'll float away. And like in space, there are forces acting on us. Instead of gravity, we've got river current. Like in space, if we drift without thrust, we'll bump into something."

"You mean crash into something. Let's not do that."

"We won't. We can control it." They must have a way to turn the ship.

Lee climbed up a ladder onto the second deck. A catwalk led over the hulking engines and giant side wheels, and down a ladder to a work area at the back. Tied to the back of the tug was a raft with hundreds of two-foot pieces of wood in neatly stacked piles. On each side was a giant firebox, already blazing heat. Ahead was a boiler, and two sets of cylinders, one for each engine.

Lee tapped a gage. Plenty of pressure, the old crew must have fired it up hours ago.

"In space, we use the thrusters to pivot the ship in three dimensions. I think it's the same here, but in two. If we want to go anywhere, we put speed on one of those wheels. Those are probably the power controls." Lee pointed to a lever next to a boiler, connected to a wheel and a chain. "Like on a car. If one goes faster than the other, the boat will spin. I'll bet those two levers control the power, or steam, to the cylinders. More steam equals more speed. Then when we point the right way, we put them both in forward."

Dena looked around the deck. "That kind of makes sense. But we can't see over the barge from here. And there's no wheel. How do we steer from here?"

"We go to the bridge. This is the engine room."

The hull was made of wood, as was the lowest deck, where the engines sat. The stairs and catwalk were metal—it looked to be part of the engines, probably included when they were shipped. All the linkages to the cylinders and wheels were metal as well, but the rest of the tug above them looked like badly hammered wooden planks.

"This isn't a room, Lee. This is a deck or something. One good wave and we'll all be washed overboard."

"Same as a spaceship engine room. In the engine room, you can control the engines directly, but you can't see where you're going or how to dock. All the cameras and sensors are mounted on the hull, and they repeat to the bridge. The engineering controls are duplicated on the bridge. Look at those chains and pulleys running up. Climb up with me." Lee ran back up the stairs to the catwalk over the engines and climbed upstairs to the next level. Here was a square wooden rectangle, with rickety railings, and posts holding up the next level. Another steep set of stairs and they reached a control center. More rickety rails, but there were two control levers at the front, a set of gauges, and a traditional ship's wheel.

"Outstanding, as the centurion would say." Lee bent over. "Look, those levers turn that ratchet, which is linked to those levers down below. That's the speed controls. The wheel we can use when we're moving at full speed to turn without messing with the engines."

"And what about these gauges?" Dena studied them. "PSI. I know that. Pounds per square inch. That's the pressure for the boilers, I remember that much."

"But how much pressure is good?" Lee asked. "What are the acceptable values?"

"Middle," Dena answered.

"How much is middle?"

"Doesn't matter. I know that from all the old systems on Rockhaul. Analog stuff is always calibrated so that acceptable values are in the middle. That's the green area. Too far to the left and whatever you're looking at is too slow, or too small. Too far to the right, too much, too big, whatever."

"But what's the actual value? What number of PSI?"

"Whatever's in the middle. That's it."

Lee shook her head. "That's it? That's all you need to know. That's kind of dumb, not knowing the parameters you need."

"I think it's dumber than trying to remember a hundred numbers that have no relation to each other and getting it wrong. Are we going to stand here and argue about how to construct low tech equipment?"

"Good point. We've got company." Lee pointed to shore.

A line of cars drew out of the woods onto the dirt road above the parking lot. "Well, isn't that great. Scruggs is going out to talk to them."

"Talk? Scruggs? I think—"

BOOM. CLICKITY BOOM.

Dena wiped her brow. "I think that's how Baby Marine talks now. I'll run down and start casting us off. Get us ready to get out of here."

Clara jumped. "Who's she shooting at?"

"Nobody, looks like," Gavin said. "She fired in the air. Showing them she's armed. Have them back off."

"She doesn't want to hurt them?"

"She'll hurt them all right," Gavin said. "But only if necessary. She's become a bit cold-blooded about the whole thing. A few months with us, and especially with the centurion, and your attitude to violence changes." *As does your attitude to the Empire, the Nats, spying, and loyalty, doesn't it, Gavin?* "Get the truck on board now."

Clara climbed back into the cab, clashed the gears, and eased the truck farther onto the dock. The dock sank another few inches, but still floated. She edged across it.

Gavin held up his hands for her to stop. He and Cleon shoved the posts. Both front and back wheels had to line up. "Straighten your wheels. Inch to the left."

He spun his fingers to give wheel directions until both wheels were set. Then he stepped back. "Forward about six inches."

Clara eased the truck, clashed the gears, and the truck jerked ahead, then stalled. She cursed and started it again.

Gavin kicked the right-hand pile of posts, then kicked it again until it moved another half inch. "The wheels are lined up. You'll have to climb up the four inches onto the posts, then up and across the ramp. Go slow."

Clara gave a tiny spurt of power. The wheels rolled and the truck paused as the leading edge of the tire hit the posts. Gavin gave a thumbs-up. She boosted the power, and the truck climbed up and onto the ramp of posts.

The posts all lifted on the far side as the truck's weight came onto them. She edged down the ramp. The outer left beam bounced away.

Clara braked hard.

"You're okay. You're okay." Gavin waved her forward. "Still centered. Keep going, keep going."

Clara leaned out the driver's side door and edged the truck forward another two feet. The left wheel was centered on only five posts, the right in the middle of all six. Still two more feet. Another foot. Look back. One more foot. Forward ten inches. The rear wheels touched the ramp. She pulsed the power, and they climbed up.

Dena ran down the deck and grabbed the watching Cleon. A quick discussion and they ran to the midship lines and started tugging on the ropes, plopping them into the water.

The posts groaned as they took on the truck's weight. Gavin kept directing her forward, she kept going straight, keeping the wheel centered.

Gavin crossed his arms in the universal 'stop' symbol. He glanced under to the truck to get a view of the rear wheels. "A tiny bit to the right. Finger's breadth."

Clara turned the wheel two inches and pulsed the power again. The truck groaned forward, barely leaning to the right.

Gavin stopped her again. "Straight now."

Clara straightened the wheel and plowed ahead. The truck thumped onto the deck. The barge shivered.

Gavin waved stop, then ran from side to side to check the wheel alignment.

Clara inched the truck along. The slope was down now, so it rolled down without any power. She let momentum carry it onto the deck and roll across. Gavin walked backwards, waving her forward.

BOOM. CLICKETY BOOM. Scruggs's gun rang out behind them.

BANG. BANG. BANG. Guns fired behind them. Gavin looked past the truck, blanched and dropped. Scruggs's opposition returned fire. Some of them targeted the barge. Dena grabbed Cleon and dove for cover behind the metal bollards.

A fusillade of shots banged into the piles of wood, the deck, the deckhouse, and the engines. Metal bullets twanged off the boiler and drive wheels.

Gavin rolled sideways. Clara was still inching along. The truck must have been hit, but nothing penetrated to the driver's cabin. She added power, then more, and more, moving forward, guiding the rear wheels off the posts.

More shots banged out. Gavin ducked. *If I stick my head up, it will get shot off. Scruggs needs to keep them off us or we're going to be in trouble.*

The barge slid sideways. Either a bullet had hit a steam line or Lee had grabbed a lever. The truck lost direction as it rolled forward, and both rear wheels dropped off the planks.

Clara was caught. Three wheels were over the barge. But the driver's side rear hadn't quite made it. It slammed off outside of the barge deck. The truck teetered, one wheel over the water, the others onboard. Clara floored the accelerator, but she stuck there, over the water.

Chapter 27

"I'm sorry, you're who again sir?" the logistics junior chief on Devin's screen asked.

"Tribune Devin, the Lord Lyon. Governor of the Verge Sector." Devin frowned. "Executor of miscreants. Surely you've heard of me."

"No sir, I mean, yes, my lord. Yes. Of course I have. You'll be wanting fuel, of course. Vector right in and we'll load you up. No problem at all."

"Fuel?"

"Yes, my lord. We have plenty."

Devin stretched in his seat. The ISS *Pollux* and its associated escorts had micro-jumped into the Hvalford system and screamed across the jump line. They now orbited the biggest gas giant in the system, and sole military system present. Fleet Refueling Station 733. It had been a short jump, but he'd practiced his threats while waiting.

"We're not here for fuel."

Lionel waved from outside of the video pickup and mouthed 'yes we are.'

"What? Oh well, we'll take some. But mostly, we're here to take over control of the system. We're occupying it in the name of the provisional government of the Empire. PGOE."

"PGOE?" The junior chief wrinkled his brow.

"Provisional Government of the Empire. Put your officer on the channel. Where is she?"

"No officer here sir. Just me. Junior Chief Classdir, at your service."

"You're in charge?"

"Yessir. Of all fifteen of us. But only seven of us on station right now. We get a week on the planet every three months. The others are away, those lucky—I mean, on leave. Yes sir."

"And you dispense fuel? With fifteen people?"

"It's all automated, but yes sir."

"But you're the largest, and busiest, military fueling station for five parsecs." *Did I take us to the wrong place? I need Dirk's intelligence.*

"Don't know anything about the largest sir. But yes, fuel. We have that."

"Well, I'm occupying your station in the name of the PGOE."

"Yessir."

Devin waited. Chief Classdir stared at him. Devin stared back. Chief Classdir blinked first. "Um, you and that assault carrier with you should just sidle up sir. We can't maneuver, so you have to match orbits and hang with us. The fuel booms extend automatically, all your crews need do is attach the couplers. We can have both of you out of here in two shakes of a tabbo's tail."

"You've never heard of the PGOE? Of me?"

"No sir."

"Nothing about the Empire, the Verge, me, anything like that?"

"Um." Classdir looked worried. "We didn't get many direct messages sir. We're all maintenance people. We monitor the pumps, the radios, life support. If something breaks, we fix it. There's me and an admin clerk handle the paperwork. Honestly sir, we don't get a lot of orders here. We did get one flash order last week, top clearance. Critical to all Verge units, it said."

"All Verge Units." Devin smiled. "Very well. What was it about? Did it mention me, Tribune Devin?"

"Ah, no sir."

"The *Pollux*?"

"No sir."

"The rebellion?"

"No sir."

"Well, what was this critical memo about, Junior Chief?"

Classdir typed on his screen. "I'll bring it up here sir. Critical Importance. All units. From now on, during all ceremonial circumstances, the System-ID tag should be worn on the left breast of your dress uniform above your planetary unit tape. Not below. Reply received by return courier."

"You got a classified courier message about uniform changes?"

"Yes sir. Of course we complied immediately."

Of course you did. Jove save the Empire. "How'd you do that? Can you sew? Did you move your tag manually?"

"Um." Classdir took a deep breath. "Well sir. We're not attached to a planetary unit, we're a naval station, so we don't rate a planetary uniform tape."

"You don't?"

Classdir shook his head, but didn't speak.

"How would you comply, then?"

"No problem complying sir," Classdir nodded. "I had a staff meeting and introduced everybody to the changes. Then I routed the paperwork to each of them and confirmed they understood the uniform change and were prepared to abide by it. Then I collected all the responses and sent them back to fleet in a priority channel, on the next courier that passed by."

"All you did was create more paperwork, then?"

"Well, important paperwork sir."

Devin rubbed his head, then squared up to the camera. "But nothing was done to your uniforms, then?"

"Well, truthfully, sir. We're not issued dress uniforms out here. I've never had one."

"Never?"

"Not even once sir. In seven years."

"Can you fire a gun, Classdir?"

"No sir. Never been trained."

Of course not. Devin leaned his chin on his hand. "What have you been trained in, Classdir?"

"Fuel systems maintenance. Fueling, of course. Administration course. Contracting Level-1, and Level-2. Advanced contracting, that's really Level-3. Computer system backup and restore—"

"There's a class on backing up and restoring computers?"

"Three classes sir."

"You spend a lot of time restoring computers?"

"No sir. We really have nothing to do."

Devin regarded the screen. "Don't you need to… go out and skim gas?"

"No sir. Contractor from the planet does that. They come out, skim, load us up, go skim some more then head to the starport. All automated. Never had a problem."

"Never?"

Classdir shrugged. "We measure how much they pump in, comm the planet and they get paid. More fuel they deliver, the more they get paid. We get maybe two naval ships a month. Couriers, a few fleet transports. The occasional warship every so often. Your unit there, that's more ships than we've seen at once in a year. The few we do see, they fuel here, then head to the system starport for R&R."

"They never board?"

"Why would they sir? Nothing here. We don't even have an officer's club."

"I see." Devin regarded the screen. "Carry on, then. We'll speak more later."

"Sir. Thank you sir."

"Thank you? For what?"

Classdir shrugged. "Gets pretty boring here. Even a comm call is excitement."

Devin watched the refueling operation from his office. "Should we blow it up?"

"Why?" Lionel asked. "Because they didn't know who you were?"

"To keep the enemy from using it?"

"The enemy will carry on to the starport. They'll get fuel there."

"But not as conveniently."

Lionel brought up a course projection on his screen and mirrored it to Devin. "Let's see. Add a day. Maybe two. Less if they keep accelerating in-system. You want to destroy a valuable Imperial asset to delay an enemy for a few hours?"

"How do we stop them using this system?"

"Blow up the tankers and the skimmers."

"Then the planet will be in trouble. As will any ships that transit here."

"They can ship from the planet." Lionel nodded. "If they're equipped."

"You're not helping." Devin shut the screen off. "I'm not destroying infrastructure on a whim. If Imperial forces were here..."

"Fine." Lionel brought up his own screen back up. "Let me play devil's advocate. Shut the station down. Take the crew off. Cancel the contract. Drain the tanks. Then put somebody at the starport to keep them from refueling any imperial units who come through here."

"How?"

"Something administrative. Hire all the fuel guys off to go fishing or something."

"Fishing?"

"Best I could do. But you're right, we can't destroy everything. Well, we can, but we shouldn't. Instead, close things down, collect up every Imperial Army, Navy, and whatever other units you can find and bring them along with us.”

“They’re fighting the rightful Emperor.”

“First, that would be you, remember, we’re the rebels, and second, with what? They’re refueling us as we speak. Doesn’t sound like fighting.”

Devin glared at his screen. “This rebellion thing is hard.”

“Hard if you don’t want to start blowing things up.”

“I don’t want to do that.”

“Yet. You’re going to have to at some point.”

Devin grimaced. “Not yet.”

Fueling station 733 was efficient and organized. All his ships were fueled in three hours, then the rest of the fuel dumped into space. Lionel seized two of the skimming equipped tankers and docked them on the *Hydrogen Queen*.

Devin wanted to leave some Marines behind with orders to blow up the fueling systems at the starport if enemies arrived, but his entire staff talked him out of it. Leave only a few, and they’d either be asleep or overrun if an enemy arrived. Leave enough to ensure the destruction, and it was a waste of excited staff.

“We need more people,” Lionel said to the staff meeting.

“My Marines can kill ten times their number,” Brigadier Santana said.

“It’s not killing people that we have a problem with,” Lionel said. “It’s feeding them, getting fuel for them, and fixing their ships. That’s where we have a problem.”

“The crews from the station support the rebellion,” Devin said.

"No." Lionel shook his head. "The crews have no idea what in Jove's name is going on. All they know is that a Tribune said 'follow me' and dragged them from the most boring station near the Verge, and they're going on an adventure. They're still getting paid, and they heard Imin's a superb cook. They've been eating cold trays in the dark for the last two years. Wouldn't you want to leave? Besides, they don't believe there is a rebellion. This is some sort of game between nobles. In a few months, you'll forget this rebellion thing, go off and join the Imperial professional ping-pong circuit and they'll get posted somewhere interesting."

"Professional ping-pong? You made that up."

"It's a thing. I checked. Very competitive."

"Do they believe that? Do you believe them?"

"That ping-pong is competitive? Surprised me as well."

Devin gritted his teeth. "Do you believe that this rebellion thing is a game between nobles?"

"Doesn't matter what I believe." Lionel crossed his arms. "Matters what they do."

The fleet jumped away, heading to Devin's next target, another fueling station. Lionel spent the entire jump trying to talk Devin out of chasing down more fuel bases.

"I want to cripple the potential of the enemy to re-supply their fleet in the Verge or the adjacent sectors," Devin insisted.

"Too many places to fuel, too many to occupy, too many are run by civilians, too much collateral civilian damage if we try to occupy them, and they can just suck fuel from a gas giant. We're wasting our time."

"How do we restrict their movement?"

"We don't. We encourage it. They chase us, then maintenance will be the problem. Let them fuel. The farther they go and the faster they go, the worse shape they'll be in."

"They can repair their ships, like we can."

"We have excited, motivated crews," Lionel said. He sat up straight in his chair. "Helm, are you feeling excited and motivated today?"

"Sir!" Trevor the Helmsman gave a cross-chest salute. "Very excited sir. But not motivated."

"Not motivated? Why not?"

"Not my day for it sir. I'm excited on alternate days. I'll be feeling motivated tomorrow. Today is Lukas's—" Trevor gestured at the sensor officer "—day to be motivated. Tomorrow, he'll be excited, I'll be motivated."

"Teamwork, I like that. Thank you, Trevor." Lionel turned to Devin. "Our people know their jobs, and they can do their jobs, and they're experienced in their jobs. But compared to the rest of the Empire, we're the exception. The Verge fleet is the working fleet. The Core fleet is all about promotions, exercises, and parties. They're never more than a half shift from a fleet repair base. They never sail anywhere."

"Has the Empire entirely abandoned all of the sectors? Not just the Verge?" Devin asked.

"We've been busy in the Verge," Lionel said. "Pirates, invasions, border incidents, cranberry picking, all manner of dangerous things going on."

"But where are the fleets? There should be battleships, or at least cruisers and warships traversing the area."

Lionel laughed. "Feeling bad that the Empire doesn't consider you a threat?"

"I have battleship envy, true. But if not here, where are they?"

"All in the Core. But don't worry, we'll see some soon enough."

"How do we defeat them? I can't take on a battleship with a frigate."

"With this frigate and this crew, you could." Lionel shrugged. "The problem is that nobody will believe that. They might stand and fight, which would be bad. For them."

"So what do we do?"

"Harassment. Capture supplies. Jump on isolated stations. Occupy key locations. We've captured and decommissioned a fueling station, without a fight. Next stop should be a few parsecs away. A logistics base, for example. Seize all the ammunition and parts. We can get a couple of freighters haul everything away. We're used to working without much. The Core fleets aren't. We keep pecking away at them, at some point, we'll have local superiority, and we'll be able to take advantage of that. Then we attack. But first, a logistics base."

"You have one picked out already?"

"Yup," Lionel said.

Devin pursed his lips. "You say win this rebellion by never fighting?"

"Not never. Not yet. First, we make ourselves a minor annoyance. The Chancellor will ignore that. Then we make ourselves a nuisance. The Chancellor will send some minor reinforcements. Small ships. We can capture those. Then they decide that we've been upgraded to a problem. Then they send out an intermediate fleet, and we trap them."

"Annoyance. Nuisance. Problem. I like it." Devin rubbed his hands. "Seize fuel depots and logistics depots. Then attack the intermediate forces and add them to our fleet."

"That's it, Tribune."

"Then trap the large fleet sent to squash us."

"Exactly, Tribune."

"Uh huh." Devin rubbed his head. "How will the trap work?"

"Don't know."

"You don't know?"

"Nope." Lionel shrugged. "I'm just a podunk Prefect who got promoted above his ability. You're an Imperial Hero. Honest. Upright. Hard-working. Diligent, self-effacing, modest. You'll come up with some idea."

"I'll apply my tactical brilliance to it," Devin said.

"Tactical brilliance?"

"I'm not only good-looking, I'm smart too."

"Remove modest from my list of characteristics." Lionel checked the jump counter. "We're coming out of jump in two hours. We'll need that time to draft new orders to the fleet and get them sent out."

"Your idea is to act like pirates until we get a serious response, and seize that."

"That's my plan. I mean, your brilliant tactical expertise."

"We're going to be raiders, stealing parts, then capturing the ships sent to hunt us down."

"That's it."

Devin thought about that. It would work. And he wouldn't have to kill any loyal ships' crews. Yet. "We can do that. But on one condition, Prefect."

"Yes, Tribune?"

"Eyepatches for everybody."

Chapter 28

Scruggs brandished her shotgun. She had positioned the governor's town car sideways to the dirt road. Now she could stand behind it and shoot at the approaching rebels, while hiding behind its bulk.

The pursuing convoy was two small cars and a flatbed truck. The car doors were emblazoned with 'Bart's Best Baking' and a picture of a white chef's hat. The trucks had a picture of a stylized blue cogwheel on the doors and hood. The first car had stopped halfway down the dirt road to the parking lot, the other right behind it. Scruggs couldn't see how the Marines had counted, but there couldn't be more than four in each car given how small they were.

When she yelled and pointed her shotgun, the first car halted. After a minute, it edged forward. She fired, once in the air, once in the dirt in front of the lead car. The convoy stopped again, and doors swung open, and guns poked at her.

Everyone in the lead cars had weapons. The same types she had seen the Planetary Guard with. And half had Planetary Guard uniforms too.

Too short to be rifles, must be carbines. That was good. The centurion said rifles were only accurate with a skilled shooter. Carbines were even worse. Centurion would say there was little risk as long as they didn't have automatic weapons.

"Who are you?" one of them yelled.

"Back, back. Sideways. We have no allowance. Keep the food coming. Hupphf. Huuppf. Huppf. No way to go. Stay. Stay. Stay. Ruspah! Radishes We shoot." Scruggs yelled random words and watched the enemy exchange glances. Centurion had told her that the easiest way to confuse an uncertain assault was to keep yelling nonsense at them. While they were trying to puzzle things out, they wouldn't attack.

"Where are you going? Who are you? That's the governor's car. He's not allowed to send anything out of the city while talks are going on. And he's not answering our comms. Why?"

"Talks are overrated. Radishes continue. Tell me more about radishes."

"Radishes? What's that have to do with it?"

"Important radishes. Contain the inevitable."

The four in the front huddled behind the doors and argued. They were barely onto the parking lot and blocked the path of the second car. A skinny man in a red and blue coverall stepped from the passenger door of the second car and held up empty hands. He walked to the first car and exchanged words with the occupants. After the discussion, he spat more than a mouthful of chew leaf on the ground and faced Scruggs.

"We haven't been paid," he yelled. "RC owes us for the last two shipments. Kel says no more outbound shipments 'til we get our money. That's the deal. RC's not answering his phone, so no shipments."

"I don't know anything about that," Scruggs yelled back.

"No money, no shipments, Kel says. Pay up and we'll let you go."

"Why did you start this rebellion?"

"Rebellion?" The skinny man dropped his hands and laughed. "This isn't a rebellion. We're not rebelling. RC said he was going to use the other families for our shipments. We warned them not to take his money. The gems are our business, not theirs. If Narla and her family had stuck to teak and the rice, we wouldn't have cared. They didn't listen, he didn't listen. We had to put them in their place. This is all his fault."

"What's his fault? I don't understand." Scruggs kept her shotgun pointed at the man.

"We know you're new. He probably lied to you. We only want what's ours. We had a deal. Gems for cash. RC would sell them off planet and split the money with us. But he hasn't paid us for the last two shipments, then we find that Narla and her gang are undercutting us. Can't have that. But that's our problem. We're dealing with them."

"Dealing with them?"

The skinny man pointed back at the smoke from the city. "Dealing with them. They won't cross us again. Now, you folks come back here, and give us your shipment and you can go. We don't want any trouble with the Empire."

"We're Imperial Citizens," Scruggs yelled. "Mess with us and you'll get a boatload of Marines here. Imagine what will happen then."

"Nothing will happen," Skinny said. "I'm not worried about Marines. RC can't afford that to happen. He'll take care of the Empire. That's our deal. He deals with the Empire people, we deal with the Andaman people, and we all get rich. Now give us our shipment or we take it. In case you missed it, we're armed."

"You can't shoot Imperial Citizens. There will be an inquiry."

"Who's talking about shooting? You were never shot. You went on some weird camping trip and fell into the river. River rats got you. Shame, but what can you expect from off-worlders? They should take better care." Skinny stepped forward. "Now, clear off and let us get what's in the truck—"

Scruggs focused the shotgun at him. "Stay back or I'll shoot."

A red-haired woman with a blue-yellow headscarf stuck her head around the door, pointed past Scruggs and yelled, "They're driving the truck on board, and they have steam up."

Skinny waved his companions out. "Let's go. We need to get them before they go."

"Stay put—"

"No." Skinny shook his head. "Listen up, little girl, step aside and I'll let you live. Otherwise, you'll be the first I shoot."

Scruggs thought about that for a microsecond. *Never let others dictate the pace of battle.* If you're going to delay, delay.

If you're going to run, run when you're ready. But if you're going to fight, fight, Centurion had always said.

She was supposed to protect the rest of the crew and keep these bandits away while they loaded the barge. What was the best way now? Delay? Run? Fight?

Fight.

BOOM. CLICKETY. BOOM. Scruggs shot the skinny man in the chest, then aimed a shot at the yelling woman. Skinny dropped, so did the woman. Scruggs was sure Skinny was out of the fight, not so sure about the other.

She stepped behind the car. The bandit group opened fire. At least two different types of weapons by the sounds. Bullets pinged off the town car, barely scratching the hood. More flew by to rake the barge.

With the driver's door open, Scruggs had a perfect view through the armored passenger side window. Skinny rolled on the ground. A pair of hands dragged the yelling woman behind the first car. A short man in a faded Planetary Guard uniform stood and pointed a carbine at the car, banging away. All four in the second car were dressed similarly. Three of them stood, firing carbines. The fourth had a more elaborate cap and a pistol. The crew on the flatbed on the bluff were firing over the cab.

Scruggs waited for the fire to slacken. This was panic fire, a reaction to her first shot. She wasn't in much danger from untrained, inexperienced troops. Centurion had always said one calm, trained shooter was worth ten scared untrained ones.

Of course, that meant that she was still outnumbered two to one.

Scruggs jogged to the front of the car and ducked. The first car was visible, but the angle shielded her from the other vehicles. She leaned into the bumper to steady herself and put two shotgun blasts into the first car. One shattered the windshield, the other peppered the open passenger doors. The yells redoubled.

She scooted back to the open driver's door, taking care to keep her feet behind the wheels as much as possible. She didn't think any of them were smart enough to drop low and shoot her feet, but best be careful.

She hopped inside and reloaded the four rounds she had shot—the shotgun took six—and peered through the windows to get the angle right. After a long look, she rolled out and skittered to the back. This time, she stuck her head up over the rear trunk and braced the shotgun with both hands. She put two rounds into the second car, shattering windows and blowing out a headlight. All four of the shooters dove behind the vehicle. One dropped his rifle. *Centurion would make me run fifty miles without stopping if I dropped a weapon.*

The crowd on the flatbed truck opened fire at her, but firing downhill, their shots missed. This time, she aimed for the driver. Two shots in the windshield, and the driver panicked. The flatbed engine roared, and it jerked backwards, spilling passengers into the brush and backing out of sight. It tilted to the left as it ran into the ditch, and figures bailed out.

Well, look who's here. One of the figures bailing out of the flatbed was the governor's social secretary. The broad shoulders and square jaw were visible even this far away. *Now we know how the gangs have been getting info from Empire House.*

Scruggs put one more shot into each car, then huddled behind a wheel and reloaded from the cartridge case on her belt. Once she was finished, she looked back to the barge.

Crap.

The riverboat had come loose at the front. The bow was swinging away from the dock, pivoting on the end of the barge. The barge was still tied up. And the truck—the truck was stuck, hanging over the side of the barge. It looked to be teetering, ready to drop into the river any second.

"I didn't do it," Lee said. "I didn't pull any of the levers."

"Well, we're moving," Dena said. "Cleon and I dropped the ropes like you said. Aren't we supposed to drift away?"

The rising sun blazed off the water. Lee shaded her eyes. "We missed one. There's a still a rope attached at the rear. We're pivoting off that."

"That's good, right? We'll get away."

"We need Scruggs. And we need that truck on board. It's hanging over the edge."

"Jove's ankles with the truck. Get Scruggs."

Cleon yelled up from below. "Bring us back into the dock. Clara's stuck in the truck, and it'll drop in the water any second."

"We can't. Get it on."

"We need more time. Gavin is going to get a rope, or a winch, or something."

"We'll go as soon as Scruggs is on. Truck or no truck," Lee said.

"My sister's stuck in the truck."

"Emperor's nature studies." Lee jerked the left lever forward, at the same time pulling the right lever back. The sidewheeler tried to pivot, but stuck and strained on the attached line. The balance of forces wanted to turn, but the rope stopped it. Instead, it slammed sideways into the dock, sending the truck teetering even more.

"Scruggs. SCRUGGS! SCRUGGS!" Dena yelled.

Scruggs waved. She was sitting with her back to the governor's car, reloading. The opposition had stopped firing. She cupped her hands and yelled, "I'm fine here as long as the ammo holds out. What do you need?"

"We need you onboard. Get back here. We're leaving."

"What about the truck?"

"It might fall off. Doesn't matter. Get out of here before we get shot. We don't need the truck."

"I told you," Cleon said. "My sister is in there."

"You go get her if you want her," Lee said.

"Come on, Scruggs! Make like a tree and go leave."

"How she going to get down that dock without getting shot? It's wide open," Lee said.

"Scruggs, let us know and we'll cover you."

Scruggs waved again. "Don't worry. I'll take care of it. Get ready to go."

"How?"

Scruggs didn't answer. She snapped the shotgun shut, stepped up, and fired six aimed shots. Two hit each opposing vehicle. This time, a fusillade of return fire rocked out as she stuck her head up.

She ducked back behind the bulk of the car, threw the shotgun inside, climbed in and closed the door.

"What's she doing? We don't need the car. Just run," Lee said.

"How's she going to—Oh."

Scruggs backed the car up, executed a perfect two-point turn, faced the dock and drove up the dirt ramp and onto the finger pier. Behind her, every gunman in the bandit cars chewed shots at the rear of the town car. One of the tires took a shot, drooped, then re-inflated as the governor's safety package activated.

"She still has to get out at some point," Cleon said. "Then they'll have her."

The town car crunched onto the pier, the engine revved and Scruggs fired off down the pier.

"Watch," Dena said. "She's not getting out of the car."

The town car passed the tiedown, Scruggs making minor corrections. Midway down the pier, the driver's side door pushed open.

"She needs to slow down," Cleon said.

"She needs to do the exact opposite," Dena said. "She's thought this through. Watch."

The heavy car flew down the pier, crossed the T-dock at the end, roared up onto the remaining wooden planks, and slammed hood first into the teetering truck. The impact shoved the truck forward onto the barge deck, and across into a pile of teak timbers.

The car followed, roaring down the ties and into the bulwark. The car's momentum pushed the barge, pitching the stern out into the river. The restraining rope parted with a crack, and the barge pivoted into the river. The town car hung for a second, then tipped sideways into the river. It dropped like a rock, sideways down, floating away, taking Scruggs with it.

Chapter 29

"We're going to hit the dock!" Dena yelled.

"I know," Lee said.

"Reverse. Forward. Hoist the sails. Something." With the rope holding the back of the barge snapped, the spinning side wheels spun the entire tug-barge combination clockwise. In seconds, they had reversed their previous spin, and now they crunched the bow into the dock. The barge flexed, and a pile of planks dropped over the side. The bow ground along the dock, and the stern pivoted farther out into the river.

"We're a tug. We don't have sails." Lee pulled the left engine lever back and shoved the right forward. "Where's Scruggs?"

"She knocked the truck—she's in the water. I can't see her. I need to help her." Dena dashed out of the bridge, and climbed down the ladder, sliding the last few feet. Then she ran to the back of the tug and vaulted over the railing onto the barge.

She ducked left and ran along the gunnels. Gunshots banged from the shore. The river pushed the tug-barge sideways down the river, threatening to override the town car floating in the river beside it. The truck was onboard, on its side, stuck in a pile of wood. Cleon climbed up one side.

"Where is she?"

"In the truck."

"Scruggs is in the truck?"

"Clara. Scruggs is in the water."

Dena kept moving. Gavin was hauling a rope in, one-handed. The barge tipped sideways, and metal screeched. Lee's reverse was stressing the connections.

"Help me with the rope," he yelled.

"Where's Scruggs?"

The river current had grabbed the tug-barge. They were pushing downriver, riding up over the town car. It was still floating, but had rolled sideways, driver's side up. The door had shut, but the window was open, and waves washed over it, driving it farther down every second.

Dena grabbed the rope and yanked it in. Only twenty feet remained, the rest stuck back on the dock after it snapped. She coiled the greasy slime-covered rope into a bundle and threw it down at the car. The line dropped down and thumped onto the door. A hand grasped it.

"She's got it. She's got it," Dena said. "Hang on, Scruggs. We'll pull you up."

"Not through that window," Gavin said. "She'll have to get the door open. Otherwise, she'll go down with the car."

"Get the door open!"

"She can't. It's armored and weighs a ton. She needs the hydraulics working."

Something popped forward, and the barge squealed sideways again. They were in danger of snapping the tow connection.

The ship drive wheels stopped. The car floated free. Water rushed into the open window and the car dropped lower. Scruggs's hands disappeared. The rope hung free.

The sidewheels spun in the opposite direction. Now, rather than fighting the river's spin, she was working with it. They pivoted faster now, the bow of the tug pulling downriver, and the stern of the barge drifting back. They banged back into the car, which sank lower , and bounced backwards. A final wave washed over, and the car pivoted hood down, as the water overcame its buoyancy and the heavy engine dragged it under.

The car tilted up, the trunk coming out of the water, dipping to the driver's side.

"She's going. Scruggs! Scruggs!"

Gravity swung the door open. Scruggs's feet showed. She kicked it fully open, then stepped onto the door and dove free. Behind her, the town car filled with water and sank, only the glow from the rear lights visible. Scruggs swam easily but was drifting behind the barge.

"Get her the line!" Gavin said and ran away.

Cleon appeared next to them. He yanked the line back in, coiling it around his elbow. Once he had the full length coiled up, he dropped it in his hand. He ignored Dena's yelling and focused on Scruggs. He swung the line forward, back, then threw it at the end of the next swing. The line sailed out, neatly uncoiling as it flew away. The end of it smacked Scruggs in the face. She grabbed the slimy rope with both hands and hung on.

"Clara's run up to get the motors reversed. If we hang here, we can haul her in."

The barge shuddered. Both sidewheels stopped, then went into a gentle reverse. The tug-barge slid into the center of the river, bow pointing down, wheels fighting the current. Cleon and Dena hauled Scruggs in. Their freeboard was so low, once she was alongside, she was able to get her arms on the top. Dena and Cleon hauled her aboard.

"Thanks." Scruggs rubbed water off her face. "That was close."

"Stupid Baby Marine. Always wants to go swimming." Dena hugged her.

Scruggs broke the hug and eyed Cleon.

He grinned. "Glad you're okay."

"Thanks." Scruggs swallowed and gave him an awkward hug. Cleon looked surprised, then returned the hug. Also awkwardly.

Dena and Gavin exchanged grins over the two.

"I'm glad you're okay too, Scruggs," Gavin said. "Do I get a hug too?"

"What? Uh, sure." Scruggs squeezed Gavin. "Cleon, sorry about your dad's car."

"Stepdad. If he was worried about it, he should have assigned something different to the convoy."

"Would have been better if he gave us another radio," Gavin said. "That was the only one we had on the local net."

Clara ran back. "Everybody okay? Scruggs, you all right?"

"I'm fine. Thanks everyone for saving me."

"Lee says she needs some help with the controls. It's hard to steer and reverse, she says. And we'll need to shovel some more wood in. And make sure we have food. A whole bunch of things."

"And." Gavin grimaced and held his arm. "She'll need to look at my arm again. I wrenched it during the excitement. Did her med kit get onboard?"

"I think so." Scruggs squirmed out of her coveralls and squeezed the water out of them. She only had on a wet t-shirt and panties underneath. "I threw the ammo and the food and all our packs onto the barge near the back. There's a pile of gear there. I think her kit is there."

The *Heart's Desire* crew had been together for a long time. They'd seen each other bleeding, knocked out, asleep, nude in a medical pod, and doing sweaty workouts. In the close confines of a spaceship, you got over things quickly.

Cleon had never been in a spaceship. Clara took in where his eyes were and slugged him in the ribs. "Her eyes are up here, brother."

"Sorry." Cleon gulped. "Sorry. Um. You should get dressed."

"Sorry about what?" Scruggs squeezed her coveralls again. "And these make me sweat, they don't have any armor rating, and they're a pain to dry out. I might as well not wear them at all."

"Probably wouldn't have many objections around here," Dena said. "Scruggs, are you okay?"

"Yes, I'm fine."

"Well, the way I read the map, it's three days downriver to the starport on this slow boat, so we should get organized. Mr. Super-engineer, maybe get with Lee and get your arm fixed up. And we'll set up some sort of rota for shoving that wood into the boiler. I know this much from Rockhaul, it's a lot easier to keep a wood fire fed than it is to restart it. I'll go look at that. Clara, you've been on these ships before, right?"

"I've been on the electrical ones, not these old wood burners."

"You think you can steer for the first while? Lee will need to see to Gavin."

"I can do that."

"I'll check out the wood situation and see if any of those valves make sense. Scruggs, there's like cabins or something up on the second deck of the tug. You and Cleon get our gear under cover, get Lee her bag, and tell us how much food and water we have."

"Wilco," Scruggs said. "Let's go, Cleon."

"Ummm." Cleon stared intently at her face. "You going to put your clothes back on?"

"Why?" Scruggs glanced down at her soaking underwear and see-through t-shirt. "It's boiling out, and for once, I'm not hot."

"You're hotter than you think, Baby Marine." Dena smirked. "But you'll want pockets somewhere to hang weapons, right?"

"Good point." Scruggs grabbed her damp coveralls and slid them on.

"Right." Dena looked around. "So far on this planet, we've been shot at, exploded at, had bridges blown up at, car chased at, fallen into frog ponds, and chased into a killer river. I think we're safe now. There's not much else that this planet can throw at us."

The barge shuddered and stuck. They all fell except for Clara, who grabbed a stack of wood. The barge slewed sideways as the tug caught on a hidden sandbar.

Dena looked over the side, at the river rushing by. "I hate planets. I'm never leaving the ship again."

They were lucky. Lee hadn't got any news from the deck, so she'd kept the engines in neutral, so they only stuck lightly onto the sandbar. Once the rest of the crew climbed back up on the bridge and she knew they were safe, she hauled them sideways off the sand. Clara took the wheel and showed Scruggs how to scan for the dappled water that signaled shallows. Lee took Gavin down a level to the cabins and lashed up his arm.

She gave him another shot for the pain. "You need to not use that arm, otherwise, it won't get any better. And if you keep hurting it, you'll get permanent nerve damage."

"I'd like to, but life kind of got in the way." He flexed his fingers. "Feels better now."

"Don't use it at all for at least a few days."

"Fine."

Dena stuck her head up the top of the ladder. "We need Gavin's toolbox. This fire grate thing is stuck. There's a chute that you shove the wood down, and it's too narrow. We need to pry it open so we can shovel bigger pieces of wood down it."

"It's in the truck," Gavin said. "Doctor Lee says I can't use my arm, but I'll show you where it is."

Lee went up to see Clara. Dena, Scruggs, Cleon, and a crippled Gavin headed for the truck. Gavin supervised while they pulled the splintered planks out of the way.

"How we going to drive this off now?" Dena wondered. "On its side and all."

"There's a crane at the front." Gavin pointed. "It's more for dragging stuff, or probably hauling this into a dock. But if we brace things right, we can haul the truck upright. The engine's probably fine, but we need to get it on all four wheels."

"Well, first, we need to get this door open." Scruggs yanked at the locking bar. "I'll need some help..." Dena and Cleon lent a hand, and they yanked the door loose. The left side door flopped down to the deck. The right one hung loose.

"Right, we need to—"

CRUNCH. Wood splintered inside the truck.

Cleon jumped back. "In the Emperor's name—"

Scruggs produced a revolver from a pocket. Dena pulled out her slingshot. Gavin ducked behind a pile of teak, grabbed a balk and readied to throw it.

"Um, shouldn't we..." Cleon said.

"Shoot first." Scruggs stepped left and cocked her gun. "Yes. Dena, I have right and high."

Dena stepped right and aimed her slingshot. "Left and low."

"That's a slingshot," Cleon said. "What's that for?"

Gavin grabbed Cleon and hauled him behind the wood pile. "Yes it is, to answer your first question. Crushing your skull, to answer the second question."

"Shouldn't we wait 'til we—" Cleon asked.

"NO!" the three crewmembers said together.

CRUNK. CRUNCH. More wood splintered inside the truck.

"Who's there?" Scruggs yelled.

"I'm coming out. I'm unarmed. Don't shoot," a voice said from inside the truck.

"Come out. Keep your hands where we can see them. Move slow." Scruggs pointed her gun.

A hand grasped the underside of the hanging door, then shoved it upright. A figure in a standard issue Imperial Navy skinsuit appeared from the gloom. He ducked under the door, crawled through, then dropped it.

The man stepped out into the light, hands held high.

"I'm unarmed, as you can see." It was Stafford Rafe Cardigan, the governor. "I heard the noise, figured you were opening up." He peered around. "Not the type of welcome I expected. This isn't a starship."

"No, it's a barge," Scruggs said. "What are you doing here?"

"Getting off planet, of course. Or rather, having you get me off planet. That's what this is all about, you see. Getting me out of here. I figured if anybody could escape a bunch of crazed rebels and get me off-planet, it would be you folks. Like calls to like. Low-class thieves and scoundrels, the lot of you."

He glanced at Dena. "That looks like a slingshot. What are you going to do with that?"

"Shoot you if you move."

"With a slingshot? Ha." RC grinned. "You? The dumb barbarian girl. Give it your best shot."

He dropped so fast after Dena shot him, he didn't even manage to get his hands out to break his fall.

30

Chapter 30

"**S**ensor suite number one reports that Freighter *Sweet Campari* has returned to station," Spaceman 1st Silaski said.

"What reports?" Hooper looked up from updating the ship's log. "Sensor suite what?" Monti had finally taken a nap, leaving her in charge. Hernandez was swanning around with her new personal pinnace boarding freighters. She'd been gone almost a full shift, far longer than expected. *Must be doing something right, though, the whole second column is getting in line and staying in line.*

"Sensor suite number one ma'am," Silaski repeated.

"What's sensor suite number one?"

"It's the first sensor suite ma'am."

"I know what the number one means. But which sensor system is it?"

"The first one ma'am."

Hooper rubbed her eyes. "Is it the radar, the laser range finder, the telescope, the IR, which? It says there right on the sensor console."

"It's the first one on the screen ma'am. That's all it says."

Hooper unbelted and ducked under the equipment hanging over her head—what idiot put the thruster ready lights up that high—and climbed up to peer over Silaski's shoulder. The *Collingwood* was shepherding the recalcitrant freighters under one-quarter-G thrust, still on its way to the jump limit. She grasped the back of Silaski's chair and let her legs float up. "Show me."

"Right there ma'am." Silaski pointed to the radar display. The top of the screen was labeled 'Sensor suite number one'

"Silaski, did you reset this console?"

"Yes ma'am. I've been reading up on it. Each watch stander sets their own settings so they can have a board customized to their job."

"This is true. Why did you choose this setting?"

"I copied my settings from the default and saved it ma'am."

"Are you sure you didn't erase all the settings and set the console back to factory defaults?"

"I don't think so, I mean, can I do that ma'am?"

"Were you watching the news again, Silaski?" Hooper had seen Silaski's program on screen twice last shift. It was more scandal than news.

"Umm...."

Hooper shook her head. "Never mind. For now, call sensor suite number one by its more common name, radar." She floated back to her seat, strapped in, and continued to update the log.

Four hours later, a refreshed Monti pulled onto the bridge.

"What are you doing here?" Hooper asked. "You're supposed to sleep for two hours more."

"Good to see you too. And I'm the captain. You're supposed to say 'Captain on the bridge.'"

"There's only me and Silaski, and she's asleep. Don't get angry at her, I told her she could."

Silaski's head was on her chin, and drool was pooling on her uniform. Monti grunted. "She's not going to thank you when she wakes up covered in spit. Why did you let her sleep?"

"No course corrections in the last three hours. Our in-house spy has been scaring the Bejoves out of the freighter captains somehow. She's visited eight of them, stays for twenty minutes, then moves on to the next. After her visit, they sedately maneuver into position and stay there."

"The convoy is forming up?"

"Forming up and staying formed up. And being quiet. No comm request either."

"Everything is going well?"

"Everything is going splendidly!"

"Why don't I believe you? Where's Weeks. Is he asleep too?"

"Yes, in engineering."

"And how is engineering? Anything to report?"

"A good shift."

"What does that mean?"

"Did you know that door lubricant is flammable?"

"No."

"Neither did Spaceman 3rd Castin, but he figured it out after he shorted a door motor and started a fire. But he fixed that problem before we had to vent the whole compartment. That's the only excitement we've had back there all shift. That makes it a good shift."

"I suppose I'll read about it in the log."

"I suppose you will if somebody puts it in there. Listen, we do have one kind-of-big problem."

"Which is?"

"We're burning fuel much faster than normal chasing all these freighters. At this rate, we might not have enough to jump. And even if we make the jump, we'll be dead in space afterward."

"You've told the flagship?"

"Three times. Once last shift, and twice this shift."

"And?"

"Acknowledgments only, no instructions. They've gone dead quiet. Nothing new from them in hours. I figure they're too busy setting up court-martials for anybody the admiral doesn't like."

"Bron, don't talk like that, you'll get in trouble."

"What type of fleet commander doesn't let his escorts fuel?"

"This one." Monti bit her lip and spun in the low gravity. "Call the *Hydrogen Pride* and ask for an underway refueling. I'll bet they'll let us do it."

"I'll bet they will. And since Hernandez has to get back sometime before jump, we can pick her up there."

"I'm sure she'll be as glad to see us as we are to see her."

Silaski jerked awake when the two women giggled.

Hydrogen Pride agreed to the underway refueling when contacted. Monti signaled the flag to say she was 'utilizing organic refueling units as per standing orders' and received another acknowledgment.

"Maybe they're all asleep," Monti said.

"Maybe the new admiral's aide doesn't want to pass any messages along."

"Maybe they don't want to ask what organic means."

Both woman were tense during the refueling, but their novice crew didn't blow anything up or break the ships.

"That's the worst fueling party I've ever seen," Hooper said.

"I can send you out if you want?"

"Nope. More fun to watch. Besides, you need me here when Hernandez comes back."

"I do?"

"To remind you that she lies all the time."

"Don't need reminding." Monti called the other two corvettes under her command and had them top up fuel as well. Theoretically, she was supposed to order them around all the time, but in practice, she'd been too busy handling her own under-crewed ship to bother.

All the corvettes buzzing through the convoy attracted attention. The flagship sent new instructions. They and another corvette were to jump ahead to the next system, do a high speed pass, scan for hostiles, then return. The name on the orders was the flag captain, 'on behalf of and for Admiral Lord Bracebridge.'

"Somebody has an idea what they're doing over there," Hooper said.

Monti grimaced. "Hooper, stop criticizing the senior officers in front of the crew. It's disloyal."

"The crew can't hear us." Hooper pointed at Silaski at the helm. "She's got headphones in. I told her to try to learn her job better."

"Fine, the crew can't hear us. It's still disloyal."

"No, declaring independence from Imperial control, seizing warships, operating undeclared war against the Nats and the Confeds, destroying pirate ships without authorization, all that stuff that Devin the traitor did, that's disloyal. I'm just incompetent."

"He does set a high bar."

"I'll get us to the jump limit. Who's coming with us?"

"We'll take the *Moncton*," Monti decided.

"Best ship for the job?" Hooper asked.

"No, I hate Lieutenant What's-his-name less than the other guy."

"Oh yes, Lieutenant What's-his-name and Lieutenant Other-guy. Great officers. Let me check their service records."

"Shut up. Get me a course to the jump limit. Then program a jump. Sooner we get out of here, the better."

"I thought you were doing the navigating?"

"You're better at it."

"Prove it. Records say otherwise."

"I'm the captain."

"Temporary, acting rank."

"Fine. If you don't do it, I'll get Silaski to do it."

Both women turned to Spaceman 1st Silaski, seated at the control panel above. She was watching a tutorial on how to operate the thrusters.

Hooper grinned. "Dare you."

Monti unbuckled, ducked under the overhead equipment, and tapped Silaski's shoulder. Silaski jerked, then took off the headphones.

"Silaski, as a helmsman, you're supposed to know how to do emergency navigation. Have the computer calculate a crash jump to the next system."

"I've never done that ma'am."

"But you trained for it. Says so on your record." *And we all know how reliable that is.* What is the Empire coming to?

"Yes ma'am. Um, we talked about my record. You know that I—"

"Cheated and lied. Yes, but I'm used to that now that I'm spending more time with the Wavy Navy."

"Oh, thank Jove." Silaski smiled. "I was worried that was going to be a problem."

Monti glared at her. "You know I was being sarcastic, didn't you?"

"Uhhhh. No ma'am. Sorry ma'am."

"Never mind. Calculate an emergency jump to the next system. Lieutenant Hooper?"

"Yes, Captain Monti."

"What's the next system called?"

"Only a catalog number. 800-463-3339. Plenty of fuel, no habitable planets."

"Very well." Monti turned to Silaski. "Pretend we absolutely positively have to get there right away and use the computer to calculate a crash jump." A crash jump was an emergency procedure. The computer calculated the quickest jump to the vicinity of an adjacent system. For safety's sake, it dumped you so far out-system on your target to avoid any potential planets or moons and was so far from any fueling stations or habitable planets as to be useless. But it was safe.

"Um, yes ma'am, I'll look up the details."

"Carry on." Monti slapped her on the shoulder, swung past the drive output thrust repeater display, and squirmed back into her chair.

"See?" Monti told Hooper on a private channel. "Motivating them properly is all it takes. She'll have a course for us."

"Hope she doesn't kill us."

"Me too. You know I expect you to double-check her, right?"

"And I expect you to triple-check me."

"Will do. Give her a head start."

The two lieutenants sat and worried. Hooper worried about slamming the ship into a black hole or emerging from jump inside an ice moon. Monti worried about that, but also wondered if the admiral would court-martial her, or if the rubber bands tying *Collingwood's* engines together would unwind, leaving them dead in space between stars, forcing them into cannibalism. She'd reached the point of starting to organize the crew by weight and edibility in her head when Monti bonged her channel.

"What?"

"I've got a course to the jump limit."

"Okay. Who's fatter? The weapons techs or the engineering ratings?"

"Umm. I don't know."

"Can we look it up?"

"If we need to, we can have some sort of crew weigh-in. Why?"

"Never mind. You happy with the course?"

"Nothing between here and the jump limit. I'm starting my own jump calcs. How's super sailor doing up there?"

Silaski had a tutorial up on one screen, and one of the control screens on the other.

"She's doing something. Should I jog her elbow?"

"We have time yet."

Silaski typed, then slapped an execute button on her screen.

"What's she—hey, my console reset."

"How did...mine too." Monti brought up the intercom. "Silaski? Silaski?"

Hooper waved. "She can't hear you. We cut her out of the intercom, remember?"

"Cut her back in!"

"That button has disappeared."

Monti cursed. She unbuckled, ducked under the monitors and slapped Silaski on the shoulder. "Well?"

"Making progress ma'am. But one question."

"What is that question?"

Silaski pointed at her screen. It had a lot fewer options than Monti remembered, and it was a different color.

"Yes ma'am. I've been following the tutorial."

"Oh…" Monti swallowed. "Did you reset all the console controls again?"

"I don't think so ma'am." Silaski pointed at the generic listings on her screen. "But for starting, should I be using navigation system number one, or navigation system number two?"

"How bad is it?" Monti sat next to Hooper in the galley and pulled a tray out of the warmer.

Hooper spooned red sludge from her own tray into her mouth. "You want the good news or the bad news?"

"Give me the good news first."

"Don't have any."

"Make some up."

"Well." Hooper licked her spoon. "It only affects the bridge consoles. Not the underlying systems, not the sensors. They all check out. It's purely a display problem, not an operating system thing. She reset all the consoles to factory default, like if they were brand new. They haven't been calibrated for this ship."

Monti pried the top off her tray and spooned red sludge. "Isn't this supposed to be hot?"

"Yes."

"Put that on the list to be fixed. What do we do with the consoles?"

"Now the bad news. We type the specs in. For example, the sensors, we manually specify the range, sensitivity, angular corrections and so on. That tells it what to display."

"That doesn't sound bad." Monti tasted her spoon. *What's in this? Tabbo hooves?* "Never mind fixing this. It's as bad hot as it its cold. "

"Understood."

"Where do you get the settings?"

"Online manuals."

"How long to put in all the specifications?"

"I can type in dozens every hour. So it's just a matter of math."

"How many specs are there."

"I don't know them all. But the telescope, for example. That's one of our simplest sensors. It has…" Hooper pulled out her comm. "Three thousand, six hundred thirteen possible settings. Which, at six per minute…"

"Never mind. What's plan B?"

"There's an auto detect function. Press a button and it scans and queries the attached equipment, gets a model number, looks it up in the database, and auto-loads all the settings."

"Super Zeus! Detect away."

"Will do. If you order it."

Monti put down her spoon. "What aren't you telling me?"

"Well, that was the bad news. The auto-detect thing."

"Bron, why is this bad news?"

"Well, I looked it up. This is normally done at a shipyard, by a technician right after they install a new piece of equipment. They check what's detected against what they installed. Sometimes they have to update the ship equipment database with files for the new equipment installed. And they know what was installed."

Monti thought about this. "What if the detection software gets an answer it doesn't understand?"

"It guesses."

"Well, that's fine. We'll let it load up all the systems automatically, and all the ones that it flags as guesses, we'll double-check."

Hooper kept chewing.

Monti sighed. "Let me guess. We can't tell which is which. We're going to have to check them all."

Hooper grinned. "And that, ladies and gentlemen, is why Mama Hooper's daughter didn't want to be captain."

Monti worked in her cabin. The software reset bug was limited to the bridge. Her captain's console in her quarters hadn't been affected, nor had the console in engineering. She'd decided to let the bridge consoles auto-load, and she and Hooper then cross-checked the detected items to make sure that they matched.

"It might not be correct, but at least we won't be in worse shape than before," Hooper said. "Think of it as a crash introduction to understanding ship systems."

"And that's what I've always wanted, a deeper understanding of one of the worst designs in Imperial history, the corvette class escort."

"There are hundreds of these in the Empire!"

"Which means there are hundreds of short-ranged, underpowered, poorly armed shoddily built escorts carrying their crews one software glitch from having all the power shorted out."

"Somebody's grumpy today. Radar system number two shows as Model 700-LR-X3L.

"700-Lima-Romeo-Xray-3-Lima. That's what I have."

"Outstanding. Next, external camera system-1 is Model 22314-7234-A."

"And...no. Read that back?"

Hooper did. Monti shook her head. "Nope. I've got 22314-7234-Av2."

"Must be version 2."

"Must be."

"Wonder if there's a big difference."

Monti sighed. "Hope not. It's just a camera. Move on."

"Understood. Stand by." Hooper went silent then came back. "Hernandez's pet pinnace is coming back. They're docking now."

"Wake up Weeks, put Hernandez on the bridge with you. She and Weeks can cross-check the engineering systems and life support. We'll finish up with weapons and navigation, and helm."

"She'll love that."

Four hours later, they approached the jump limit. Hernandez had returned from her package delivery, and didn't even do them the courtesy of making up a decent lie, instead going right to sleep until her shift. After waking, she'd been friendly, relaxed, hardworking, dedicated, and willing to do anything Monti asked with a cheerful grin.

This made Monti's head hurt with paranoia so much, she had to take pills. She considered wearing her sidearm on watch, ready to shoot Hernandez during her upcoming sudden but inevitable betrayal. But she consoled herself that Hooper seemed to feel the same way and could probably hold Hernandez long enough so that she could beat her to death with a crowbar.

"Approaching jump limit," Silaski said.

"Thank you, Spaceman." Monti keyed her comm. "Engineering, how does it look?"

"In all respects ready for jump ma'am," Weeks said. He was always polite.

"Very well, thank you, Engineering."

"Ma'am."

Monti keyed the intercom again. "Weeks, do we have any crowbars on board?"

"Crowbars? Somewhere. Why do you ask?"

"Just a thought. Thanks. Control out."

Hooper turned from the navigation station and ducked her head under the roof-mounted displays. "Crowbars?"

"Just a thought." Monti looked at Hernandez. "Just a thought."

"I've got a gun, Monti." Hernandez didn't take her eyes off her screen. "I keep it with me all the time. Want to try it?"

"I have no idea what you're talking about." Monti said. She turned to Hooper and mouthed 'damn.'

"Clear of jump limit," Silaski said.

"Hooper?"

"Board is green. We can jump any time."

"You're happy with your solution?"

"Yes. In fact, we've got two to choose from. My calculated one, that you checked. And the auto-generated one that Silaski brought up."

"Silaski got the auto-gen one to work?"

"She did. All on her own."

"Silaski, well done." Monti clapped her hands. "You have a future in the Navy."

"Um. Thanks ma'am. The real Navy or the Wavy Navy?"

"Let's not get excited here, Silaski."

"Sorry ma'am. Ready to jump."

"Very well. Jump."

Silaski tapped her console. The main screen darkened and the blue-green light of jump space displayed.

Alarm lights flashed. And flashed. Then flashed more. Alarms bonged. Hooper and Monti ran their fingers over consoles, silencing alarms and checking settings.

"That's not normal," Hernandez said. "What's going on?"

Monti looked at her display. "Silaski?"

"Ma'am?"

"When I said jump, which jump solution did you pick?"

"Ma'am?"

"Did you pick the carefully calculated, triple-checked one created by Lieutenant Hooper over there, or did you stab at the auto-generated emergency jump that you calculated on your malfunctioning console, as an exercise."

"My calculation was an exercise?"

"Yes."

"Oh. I thought when you said it was good. I mean. Oh." Silaski's hand went to her mouth.

A single alarm bell bonged slowly. Hooper slapped it down. The bridge sat in silence.

"Well, I wouldn't worry about it," Hooper said. "I mean, all we're doing is traveling trillions of miles inside a compressed space-time mini-universe that we've artificially created. I mean," Hooper shrugged, "what could possibly go wrong?"

Chapter 31

"**S**he's a menace. Completely crazy," RC said.

"Um-hmm." Lee shined a penlight in RC's eyes. "Doesn't look like a concussion. Or if it was, it's gone. But you did pass out. No issues with your breathing?"

"She shot me. Without warning. She's a crazy woman."

"Lots of talking, so I guess your breathing is okay. You asked her to. With Dena, you don't ask her to shoot you twice. Right, you're fine. Back to work." After Dena had knocked him out, the crew had carried RC up to the deck under the control room where Lee kept her medical kit.

"Work?"

"Nothing free on this ship. Wood shoveling. Need to keep the boilers fed." Lee put the penlight back in her medical kit. "If we want to keep moving."

"Why did you leave with this stupid barge? We were supposed to be on a starship."

"Didn't you hear about the revolt? The bridge being destroyed?"

"What bridge? What revolt?"

"You don't know?" How could somebody this stupid become governor? Who are they hiring these days?

"I was in a box. A box that you blew up."

"We need to talk. Everybody needs to talk." Lee stuck her head over the edge of the deck. "Gavin! Everybody. RC's awake. Take a break, grab some food and meet up in the control room."

"The bridge," RC said. "We're not on a starship, we're on a boat. It's called a bridge. Not a control room."

"Fine, we'll act like we're on a boat," Lee said. "Is that a good idea? You okay with that?"

"Why wouldn't I be?"

"Because, if I remember from my reading, on a boat, we just throw stowaways overboard."

Everyone climbed up onto the top deck, and sat, staring at the river. Scruggs carried up a box of ration bars and two containers of water in her ubiquitous backpack.

Clara volunteered to steer. "I can do this for four hours," she said. "But I'll need a break in the middle."

"Is it all like this?" Lee gestured at the water. The river was muddy brown water, frothing where it ran over hidden sandbars. No river bank—the high water flooded into the forests and covered the tree roots. "Nowhere to land or tie up. Just water and trees everywhere."

"Amazing planet, isn't it?" Clara said. "Wonder why we wanted to leave."

"Speaking of leaving. What are we going to do with the governor, here," Cleon said.

"For Jove's sake," RC hissed. "I've told you not to call me that. Call me Dad."

"You're not my dad. You're my stepdad. And you weren't even good at that."

"I did my best for you."

"For our money, you mean," Clara said. "Mom's money. That's all you were interested in."

"Don't talk to me like that. I loved your mother. That's why I married her."

"You're lucky she put up with you."

"Yes." RC nodded. "I'm very lucky. I was very lucky. Luckiest man in the universe when she said yes. Lucky every day after. Every day until the accident." RC blinked away tears and turned away.

The others exchanged uncomfortable glances. This grief was unexpected.

Gavin cleared his throat. "The accident?"

"Mom died in a fall," Cleon said. "A stupid, dumb accident. She was walking down the main stairs at Empire House, and she tripped. Nothing special, she tripped. No drugs, no alcohol in her system. Nobody near her. Just a stupid accident."

"She left everything to us in a trust." Cleon pointed at RC. "Not to this one here. Otherwise, we would have been suspicious. He's worthless."

"I made your mother happy, didn't I?" RC said.

Cleon grimaced.

"Is that true?" Gavin said.

Both Cleon and Clara nodded. "She was happy enough," Clara said. "I think she didn't mind being out at the edge of nowhere here. She had a big house, and we had good teachers—she hired tutors from the Core for years. With all the help she had, we were pretty easy kids. She was big on education, Mom was. And I'll admit, she enjoyed running those parties and talking to the locals. That's what she called them, 'the locals.' She was the queen bee, and she ruled over all of them."

"Mom was a snob, truth-to-tell," Cleon said. "That was her only flaw."

"That and marrying Mr. Profligate here," Clara said. "He's been wasting all our money since Mom died."

"Well," Lee said. "From what Dirk told us, he's been wasting your money long before your mom died. Long before he met you or her, that is. Isn't that so, Governor?"

RC wiped his eyes. "Nobody ever accused me of being good with money. But I did my best for the two of you."

"With our money," Cleon said.

"Whose was I going to use?" RC shrugged. "I didn't have any of my own. Everybody knows that. Your mom knew that. She knew that before she married me. I'm not good with that sort of thing. Even if I had a business idea, only a drunken blind banker would lend me money to start it. But she wanted a title, and I had one. She wanted to be at the top of the social pyramid, so I bought a job out here. She ran the social side, she spent time with you kids, arranged your education, and I did all the dreary things required to run a planet. I dealt with the families, the companies, the Marines, the Empire, all of that. She bought shoes and had parties."

"Sounds like fun," Lee said. "Did you have to steal the locals blind?"

"The locals, as you call them," RC said, "steal each other blind. They did before I got here, and they'll keep doing it long after I leave. I kept the stealing within bounds, made sure some of the money went where it was supposed to. Most of the roads got paved, the starport kept functioning, the schools worked. Yes, imports cost more than they should have, and the workers didn't get as high wages as they could. But nobody starved, there were hospitals and schools and things, and more importantly, I kept the violence out of it, until now."

"And got rewarded handsomely for your troubles." Clara frowned. "Sandbar ahead. Hang on." She threw the starboard engine into neutral and swung the wheel right. The barge skidded sideways against the current. She threw the starboard engine into reverse, pivoted some more, then threw both wheels to full power ahead. "Hold tight, I need to pivot us." They pointed to the right side of the river, but they were drifting down on a sand island dead ahead. "One more pivot." Now she reversed the port engine and pushed the starboard forward. The barge pivoted behind the tug from left to right, and they ended up sliding by the island, the tail of the barge sliding past.

"Well done, sister," Cleon said. "Those classes paid off."

"The classes I let you take," RC said.

"You wanted us out of the house so you could have your women over."

"Your mother was dead and I was alone. What would you have me do? Invite them to dinner with the two of you?"

Cleon and Clara were silent.

"That's old news anyways." RC pushed his hair back. "It's time to get off this stupid planet. You two are old enough to go your own way, and I haven't stolen your money. It's still safe off planet. Enough to put both of you through college or the Imperial academy. And you'll be going as the children of a noble, not commoners, and you're welcome. Most of my money from here is in that truck."

"Great speech." Dena clapped. "What happens now?"

"We need to talk about where we're going."

"No, we do not. Or you do not." Dena crunched a ration bar. "Baby Marine, this is disgusting, as usual."

"It's not." Scruggs took a big bite of hers. "It is a bit unique-tasting, is all."

"It tastes like unique burned sawdust mixed with motor oil. Are we eating wooden bars?"

Scruggs looked at the package. "Says 'contains cellulose as a filler.'"

"Told you so. Wonder what the motor oil is used for?" Dena crunched. "I suppose it does make the sawdust stick together."

"Enough of this, you crazy slingshot girl," RC said. "About where we're going—"

"We're going where this river goes. First because we don't have a choice. That's how rivers work. Second because we told Dirk that we'd take this truck to the starport and put the datapaks on the ship, then pick him and the centurion up."

"And Rocky!" Scruggs said.

"Who's Rocky?" Cleon asked.

"He's our attack space whippet," Scruggs said. "Our dog. He helps guard the ship, and he keeps animals away. He kills snakes and he attacks machine guns."

"He attacks machine guns?"

"Well," Scruggs said. "That was me. But he helped."

"You attacked a machine gun?"

"That's when the centurion got hurt. He was covering me while I stormed the machine gun on the drive in here."

"You and that old man attacked a machine gun?" Cleon asked. "Wow."

"Look," RC said. "I don't care about what some lying girl says—"

"I'm not lying." Scruggs glared. "And don't call me a girl."

"I'm an Imperial Governor. I'll call you what I want. Girl."

Scruggs put down her bar and stood. Her face reddened. She put her hand on her revolver.

"Sister Scruggs." Lee raised a hand. "Before you shoot the governor, could you get me another ration bar, please? Something different. From the box on the main deck?"

Scruggs glared at the governor, nodded at Lee, and climbed down to the main deck.

Gavin, Dena, and Lee waited until Scruggs disappeared below deck level, then tossed their uneaten ration bars over the side.

"You understand," Lee said, "that if she shoots you and throws you over the side, none of us will stop her."

"I'll help," Dena said. "But she doesn't need any help. But I'd do it for fun."

"We can't shoot him." Cleon looked worried. "Can we?"

"*We* don't have to do anything," Dena said. "But get Scruggs angry enough, and *she* will take care of the problem. We can watch."

"Did she really attack a machine gun?" Clara asked

"You saw her face down twenty people and three vehicles, shoot them up and scare them all away. What do you think?"

"I was in the truck...Cleon?"

"She did. Is it true about the old man too?"

"And the dog, yes." Lee nodded. "So, RC, I'd be more polite."

RC reddened. "You need me—"

"I don't think we do," Lee said. "Gavin, what's in the truck?"

"Money, like he said." Gavin shaded his eyes. "Look at those birds. Look at the colors." A flock of mustard-yellow birds with bright red beaks flapped by. "Really neat animals here. Wow. I should take pictures?"

"Later. The truck?" Lee asked.

"We've opened half of the boxes. They're full of money."

"That's my money!" RC said.

"Funny, that," Lee said. "A governor sneaking off his planet with boxes full of money. Doesn't sound legitimate. What type of money, Gavin?"

"Gold and platinum bars. Lots of raw gems, wrapped in paper. Green ones, they look like emeralds to me, but I'm not an expert. Blue ones could be sapphire. And other ones. None polished. Wonder how he got it."

"Stole from the locals," Lee said. *Should I make him give it back?*

"Maybe he—aha! That's why the codes." Gavin laughed. "I wondered about that. Why commercial codes? You were playing the different factions against each other. You used commercial codes with them so they couldn't see what you were talking to the others about."

"That's why Jack was with the group shooting at us!" Scruggs explained about Jack Boone, the governor's aide, helping the shooters. "He would have given them the commercial codes."

Lee nodded. "Giving away Imperial codes is treason. The Marines wouldn't stand for that. But giving commercial codes, that's not illegal. They each figured out they had a special deal with the governor." *This gets worse and worse. Who are they sending out to run planets these days?*

"Until they didn't." Gavin nodded. "There's two boxes with your datapaks, Lee, and two other boxes." Gavin grinned. "With two more datapaks. Not the ones that you took. Different ones."

Lee looked at RC. "What's on the other datapaks?"

"Data," RC said. "And none of your business. Look, I'm the governor of this planet—"

"Were the governor. You left. Dirk is in charge now."

"Only a representative of the Emperor can dismiss—"

"Dirk already did that. He's an Imperial Duke, and he's been appointed by Tribune Devin to deal with this sort of things. You do remember Tribune Devin, don't you, RC?"

RC gulped. "I'll give you half of the money if you deliver me to the starport and fly me off here. And fly the kids where they want to go."

"Why not throw him overboard, and take all the money?" Dena asked. "We're due some payment."

"That's one plan," Gavin agreed. "Lee, any issues with that?"

"You can't do that," RC said. "You need me to give the control code to decrypt those datapaks when you hand me to my representative."

"You said that your contact would have the codes."

"I lied," RC said. "Without me, the data's useless."

"Well," Lee said. "I didn't lie. I told you that if your contact didn't have the codes, then all your boxes would be out the airlock. Since you just told me the contact doesn't have the codes, then your boxes are going out an airlock, and since you came out of a box, you're going out an airlock. Or, what's the river equivalent of an airlock?"

"Walk the plank?" Gavin said. "We shove him off the boat."

"That sounds fun," Dena said. "Let's do that."

"Plenty of planks," Gavin said. "I can set something up."

Clara cleared her throat. "Much as I agree with a lot of things you say, he was a governor, and he did keep my mom happy. I can't—"

Scruggs climbed up onto the deck and dumped her backpack. "I got different ration bars, and I got these tins of food from a crate in the truck. Caviar, duck a l'orange."

"Those are mine!" RC said. "I had those shipped all the way from the Core."

"Well, they're ours now." Scruggs handed everybody another ration bar, and then gave everybody two tins. "Eat up."

Dena, Gavin and Lee popped the tins open and started digging in.

"This is amazing," Dena said. "What's a marlin?"

"Big fish," Gavin said.

Scruggs munched her ration bar and poked at her tin. "What did we decide?"

"We're rich," Dena said between bites. "RC lied to us. Our contact doesn't have the codes we need to decrypt the datapaks, so we're taking all his money. Emeralds. Gold, stuff like that. Then we're going to drown him in the river."

Scruggs crunched on her bar. "Wouldn't it be easier to shoot him?"

"Nobody's shooting me!" RC grabbed at his ankle. His hand came up empty.

Lee swallowed a bite of canned duck confit. "Took your holster off while you were knocked out, sorry."

"I'll shoot him." Scruggs opened her can. "Can I finish lunch first?"

"Sure," Dena said. "Always give rich people time to eat."

"How rich are we?" Scruggs asked.

"Boxes and boxes of gems," Dena said. "After we sell them, I'll..."

"You'll what? Retire to Rockhaul and build a big cow farm?"

Dena shook her head. "They're called ranches. But you know, I don't know what I'll do. I mean, money is great, but I don't want to go back there. I still want to travel."

Gavin shrugged. "We travel all the time."

"And you get to shoot people with your slingshot," Scruggs said. "And you meet different men on every planet we go to."

"I do like the men." Dena nodded. "I guess I'll stick with you guys. Lee, what about you? What will you do with your share of the loot?"

"I'm on the Empress's business," Lee said. "And helping Tribune Devin helps the Empress, so I'm going to stick with him. He can use a praetorian by his side."

"So says the loyal servant of the Empire." Dena licked her lips. "Scruggs, you going to finish that?"

"No." Scruggs shoved the can of 'Kobe-beef-stew' at Dena. "Take it."

"Thanks. What about you, Baby Marine? What will you do with all your money?"

"Put it with the rest, I guess." Scruggs took a ration bar out of the box. "I might buy a new shotgun. An automatic one."

"You've already got five," Gavin said. "Why do you need more?"

"How many different wrenches do you have?"

"That's not the same. They're tools. They help fix problems."

"So are shotguns. But different problems. You staying or going, Gavin?"

Gavin shrugged. "I'll stay. I like it here. None of you are trying to kill me."

"Except maybe the centurion."

"Yeah, but he's got a lot of people on his need-to-be-killed list. It will take him forever to get to me."

Everyone nodded at that.

RC shook his head. "You people are all crazy. I'm offering you piles of money, and all you're discussing is how you'll kill me, or each other, and what type of rifles you want to buy."

"Shotguns, not rifles, totally different thing." Scruggs swallowed the last of her lunch. "And why should we care what a governor who pushed a planet into rebellion thinks?"

"That wasn't me," RC said. "Can't blame that on me. I had a good thing going here. The kids could go to school, I had my...business activities...but the stupid chancellor messed everything up."

"So this little rebellion is all the Chancellor's fault?"

RC crossed his arms. "We used to have a Marine battalion here, and four ships on anti-piracy patrol based here. They cut the battalion in half two years ago and took half the ships. They did it again last year, and then three months ago, they took all the ships and cut the Marines down to a skeleton force. And told me to be prepared to have the remaining Marines leave in six months. The Empire needed the troops elsewhere, they said. That's when the locals starting getting ideas. Rebellion ideas."

"Where elsewhere?" Lee said.

"Didn't say. Just not here."

"You're an Imperial Governor. The Emperor didn't tell you?"

"I've never talked to the Emperor. I've only ever talked to the Chancellor or his friends."

Lee nodded. "You bought your job here, didn't you?"

"Some money changed hands, but that was years ago." RC shrugged. "Long as I kept the taxes up and the pirates down, and didn't steal too much from the locals, nobody cared. But import duties went up last year, and again a month ago. When word leaked that the troops were going, things heated up. I didn't figure there would be open fighting right away, but I wasn't surprised. I made contingencies. Besides, the locals still won't attack Imperial assets. The Empire has a long memory."

"Not long enough, apparently. This is news to me," Lee said. "It's interesting, but we promised Tribune Devin—"

"All right. All right. You two win. New deal. Can I have one of those bars?"

Scruggs dug into the box and handed RC a ration bar. He crunched into it, made a face, then swallowed. "I know a few things. I still have friends coreward. The Emperor and the Empress haven't been seen in public in over a year. The Chancellor is running things. He's been quietly recalling troops and ships to the Core. This isn't the only planet that has lost its garrison, or its ships. There's a lot of unrest out there. And a lot of it has been coalescing around my old gambling buddy, Devin, Lord Lyon. Word is the Chancellor is gathering his strength and might declare himself Emperor."

"What? Nobody will support that."

"More than you think. But not everybody. The biggest opposition is suspected to come from your favorite Tribune. The Chancellor has been gathering troops to be ready to stage a coup, and there are other nobles that will be visited by the Chancellor's forces and taken in their homes, before they can start to rebel. He figures to squash that problem before it starts."

"Devin will never let him take them!" Lee said. *I have to let Devin know!*

"That's what I think too." RC bit another bite from his bar. "I dislike that stiff-necked, arrogant, pompous twit. Thinks far too highly of himself, and he hates the little people like me."

"You're almost talking like you're on his side?"

"I'm on my side. The way I figure it, the Chancellor will win in the Core. He's got the troops, the ships, and surprise on his side. What he doesn't have is an easy way to get at Devin. That self-exile thing of his was a masterstroke. He's in the biggest and least populated sector, but he's so far away, the Core Navy can't get at him. And he's got lots of friends out here. The Chancellor will expect me to fight Devin if he comes in here, and if I lose, he'll have my head chopped off. So will Devin if I fight him. Say what you will about Devin the snob, but he keeps his word."

"He's promised to cut your head off if he sees you again."

"Which is why I'm not going near him without something that he'll trade for."

"Such as?"

"Not only Imperial movements in this sector—that's your datapak, but the list of all the reinforcements coming out to the Verge. And all the Imperial garrisons and ship deployments out here. The real numbers—not the supposed strength. I know he's got Marines and some ships. He can take half the sector over without a fight if he knows where to go first, and the other half will surrender once he's got the first half. If he knows where to go."

"You have that information?"

"That's the first datapak I put in the truck."

"You'll tell him that?"

"If he promised not to kill me, yes. But he has to do it soon."

"And why does he have to do it soon?"

"Because of the convoy coming out to reinforce all the critical imperial stations. Big convoy. Weapons. Supplies. Garrison troops. Let them get out here and it's ten times more difficult."

"A convoy? Coming out here?"

"Yep."

Devin needs to know this. "We have to let the Tribune know. Right away."

"Sure, go ahead."

"Wait." Lee shook her head. "You wouldn't have said this unless you had some sort of angle on this. What are the details?"

"Rather than what are the details, you should say, where are the details?"

"Fine. Where are the details, Governor?"

"In the second datapak. Encrypted, of course." RC grinned. "Take me to see Devin, and I'll give them to him. For a price."

Chapter 32

"Well, at least now we know where he ran to," Dirk said. "How big a resupply convoy?"

"Dozens of ships. Thousands of troops. Millions of tons of weapons and supplies," Lee said over the radio. "If you believe RC." Without the town car, they had no comm on the local channels, but RC had a radio disguised as a stove in his supplies. After the threat of plank-walking, he'd shown Lee where it was and suggested she confirm things with Dirk.

"I don't believe it." Dirk shook his head. He was in the communication room back at Empire House. "Why such a big convoy? Why not send it out a ship at a time?"

"RC says that they've been stripping the less important planets of Marines, ships and supplies, and sending them into staging points. They got them all together and put them under the control of the regular Navy to move things out."

"What units are they moving?" How could they do this without people noticing?

"No coherent units. A couple hundred Marines here or there, one ship, a Planetary Militia unit or two, and have them take their supplies with them."

"Planetary Militia? How did they get them to serve off planet?"

"Bribes. Promises. Lies."

"Lee, enough drama. Be specific."

"Trade concessions. Lowering of import or export duties. Promises for planetary independence."

"No way the Emperor would confirm those."

"The Emperor never hears about it. Not this one at least. Oh, and guess who the Naval Intelligence liaison is, according to the records?"

"Who?"

"Our old friends, Hernandez and Weeks."

"Not those two." Dirk and the crew had a number of dealings with both over the last few months. Ana called them the Tribune's tame spies. They'd been involved in a number of shenanigans that affected him. Scruggs had been more or less kidnapped by them, before escaping and saving their lives. But Devin trusted them. Something else to worry about.

Dirk clicked off the microphone and drummed his fingers. Colonies had Imperial-appointed governors, paid taxes and were restricted in the tech level they could import. And their inhabitants weren't imperial citizens—they couldn't vote for the Senate. Independent planets had self-government, control of their own taxes, a senator, and most importantly, their own armies. And if an ambitious warlord on an independent planet decided to capture the place and make herself rich, well, that was for the independent government to deal with, not the Empire.

But, how could he use this information to help Devin? How did the convoy change things? And what type of help would he need if the revolt went full steam ahead?

Dirk clicked the microphone. "Lee, are you sure? He could be lying."

"I'm sure he's lying about lots of things, but there's so much information there that we need to get it to the Tribune."

"Well, you're right about that."

"And, Dirk, he didn't have to tell us about this radio. We'd never have caught it unless he showed it to us. We can count on his own self-interest. He's committed. He needs to get off this planet. We've got him, his money, and his kids."

"How much longer 'til you can get to the starport?"

"We can't travel at night, we'll run aground. We're tied up to the shore right now. Clara says we can leave in the morning. We can make it to the dock day after tomorrow, unload all this stuff and be on the ship by nightfall. Provided the Marines let us on, and none of the local factions bother us."

"I could come and get you. The Marines at the starport have one helicopter—"

"And the rebels have at least one surface to air missile. You want to go first? We're pretty secure on the river here. What about the Marines?"

"The Marines won't bother you. They want to be left alone. They're kind of confused out here. Did you know that most of them left a few months ago?"

"RC told us. According to him, the Chancellor has been stripping planetary garrisons to reinforce the Verge forces. That's what this convoy is for. They've been picking up troops from isolated garrisons, like Andaman."

"Let me think about it."

"What about the local... warlords?"

"They've been leaving us alone. One group won over the others, or they've come to some sort of agreement as to who's top dog now. No fighting in two days, and the stores are re-opening."

"Hope that stays in place."

"Maybe. One group sent a note, said they wanted a meeting. I'm stalling them."

"How much longer can you stall them?"

"Not long enough for you to get down the river, load up the ship, and get back here. They could have a couple hundred troops shooting at us real soon now."

"The Marines will stop them. And they won't shoot at Empire House. They're too scared of Imperial retaliation."

"Maybe before. Not sure now. And your barge isn't Empire House."

"How's the centurion?"

"You're asking about the old man now? Listen to you."

"He's part of the team. Him. You. Even Rocky."

"Doctor says he's stable, but needs to stay in the pod while the drugs do their work. Surgery was successful. All the sutures and ties and things are closed. We have to wait."

"Don't wait too long," Lee said. "We need to get out of here."

Clara steered all the next morning, relieved for breaks by the others. She pushed the engines to maximum speed, but after bouncing off two mud banks, throttled down. Gavin talked Scruggs into spending the day on wood-shoveling duty. She was the youngest and fittest, and the best suited for a full day of physical exercise.

Plus, she got to work with Cleon, and he took off his shirt.

"He is a nice-looking boy." Dena swung a hammer. She was punching holes in the truck cab to feed tow lines in. "I might be interested in him myself."

She and Gavin had rigged the crane to haul the truck vertical. Because of his arm, Dena did the actual rigging with Gavin supervising.

"Punch a hole in the side there, on that metal support, then feed this cable through there, and back on itself."

"Why on this side? Why not closer to the crane?"

"If we attach it on the other side, it will drag closer. This way, we'll lift the far side up, and once it's high enough, gravity will take over and it will topple over and land on the wheels."

"You think?"

"I know. I know cranes. I also know that the way Scruggs is looking at that boy, you touch him, and she'll cut your fingers off."

"She'll cut my arms off. She's infatuated."

"He likes her too."

"He's scared of her."

"So am I." Gavin shrugged. "We all should be. She's smart as a whip, motivated, and gets more and more experience in fighting all the time."

"We all have." Dena fed the cable through the holes. "Clip like this?"

"Yep. Like that. Now back to the winch and haul."

Gavin was good as his word. It took fifteen minutes of turning the winch handle, but the truck lifted off the ground, then inched higher and higher, until a passing wave rocked it upright and over. It landed solid on all four wheels.

"I can't believe you're stealing my money," RC said. The crew let him wander, but Lee had checked his bags for weapons, confiscating several. The rest of them were armed, including the twins. He'd complained, until Scruggs said he could pick any gun he wanted. Then she'd pick one, and they'd put both them on the floor. Then Lee would start counting, and if RC was still alive by the time Lee reached ten, he could keep it. If he wasn't, Scruggs got to keep his gun.

RC declined.

"It's not your money. It belongs to the Empire, in the person of Tribune Devin now," Lee said, coming up behind him. "Good job with the truck."

"I can't believe Devin is stealing my money. I can't believe he'd stoop to this."

"Believe or not believe, it's not yours anymore," Lee said. "Guys, it's getting late. I'm going to get Clara to stop for the night and get moving first light tomorrow. Then we'll only be a couple of hours to the landing."

"What happens there?"

"You hide in the truck. We all get onboard, drive off the barge, up to the starport, and onto the *Heart's Desire*. Then we fly back to Empire House, pick up Dirk and Ana and Rocky, and go see Devin. You keep hidden and nobody will know you're here."

"I could help get us past the Marines at the starport."

"Dirk's already arranged that."

"What about the bandits? If they're at the landing, there will be trouble."

"Dirk's dealing with that right now."

"How's he going to fix that problem?"

"In his own inestimable way."

"What does that mean?"

"It means trying to estimate how he'll do it is stupid, because nobody has any idea."

"Sure. No problem. Right away," Dirk said. He sat behind RC's old desk in Empire House. He folded his hands and waited for his visitor to continue.

"And if you disagree—wait. What?" Narla said.

"More local control is fine. I don't need to talk to anybody. I'm the acting governor. I'll appoint you as a member of my advisory council. You and say... four others. Five total. I'm appointing you as advisors on local government issues. I'll issue a temporary charter for a city council, and what do you call em? Counties? Do you have counties?"

"Yes."

"What's the head of a county called? A mayor?"

"The governor calls them wardens." Narla tilted her head. "You're giving us control? What's going on here?"

"It's time for the citizens of Andaman to participate more fully in their local government." Dirk remembered Narla from the party. He was hazy on which family she represented, but she had worn sapphires that matched her eyes, and her orange and gold dress had hugged a pleasing shape. He liked pleasing shapes.

He'd told the Marine to pass the word he wanted to talk to the head of the 'orange and gold' people. Narla and two guards had arrived to talk. "I don't want any more of the... activities... that have occurred here recently. The best way is to give you more control of your own affairs."

"But you can't do that. We have to..." Narla blinked. "There has to be an election. And a petition to the Emperor. And the Senate has to have hearings and send out an investigation board to report. Then there's a consultation period."

"Impressive." Dirk nodded. "You learned that in school?"

"I did." Narla glared at him. "I'm not dumb. I'm a civil engineer. I studied in the Core."

"Pretty and smart." Dirk smiled.

Narla didn't smile. "I don't think you're used to smart women. You like your women dumb?"

"Of course not." But it does make things much easier. Best change the subject. "And you came back here why?"

"I was tired of your superior Imperial snots always looking down on me. There, I was an unwashed colonial. Here, I'm one of the first families."

"Better to rule in hell than serve in heaven," Dirk said.

"Milton. Boring book. I had to read it in university." Narla shook her head. "Where's RC?"

"No idea right now." It wasn't a lie. Dirk hadn't looked at the river map.

"You kill him? You want to take his place?"

"You think a superior Imperial snot would kill for this planet?"

"No, I do not. And certainly, Dirk Friedel, the Butcher of New Madrid, wouldn't."

"You know me?"

"Know of you. We do get some off-world news. Friend of the Empress. Close friend of the Empress, some say. Convicted of treason. Pardoned by a certain Tribune Devin, Lord Lyon. Who is currently in charge of the Verge Sector."

"Good intelligence. Know anything else?"

"Why have all the Marines and ships been swept out of here?"

"Why do you think?"

"I think it might be a good time for a revolution, if we wanted to get rid of the Empire."

Dirk drummed his fingers on his desk. "Think you could overrun Empire House?"

"Wouldn't touch it. Too easily defensible. The starport, on the other hand, we could take that in an hour. Too big, too open, not enough Marines."

"Interesting point. Drink?" Dirk stood and wandered to RC's liquor cabinet. "Lots of stuff in here."

"Pour the rum," Narla said. "It'll be the best."

"There's some imported Imperial wines here..."

"They are prestige items. Imported at great expense, but they're vile. The transit ruins them, but everybody pretends to like them because they come from the Core of the Empire. We have sugar cane here, and limes and lemons. Which means we have an excellent base for fruity drinks. Do you know how to make a rum punch?"

"No idea."

"Useless Imperial twit. Like all you useless Imperial twits." Narla stood, and pointed at her guards. "J and K can wait outside. Your Marines can join them."

Dirk nodded at the Marines, and the room cleared until it was he and Narla. Dirk sat on the edge of his desk and watched her mix drinks.

"First the rum. Dark rum." Narla dug through the bottles until she found the blackest and poured two generous mixes. "Class 7 colonies don't have elected city councils, or any elected councils for that matter. All officials are appointed by the governor."

"But Class 3 colonies do. Local councils, local elections. All towns and cities have mayors. All chosen by popular election. The governor has a council to assist in governing. He can appoint people, or have them chosen by election. I'm going to appoint. And he can delegate certain powers to the council. Management of the local elections. Certain taxes. I appoint you and your friends to the council, you run things here for the next few years. I want five names before you leave here. One of them has to be you."

"You want me on the council?"

"I require you to be on the council."

"Why me?"

Dirk grinned. "You have pretty eyes."

"You're giving me supreme executive power because I have pretty eyes?"

"Better than making a lady in a lake throw a sword at you."

Narla pulled open drawers until she found a white powder. "Need sugar to cut the juice. My father will want to be on the council."

"Put him there. Or your mother. Or both. Or not. You pick. Five names including yours, but I want them before you leave."

"I could put my whole family on there."

"You could, but you won't."

Narla smiled. "Why won't I?"

"Because this fight thing, the one that just happened? You lost. Or, at least, didn't win."

"We didn't lose."

"Sure you did. I saw the burned buildings. It's a setback, but not yet a disaster. The real power in this planet is the rural areas. I'll bet your real power is outside of the city, plantations, factories, mines, regional towns. The others can't touch it. And I'll bet you were against this fight from the start. You're young, you're smart. You have a plan. Long-term plan. Your father doesn't like it, but he won't live forever. While he's alive, though, nothing will happen. I've never met him, but I know him."

Narla smiled wider. "Oh? Tell me about my father."

"This has been a lifetime thing for him. He wants a free Andaman, or power to the people, or something like that. He's been working on it for years. It defines him. The principled freedom fighter. He's never been off planet, has he?"

Narla shook her head. "No. So?"

"But he likes his position, he doesn't want to do anything. This planet is stuck in the status quo. I've seen this before. Lots of families, all locked in petty disputes, keeping each other down. He made a play to grab more of the off-world smuggling that... Kel? Colonel Kel? That's his name. Kel had the lion's share of the old governor's smuggling. You all do some, but he was the best of it. Your dad made a deal to get some of that, Kel didn't like it. First chance he had, he put a stop to that."

"You have a very strange mind."

"You ever going to finish that drink?"

Narla opened the refrigerator and pulled out a pitcher. "Lime juice." She topped up both glasses. "Now we need some herbs."

"What type?"

"We have a local mint analog." She rummaged through the fridge. "Here." She yanked a bunch out and shredded leaves onto the drink. "So my father is slowing me down?"

"He doesn't see beyond the current situation. Sure, more money, more power for your family. The other families don't want him to win, relative to them. It's all incremental."

"You're not making sense."

"What I'm saying, is rather than fighting for the scraps in the pond, make the pond bigger. Rather than being the most important resource extraction family on a Class 7 colony, be the most important political family on a Class 3 colony. And Class 3 colonies always become Class 1 colonies eventually."

"Now you're promising a Class 1 colony? Why not an independent planet?"

"Not big enough population. That's a hard limit. You're not there yet."

Narla shoved the drink at him. "Try this."

Dirk took a big gulp. "Tasty. Refreshing. Can't taste the alcohol at all."

"It sneaks up on you. How would you do this?"

"I'm the governor. Temporary, but real. I submit a proposal to Tribune Devin that you be raised from a Class 7 to a Class 3 colony. He endorses it."

"The Tribune is not here right now. How will he endorse it?"

"I have one-use codes to approve legislation. I can make it official." *I hope that Devin doesn't ask too many questions when he finds out.*

"Really? He must trust you a lot?"

"He does." *Not as far as he can throw a tabbo, but if I get things fixed here before we leave, he might not stab me.*

Narla sipped her drink. "We're not in the Verge sector here. Tribune Devin is the governor of the Verge sector."

"So what? He's still a Tribune. He's the Empress's brother. He has consular power. He can sign proclamations. And after it's signed and published, it's official. Nothing to be done about that."

"So you put me and four others in charge of the planet?"

"You. Pick a couple from your family, or closely aligned ones. Smart ones, ones that might not win an election, but everybody knows are bright. A cousin, one that runs a mine or some heavy industry. And one of your best friends from college. The one who studied economics or finance. They'll know they owe their position to you, so they won't cross you. But they're smart enough to give good, disinterested advice, and non-threatening enough you'll take it. That way, you have a majority."

"You've got this all thought out."

"I'm an Imperial Duke. I've been doing political calculations with my family since I was a kid."

"Why didn't you go into the Senate?"

"It's boring. And my family already has a planet."

"Mine doesn't. Who will be the other council members?"

"One older one, head of a different faction. Conservative. Thoughtful. Keep the old people on your side. A friend of your dad, but not a close friend. And another young person, head of another different faction. Some guy who's in love with you. He'll go along with what you say as long as you flash your eyelashes at him."

"That's your political advice? Flash my eyelashes?"

"That's my human nature advice. And get a couple non-voting members at the meetings— other groups you need to keep sweet. Small ones."

Narla downed her drink. "Well well. I get all these wonderful things. What's the price? Do I have to sleep with you?"

"As fun as that would be, it's not a requirement." Dirk grimaced. "Listen to me, all grown up. No, I want the same thing from you any feudal empire wants."

"Which is?"

"Followers." Dirk figured if they could organize their own militia, they could organize getting it off planet. And every rebellion, even Devin's, never had enough troops. "Tell me about this Planetary Guard. How big? What type of weapons? And how reliable?"

Narla grinned and walked to the bar. "Sit down. I'll make us another drink."

Dirk sat.

"What are you going to have the Planetary Guard do?"

"You mean the Governor's Own?" Now Dirk grinned. "Why, their duty to the Empire, of course."

Chapter 33

"Electric junction boxes, breaker boxes, and switching modules sir." Imin checked the sidearm he'd been issued. "And while I'm there, I'll keep a lookout for any sort of berries. Even strawberries. And I'd like some honey, and I'm short of cream of tartar. Could really use that. And I wouldn't mind some balsamic vinegar."

"This is a combat mission, Imin," Devin said. "Not a shopping trip."

"I heard the Prefect call it a raid."

"Well, yes. We're raiding things now."

"Raids always capture things, don't they sir."

"Regardless, there might be some opposition."

"Of course sir." Imin handed his pistol back to Devin. "As you say, Tribune."

"What? What's this?"

"That's an officer's sidearm sir."

"I know that." Devin frowned. The *Pollux* battle group had jumped into the Lasadaris system and sped directly to the one inhabited planet. Santana's Marines had seized the naval station and were awaiting 'a naval liaison mission' to assess what items from the naval station's stores should be requisitioned. The word 'looted' was never mentioned.

Bosun McSanchez had assigned a crew, and Imin came along. Lord Devin had gone to the airlock to address the assigned crew. Prefect Lionel was behind him saying he planned to 'observe the Tribune's oratorical skills, and profit from his fine example'."

"With respect, Tribune." Imin gave back the pistol. "May one ask why you asked, then?"

"No, I mean, I know what it is. But why are you giving me this pistol?"

"Won't be needing it sir."

"Imin, I understand that the Marines have cleared the station. But there may still be disaffected naval elements around. You'll have to deal with them."

"No time for shopping, then."

"Right." Devin stared at him. "If you're not shopping, and if you have to engage with naval forces, won't you need the pistol?"

Imin laughed. "The Tribune is pleased to make a joke. Need a pistol to deal with naval forces? Very funny."

The line of naval crewmen behind Imin snorted and poked each other. Imin turned his head and furrowed his brow. All the crew shut up and snapped to rigid attention.

Devin glanced over the now-silent detachment. *They never act that scared of me.* What do they know that I don't? "Assume for the moment, Imin, that you don't need the pistol to deal with the naval crew that are below, how would you deal with them without a weapon?”

“Well sir.” Imin cocked his head. “The naval crew? They’re either going to be armed or not.”

“Yes.”

“If they’re not armed, I can take care of any…physical issues myself.”

“And if they are?”

“Well, if they’re armed, they’ll have some sort of weapon. I’ll take it from them. That usually satisfies things, and they stop arguing.”

“Won’t they resist this taking?”

“Attempt to resist, yes sir. Some will, I’m sure.”

“And will this resistance involve them trying to shoot these weapons at you?”

“It could sir. I’d rather they didn’t.”

“Because you don’t want to be shot?”

“Don’t want the station damaged sir.”

“But, what about yourself? Won’t you be damaged?”

“How will that be sir?”

“If they shoot you…”

Lionel interrupted, “Tribune. I think you’re confused. You’re conflating ‘shooting at’ with ‘hitting.’ Your steward doesn’t think they’ll actually hit him when they shoot.”

Devin swiveled his attention from Lionel back to Imin. “Imin, you don’t think the naval ratings will hit you if they shoot at you?”

Imin shrugged. “Never have yet sir. And I’ve given them plenty of opportunities.”

Devin fiddled with the pistol. "You don't need a weapon to deal with the Navy."

"No sir."

"Then." Devin held the pistol up. "What was this for?"

"The shopping sir."

"Shopping?"

"Yes sir." Imin nodded. "The berry people can be rough. And cream of tartar, well, let's say the real stuff is expensive and hard to get out here. Lots of money in that. Gotta watch your step with the tartar mafia people. They can get physical." Imin shivered. "Very scary."

"You're scared of a bunch of armed grocers?"

"Not scared exactly sir. Just careful." Imin shuddered. "But it's a good thing we're not looking for maple syrup. Those people are animals sir. I watch my step with him."

"You'll willingly attack an Imperial Naval station full of armed sailors, but you hesitate to steal tree sap?"

"Boiled tree sap. And yes sir. It's all about conducting a proper threat assessment."

"Which apparently I haven't done. Very well, do your shopping." Devin handed the pistol to Imin. It disappeared into his belt. "Prefect? Anything to add?"

"Excluding the grocery shopping, I heard that all you're taking is electrical junction boxes. Why not others, Imin?"

"Got that from the bosun sir." Imin nodded. "Asked him what he'd miss the most if it was in short supply. Military-grade electrical components, he said. Electrical, not electronic. If you can't get power to a weapons mount, or a sensor, doesn't matter how much computer capacity you have, or what type of sensors. Everything—life support, fuel pumps, sensors, bridge monitors—all need electricity. If the distribution goes bad and you don't have spares, you have to start to cannibalize your own ship. And he says the first thing that goes bad in combat is the electrics. Breaker boxes, switching units, that sort of thing."

"Can't they use civilian ones?"

"The bosun said they're not shielded, and they can't take higher voltages the military components use. Didn't realize it myself sir, but there are dozens of types, and they break all the time. Smart man, the bosun is."

"Indeed. Tribune, this sounds interesting. Perhaps I could accompany Imin while he does this supply run."

"As you wish. Carry on, Imin. Prefect."

Imin and Lionel saluted. Devin returned the salute and marched off.

Lionel regarded Imin. "So your plan is to hold the crews hostage while you loot the warehouse."

"Not exactly sir..."

"This," the supply clerk said. "This is a form IS-DD-214. Request for transfer of components from inactive storage."

"Correct, Senior Clerk Level-3—" Lionel leaned across the counter and scrunched his eyes. "Senior Clerk Level-3 Gallego."

Gallego was a middle-aged redhead. Tall, skinny, fit, she looked like she played volleyball in her spare time. "This is a long list. Mr....?"

"Steward Imin. Indeed." Imin nodded. "Comprehensive, in fact."

"I'm not sure we have everything on this list, Steward Imin." She frowned. "And I notice some of these are listed as 'all in stock'."

"We have extensive needs ma'am."

"I can't issue you everything. I need a quantity."

"I figure you can calculate that number, figure it out by yourself. Then tell me what I'm getting, and I'll sign for it." Imin gestured at the two heavily armed Marines standing behind him. "We'll do a count before we leave, of course. But as long as all the items in question have been reduced to zero, we'll take your word on it."

Gallego blinked, then grinned a broad smile. "Why, that's an excellent choice, Steward Imin. We can do that right away, no problem. It will only take a few minutes to get things sorted out. In fact, if you send a loading crew to the back, I can start issuing them boxes right away."

"Thank you ma'am."

"In addition, Steward Imin, I have some familiarity with these types of issues. Normally, other items, necessary components accompany them. I can add those to the bottom, correct?"

Imin grinned back. "That would be fine ma'am. Just one thing, this list was prepared by the bosun originally, and he'll need to be satisfied that he's receiving correct items."

"I'm sure we can take care of the bosun's concerns. How involved in this transaction is he?"

"Very involved ma'am. He feels that supply and operations are equal partners in the fleet's success."

"Equal partners?"

Imin nodded at the two armed Marines on either side of him. "He has a lot of responsibilities to take care of."

"Understood. I can get on this right away."

Lionel cleared his throat. "I'm not sure I understand what's going on here. We're here for spare parts, but I haven't heard of—"

Gallego glared at Lionel. "Who in a hydrogen blaze are you?"

"I'm Lionel, I'm—"

"Mr. Lionel is an associate of mine." Imin grabbed Lionel's shoulder. "Please excuse me while I explain a few things. Step over here." Imin stepped back from the counter and waved Lionel back.

Lionel didn't move. "What I want to know is—hey!" At a signal from Imin, the two Marines had spun, lifted Lionel high enough so that his feet cleared the floor, and brought him down the hall. Imin stepped back another two meters until they were out of earshot.

"Put him down here."

"Imin!" Lionel hissed. "What's going on? And you two. What's the meaning of that? You can't manhandle an Imperial Prefect!"

"Yes sir. Sorry sir." The Marine didn't sound sorry. "Brigadier Santana was very clear sir. In any sort of combat situation, or potential combat situation, we were to take Mr. Imin's orders sir. He seemed to want you moved down the hall, so here we are. Sir."

"I'm an Imperial Prefect."

"Yes sir. A *Navy* prefect."

"I'll speak to Santana about this."

"Yes sir. Of course sir. Brigadier Santana is always interested in the Navy's viewpoint. I'm sure he'll give it all the attention it deserves."

Lionel glared. "I obviously don't get it. What did I miss?"

Imin ran a hand through his hair. "We gave her permission to sell everything in there. She's going to give us probably half of what is in the depot. Everything we ask for, plus some other stuff. We get everything that we want, and she gets a paper saying we took piles and piles of other things. She'll sell everything to locals, zero out the stock, and it's not her fault."

"Oh." Lionel looked up. "That's why you didn't ask for specific numbers. She can fill in whatever numbers she wants."

"Right. And this way, we haven't done anything wrong. Nor has she. Nor has anybody. Not according to the paperwork. We empty the place, or she does, and if some other task force comes through here, there isn't anything."

"And that discussion about the bosun…"

"Lets her know we're serious sir."

"I put my foot in it, didn't I?"

"We can recover sir. Just follow my lead."

Imin led them back. The clerk stood with her arms crossed. "Sorry," Imin said. "Just some confusion here. Some numbers that didn't work out. But we've fixed it."

Gallego raised her eyebrows. "Is that so?"

"Everything's fine," Lionel said. "All taken care of."

"Well." Gallego shoved a tablet across at Lionel, then picked up her comm and typed. "Let's get this show on the road."

Lionel watched as the crew from the *Pollux* loaded box after box onto the shuttle. Another shuttle was dispatched to take the overflow, and cargo shuttles from the *Hydrogen Queen* arrived to collect even more.

Thirty minutes in, more people arrived at the loading dock, usually groups of two to four, in merchant ship coveralls. They came around the corner and did a double-take at the Marines and Navy personnel loading up. Gallego called them all by name and brought each one of them into a private office.

The office discussions lasted only minutes. The new arrivals re-appeared, and Gallego sent one of her crew into the shelves. Within five minutes, they were on their way. During the four hours that Lionel supervised the loading, a steady stream of naval ratings stuffed the shuttles with boxes large and small, and an equally steady stream of merchant crew carried their own piles of equipment away.

"Kind of like a day at the fair," Lionel said to Gallego.

"You think so, bud?" Gallego was curt. She hadn't been properly introduced, and Lionel had no plan of letting her know how high ranking he was.

"Like those ball-throwing booths. Everybody gets a prize."

Gallego cocked her head. "I guess so. Everything okay, Steward Imin?"

"Everything is fine, Senior Clerk-3." Imin nodded. "Looks pretty bare in there now."

"Your crews have been kind enough to help us in shifting some pallets. That makes it easier to access some of the more hard-to-reach items. We've encouraged the local Naval Reserve units put in their requests while we have available loading personnel."

"Nice of you to think of the Naval Reserve units," Lionel said. "They often get short shrift."

"I'm a patriot that way," Gallego said.

Lionel's comm bonged. "It's the boss, stand by." He stepped away and assured Devin that things were going well, and they'd be ready to go by the end of the shift. When he came back, Gallego eyed him.

"Who's that?"

"Our boss." Lionel looked at Imin. "The Tribune, Devin, Lord Lyon?"

"You work for that guy? The Mad Dog of the Verge? The one who single-handedly attacked the Nats and destroyed those task forces? And reoccupied that Confed planet?"

"That's him," Imin said.

"The Mad Dog of the Verge," Lionel said.

"I hear he cuts people's heads off with a big sword."

Both Lionel and Devin nodded.

"And whips his crew when they don't do what he wants?"

Lionel nodded.

"And makes them live on ice planets for days and days."

"Well, he's been on some ice planets—"

"And I heard." She lowered her voice. "I heard that he chops up his enemies with his sword into little bits, and then he has them put into stews and serves them to his crew. His crew eats all sorts of weird things—he makes them eat these tarts out of boiled bones, and stews flavored with human flesh." Her eyes were wide. "Is that true?"

"Don't tell anybody," Imin whispered, "but sometimes I have to make his stew. His special stew. That's what the cream of tartar is for."

"Special stew?"

"He loves it." Imin nodded. "He'd eat my stew every day if he could."

Gallego put her hand to her mouth. "Well, I certainly don't want to get on the wrong side of somebody like him. Anything he wants from here. Something I can get?"

Imin shook his head. "Nothing that you have here—"

"You got any berries?" Lionel asked. "Fruit berries?"

"Berries? What type?"

"Well, raspberries, strawberries, blueberries, blackberries, um...white berries, green berries?"

"Never heard of green berries."

"Yellow berries, then?"

"Yellow? Oh, bakeberries. We got lots of those."

"He loves those whatchacallit? Bakeberries? Especially."

"Frost! Heiml! Slater! Over here!" Gallego yelled at three of her staff lounging nearby. They held a whispered conference, and the three raced off.

"Give me a few minutes. I'm calling in some favors. I'll have everything you need shortly. We're almost ready to give you the last of your list anyways."

Lionel stood with his arms crossed, watching the last of the crews scuttling along. *Either they've all got what they want, or everything of value has been stolen. Or both.*

"Mr. Lionel," Imin said. "Next shuttle will be the last. Marines are ready to pull out at the other airlock." He waved to the two Marines lounging near them. "We don't need you two anymore. Check in with your gunnery-sergeant."

The senior Marine shook his head. "Gunny said we're to do what you say 'til you release us. If you say get on the shuttle, you're getting."

"That okay with you, Pre—I mean, Mr. Lionel?"

"If it isn't, will it make any difference?"

Imin shook his head. "Nope."

The three workers Gallego had sent off returned when the shuttle was nearly loaded up. They dumped plastic bins at Imin's feet.

Gallego came out and opened the top one. "Here's a present for your boss, the Mad Dog. Blueberries and raspberries in this one. From imported stores. Next one is all blackberries and mixed yellowberries. Bottom one is all bakeberries. You know how to use those?"

Imin nodded. "I've done them before. Dry them first, then grind them up. Tastes a little like currants."

"Exactly," Gallego said. The crew was back on the shuttle. The Marines stood waiting. Imin checked his comm and then pocketed it. "Looks like you're ready to go."

"Pleasure doing business with you." Imin shook Gallego's hand. "And thanks for the extra present. The boss will love this."

"Glad to help. He scares me." Gallego extended her hand to Lionel.

Lionel reached out and shook it. "Efficient operation you run here. Thanks for everything."

"Glad to help out."

"You did such a great job with the berries," Lionel said. "Next time I need something, we'll come back here."

"Thanks. Anything you need, ask."

"Well." Lionel pursed his lips. "Think you could get us some maple syrup?"

Gallego's face turned white. "Mmmm-aple syrup? You want me to get maple syrup?"

"Sure," Lionel said. "Shouldn't be too hard, for some-body—"

Gallego slapped her hand over Lionel's mouth. "Shsss. Shsss. Shsss." She glared at Imin. "What is wrong with you? You want to get us all killed?"

Imin gestured at the Marines. "He goes on the shuttle, now."

The two Marines picked up Lionel and hustled him back to the airlock.

"I was just—"

The biggest Marine put his beefy hand over Lionel's mouth. "Not right now sir."

Gallego shook her head. "Can you imagine?"

Imin nodded. "He doesn't get out as often as he should."

"Well," Gallego said. "A crazed mad dog who kills his ene-mies with a sword, chops them into bits and eats their flesh in stew, that's one thing. But the crossing the maple syrup people." She shuddered. "That's just scary."

Chapter 34

"The jungle is creepy," Scruggs said.

"Creepy? Jungles aren't creepy," Cleon said. "They're... majestic."

"The chirps. Buzzes. The noises. The water. Everything. Listen."

Cleon tilted his head to listen. Clara had lashed the barge to the trees on the outer side of a river bend, where the water was deepest. Everybody had gone to bed for the night, but Lee had assigned night sentry duties. Scruggs got the second shift, with Cleon relieving her after four hours.

The docking lines creaked and groaned as the barge spun with the current. Water gurgled past the hull and against the transom. Swarms of insects buzzed, and a light wind rustled the trees.

"All I hear is night sounds," Cleon said.

"But they're so loud. Why do they get louder at night?"

"They don't. The jungle always sounds like this. You don't notice it when the suns are out. Turn on a light and it won't be so loud."

"No. No lights." Scruggs's headshake was visible in the glow from the two moons on the horizon. "Lights attract notice. We don't want notice. And I'm not sure what's out there."

"There's nothing out there, Ms. Scruggs."

"Think again. Try these on." Scruggs leaned in to drape her sensor goggles over his shoulder. Her hands fumbled as she adjusted the straps over his shoulders. *Strong shoulders. Good muscle tone.* "Um. Look into the woods."

Cleon's hands lingered on hers as he adjusted the straps and fixed the goggles over his eyes. *Had he squeezed her hand? Maybe?*

"These are—wow. It's like daylight. I can see the deck, the truck. All the trees. It's almost like noon."

"That's the light-enhancing module. Click here." Scruggs pushed the status stud. "That one will show blues. Dark blue on the ground, the sky will be lighter. You might see a few bright spots in the sky."

"I see one. What is it? Stars?"

"Nope. Satellites. Radio frequency sources. Now click again."

"Everything's red. Oh. I see lizards. Two, three of them on the trunk. There's a gecko." He turned his head. "The ship is bright. Is this infrared?"

"Yes. The ship is the biggest heat source out here. But you'll see animals."

"These are amazing. Core technology. They must be very expensive."

"Very, very expensive. And hard to find."

"Did your Duke buy them for you?"

"My Duke? The Pilot?" Scruggs giggled. "No, he spends his money on food, alcohol, and women. I paid for these. The centurion had a pair, and I wanted my own. Stand up and do a scan. Full three hundred and sixty. The processors have pattern recognition. If they sense a person, they'll flag them."

"Like this?" Cleon scanned the jungle. "All I see is birds, bugs, and lizards."

"Look up and down river too. Look for other boats. And look up at the sky. Check the weather. We need to know if the weather is changing."

"There's no boats on the river except us. Nobody would travel at night. And why not just check the forecast?"

"Bad things happen at night, unless you pay attention. I remember..." Scruggs talked about her adventures with the crew. Almost getting flattened by a volcano. Visitors at a dinner killing the other guests. The pilot getting lost in a sandstorm. Sulfur rain. Wild dogs attacking them in the dark. Snowstorms. Floods.

"You got attacked by wild dogs?"

"In the snow. That's where we found Rocky."

"And people tried to kill you at a dinner?"

"Not us. Each other. That was where we got Dena."

"She was running away from the killing?"

"Um. No. She started it." Scruggs coughed. "I'm not—you better ask her if you want to know more about that. But all those things, that's why we always have a sentry. Keep an eye on things, in case something unusual happens."

"You are the most interesting girl I've ever met."

"I'm not a girl, I'm... never mind." *Should I try to kiss him?*

"Sorry. Woman."

"It's okay when you say it. Anyways, you must know lots of women. All those girls at the governor's ball. Those families."

"The locals?"

"That's a mean way of putting it."

Cleon's shrug was visible in the dark. "That's how they'd put it. We're the foreigners. They all were born here, grew up together, raced boats on the river together, went camping in the jungle together, went to the same schools. There's only a couple of reasonable schools on the planet, all the upper-class kids graduate together. We're just the latest Imperial scum come to steal their money."

"Do you steal their money?"

"Not as much as they steal from each other. RC isn't the nicest person in the world, but he told the truth. This is kind of like a little pot full of frogs. All the frogs jump up and down and try to drown each other. They're way meaner to each other than they are to us."

"How can you hate them so much if you've been here for years?"

"We've been here for years, but we're not from here. Dad died when we were young. We were kids. Then Mom married RC. Last few years, we've been out here. We had tutors. We lived in Empire House. We met everybody. They know us, but they don't like us. Everybody comes to the governor's parties and events. We see everyone there, but they never invite us anywhere. We're pretty much on our own. That's why we joined the Andaman guard. And why we want to leave."

"The governor's private army?"

"No, the planters' and the mine owners' private army. Household troops. Technically, they're 'unorganized Imperial Reserve units,' but they're really private armies. The officers all train together and we have dinners and things, and I've had to do field training. The families all ponied up some money, and RC let them buy uniforms and communication equipment and some weapons—for a commission, of course. Imperial surplus, of course. Old Imperial surplus, the older the better."

"That's news to us." Scruggs sniffed. "That smell. It smells like…"

"Mud. Dirt. And decaying trees. Whole planet stinks of it."

"If you're going to wear those goggles, you need to do a sweep."

"Who will know if I don't?"

"Me. And everyone. We write them down and save the sensor reports."

"Really?"

"Keeps everyone honest."

"Sorry." Cleon did the search. Scruggs coached him in how to report, how to save a snapshot of the weather, how to check close by the barge.

"We never did this in the guard. Half of our sentries sleep all night."

"If Centurion found a sentry asleep, he'd beat him half to death."

"Wow. You folks are hard core."

"It's a dangerous galaxy."

"If you found a sentry asleep, would you beat him up?"

"No." Scruggs shook her head. "Not me. Not a man."

"Why not a man?"

"I'm a small woman. Men are stronger. They're hard for a woman to beat in a physical fight."

"You'd let him get away with it?"

"Of course not. I'd shoot him."

"Shoot him? What?"

"Sure. That's what a gun's for. Shooting people. And a sentry who falls asleep puts everybody in danger. They need to be punished. Easiest way for me to punish them is to shoot them. I shoot them, everybody wins."

"You have a strange definition of winning."

Scruggs laughed. "Am I still the most interesting woman you've ever met?"

"Yes. And the scariest." Cleon's teeth gleamed in the dark, but he stepped slightly back from her.

Should have kissed him before. Too late now. Scruggs saved the sensor readings in her log. "How big are these armies?"

"Depends. Somewhere between one hundred and five hundred per family. We have way more officers than we need, and the families run them. Kel's family—you remember him?"

"The jerk with the nice gun."

"That's him. He claims he can raise five hundred soldiers if needed. They bought five hundred of everything, rifles, uniforms, that sort of things."

"Who pays for this?"

"Not the Empire. The locals, as you would say. They get uniformed bully boys, RC gets his cut, and we have parties. The officers at least. We're way over officered, that's for sure."

"You're in this?"

"Both Clara and I. Because we're the governor's kids, we're attached to the battalion headquarters. We do training, but we don't have to go live in the jungle."

"What type of training?"

"That's up to the companies, which means the families. Some do more than others. I've heard of some units doing cross-country marches, field maneuvers, but not many. Bullets cost money. Trucks cost money. Training costs money. Most of the families want to spend as little as possible. A couple times a year, everybody puts on their uniform, meets up for a display somewhere, does some marching, drinks beer then goes home."

"I saw uniformed Andaman guards at the governor's residence."

"You saw rich kids playing at being soldier and acting as self-important administrators. They're not real soldiers. The Marines despise them, but they have to put up with them because RC is their honorary colonel."

"Huh. That explains the troops on the road." Scruggs explained the different hijacking attempts on the way into town.

"I didn't know any of this. You said troops were blockading the starport?"

"Yes. Whose were they?"

"From the description, Kel's. His family. That could be a problem. He doesn't like me much. And I know he doesn't like you and your friends."

"And those truck types back at the loading port. They said they worked for Kel, and that RC was stiffing them."

"Looks like they decided to take things into their own hands."

"Sure does. Well, I need to get some sleep. Enjoy your shift."

"It's been nice talking to you, Ms. Scruggs."

"Sandra. Call me Sandra."

"Nice talking to you, Sandra. Good night."

Scruggs went to the ladder to climb down to her bedroll on the lower deck.

"Sandra?"

"Yes?"

"What happens at the unloading point? If Kel's people are there."

"Pilot will figure out something. He always does."

Clara got them moving at dawn. "Pull the ropes!"

They'd run a rope onto shore, around a tree, and back onboard. Cleon, Scruggs and Dena untied then hauled the ropes back in.

"Clara's good at this," Dena said. "She'd make a great boat captain."

"She wouldn't mind being one," Cleon said. "She hasn't decided what to do at school. She was talking about engineering, but..."

The paddlewheels thrashed and the tug and barge pulled out onto the river. The water rushed by.

"Feels different today." Scruggs walked to the crane. "Slower. Everything tied up like normal, right?"

"That's because we're going to get off this wooden plank boat and back onto a real starship. You're getting anxious. I want some air conditioning. The humidity is getting to me."

"I wouldn't mind a shower," Lee said.

Scruggs peered into corners. "Too much water."

"For a shower? On the ship?" Lee shook her head. "Never use too much water for a shower. And we recycle the water."

"There." Scruggs pointed down the hatch next to the crane. "That well thing. What did Clara call it? The bilge? Down there. It's full of water."

Gavin leaned over the edge of the barge. "Hey. We're lower in the river. Yesterday, the bolts on the side were visible. Today, they're under water."

Cleon ran to get Clara. Lee spelled her at the wheel. Clara hopped into the well and crawled under the deck. Scruggs and Dena made inane suggestions.

"Well?" Dena asked when a soaking Clara climbed out. "Tell us there isn't a big leak."

"There isn't a big leak."

Dena let a breath. "Good. I was worried."

"It's not a big leak," Clara said. "It's a giant leak. We're sinking. Well, the barge is sinking. There's a big crack halfway up the starboard side, the hull is flexing and water rushes in every time it strains."

"How did that happen?" Dena asked.

"Remember when we crashed into the dock? We hit hard. Must have cracked a weld."

"Why didn't we notice before?"

"Not sure. If I had to guess, the crack is smaller, deeper down. I can't see under the water, but we've probably been leaking since we left. The more we leak, the lower we go. The lower we go, the more the crack is exposed, the more water we get. So we're taking on water faster and faster."

"So we fix it, right?"

"You have any welding equipment and metal plates hidden under that dress?"

"Not that what I'm wearing doesn't generate heat, but... Gavin!"

"What?"

"You have welding equipment and metal plates?"

"Sure." Gavin nodded. "On the ship."

"There? See?" Scruggs clapped her hands. "We get to the ship, and Gavin can get his gear, and fix it. No problem."

Everyone stared at her.

"Oh, right. We need to get there first. Um, how much longer 'til we—"

"Don't know." Clara headed back to the tug. "I need to check the bilges on the tug. If that's taking on water too..."

Clara checked the well. It was bone dry.

"Right. The tug will stay up. We won't drown."

"But the barge will sink," Dena said.

"Eventually. But we're only a couple of hours from the landing. We can keep it up that long."

"But when it sinks, won't it drag us down…"

"We need to unload the truck…"

"Can we fix the leak…"

"Let's uncouple from the tug…"

Everyone shouted. Everyone argued, and Lee yelled down to find out what was happening. Everyone yelled back.

"Shut up," Lee yelled. "Clara, you said when the hull flexes, it takes on water."

"Yes. The more flex, the more water."

"What makes it flex?"

"It flexes when we pull, every time we turn."

"What if we push the barge rather than pull it?"

"Well. Yes. That will work. We won't flex as much."

"Get up here and turn us around. Dena, get down there and get a look at that leak, see if there is anything we can do to cover it. Or stuff it closed. Seal it shut. Gavin, take a look at the tow connections, those cables and those bars. See if we can cut the barge loose. Scruggs, Cleon, get the datapaks off the truck. Any weapons and food as well. Get it on the tug. Go."

"Who put you in charge?" RC yelled up.

"We all did," Dena said.

"What about my money?"

"Move it or not, your choice," Gavin said. "Let's go, every-one."

The crew scattered. Clara steered them into the middle of the river and did a wild spin. Waves washed over the sides as they came broadside. When they were done, the barge was plowing down the river stern first, and the tug had both wheels in full reverse, pushing it along. Now the rear of the wheelhouse blocked the view. Lee steered while Clara hung out of the window and yelled instructions.

"That was fun," Dena said. "I want to learn how to do that."

"Maybe later," Gavin said. "What's up with the crack?"

"It's huge, and it goes down about three feet. I can get my fingers in it. Get me some blankets or shirts or something, and something to pound with. I'll try to jam it."

"Hammer and chisel in my tool kit," Gavin said. "Scruggs, can you get the blankets from the cabins?"

"On it."

"Cleon, can you help me try to unjam some of these clips holding us together?"

"I'm supposed to be on wood-shoveling duty," Cleon said.

"Fine. Mr. RC, can you give me some help?"

"I'm not a stoker."

"True, you're not. Well, I guess we need to lighten our load. We could dump those gold bars first. They're heavy."

RC cursed. "Show me these clips."

They met at the wheelhouse so Lee could hear.

"Left. Left. More left," Clara said. Lee spun the wheel.

"Lee, you're turning the wrong way," Dena said.

"We're going backwards, so I turn right to go left," Lee said. "Rudder's in front of us now, so it works backward."

"That makes no sense." Dena watched the river. "But it seems to be working."

"Did you seal the crack?"

Dena shook her head. "I tried, tried jamming the blankets in. Cut different pieces. They stick for a while, then either the flex or the water pushed them out. I marked the wall where the water was to measure the flow."

"Bulkhead."

"Whatever. The water level is rising. I can keep jamming things in there, but the water's climbing."

Lee turned the wheel slightly. *This is worse than I thought.* "You can't stay down there. If we get too much water coming in, we'll go down quickly. If you're down there, you'll drown. Stay up here. Gavin, what about the towing clamps?"

Gavin shook his head. "Those clips holding us together are rusted shut. They haven't moved in years."

"Can you cut them?"

"They're metal bars. Not chains. Even if we take axes to it, we'll just dent them."

"Scruggs?"

"The datapaks and our gear is below. Um, the datapaks are heavy, they won't float. And I don't think the boxes are water-proof. We can't let them get into the water."

"Outstanding," Lee said. "Cleon?"

"We've still got lots of firewood. Lots and lots. We could burn things twice as fast, and still have plenty of wood left."

"For what that's worth."

"Lee!" Clara yelled. "More wheel. More left."

Lee spun the wheel all the way to the stops. "Hard over."

"Hard over?" Dena said.

"Ship talk," Cleon said.

"It's going to be close. Hang on." Everybody grabbed the wall or the door. They slid majestically to the left.

The barge swung as they surged around a sharp corner. They brushed the overhanging trees. Once they were past, Lee centered the wheel again.

Clara stuck her head back in. "The barge is so low and has so much water, it steers like a pig. We're barely making these turns."

"Use the engines?" Gavin suggested. "Pivot with them in opposition?"

Lee shook her head. "If we pivot, we'll warp the barge and break that crack ever wider open. Then we'll sink faster. Clara, how much longer to the Landing?"

"Less than an hour, at this speed."

Outstanding. "Are we going to sink before we get there?"

"It's hard to be sure."

"Guess."

"Probably, yes. At the rate the water's coming in, with the reduced freeboard. We'll all be okay if we all stay on the deck. We won't go down that fast, we'll swamp and sink slowly."

"Who can't swim?" Dena asked.

"Don't need to swim," Gavin said. "All that wood piled on the deck, that will float off. We can hang on to that."

"Trucks don't float," Dena said.

"We need to save the truck," RC said.

"You mean save your money." Lee spun the wheel an inch. "We're in trouble. The barge is sinking, we can't cut it loose, and all our data and equipment will end up at the bottom of the river." Clara waved, and Lee turned an inch left. "I have an idea. Cleon, you sure about how much wood we have?"

"We have more cut wood than we'll ever need. If we run out, we can burn the deck cargo."

"Right. Everybody get your gear on deck and tie it to something that will float. Then get back up here. I've got a plan."

Chapter 35

"**B**ut I don't understand how you talked to them." Dirk looked across the gorge. Three soldiers in Narla's colors stood at the opposite end of a rope bridge, next to a truck. "Radio net is down. Comm net is down. Everybody is jamming everybody. How are they here?"

"I called them on the phone." Narla grabbed the upper guide rope. The rope bridge was pedestrian only.

"Phone? Like a comm?" He and Narla had struck a deal. She and her allied troops would help him get the others off-planet, taking on Kel if necessary. They'd get a signed warrant from the Tribune declaring them a Class 3 colony, with her in charge of the council. She'd promised him five hundred Andaman guard for 'external operations.' He was a bit hazy about the external operations, but he had some ideas. She'd demanded concessions. He'd agreed, without thinking too hard about what she asked for.

"You call them on a telephone? A radio telephone?"

"This one doesn't use radio. This one uses wires."

"Wires? You mean like... physical wires? Like fiber optics?"

Narla shook her head. "We don't have the technology to make fiber optic cables here. Or radios. We're too small. We import all that stuff. Costs a fortune. But we make cables for the mines, and we have lots of metal. We make copper cables. Insulate them with sap from the trees. Roll them in it, it hardens up nicely and acts as an insulator. When we put in a road to a mine or a jungle camp, we put in some cables and a phone."

"You talk to your mines on metal wires covered with tree sap?"

"We don't have a satellite network. Too expensive. We don't have a cellular network except for the one based at Empire House. Also too expensive, and we couldn't maintain it even if we had one. We have radios, but those are line of sight. We don't have orbital repeaters. That's core technology that we can't repair. But we can make wire, and we can make telephones, and they work fine. We're not some rich core planet where we have everything. Now, are you crossing this bridge, or are you going to keep staring at my butt?" Narla flounced onto the rope.

"Can't I do both?" Dirk climbed up behind her. One look down into the canyon, the very deep canyon, and Dirk decided that that staring at her butt was much safer. *That's my story and I'm sticking to it.*

At the far side, they climbed into a waiting truck. Two others filled with troops sat ahead of it. "I thought the bridge was blown?" Dirk asked. "How did you get the truck here?"

"It was already on this side of the bridge."

Dirk glanced around the cab. "Never seen a truck like this. You make them here?"

"They come in parts. We put them together. And we order just the parts we need, the ones we can't fix or make locally."

"How'd you call it if the wires were down?"

"Wires didn't go over the bridge that blew up. They've got their own connection. Kel has twenty-two people at the starport watching things, searching the trucks. I've called in twenty-five of mine, and my friends are sending another thirty-five. That will be enough to get your friends. You're sure you can give me what I want?"

"I've got the proclamation all set," Dirk said. "Soon as we're back at Empire House, I'll broadcast it."

"My troops are coming with you to Empire House."

"I know, I know. You told me. But not all of them."

"Just to make sure. I don't entirely trust you."

"I don't see why not." Dirk smiled. "Why would I lie to you? What's in it for me if I do that? I want your help, I want my friends on our ship, I want Kel out of the way."

"And you want your sick friend in the med pod off planet, which you won't get unless I get what I want." Narla had insisted on leaving Ana behind in the med pod, in care of the Marines and Rocky. Dirk agreed. After seeing Ana's awards, the Marines would take good care of him. And if anything went sideways, he wouldn't be any help in his current condition, regardless.

Rocky had protested, but after Dirk used the word 'guard,' he'd gone back to the med pod and lay in front of it, growling at any strangers who came near.

The truck rocked past another corner. "How long to the main road?"

"Not going to use it. We'll stay north of it, and come to the starport from the far side, then down to the landing. We'll meet your friends there, and deal with Kel, all at the same time."

"You don't like Kel very much."

"I don't care about Kel. He's a pompous, self-centered, irritating twit who thinks he's Jove's gift to women, but I could deal with that. We dated for two years."

"He was different when you first started dating?"

"No, he's always been an ass. I've known that since childhood."

"But you still dated him?"

"Small planet. Limited dating pool. But mostly, it ticked off my dad."

"You dated someone you hated to make your parents angry?"

"Haven't you ever done something incredibly stupid just to irritate your parents?"

Dirk laughed. "That's why I joined the Navy."

The truck ahead crashed over a hump and spewed up a particularly dense cloud of dust. Dirk gasped and waved the dust away. It didn't work, instead coating his face and gumming up his hair. He spat out a mouthful and peered ahead into the gloom. *Join the Imperial Navy. See the stars. Eat their dust.*

Two hours and twenty dusty minutes later, the road swung around the side of a cliff. A mud-red river snaked below them, jungle running right up to the edge. The river was so wide, the far shore was a thin green line. The leading truck honked its horn five times in a row, then stopped. The two trailing trucks skidded to a stop. Narla hopped out and conferred with the other drivers. Dirk climbed out to ease his aching back—suspensions seemed to be a technology that Narla's people hadn't bothered to order.

The three drivers and Narla were shading their eyes and staring upriver. A giant plume of smoke stretched into the sky from the middle of the jungle. The four of them had a rapid conversation in a language Dirk didn't understand.

"What language is that?"

"Local dialect. Not important."

"None of the briefing mentioned you having your own language."

"We don't use it around outsiders. We all speak standard."

"What's it called?"

"It's called Outsiders-don't-know-everything. Mount up." The crews climbed back into their trucks.

Dirk pointed at the smoke. "That's a lot of smoke. What's burning?"

"No idea. The guys don't know either."

"What's out there?"

"River and jungle."

"Can the jungle burn?"

"Never has before."

"So what is it?"

"A surprise."

Dirk thought about all his time in the Navy, all the time on *Heart's Desire*, dealing with Tribune Devin, his crew, the Empire, the Emperor, the Empress, and all the other things that had happened in his life.

"You know what?"

"What?"

"I don't like surprises."

The three trucks passed a sign that read 'Starport 5km' that pointed up and to the right. Instead, they turned left and followed switchbacks from the plateau down to the river valley.

"Shouldn't you be going up to the starport and arresting the troops there?" Dirk asked.

"Is that what you call it? Arresting?" Narla asked.

"You will be the executive council, so yes."

"But we're not yet."

"I'm the acting governor. I can order them arrested."

Narla shook her head. "If some outsider starts telling my boys what to do, then they'll do the opposite they're told, and all the other families will band together to resist the outsider."

"You hate outsiders that much?"

"The only thing we hate more than outsiders is each other."

Dirk slid sideways as the trucks rocked down a hill. "Shouldn't you be looking for ambushes?"

"With what? Our secret satellites that we don't have?"

"A squad of men with good leadership could easily block this road."

"Good leadership, huh. I could have sent half of my boys to block the road to the starport. Know why I didn't?"

"No."

"Because I can only trust them when I can see them. We don't have any decent officers. I couldn't even put my dad up there, even if he had come along. He'd want to make a speech and then leave for some rum punch. I do have one cousin who's competent. I'm putting them on the council." Narla cocked her head. "How'd you know I had a cousin I could trust?"

"Every family has that one cousin, the one who makes it work. It's a law of nature."

"Anyway, he's back in town keeping an eye on things, making sure my boys don't start a bigger war by shooting at Empire House. Out here, everyone is under my eye. And if something goes wrong, they'll look to me to sort it out."

"Outstanding." Dirk grabbed the window as they bounced over a pothole. "Do you want me to talk to Kel's people when I get there?"

"That is exactly what I don't want you to do. Just keep your mouth shut and I'll take care of this."

"You sure?" *She might do a better job as council president than I thought.*

"I'm going to be on the Planetary Council. People need to get used to taking my orders."

The bluffs climbed behind them, a sea of green trees with lines sliced out below where the road appeared. The trucks screeched around the final corner and arrived at the landing. The road down had been paved thus far, and wide enough for two trucks at a time. It arrived on the flat land and ran out to nothing. The convoy swung left, bumped down the bank and onto a flat dirt plain. The river was two hundred yards to their left, separated by the muddy field.

They roared along, beside the river bend, and then a dirt causeway appeared in front of them. The ground had been bulldozed to form a ramp up to the top. The causeway stretched off to their left, into the river. Twenty feet into the water wooden rafts replaced the dirt. Fifty feet later, the rafts connected to a floating dock.

"What the heck is this?"

"Docks float. River is up, or river is down, docks are at water level," Narla said. She leaned sideways and spoke to the driver. "The docks and those rafts get towed here as the water level changes. We bulldoze a dirt path to the floats. Make it shorter or longer as needed."

"Slick."

"We're poor, not stupid." Narla blew the horn five times. That must have been the 'everyone stop' sign because the first truck slid to a halt, the others following.

"Move. I need to talk to the drivers." Dirk climbed out and waited. Narla hopped out, conferred briefly with the drivers, then hopped back into the truck, Dirk following. This time, their truck took the lead. They drove up onto the ramp and onto the causeway. The second truck followed.

Dirk craned his neck. The third truck stopped at the land end of the causeway. Soldiers spilled out of the third truck. "Where's Kel's people?"

"Don't know."

"Where are your other friends?"

"Don't know."

"Where's the barge?"

"Don't know."

"This going to war without radios is a problem," Dirk said.

"Communications are a force multiplier that we don't have," Narla said. When she caught Dirk's look, she grinned. "Didn't think the peasant girl knew all your fancy military terms, did you? Like I said, we're poor, not stupid."

The first truck slowed to a crawl, and edged onto the floating rafts, then drove down to the T-junction. The other truck stopped behind them, engine running.

Narla shouted orders and waved her hands a lot. When finished, their truck was pointed back inland, with the rear facing the river, ready to be loaded. The second truck had returned to the dirt ramp, also facing inland. Soldiers surrounded each truck, carrying rifles. The sergeant or whatever the leader was called handed around large green leaves.

"We're all set." Narla pointed. "Base of the ramp is protected so we can't get blocked in. We're out here to load up whatever your friends bring in. The middle truck keeps unfriendlies from getting close to the shore end of the pier."

"Good tactical sense," Dirk said. "Glad somebody paid attention in college."

One of the troops yelled and pointed upriver. A huge plume of smoke curled to the sky around the nearest bend.

"Is the boat on fire?" Dirk asked.

"Could be," Narla said.

"That could be a problem," Dirk said.

"It could." Narla shrugged. "But I'm not worried about that right now."

"And why not?"

"Because." Narla pointed at two vehicles sweeping down the dirt from upriver. "That's our problem right now. Kel's here."

Chapter 36

Mud spattered from the wheels of the four-door station wagon as it skidded to a halt at the water's edge, the loaded pickup following. Kel opened the car door and leaned on it. "Squad, spread out." Six men and two women jumped down from the back of the pickup truck behind him, and formed a loose group behind him, rifles in hand.

"Hello, Kel." Narla waved from the dock's end. "You're looking handsome as always." She leaned on the side of her truck. Her crew ranged behind her, covering Kel with their rifles. Her other squad had done the same. Only the vehicle onshore was still loaded, engine running, the driver watching.

Dirk stood. "I'll go—"

Narla shoved him back behind the truck without looking. "You'll stay there 'til I tell you otherwise, thank you very much."

"Narla. What are you doing?" Kel yelled. "Have you gone completely insane?"

"Now that's no way to talk to an old friend, Kel. I thought we parted on good terms. It didn't work out, I know that, but

I thought we really had something there. Something special, something different."

"Narla, you're completely off your rocker. What are you doing up there? Why the guns?"

"Waiting for my special off-world shipment to arrive." Narla smiled. "Or I should say, the special shipment that I'm going to send off-world. It's coming down the river."

"Narla, you know that my family takes care of these things. We do the special shipments. We've got a deal with the governor."

"Well, things have changed, Kel. RC isn't in charge. There's a new governor. Tribune Devin has appointed Duke Dirk Friedel the new Governor of Andaman."

Kel pointed. "That Dirk Friedel?"

"Yes."

"The Butcher of New Madrid?"

"That's the one."

"Narla, you can't trust him. He's just another overdressed pretentious Imperial twit with his nose in the air and a stick up his butt who spends his time avoiding responsibility, wasting his family's money, and slouching along with low-class women. Whatever he said to you, it's a lie."

"Hey—" Dirk started to stand.

Narla shoved him back down. "Stay put," she hissed, then turned to Kel. "I disagree completely."

A gabble of yells distracted them. The truck crew pointed upriver. A shower of sparks filled the plume of smoke at the bend.

Kel's people readied their guns. "You disagree with what?"

Narla shrugged. "Well, I think he has good fashion sense. But the rest is all true."

Dirk stood. "What? Ouch." He ducked back. This time, Narla had slapped his head.

Kel crossed his arms. "So why are you here? We don't need your help. And we certainly don't need his help."

"Well, Kel, the new governor and I made a deal. You're looking at the new head of the executive council."

"The executive council? We're a Class 7 colony. We can't have an executive council, we need, um, something. The planet needs to be voted on, or whatever."

"We're going to be Class 3 Planet. We're going to have a council. Me and four others. I think probably...Mywint. Lwin. Chee. And Zan."

"Two of your cousins."

"Zan's your great-uncle."

"You know he and Dad don't get along."

"Sounds like a family problem to me."

"And Lwin can hardly stop slobbering on himself when he sees you."

"That's true." Narla smiled. "It's kind of cute." She ducked down and whispered to one of her rifleman. "Thul. When the shooting starts, empty your magazine into the car. Then run back to the other truck and tell Tak to bring his squad down onto the flat and get behind those losers. Stay out of our line of fire. Shoot to wound if they can. And a hundred credits to anybody who hits Kel in the butt."

Narla stuck her head back up. "Sorry, internal matter."

"Who's going to be the president of the executive council?"

"Me."

"Seriously, Narla. Who?"

"Me. The governor has graciously appointed me his chief advisor."

"He can't do that." Kel shook his head. "For one thing, you're a girl."

Narla bent and tapped Thul again. "New plan. One hundred credits for anybody who shoots Kel in the butt. Two hundred for anybody who shoots him in the groin. Understood?"

Thul gripped his rifle and nodded.

"Narla, we can still work this out," Kel yelled. "Come down here and talk to me."

"Why don't you come up here and talk to me."

"You don't—" Kel looked over her shoulder and stepped back. "Jove's giant forehead."

Dirk and the truck crew looked upriver. "Well," Dirk said. "You don't see that every day."

"No, I don't know how it happened, and I don't care. It doesn't matter now." Gavin coughed. "We need to go faster. We're nearly under."

"I can hardly see anything." Lee waved her hands in front of her face. Smoke poured into the wheelhouse "And I can't breathe."

"I saw them through the smoke. There's a dock up ahead, less than a mile, with some trucks on it. Must be them."

"Left, left, raaaagh!" Clara yelled.

Lee spun the wheel left. "That far enough?"

"I don't know, I can't see. Hang on. It's—right. Right. Hard right."

Lee spun the wheel in the other direction. The sidewheeler was careening down the river. The current caught it and turned it ninety degrees. Now it was heading directly into the riverside.

The smokestack belched a constant billow of black flame. The firebox glowed a dull red. Every few seconds, the stack belched burning embers in all directions. Three piles of wood on the barge had caught fire—two small ones on the port side forward, and a larger fire middle of the back. The deck cargo of teak was dry, seasoned, and burned nicely.

Gavin sniffed. "When you can breathe, that teak smells nice, kind of foresty."

"Can we get to the truck?" Lee spun the wheel to hard lock. "Get those fires out before we burn our transportation?"

"Too hot. Everybody is stuck where they're at."

Below, Scruggs, Cleon, and Dena dumped armfuls of wood down fire chute. Once Clara had established they were sinking, Lee had increased speed to the maximum. She demanded more wood to keep the steam pressure up. Their combined efforts had filled the firebox with more wood than it could handle. The resultant increase in temperature had scorched the deck. An explosion of sparks had blanketed the boat. Now spot fires burned all over, including on the top and front of the wheelhouse, drenching them in smoke as they tried to maneuver.

"I've got your datapaks here." Gavin hefted the backpack Scruggs had loaded up. "But if I go in the water, I'll sink like a stone. I don't swim well."

"Give em to Scruggs, then."

"How do I do that? The railing is red hot."

Clara broke in. "Lee, Lee, we're not going to make this turn. Use the engine."

Lee let loose a string of curses, then pushed the starboard control to full forward. The boat was facing backwards, so they spun in the opposite direction. The bow of the barge checked, then swung sideways. The water in the bilges surged forward, digging the bow under. Another wave sizzled as it ran across the hot deck, flashing to steam as it hit the hot spots.

Lee ducked her head to see through the steam. Forward was a mass of boiling vapor, so she looked back, to see if it helped. She caught a brief glimpse of green spinning across the bow, then brown. *We made the turn. Center everything*. She centered both engines. The brown flashed in front of her vision, then stabilized.

Clara stuck her head back into the wheelhouse, coughing. "We're on a straight course, I can see the dock. Bring us up to it and then kill the engines."

The ship tilted to the right. Wood crashed, then steam sparked up everywhere. Lee cursed, turned away from the smoke, faced backwards, and used their back bearing to stabilize their drive down the river.

The steam billowed over the wheelhouse, then cleared. The barge was now awash. Waves splashed the length of the barge deck, sizzling on the hot metal. The piles of wood had tilted, and single pieces bobbed alongside. The truck sat in the middle of the deck, small waves flooding under the wheels, sliding it an inch at a time.

Cleon yelled from below. Something clanked, then crashed, then hissed. Lee tried to keep the boat centered in the middle of the river using reverse drive.

Gavin stepped back inside the wheelhouse. "They're coming in."

"Who?"

Scruggs, Dena and Cleon and RC coughed their way into the wheelhouse. Lee couldn't tell them apart in the gloom. All were covered in black ash, rivulets of sweat making clear trails down their arms and shoulders. Ripped cloths covered hands.

"What in Jove's name?"

"Deck's on fire," Scruggs said. Lee could only tell it was Scruggs by the voice. "Had to get out of there. Something melted and flared up. The oil, I think. Wind is blowing the smoke."

"What's wrong with your hands?"

"Everything metal is red hot. How long 'til the dock?"

"Can't be far," Lee said.

Clara stuck her head back in the wheelhouse. "Dock ahead. Two hundred meters. Slow us down to dead slow, turn left about twenty degrees, we'll make it."

"Thank Jove." Lee pushed the levers until the wheels were barely ticking over. "We've got to get off right away. Will we be able to climb down?"

"Maybe not," Scruggs said. "But it's only twenty feet to the water. Jump off the river side."

"Some of us don't swim well..."

"Prefer to burn?"

Gavin coughed. "We'll learn quickly. How are we going to tie up to that thing, if we.."

CLANG. The boat shook, then slewed left, toward the shore.

"What was that?"

Lee pulled the starboard lever back, then pushed it forward. It moved without resistance. "Starboard lever is broken. Engine's control isn't responding."

Clara stuck her head in. "One of those teak beams is jammed in the paddle wheel."

Lee flipped the starboard throttle back and forth again. "Nothing happening here. Something's busted up." She swung the wheel to correct. The boat struggled, but the turn slowed.

Clara stuck her head in again. "Dock is fifty meters ahead. Give us some reverse."

Lee was tired, hungry, dirty, and crying from all the smoke. She coughed once, twice, wiped her eyes, then pulled the remaining throttle to reverse. Which would have been fine, if they were pointing forward, not backward. Then pulling the lever would put them in reverse, pushing them forward. Instead, with everything messed up, she got confused, and pulled when she should have pushed.

SCREECH. The remaining engine went to full speed. The unbalanced barge pivoted left. The shearing force snapped the metal tongue connecting tug and barge. The barge swung farther left, heading for the dock at full speed. The smoke cleared, and Lee realized her mistake. She grabbed the wayward throttle and pushed it forward as hard as she could.

The lever stuck in place and didn't move.

Dirk nodded. *What an amazing pilot Lee was. What incredible spatial understanding.* Even with two different watercraft coupled together, she'd executed a sideways turn, edging the tug train in closer to the dock. All this with smoke billowing out of the stack, and small fires burning all over.

"What in the name of a desert tabbo is she doing?" Narla asked. "They're turning in to the shore."

"She's pivoting the boat to come in close to the dock, facing upriver. Bring it in slow enough, then reverse the other wheel, and she'll glide alongside. Watch. She's aiming the boat dead center of the dock, now all she has to do is reverse the outboard engine, and the boat will pivot away, stopping parallel to the dock."

"Hard to judge when..."

The engine noise increased. "See?" Dirk smiled. "She's good at it. She'll slip the boat right—"

"The turn is getting tighter." Narla cocked her head. "Did she go the wrong direction? Or did something happen."

"I'm sure she'll figure it out." Dirk cocked his head. "She is going a touch fast. Faster than I would, but she's the pilot. Pilot always chooses, and—"

CRACK. A metal flange snapped at the linkage between the tug and barge. The barge sagged to the left but kept moving. Smoke gushed out of the engine as the paddle wheel roared at full speed. The tug steamed toward them.

"They're out of control!" Narla yelled.

"Run." Dirk grabbed Narla and they ran down the dock, away from the junction. They raced for the end away from the smoking, burning river barge monster.

The barge thundered in. CRACK. Another piece of linkage burst up and the barge jerked. Now it pointed dead onto the end of the dock. Half of Narla's squad on the dock ran for the floating rafts and shore, the other half to the top of the T-junction.

The driver of their truck climbed in and floored it. He raced down the dock, hammering his horn. His crew scattered, diving into the shallow water. He bounced from raft to raft, and almost made it. The last raft dipped too far, slammed onto the bottom, and broke in two. The truck dropped two feet to the riverbed and stalled.

The barge rushed in, the fires smoking. It clipped the downriver end of the floating dock, shearing it off. A three-foot bow wave of dirty brown water pushed ahead. Kel's crew, standing on the muddy beach, gaped at it, tossed rifles and ran for their lives. Kel, the closest to the water, ran for the dirt berm.

Neither of Kel's drivers made it onto their cars. The barge slid onto the shore, crunched into the sedan and drove it under. Piles of teak beams spilled off. After riding up over the sedan, it banged into the heavier truck. The truck shoved forward. Its passenger side wheels dug in, and it tilted sideways, toppled and slammed over. The barge slid to a halt. The wave of water splashed onto the berm, bouncing back onto the barge, the spray smothering the remaining fires.

The tug, separated from its load, accelerated. The right-hand wheel smacked the bottom. Pieces flew off it as it smashed itself to bits. The tug slewed left, then tilted right as the hull gave way and water rushed in. The mangled steam system collapsed. Pipes cracked and high-pressure steam whistled out from a dozen breaks. The engine slowed, then seized. Inertia pushed the tug along a dozen more feet, then it stopped. The list increased as water rushed in the shore side of the hull, and it tipped sideways. More river water flashed to steam as the hot ladders and deck house contacted the river. Steam, smoke, a few embers, and a sizzling cloud enveloped everything.

Dirk and Narla poked their heads up above the pile of scrap wood they had hidden behind. The crashed tug loomed over them. The height of the berm had saved them from the rushing water, and the bulk of the wood had shielded them from any shrapnel, and the shallow water had kept the tug from squishing them.

"Well, look who made it." Narla pointed. Her troops were pulling a groaning Kel up onto the berm. He was covered with river muck from head to toe.

A smoke-blackened figure dropped from the wheelhouse into the water. With the tilt, it was only ten feet. She—that was all you could tell—climbed out of the water onto the berm and faced the boat.

"Throw it here." It was Scruggs.

A backpack flew from the steaming upper deck. Scruggs caught it and turned to Dirk.

"Pilot."

"Private."

"Is the centurion okay? How is he?"

"He's fine, Scruggs. The doctors say everything worked great. He's in the pod recovering. They kept him there so the drugs could do their work."

"And Rocky?"

"He's fine. He's guarding the centurion."

"Oh! Great news. I was so worried." Scruggs extended a soot-blackened arm, holding the backpack. "Here's the data-paks you wanted us to bring you."

Dirk took the backpack. "Thank you."

"There's some other stuff too. On the barge. From the boxes."

"What's in the boxes?"

"Lee and Gavin took care of it. Nothing important. Just gold and gems and stuff."

"Just gold and gems. I see." Dirk nodded. "So nothing important."

"Nope. We have a lot of wood, though."

"Yes, I see that."

"Teak, Dena says. She says it's good for furniture. Maybe we could take some?"

"We don't have wooden furniture on a spaceship, Scruggs."

"Oh, right. That's too bad. It smells nice when it's burning. Hello, Ms. Narla."

"Hello... Sandra?"

"Yes." Scruggs indicated the destroyed barge, and the still steaming/burning tug. "Sorry about your boat. We kind of wrecked it."

"You did. But it's not my boat."

"It isn't? Oh good." Scruggs frowned. "But we'll have to contact the people who owned it. Explain things."

"Um, Scruggs?" Dirk asked.

"Yes, Pilot?"

"I think we'll wait 'til they call us, how about that?"

"Of course, Pilot."

"Everybody—how are you? Are you coming?"

The crew, Cleon, Clara and RC all yelled from the wheelhouse. They were fine. Everybody was fine. The cargo was fine. They'd wait until the ladders cooled, then come down. Nobody else wanted to go swimming.

Scruggs surveyed the smashed rafts, the crushed cars, the piles of wood, the burning barge, and the wrecked tug. "We kinda messed up things here, didn't we, Pilot."

"Nothing important, Scruggs."

Scruggs wiped the soot from her face, then turned and examined the steaming, hissing wreck of the tug behind her. She wiped some more soot from her nose, then looked at the smoldering pile of wood and metal that was all that remained of the barge. Their truck sat balanced in the clear spot in the middle. The remains of Kel's vehicles were smashed up onto the beach.

"I like boats," Scruggs said. "They're fun."

Chapter 37

"But how did you get a Marine star?" Dirk asked. He led his mixed group of Imperial Marines and Planetary Guards past a group of office workers packing boxes in the corridor of Empire House. "I looked it up. That's a prestigious award. Almost as prestigious as a Navy award."

Ana leaned on his canes and glared at Dirk. He was out of the med pod and moving. Barely. The Imperial Marines escorting him stopped and glared as well. Rocky, following along behind, showed his teeth and growled.

"What?" Dirk raised his eyebrows. He turned to the Marines behind him. "What did I say?"

The lead Marine, Suprapto, energized her rifle and glared at Dirk. "Just say the word, Senior Centurion. Just say the word."

"No." Ana's voice was shaky. "He can't help it. He's Navy. It's what they do. It would be like shooting a tabbo for eating grass."

"A dumb tabbo."

"A stupid, dumb tabbo," Ana agreed. "But all the same, we don't shoot Rocky just because he licks his own testicles. He's a dog, it's what dogs do. This one here—" Ana jerked his head at Dirk. "He's just a Navy guy. He does Navy things, like Rocky does dog things."

"At least our furry little killer here has testicles." Suprapto smiled at Rocky.

Rocky wagged his tail. He liked the tiny woman. She smelled like the big man, and she let him kill lizards.

"Navy is surprisingly brave when he has a spaceship strapped to him," Ana said. "Which, from our point of view, is when he's supposed to be brave. So we can forgive him his other transgressions." Ana coughed and held his canes tightly. "For now."

The procession entered the main courtyard in the center of Empire House, pausing as a group of more formally dressed office workers carrying boxes waddled by. The two Planetary Guard escorts snapped to attention as a woman in orange and green approached. Suprapto turned to Ana. "Senior Centurion?"

Ana glanced at Dirk. "Well, Navy? Your friend approaches. Or is she..."

Dirk waved at the approaching woman. "Not 'til tomorrow noon. Hello, Councilor Narla."

"Acting Governor Friedel." Narla nodded at the others. "And the senior centurion I've heard so much of. Thank you for your service."

"Ma'am. I'm sorry, but I can't salute. Not without dropping onto the courtyard."

"Well, we can't have that." Narla smiled. "If that happened, your Marines might shoot me."

"Not true ma'am." Ana coughed again. "They'd prioritize helping me up." Ana grinned. "Then they might shoot you."

Narla smiled. "Would they?"

"Might."

"Mine might shoot back," Narla said. The two Planetary Guard troops behind her stiffened. The Marines laughed.

Narla glared at them, then turned back to Dirk. "You owe me a planet."

"You owe me a starship, safe passage for a bunch of people, medical supplies, oh, and by the way, a battalion of Planetary Guard."

"A reinforced battalion," Narla said. "With support staff. Total will be approximately two thousand when we're done. First contingent of two hundred will be ready in a week. You can arrive to transport them when you're ready. And another company every week thereafter. All taken care of. Ready to go."

Her voice disappeared in the growl of a starship engine. The *Heart's Desire* roared overhead, descending to land near the river. "And there's your starship. Landing at the docks, the one you banged up when you left. But we won't charge you for that. There's an ambulance outside. Two, in fact, one for the senior centurion here, and the other for various supplies."

"And passage off-planet for the governor's staff?"

"All forty who wanted to leave?" Narla nodded. "Already organized. We've contracted with a shipping company at the starport. They can leave anytime in the next thirty days, passage paid up."

"Only forty?" Dirk shook his head. "Are you sure? I thought more—"

"Maybe this backwoods planet isn't as bad a posting as you think." Narla shrugged. "We offered everybody jobs in the planetary administration. With raises. Good jobs by local standards. We need their expertise. Most everybody took us up. Good jobs, good pay, doing something they understand. Even that social secretary, Jack. He's a bandit, but he knows things. Oh, each of them will get three understudies, and we'll be replacing them in a few years, but for now, they can teach us and get good wages."

"That's very... efficient of you," Dirk said. *She's going to be a great planetary executive. Maybe I could stay. No, she'd have me shot sometime. Sometime soon.* "Since you've only had a few days to organize things. Why do I feel like I'm missing something?" He looked at the boxes of personal items piling up in the corridors. "I'm getting screwed over here, somehow."

"As the newest Class 3 colony government in the Empire," Narla said, "the people of Andaman are pleased, and proud, as a sign of their devotion to the Emperor to fulfill all of their obligations. In fact, I think we'll be able to provide those troops to you faster than anticipated. We should have the whole two thousand ready within two months."

"You can train two thousand soldiers in two months?" Dirk asked.

"Of course, as specified in our agreement." Narla smiled.

"What am I missing?" Dirk looked around. "Centurion?"

"You idiot naval puke." Ana shook his head. "I need to sit." One of the Marines ran into a nearby office. There was a shout and a smack, and she returned with an office chair. Ana slumped into it. Five seconds later, a Planetary Guard trooper came out, holding his head, saw the entire Marine Platoon glaring at him, and retreated inside.

Ana took a breath. "Did you read the proposed TOE?"

"What's a TOE?"

"Table of organization and equipment. You didn't read it, did you."

Dirk shook his head.

"Imperial credits or local currency?"

"Well, this is the Empire, so…"

"Do you pay the troops directly, or their officers on their behalf?"

"Neither. We pay Narla here—"

Ana laughed. "That would be funny if it weren't so pathetic. Well, Ms. Governor?"

"Yes?" Narla glared at him.

"Can they all read?"

"Yes. All of them. But…"

"Not standard?" Ana said.

"Enough of them will read and write standard to explain things to the others," Narla said. "They've all been to school, at least here."

"Did they graduate school?"

Narla shrugged. "Most."

"Well, thank the gods," Ana said. "Personal weapons? Rifles? Grenades?"

"Rifles."

"What type?"

Narla smiled at that. "The best the Empire would sell a Class 7 colony."

"Blessed Jove of blessed memory. That bad?"

Narla crossed her arms. "If you wanted us to provide better equipment, you Imperials should have sold us better equipment. But they all have rifles."

"Have they at least fired those rifles?"

Narla shook her head. "Ammunition is expensive."

"Zeus and his fingertips. Squad level weapons? Machine guns? Mortars?"

"Not in the TOE."

"Transport?"

"Not in the TOE."

"Heavy weapons? Artillery?"

Narla laughed.

"Of course not." Ana grunted. "Well, congratulations, Navy, you're now paying Imperial Marine level wages for all the high school dropouts that Governor Narla can convince to put on a uniform and go on an all-expense paid trip to the stars. Hopefully, she'll feed them well enough you don't get a riot on your hands. Hope you've got a use for them."

"About that." Narla turned back to Dirk. "I don't know if you read the section on rations, but there will be a lot of troops out at the starport soon, and they need to eat, so you'll need to do something."

Dirk's eyes were wide, like he saw a herd of drunken tabbos stampeding toward him.

"You idiot." Ana coughed. "We're never letting you out of the ship again."

They got the truck onshore via extravagant usage of teak beams as ramps. After looting everything they needed from the barge and loading it into the (former) governor's truck, they had driven with Narla's convoy to the spaceport.

Kel's local guards there had suggested searching the truck and confiscating contraband. Dirk had suggested revoking the planet's new status and Narla's new appointment. Scruggs had suggested shooting everyone in the way. Narla had suggested they all follow their new planetary executive in collecting the piles of beams to fix the blown bridge down the road and simultaneously searching the wreckage for anything that Dirk's group might have missed.

Dirk stayed with her and the scavengers and returned to the city. The others entered the starport and loaded the *Heart's Desire*.

Kel had disappeared in the mess, along with most of his troopers. Narla was evasive about what happened to them, and Dirk didn't press. Not his planet, not his problem.

RC hid in the back of the truck and snuck onboard. Some of the soldiers saw him, but the greasy soot-covered man with half his hair scorched off didn't look like an Imperial Governor. Cleon and Clara helped around ship. Lee piloted them to a flat spot near the city docks to land. They planned to lift as soon as Ana and the others were on board.

"Centurion!" Scruggs beamed as Ana thumped up the ramp. "You're walking. You're okay. And you brought Rocky!"

Rocky raced past Ana and jumped up to lick Scruggs's face. Then he jumped onto the seats in the lounge and rolled on his back, barking with delight.

"I'm not okay. I'll live, but I still need some work." Ana climbed into the lounge and sat. "Dr. Lee will set me up."

"Not Doctor Freak?" Lee climbed back from the control room.

"Not for a long time. Could I have some basic, please? I need to take some pills."

"The spigot's over there, Old Man." Dena pointed to the basic dispenser six feet away.

"And I'm over here. Could you get me a glass? Please."

Dena raised her eyes. "I don't think you've ever said 'please' to me before."

"I don't think you've ever seen me shot in the lungs before. Slows a man down."

"How are you, really, Centurion?" Scruggs asked.

Gavin popped his head into the lounge. "Wow, you look horrible, Old Man."

"Good to see you too, punk." Ana took the glass of basic from Dena and sipped. "Aha. Thank you."

"Be brave, Scruggs," Dena said. "You have to be brave."

"Why?" Scruggs furrowed her brow. "What do you mean?"

"He's clearly gone insane and is dying of some sort of fatal brain disease that affects his vocal cords. He's said 'please' and 'thank you.' Both. And within five minutes. He's clearly gone nuts."

"Bite my hairy mercenary buttocks." Ana drank more basic.

"Okay, maybe not dying quickly," Dena said. "But soon."

"But, Centurion—"

"That shooting in the lungs, I don't recommend it. Wouldn't do it again." Ana sighed. "That was the second stupidest thing that's happened around here recently."

"Which means we have to ask what the stupidest thing was," Gavin said. "Gonna help us out there, Old Man?"

"Putting Navy here in charge of the planet."

"He got the locals to come help us get to the spaceport," Gavin said. "And helped us load up the ship."

"And hide he-who-will-not-be-mentioned," Lee said.

Dirk climbed up the ramp behind Ana. "And I got a reinforced battalion for the Tribune. He can use them to fight."

"First question," Ana said. "Do you know what a battalion is? How big is it?"

"Well, it's... big," Dirk said. "Very big."

"How big."

"What do you mean?"

"Exactly how big? How many men?"

"Well, some, uh, um."

"What type of weapons does it have?"

"Well, army weapons. Rifles and knives, and things like that."

"You hired a battalion of troops with knives?" Gavin asked. "Just knives."

"Not just knives." Dirk nodded. "They have rifles too."

Ana laughed. "Ask him how much ammunition they have for their rifles."

Gavin looked at Dirk. "How much?"

"Not lots."

"How many rounds per man, Skipper?" Gavin asked.

"Well, thirty."

"Thirty? One magazine? They'll shoot that off in ten minutes. Five minutes. No, two minutes." Gavin shook his head. "They need way more ammunition."

"More ammunition won't help," Ana said. "Because they haven't ever fired the ones they have. No way they'll hit anything, even if we give them more ammunition."

"They're trained—"

"No they're not."

"They're volunteer—"

"Are you sure?"

"They have uniforms and rifles," Dirk said. "They've got to be useful for something. Look, never mind about these troops. That's done. I'll deal with the Tribune on this. We need to drop from this planet, get back to see the Tribune and give him this information about that convoy you are talking about. He'll want to raid it or destroy it. And he'll be very happy to see us when we get there, and he'll find a use for all these troops when we get there. You'll see." Dirk crossed his arms. "You'll all see."

Chapter 38

"I can't say I'm happy to see you, Dirk," Devin said, facing the crew in the airlock of *Pollux*. "Given everything I've heard. Arbitrarily raising a colony's status, and promising a career criminal that I'll pardon him. And what in Jove's name am I supposed to do with two thousand untrained riflemen?"

Given their knowledge of the patrol areas, it took only two days to find one of the Tribune's corvettes, and only another day to get back to the man himself.

"Tribune, you need to look at the details of this convoy that we found." Dirk extended the datapak. "And you should look at the crew lists. Hernandez and Weeks are onboard. There are all sorts of opportunities for us there."

Devin shook his head. "You had one simple job, drop by an unremarkable planet, pick up some data, come back. Instead, the planet is in flames, there's been a rebellion—"

"Technically, your Tribuneship," Ana broke in, "it's only a rebellion if they lose. They seem to have won, so it's more like an election, with lots of guns."

"They rebelled against the rightful Emperor—"

"Met with the duly appointed Imperial Governor, who was pleased to grant them Class 3 Colony status." Ana said.

"What? Class 3? What idiot did that?"

The whole crew pointed at Dirk.

Devin rounded on him. "They were a Class 7. You could have given them Class 6, or Class 5 even. No, you had to go right to Class 3. Now they're guaranteed to be a Class 2 in three years, and a Class 1 three years after that. Do you know how many commercial connections you've disrupted, no, destroyed with this?"

"Commercial connections with people who are your enemies now, Devo-my-friend." RC stepped up between the crew. "And good to see you too, old fellow. How is your sister?"

Devin stared at RC for a full ten seconds without speaking, then blinked his eyes. "Imin?"

"Sir." Imin stepped from behind the Tribune.

"Fetch my sword. Immediately."

"Yes, Tribune." Imin cast a look at the Tribune's duty uniform. His clean duty uniform. "Would you like... a working outfit, Tribune?"

"No."

"Perhaps a pair of coveralls, then, Tribune."

"No. I want my sword."

"I could stop by the dining room, Tribune. I've got a couple spare table cloths. Very white, almost look like senatorial robes in the right light—"

"Get. Me. My. Sword. Now."

"Sir." Imin saluted across his chest.

Prefect Lionel took the datapak from Dirk. "And, Imin, bring a reader so the Tribune can read this. And a decryption unit."

"Too heavy sir," Imin said. "And that's all secret equipment. Can't be carrying it all over the ship. Have to keep it in the compartments specially secured for top-secret intelligence data. Like the bridge, and the intelligence vault."

"We can't all fit in the vault," Lionel said. "Where's the closest specially secured compartment?"

"That would be the dining room sir. Cosmic-level security classified room."

All the assembled staff, who had been glaring at RC, swiveled to look at Imin.

Lionel raised his eyebrows. "The dining room is classified Cosmic?"

"And the pantry, and the kitchen sir. Had them inspected and certified before we left the Core, years ago. But the certification is good for five years. So we're still within regs."

"Why is the pantry an intelligence vault?"

"That's where we keep the decryption equipment sir."

"You keep Cosmic Level-1 decryption equipment in our food storage?"

"I do not sir." Imin shook his head. "I do not."

Lionel shook his head. "Good. Where do you keep it, then?"

"Don't have any Cosmic Level-1 decryption equipment sir."

"But you said..."

"Only Cosmic Level-7."

The crowd sucked their breath. Lionel raised his eyebrows. Santana, behind Lionel, grinned. Devin continued to glare at RC.

Dena raised her hand. "What's Cosmic-level security?"

"Extremely high-level security," Gavin said. "Messages of high operational or strategic importance. Fleet dispositions. Combat readiness reports."

All eyes swiveled to Gavin. The Marines in the crowd put their hands on their weapons.

"What?" Gavin shrugged. "I'm a spy, remember?"

Dena snapped her fingers. "Right. We knew that. So, is seven good, or bad, or what?"

"Big good. Only thing higher is personal Imperial communications. The Tribune probably has something for that in his rooms. I've never even seen the decryption equipment. It would be interesting—"

"No." Lionel shook his head. "Hard no. Imin, why is there Cosmic Level-7 decryption equipment in your pantry?"

"No room in the food storage area sir. Too small."

"Too small?"

"Yes sir. Too small, and it doesn't work in the main dining room. It's all metal, and the dining room is more of a dark wood motif. Deep forest, burbling stream, sort of thing."

"Maybe you could make your decryption thingy burble?" Dena suggested. "Can't it play music? Or brook sounds, or just white noise?"

"It could at that. It could at that." Imin nodded. "Lots of options there."

"And you just said you had some nice white table cloths," Dena said. "Big ones. Maybe drape it and put some flowers on top. A nice arrangement. Hey, Old Man." Dena turned to Ana. "I heard you did flower arranging."

Ana coughed. "I did, years ago. My arrangements are artistic, if I do say so myself. I do a nice green and yellow combo. Restful."

Imin stroked his chin. "That wouldn't be bad at all. Bring the whole room together."

"That would be sweet," Dena said. "Something soft, relaxing. Seems like every time I've been in your dining room, the food's great, amazing food, but there's always an argument, or a shooting, or some sort of impossible actions going on—"

"QUIET," Devin snapped. "All of you. Quiet. Imin?"

"Tribune?"

"In my extensive readings of Imperial ship regulations—"

Even the Marines snorted at that one.

"I mean, what I meant, while reviewing ship readiness reports—"

The bridge officers present shook their heads.

"Okay." Devin took a breath. "I was at a party once, and while I was ordering more wine from the wine steward, I overheard two other officers talking..." Devin eyed his crowded shuttle deck. Now everyone was nodding. "Good, so I overheard the two officers talking about security protocols, and I remember three things. One, not only is that a decryption unit for regular codes, but it also functions as a codebreaker, correct."

"Yes, Tribune." Imin nodded. "Whatever encryption is on that data chip, it stands a pretty good chance of breaking it."

"Very well, that's good news." Devin nodded. "Now, Imin, I also remember, that according to regulations, you need a specially certified clerk for that equipment."

Imin nodded. "I'm a qualified cypher clerk sir, authorized to work on that equipment."

"Of course you are. Of course you are." Devin shook his head. "Learned at Fleet Academy?"

"Did indeed sir."

"Well, I guess that it's all right. But there was a third thing..."

"Wait." Brigadier Santana held up a finger. "It has to be a secure location. I haven't seen any guards on the dining room, except when the Tribune is present. What's to stop somebody from sneaking into the pantry and stealing the coding equipment?"

"My pantry room?" Imin turned on the Brigadier. "You're saying you'd sneak into the pantry. My pantry?"

"It's not your pantry, Imin. It belongs to the Empire."

"My pantry is perfectly safe. Nobody on this ship will ever, ever, break in."

"But what if somebody is in there trying to steal your cookies, or something—"

Imin stepped back and surveyed the crowd. His eyes reflected the ceiling lights in the compartment, the pinpoint of focus flickered over the assembled troops.

Even Devin stepped back. *What is that expression?* Thus did the guardians of the underworld look as they choose who was to be dammed and who was not.

Without orders, they all snapped to parade attention as his glare focused over them. Ana pushed himself as far to attention as he could. Dirk, Lee, and Scruggs snapped straight. Even Dena rocked back a bit.

Imin finished his head sweep of the compartment, then marched to stand in front of the Brigadier. "Are you planning on stealing my cookies, Brigadier?"

Santana had also unconsciously braced to attention. "No. No, Imin. I wasn't going to do that."

"I wouldn't suggest you do that sir. That would be a very, very bad idea. In fact, such a bad idea, that anybody who tried to steal my cookies would not survive the experience." Imin grinned. "At least, not for long. I would want some time with them before that."

The crowd actually shivered.

"Imin." Devin coughed. "Imin, I'd like to see what's on those datapaks."

"Of course sir." Imin looked around the compartment. "And I can make lunch at the same time."

Lunch was a seafood stew, with crustaceans in a red sauce. Imin passed out bowls of melted butter and a sweet white wine. "The stew is salted, so is the butter. That cuts the sugar in the wine."

Dirk and the crew sat across from each other at center table. Devin, Lionel and Santana occupied one end, RC, Cleon and Clara the far one. Devin had been quizzing Cleon and Clara—he'd known their mother, and they were distantly related to him.

"Well, I can't guarantee the Imperial academy right now, unfortunately." Devin gestured to his plate, and one of the stewards added more stew. "But for the next year or so, I'm sure I can find you some sort of apprenticeship in the military realm. We'll rotate the two of you across the fleet, give you some practical experience."

"The fleet?" Lionel spooned up a sea-creature claw. "What fleet would that be?"

"Flotilla, then." Devin waved his hands. "The frigate, assault carrier, and various tankers, corvettes, and gunships that we've acquired. We have a respectable force. Twenty ships?"

"Twenty-one jump-capable ships. They all have some sort of weapons, so they're not helpless against pirates. But regular warships? I wouldn't be happy about that." Lionel scraped up the last of his stew. "What's next, Imin?"

"A light goulash of sorts. Something meaty, with a rose as a transition wine."

"A goulash is unusual for you."

"Yes sir. But I needed something the furry fellow would like." Imin pointed at Rocky. "I don't think he's a seafood fan."

Devin sat up straight. "Now you're organizing dinners around the likes of pets?"

"Rocky is not a pet," Dena said. "He saved Dirk and me from a poisonous snake by attacking it and snapping its neck."

"A machine gun shot at us on Andaman," Lee said. "Rocky attacked the gunner and bit him."

"While I was in the med pod," Ana said, "he stood guard over me, and wouldn't let any of the Navy types screw things up. He's my furry buddy."

Devin swiveled to look at Rocky. Rocky sat upright and thumped his tail. Once. Devin nodded. "More combat experience than most Core officers, then. Welcome aboard, furry warrior."

Rocky thumped his tail. Twice. Then stood and wagged as Imin put an overflowing bowl in front of him.

RC spoke from the far end of the table. "With that much experience, I'm surprised you didn't put him in charge of your planning staff, Devo-me-boy."

Devin glared down the table. "I'd forgotten you were here. Probably because I wanted to enjoy my lunch. Last time we spoke, I promised to kill you. Why shouldn't I do that now?"

Imin shoved a bowl of goulash in front of Devin. "Not 'til dessert at least, Tribune."

"No, not 'til dessert." Devin sipped his wine. "Wonderful. But the question stands. Why let you live?"

"You're going to pardon me," RC said, "for service to the Empire."

"I'm going to need a lot more of this excellent wine before I do that."

"I've just delivered you a complete set of movement orders and station status reports for the entire sector, along with courier databases and the latest codes."

"You have the latest codes?" Devin asked.

"I gave them to Imin when he asked."

"Imin? Why not me?"

"I'm scared of Imin."

"But not of me?"

"No, you too. But my fear of him was more... immediate."

"Right." Devin nodded. "That's right. And what does this database and those reports say?"

"No idea." RC shrugged. "There's a lot of data on that datapak. It's up to you and your planning people."

Devin looked over his shoulder. "Imin, what happened to the data?"

Imin stepped from the pantry, holding a scoop and a bucket. "It's coming off now sir. The movement orders I've sent to your staff to examine. The status reports for stations went to the Brigadier's people to choose occupation targets. And we're breaking the encryption on the others now. We'll have something soon."

"What do we do while we wait?"

Imin held up his scoop. "Blueberry ice cream!"

Everyone was happy that they had finished dessert before they got the full intelligence download.

"A battleship," Devin said. "That's unexpected."

"We can take her," Lionel said. "*Canopus*. She's old. Under-powered. Not up to modern standards. And she's straight from the Core. Her crew won't be drilled into shape. We take her and that convoy is ours."

"But because she's straight from the Core, the crew will be loyal to the Chancellor, or at least not rebels. And this admiral what's-his-name— Bracebridge? He's the Chancellor's man."

"*Pollux* can take her," Lionel repeated.

"Fine." Devin crossed his arms. "That's the plan, then. Go charging in and take her. But I'll be sitting right next to you while you do this. Waiting. And if the ship blows up, you and I blow up with her. And what happens to this rebellion then, what happens to my sister then, with both of us gone. For that matter, assume we take the battleship, there appears to be a cruiser waiting right behind."

Lionel and Santana exchanged glances. Santana coughed. "Tribune, I don't think that the risk—"

"That's a no." Devin waved his glass of wine. "Not going to do it. What else do we know?"

"Well." Santana tapped his screen, which he had placed next to his wine glass. "These station reports are interesting. Now that we know what is where in terms of defenses, and which stations are short munitions, or supplies, we could do some interesting things."

"But they'll only be short of supplies until this convoy gets moving. It's stuffed with naval stores."

"And a battleship, a cruiser, two destroyers, and a gaggle of corvettes with her now, and even more escorts sent out to rendezvous with her," Devin said. "Which we have to keep in mind."

Ana coughed and raised his hand.

"You have something to say, Senior Centurion?" Devin asked.

"Mostly, I wanted more wine." Ana held up a glass. One of Imin's stewards stepped to refill it. "But I did have a question. You've declared a rebellion against... well, in theory, the current Emperor, but in practice, you figure the Chancellor is behind this."

"Thank you for pointing that out, Senior Centurion." Devin grimaced. "My ability to understand the obvious must appear to be lacking to you."

"So this rebellion." Ana took a sip. "How do you go about fighting it? How do you know when you've won?"

"When I stand in the Senate chamber in the Capitol and declare myself Emperor," Devin said. "As all Emperors in the past have done. That's when I know I've won."

"So why not do that? Just sail in, walk up the steps and say you've won."

"Why didn't I think of that." Devin snapped his fingers. "Oh wait, there are some fleet elements between here and there, substantial fleet elements. They would have to be defeated."

Ana put his glass down. "Define 'defeated.'"

"Well, we'd need to fight..." Devin's voice trailed off.

"Is fighting the only way to defeat them?" Ana asked.

"Noooooo...." Devin steepled his fingers. "In fact, it's the worst way to win."

"There another way to do this?"

Lionel stirred. "Most of the troops we've taken up haven't fought. Most are happy for some firm direction."

"You didn't need to fight my Marines," Santana said. "We know where our duty lies."

"Indeed." Lionel tapped his fingers. "Indeed. Senior Centurion, do you play chess?"

Ana shook his head. "Nope. Too much officer-like for me."

"Indeed. Imin?"

Imin's head appeared from the galley. "Tribune?"

"Put the specs of all the ships in that convoy up on the screen."

Two seconds later, one of the walls flashed to a data display. The freighters in the upcoming convoy, their specifications, and the cargo carried occupied one wall. The details of its escort occupied the other.

Lionel peered at the screen. "The thing about chess, Senior Centurion, is that you both start out with an equal chance of winning. Same forces, same placement. You have to figure out how to attack the other where they aren't. Concentrate your forces. Get local superiority."

"Good to know," Ana said. "And good military advice. But I don't play the game myself, and I don't see the relevance."

Devin ignored the byplay. "And the second thing, Senior Centurion, is that you never win the final battle."

"You don't?"

"No. You just put the other player in a position where they would lose, and they don't see a way out of it. The Chancellor thinks I'm starting to win, otherwise, there wouldn't be a convoy. That convoy means we're winning. And we will win, if I can convince the people on that convoy it's true."

"Odd sort of war."

"Indeed. But that's what we're going to do." Lionel raised his glass. "A toast."

Everyone followed his lead. "We're not going to fight any-body. We're going to convince them they've lost."

Chapter 39

"Emergence!" Trevor, the helmsman, said. "Sensors up. Stand by for update." The bridge of the *Pollux* quieted.

Devin had dispersed his fleet. The Marines had rushed back to Andaman to load up as much of the new Andaman Imperial Auxiliary Brigade on board the *Valhalla* as would fit.

Lionel had plotted the path of the resupply convoy and made a long jump to beat them, accompanied by the two tankers. The tankers were replenishing from a nearby gas giant and the *Pollux* would observe the movements of the convoy as it passed by and plot their next move.

The corvettes had been dispatched to a rendezvous in the Merhack system, a busy system adjacent to the convoy's path. The *Heart's Desire* had accompanied them.

While they waited, Lionel asked about the maple syrup. "They burn you alive?"

"Your entire family. Kids, uncles, aunts, third cousins. Pets. Scary people," Devin said. "Any planet that produces it, they go out and arrange to buy all your production. If you don't sell, you suffer an unexplained forest fire."

"Forest fire?" Lionel took his eyes off the jump screen. "They burn entire forests?"

"They put you and your family in it first, before they burn it."

"Wow. Sensors, any update?"

Lukas, the sensor officer, turned to Lionel and rolled his eyes. Midshipman Calroy was operating the sensors this time.

Calroy typed on his screen. "Beacons sir. Many beacons."

"Thank you, Sensors," Lionel drawled. "But are any of them warship beacons, and what should we be doing about them?"

"Ah. Stand by sir." Calroy typed on his screen.

Lionel turned his attention back to Devin. "Do you think burning your suppliers alive makes good economic sense?"

"I wouldn't think that would make people want to get into the business," Devin said. "Maple syrup is much more dangerous than I thought. But an unrelated point to consider. Since we're in a hostile system, shouldn't we be at general quarters, and running around trying to destroy any Imperial units we see out here?"

"If we were on the ecliptic, which we're not—we're way above it, and if we were anywhere near the habitable planets, which we're not—they are on the far side of the system, or if we were anywhere near any stations, which we're not, then yes, I'd put us at general quarters because there might hypothetically be other ships nearby, or transiting past us. But we're on the far side of the system from anything useful, these gas giants rarely get visited, and we're not on line to any reasonable destination either. Nothing jumps in from this side."

"We did."

"I should say, nothing would jump in from this direction except for the latest Imperial warships. Like us. In fact, we're so far from everything interesting in this system right now we're in the exact spot a crash jump would pick as the safest place to be. My unrelated point. How come you got such a great ship?"

"It was a bribe. My sister wanted me out of her hair."

Lionel checked his board. "We seem to have beaten that resupply convoy and their escorts. Are you sure this is a good idea?"

"No. But it's the best one I have for now."

"How sure are you they will react the way you want?"

"We need to be seen first. But not positively identified."

"Will anybody see us?"

"Not if Calroy has anything to do with it. Calroy? Beacons? Tell me about them?"

"Sir. No warships. Four Imperial freighters. One independent registered tramp freighter. Two Confed freighters. I've scanned them."

Lionel waited. "You've scanned them for... warranty repairs? What?"

"Sorry sir. I've scanned them with radar and IR. They match the dimensions in the warbook, and their IR pattern matches what the warbook showed for that ship design. They're almost a hundred percent match."

"Which means?"

"Likely the beacons are correct sir, if the physical descriptions match. They can't be warships, at least. I'm waiting for the scan results on the independent freighters."

"You did the Confeds and the Independent first, why?"

"Well." Calroy wrinkled his brow. "They're our enemies sir. The Confederation."

"We're not at war with them this instant, are we?"

"No sir. But I was told to look for spies from the Core sir, and they're suspicious."

"Why are they suspicious?"

"Well, because they're Confeds sir. That's suspicious. And the Independent freighter as well. Never know what they're up to."

"Let me see if I understand this." Lionel rubbed his forehead. "If you were going to spy on somebody in Imperial space, you'd choose a ship to be the only nationality that is guaranteed to attract our notice and would be easy to verify because we keep detailed scans on Confed ships we let past our borders."

"Well, when you say it that way sir—"

"And there are those Imperial freighters here, from god knows where in the Empire, who we don't have amazing records on, and you're not even bothering to check them?"

"Um. No. Sir." Calroy's face reddened.

"The Emperor's toes," Lionel said. "Lukas, help Calroy scan."

"Sir." The scan officer typed on his console. "Be a few minutes."

"Let me know if any of them don't match their physical records, such as we have. Then we'll know if they're spies."

"Beg pardon sir, but that's not enough," Villa, the comm officer, said. "We need more than that."

"Not enough?" Lionel turned to her. "Explain?"

"Sir." Villa locked her screen and turned to face the Prefect and the Tribune. "If I was going to set up a spy ship, I'd buy a couple of used standard freighters, like a Mack model 300, common as grass. Then I'd get a list of freighters with the same names that were built around the same time and use their IDs for my fake beacons. I'd pass a physical scan, an IR scan, even a boarding because they're the same type of ship. I'd upgrade the sensor suite with excellent passive sensors, keep the old active ones. Have one or two sensor operators in the crew. I could scan all day long, everywhere, and nobody would notice or care."

Devin grinned from his chair next to Lionel. "And that, Prefect, is why you hire officers who are so much smarter than you are. The better your subordinates, the more foolish they make you look."

Lionel nodded. "I agree, Tribune. That's a characteristic of yours that I've always admired. But I think you take it too far sometimes, too much of a good thing."

"Exactly, I. Hey, wait a minute." Devin scowled.

All the bridge officers, except Calroy, laughed.

Lionel turned to Villa. "That's exactly true. How do we find them out?"

"We need a database of all the freighters in the Empire, updated regularly, so we know what ships are in which sectors, and which ones are lost or scrapped, so if one of those ships shows up somewhere they can't or shouldn't be, we can zoom right in."

"I'll put that on the list," Lionel said. "But we don't have that. What should we do?"

"Get their cargo list. Compare it to the others. Ships going to the same ports should carry the same cargo. If one of them is different..."

Lionel and Devin exchanged glances. "When are you due for promotion, Villa?" Lionel asked.

"I'm kind of overdue sir. Next promotion would take me away from the *Pollux*, so I sort of—"

"I'll fix that."

"I don't want to leave the *Pollux* sir. Not right now."

"Why not?"

Villa shrugged. "You're doing something that needs to be done. I didn't join the Navy to count boxes of strawberries."

"Fair enough. Carry on."

Lionel stood. "Word with you in the day cabin sir?"

"You mean my cabin?"

"I mean the captain's day cabin, which as the captain of this ship, I have graciously allowed a visiting senior officer, to wit, an Imperial Tribune, occupy while he plots fleet movements."

"Let's go." Devin left the bridge and retired to his cabin. He waited until Lionel arrived. "Well?"

Lionel walked to the sideboard and poured some brandy. "Don't screw this up. We've got people like Villa depending on us. It's not fair to her."

"Do you think I'm screwing things up?"

"Nooooo." Lionel took a long drink. "But I think you're running out of ideas. I've agreed with you up until now. No bombardments. No destroying stations. Not shooting up Imperial real estate, that sort of thing. This should be our last show and tell."

"You mean, if we can't get this convoy the Chancellor has sent, we'll have to blow things up?"

"And kill people."

"I'm having a problem seeing myself doing that. Give me some of that." Devin waited for Lionel to pour him a glass. "As you pointed out, they're just troopers and rankers who were unlucky. To wit, they were assigned to the wrong commander."

"Do you even know what 'to wit' means?"

"Means I have to make a decision. About what to do out here, soon. You're right, I've tried to run a rebellion, without actually rebelling. But I'll have to choose soon."

"Still time to collect a few more troops with a good speech and bowl of soup."

"We only have so much soup." Devin drummed his fingers on his desk. "How long do we stay here?"

"Long enough for those freighters to react to our presence and figure out something big and dangerous is coming. Light speed delay will be a factor, but once we see them scrambling, we'll know they've seen us. If that convoy is on schedule, it should jump into the middle of this mess. Or its escorts will. Wait for some of them to get over the jump limit and spread the word, we can jump out, collect the rest of the ships, and wait until the—"

BONG-B-BONG. BONG-B-BONG.

Devin looked up at the ceiling speaker. "Haven't heard that one before."

Lionel stabbed at the intercom as the call button lit. "It's the proximity radar. Bridge, report."

"Jump emergence. Very close," Trevor's voice said. "Still calculating. We're—hang on."

"Don't tell me hang on. I'll—Jove's knees." The ship yawled sideways, and the main drive fired. Both officers grabbed for chair arms and desks and held on.

BONG-B-BONG-B-BONG-B-BONG.

"What's happening?" Devin clung to the seat. "What's that one?"

"Collision alarm." Lionel gripped the desk. "Something's going to hit us."

Chapter 40

"**S**ound Collision. Pitch down ninety. Full thrust. Helmets on." Monti slapped her helmet over her head. Hooper and Hernandez did the same.

Silaski fumbled with her helmet, fiddling with the catch.

"Silaski! Helm controls. Now."

Silaski dropped her helmet. It bounced twice, then rolled to the rear of the control room.

A warship centered on the main screen. The entire crew was at their stations for emergence. Extensive calculations while in jump space had revealed that Silaski's crash jump would bring them in far, far above the ecliptic, in a supposedly empty, and thus safe, part of the system. *I thought locking everyone down at general quarters should have been enough. Should have de-aired the whole ship and had the crew suited up.*

Silaski unbuckled and got up to get her helmet.

Monti cursed. "I've got the helm." She pushed the thrust to maximum and entered the pitch correction.

The ship pivoted forward and down, and the bridge crew floated up on their straps, then settled as the main drive fired.

Fired too slowly. Only a quarter-G at most. Enough to make a helmet-less Silaski slide back to the bulkhead, where her helmet bounced under a scanner. But not enough to lift them from their seats.

Monti slapped her intercom. "Engineering. Give us full thrust now."

"Captain." Weeks's voice came over the intercom. "The limiters kicked in and they're limiting the thrust. I can override, but is this really necessary—"

Hernandez, helmeted and strapped in, leaned left and smacked the collision alarm on the now vacant helm station.

BONG-G-BONG-G-BONG-G-BONG

"Collision? Jove's teeth." Weeks's voice disappeared. A quarter-second later, the main engine thrust climbed to maximum and they all slammed back into their seats.

They were successfully diving under the upcoming warship. No, warships. There's more visible on the scanner in the distance. Where did they come from? Why are they all the way out here? Nobody comes this far from the ecliptic.

"General quarters. Laser charging."

Hernandez looked up. "It's the *Pollux*. Devin's—the rebel frigate. And escorts. I'm scanning them now." Her voice came over the suit radio channel.

Hooper had the weapons screen up on her console. "We're within range, but they're evading. Should I target them?"

"Don't shoot," Hernandez said.

"Why not? They're in range."

"And so are we." Hernandez's fingers flew over her console. "And they're bigger, meaner, and much, much better armed. We'll only irritate them, and then they blow us to space dust."

Hooper froze her screen and held her finger over the red button. "I've got a shot."

"What's the chances of that shot hitting them? They're as surprised as we are. Hold fire. Keep running. Every second, we get farther away."

Hooper turned. "Captain?"

Monti opened her mouth, and then shut it. What to do? Her vision sharpened. The lights got brighter. Shadows dimmed. *Oh no, that means—*

Red lights flashed on all the consoles, the wall, and her suit. Major air leak.

"Hold fire unless fired upon. Maintain course and speed. Shut off that damned alarm." Monti popped her harness and swung out of her seat.

Behind her, Silaski leaned on the rear bulkhead. She wheezed for air as the compartment vented. One hand scrabbled at her mouth, the other grasped the wall. Monti slipped, lay down, and snatched Silaski's helmet out from under the scanner. She stood, yanked Silaski's hand from her mouth, and slammed the helmet down over her head. Silaski feebly pawed at it. Monti shoved Silaski's shoulders. The spaceman dropped to her butt, then Monti grasped the helmet, slammed it onto the collar, and pivoted it counterclockwise to lock. She checked that the air supply was green, then climbed back into her seat.

Hooper had two screens up, one a passive scan of the *Pollux*, the other a constantly updating laser targeting screen.

"Hold your fire," Monti said.

"And that's what I'm doing."

"Did she shoot?"

"They must have. At least once. Why else did we lose atmo?"

"You sure?"

"He's tracking us. Lots of radiation coming our way. And she's still in range."

"Effective range?"

"Well...No. Not that close."

"She hit us once. Why only once? Why isn't he still firing?"

Hooper shrugged. "I don't know."

Monti brought up the radar range measurement. "We're on almost opposite vectors."

"Shouldn't we be evading or something?" Hooper asked.

Monti cursed, then brought up the helm controls, and hit a random walk pattern. They rocked side to side, as the *Collingwood* fired its thrusters at random to confuse targeting lasers. "Engineering. Report."

Weeks voice was tinny—he must have put on his helmet as well. "The ship broke."

"No kidding. What broke? Why did we lose air?"

"It just...broke."

"What in seven Jovian virgins does that mean? The ship broke how?"

"The thrust was too much. The ship whiplashed and flexed, and a bunch of welds gave out, snapped, whatever. The thrust kind of blew bits apart."

"Are you telling me our own engines snapped us to bits?"

"Not a lot of bits, but more or less."

"How long to fix?"

"Gotta get out on the hull and weld."

"Can't you patch it?"

"There's not much to patch. We broke apart. We'll have to glue it back together. I can foam some stuff from inside, but it will still take a while."

"You've got thirty minutes and then we need to jump out of here, otherwise, those ships will catch us." Monti closed the channel and cursed some more. "Hooper?"

Hooper had changed her screen to the jump calculations. "I don't have a shot. We're clear to jump if we want to calculate a solution."

"Do it." Motion on the bridge attracted Monti's attention. Hernandez's fingers were flying over her console. "Hernandez? What are you doing?"

"Scanning. I've got clear views of the *Pollux* and all her escorts. Some big ships out there. I'm getting as much info as possible, we can pass it to the admiral when we get back."

"Pass it to the admiral?"

"Sure." Hernandez swapped screens "Wasn't that why we were here? Reconnoiter enemy forces, estimate strengths, that sort of things. That's what we're supposed to be doing, right?"

"Yes, sure. Um, in the confusion, I kind of forgot."

"Don't worry, Monti, I've got you covered. Lucky for you, I'm Naval Intelligence. I'm doing a full force estimate and identifying the ships out there as much as possible. I'll have it all packaged up, and ready for the admiral." Hernandez's screen flashed, and the long-range sensor screen appeared. "Could you work on getting us out of here?"

"Yes." Monti took a breath, then checked the scanners. They were lucky. The two forces were on almost opposed vectors when she dropped in the middle of the rebels. It would take the *Pollux* group hours to change direction and catch her, and they'd be gone by then. Gone with a report for the admiral, who hopefully wouldn't hate her. Well, couldn't hate her more than he did already.

One thing bothered her as the rebel ships drove farther away. Hernandez had the long-range sensors up and scanning. But Monti had gotten a glimpse of the other screen. Before switching to the scan screen, Hernandez had the commo screen up. She'd been communicating with somebody during their maneuvers. Another ship.

And the only other ships in the system she could be talking to were the rebels.

"Control room, now." Lionel's drink slid off Devin's desk to smash on the floor. "Run."

"Right behind you." Devin crunched over the broken glass to the door. The door buzzed red—the helm override had locked all the doors. "What in Jove's name?"

The main drive paused, and they floated free. Then the thrusters fired in a vicious pitch down. Broken glass floated out of the carpet.

Villa's voice interrupted the alarm. "Secure for emergency maneuvering in five seconds. Now. Now. Now. This is not a drill." The alarm returned.

"Chairs!" Devin yelled. He and Lionel dove for the armchairs in the cabin. Expensive cloth-covered antiques or not, every chair in the office was bolted down, and had a harness. Both senior officers snapped in.

Two seconds later, the main drive fired at full power, and they were slammed back into their chairs. They were both pivoting and accelerating, Villa must have been so scared that she didn't wait for proper vector alignment.

"What's going on? Who's attacking us?" Devin yelled.

"Do I look like a sensor suite?"

"What's Villa doing?"

"Her job. Hang on."

"Like I have a choice?"

The acceleration increased. Lionel cursed as the giant tabbo resting on his chest invited a friend to sit with him. Or he tried to curse. He mostly croaked.

The harnesses kept them from bouncing across the cabin, but didn't help with the excess thrust. Devin dropped his hands to his lap. That hurt, but he was able to link his hands side by side, close enough to tap his wrist comm. "Viiiilllla. Wasss happening. Cutttt thrust."

Villa's voice was strained, but clear. Then again, she was in a padded bridge chair. "Inadvi*sable* sir. Maximum thrust for forty-two more seconds."

"Iiiiii'm a prefect. Dooo as Iiiiii say."

"Thirty-seven seconds sir."

"Youuuuuuree relieved."

"Understood sir. Twenty-eight seconds sir."

Devin started cursing, but it came out as babbled blather. Twenty-eight seconds later, the thrust dropped from what must have been five- or six-Gs down to one, and the collision alarm stopped. The ship described a slow arc as the thrusters fired.

"Secure emergency maneuvering," Villa's voice said. "Regular maneuvering underway. General quarters. All hands to stations. This is not a drill. General quarters."

"I'll cut her head off," Devin snarled. He grabbed his helmet.

"Unless she followed regulations." Lionel headed for the door. "Emergency maneuvers are allowed in certain circumstances."

"Which ones?"

"Which regulations or which maneuvers?" Lionel asked.

"We have more than one type of emergency regulation?"

"Seventeen."

"Seventeen?" Devin waited for Lionel to type his entry code to the bridge door. "That many?"

"Yes. Didn't you know that?"

"No."

"You haven't read any of the regulations, have you?" Lionel's code didn't work. He typed it in again.

"No. I planned to, though."

"When?"

"Well, sometime soon."

Lionel glared at Devin. "Soon?"

"Very soon?"

Lionel hammered the bridge intercom. "Bridge, I can't—"

"Sorry sir." Villa's voice. "We locked down...you're clear."

The bridge hatch lock flashed green. Lionel pushed his way in and surveyed the scene. "Report. Somebody."

Villa put her image up on the main screen. They were still under power, and still at general quarters. "Sir. An unidentified ship crash emerged within our collision perimeter. It was so close, the computer didn't have time to give a proper avoidance vector. JD—I mean, Lieutenant Trevor—took emergency manual control and drove us away from the incursion. Scanning says it's an imperial patrol corvette, Matapedia class. Beacon says the *Collingwood*."

"Where is she?" Lionel said.

"We're maneuvering to come on a pursuit vector. We're nearly on reciprocals. After the emergency cleared, Trevor limited his maneuvering while I brought the ship to general quarters.

"You did this?" Lionel looked at Trevor. "Isn't he senior?"

"He was occupied at the time sir. I did what was necessary."

"Very well. Can we pursue?"

"We can sir." Trevor put a course on the board. "However, given our relative velocity differences, it would take hours to get back into range. That's assuming they don't jump."

"Which they can do at any time. How are our escorts?"

"Asking for instructions sir."

"Pursue the *Collingwood* at one-G." Lionel paused. "Did she fire at us?"

"Her weapons, sorry, her weapon—that class has only one laser—was hot, but she didn't fire."

"Well, commence pursuit while we figure out what she was doing way out here. Have the in-system freighters reacted at all?"

"None yet sir. With light speed delay, we don't expect to see activity for about ten more minutes."

"Very well." Lionel dropped into his seat. "Well done. Carry on. Tribune?"

Devin had sneaked back into his seat. His message light flashed. He tapped it, listened for twenty seconds, then typed a long reply and sent it.

"Tribune?" Lionel asked.

"Um, yes?"

"Do you have any questions for the bridge staff?"

"Stand by." Devin's message light flashed again. He listened, nodded twice, and typed another reply. "Um, well. Lieutenant Villa."

Villa did turn this time. "Tribune?"

"We had a conversation over the intercom, during the emergency."

"We did sir. The alarm and the accelerating made hearing you difficult. But I did make out the gist of it."

"Um. What was the gist of it, Lieutenant?"

"Execute, execute, execute. Did I get that right sir?"

Devin flopped into his chair. He nodded once. "Absolutely correct, Lieutenant. Execute, Execute, Execute. Prefect?"

"Tribune?"

"Carry on." Devin sighed. "And execute, execute, execute."

Chapter 41

"In addition to the *Pollux*, we got good scans of the nearest two escorts. We weren't able to get full electronic sweeps, but we got good displacement data. One approximated the tonnage of a heavy cruiser, possibly a Suffren class." Hernandez highlighted an entry on her screen. "The other was larger, and we didn't get as good a scan. But the only ship of that size in the Imperial inventory is an Admiral class heavy cruiser."

The dozen faces in the virtual meeting blinked or shook their head as Hernandez's presentation reached them. They'd strapped the *Collingwood* back together with seal foam and plastic sheeting and jumped back to the convoy as soon as they had a vector. Monti had sent in her report immediately upon emergence, and then been called in to an all-captains meeting.

Admiral Bracebridge sniffed. "Nothing to worry about, then. Two small ships. We will see them off."

The animated faces blanked as the admiral's words reached them.

Mahony, the reserve captain from the *Hydrogen Pride*, pressed the request-to-speak button. The admiral's face clouded, but he nodded to an off-camera aide to connect her.

"The data I have here." Mahony put up her own graphics, the schematics of Suffren class cruiser, and an Admiral class cruiser. "A Suffren has only slightly less powerful guns than the *Canopus*, and she's faster. Not so, Lieutenant Hernandez?"

"Yes ma'am," Hernandez answered. "According to the warbook anyways."

"These sensor readings, you based them on active scans?"

"No ma'am. Our active scanners were knocked down upon emergence. We were so close to *Pollux* when we emerged, Captain Monti had to make some very violent evasive maneuvers. The active sensors went off-line, and didn't recover until after the encounter."

"I see. No active scans. That's quite a failure, Lieutenant."

"Ma'am." Hernandez nodded. "My apologies."

Monti wiggled in her chair. *She doesn't sound sorry. And I didn't see any cruisers. What's her game?*

Hernandez continued. "Emergence was so violent, the ship nearly shook itself apart. As you can see, we're held together by leak foam. Captain Monti did an outstanding job bringing a crippled ship back to the convoy, and Lieutenant Weeks's repairs were a masterstroke."

The admiral broke in. "In the Empire, we expect nothing less than excellence at all times. Are you satisfied, Captain Mahony?"

"Yes, Admiral." Mahony smiled. "I'm confident that at least one warship of comparable strength to the *Canopus* awaits us in the next system."

"Comparable strength?" Admiral Bracebridge's brows knitted. "*Canopus* is a battleship. This other...Suffering... is a cruiser."

"Suffren, Admiral, not suffering. And she's not just a cruiser, she's a heavy cruiser. A modern heavy cruiser. *Canopus* could possibly defeat her, but you'd know you were in a fight. A hard fight. Damage to the *Canopus* would be extensive, and you could expect to take heavy casualties."

"Heavy casualties. I see." Bracebridge nodded. "Well, I'm sure with our other escort ships, we could handle her easily."

Mahony's eyes flicked down to her screen. She was looking at someone's face on her console.

The other reserve captain, Llewling, had been waiting for her signal to jump in. "Tara, that other ship, the Admiral class heavy cruiser, is that the one they call a pocket battleship?"

Mahony nodded. "Yes. They have battleship-class guns on a cruiser class hull. Over gunned, under armored, but still fast. Those two ships together, that's a problem for any battleship. Especially an old one like *Canopus*."

"Well, with that level of firepower ahead of us, I'm not sure I want to jump into that mess." Llewling shook his head. "And while the big ships are fighting it out, we'll have the *Pollux* attacking the convoy itself. And what sort of escorts did she have? Lieutenant Hernandez, what other ships did you see?"

Hernandez shook her head. "None confirmed sir. But we were busy looking at the capital ships. The ones we could see, at least."

"What do you mean, the ones you could see?"

"Sir, we were maneuvering under fire. I only had so much time, and only our passive sensors were operating, so we directed the telescopes and receivers to focus on the nearest ships. There were other anomalies in the sensor data, but we didn't have time to investigate them."

"How many anomalies?"

"Seventeen."

"Seventeen? There are potentially seventeen other ships out there?"

Mahony jumped back in. "They could be light escorts, Jim."

"Or not, Tara. What if there are more heavies out there? Seventeen is a lot of escorts."

"It's bad enough we think there are two cruisers out here. You think there are more?"

"What does fleet intelligence say, then?" Llewling asked. "Lieutenant, any idea how those heavy ships got out here in the Verge?"

"Sir, I don't even know how I got out to the Verge." Everyone on the call grinned. "But I assume somebody sent them."

"Like who?"

"Like somebody's sister," Mahony muttered.

"I see." Llewling nodded. "So to summarize, you detected at least two capital ships and escorts at the convoy's next jump destination."

"At least two capital ships. Outstanding. And we're all ready to fly into that." Mahony's eyes switched to a different spot on her screen. "Orders, Admiral?"

Sweat beaded on the admiral's forehead. "Two capital ships, you say?"

"Two modern capital ships," Mahony said.

"Well, we can't, I mean, we shouldn't..." The admiral gulped. "The convoy is of the most importance. But how did they get there? Ahead of us?"

"We're on one of the most direct routes from the Core to the Verge," Mahony said. "So they could have been picketing likely systems and got lucky."

"Very lucky," Llewling said. "And if I were them, I'd be coming for us now."

"What? Coming for us?" the admiral said.

"Yes sir. They know what system *Collingwood* came from, and where it went back to. An aggressive combat commander would collect his ships and follow her into jump and catch us back here."

"Back here? They're coming here?"

"Could be," Mahony said.

"We need to get away... I mean, the convoy has to be saved."

"With respect, Admiral," Hernandez interrupted. "We've been giving this some thought on the jump back. The Merhack system is a good alternative. It's a farther jump, but the angle isn't that bad. The convoy could redeploy easily to a vector there."

Monti opened her mouth, then shut it. *Merhack? She never mentioned that.*

"We'll do that. We'll do that right away," the admiral said. "I'll have my navigation team send new courses immediately. Execute your orders as soon as you receive them."

"Sir." Mahony spoke up. "*Collingwood* and the other escorts will need to refuel. I can give them the necessary instructions after the meeting. Permission to drop out of formation to conduct fueling operations."

"Yes. Yes, of course. Just don't delay the others. Everyone. Prepare for vector change."

The admiral disconnected without dismissing them. The remaining captains waited, then dropped off. Everybody disappeared until it was just Mahony, Llewling, and the *Collingwood* crew.

"I'll cover the other escorts, Tara," Captain Llewling said. "I'll leave the *Collingwood* to you. Smooth sailing."

"You too, Ron." Mahony waited until he dropped off, then addressed Monti. "Captain Monti, you've been quiet up to now. Anything you want to add?"

"Only to commend Lieutenant Hernandez on her quick thinking on her emergence. If she hadn't continued scanning, we wouldn't have the sensor scans we have now."

"Of course, of course." Mahony nodded. "Lieutenant Hernandez, would it be possible to see the raw scans from your sensors?"

"We can only share them with the admiral and his staff ma'am."

"What would you do if you got a request for the raw data from the admiral?"

"Wouldn't matter ma'am. We suffered a number of failures during our escape. Some of the raw logs were damaged."

"But the summaries and computer interpretations survived?"

"They did ma'am."

"How convenient. How very convenient. Well, Captain Monti, my fueling crew will send you instructions."

"Ma'am."

"I hope you know what you're doing, Captain."

"We've fueled before ma'am."

"That's not what I'm talking about. But good luck. Mahony clear." The channel fizzled out.

Monti, Hernandez, and an until-now-silent Hooper exchanged glances.

"Hernandez," Monti said. "I didn't know we had a sensor log failure."

"Fixed now."

"And our active sensors weren't working?"

"Oh, they were working fine. I didn't have enough time to activate them."

"Not enough time. During the lead up to our jump? The lengthy lead up to our jump?"

Hernandez shrugged. "I'm intelligence, not fleet. I'm not as familiar with these systems as you two. I'm sure you would have done a better job if you weren't so busy."

"Yup. Yup." Monti shook her head. "Set course for the Merhack system, then."

Hooper looked up from her navigation screen. "Hey, Hernandez."

"Yes?"

"What's in the Merhack system?"

"Fuel. Water."

"Anything else?"

"Trouble." Hernandez grinned. "Lots of trouble."

Chapter 42

Devin put a picture of the system up on the main screen. "The Merhack system. What am I looking at?"

Lukas, the sensor lieutenant, highlighted points on the screen. "Twenty-two planets. Twelve rocky ones in close, ten gas giants. Hundreds of moons and moonlets. Asteroids everywhere. The rocky ones are mostly uninhabitable, except for three that are marginal. Too cold for most anything. All three have minor settlements. Biggest one is on the outermost rocky planet. Edmunchuck is the name."

"Odd name."

"Something to do with the weather and the ethnic group that colonized it. It's over there." Lukas highlighted a planet. "Doesn't even have a station in orbit. Neighbor wise, nothing for two parsecs in any direction from this system. Long-haul merchant traffic comes from the Core, jumps in, refuels, then jumps out. Nobody comes inside the jump limit if they don't have to, they dawdle at whatever gas giant is nearby. They don't even have to transit to this side of the system, the nearest stars are only sixty degrees apart—jump in, gas up, turn sixty degrees, jump out."

"A waystation, then. How long will it take to fuel a convoy with eighty-odd ships?"

"Days, Tribune. Even if a merchant can skim fuel, their systems aren't designed for speed."

"The warships can fuel faster. And they have tankers."

"Yes, Tribune, but the convoy has to wait for the last ship to fuel up. Even with tankers, that takes time. And if they don't want to split up, then they have to pick a gas giant and move the whole convoy to it. And with so many different ships and different fueling profiles, and since they're not military..."

"Outstanding." Devin tapped his console, then highlighted a spot on the display. "Assume an eighty-ship convoy arrives at this point in say... twenty-seven hours. It needs to fuel. Pick the three most likely destinations and plot the courses. And I sent a convoy plan to your station."

"Very well, Tribune." Lukas examined the file Devin had sent him. "Sir, where did you get this convoy plan?"

"A friend of mine gave it to me." Devin blanked his expression. *Hopefully, she's a friend of mine and not a friend of the Chancellor.*

"Sir, this file is incorrect."

"Corrupted?"

"No sir. Wrong. Nobody would organize a convoy this way. Nobody smart anyways. You have the heavy fleet elements leading the center column. That leaves all manner of blind spots on the flanks and astern they can't cover. They should be in the middle. From there, they can maneuver to shoot above or behind."

"So, this is a stupid way to do things?"

"Very stupid sir."

"Then it's correct. Calculate your courses. Carry on."

"Sir." Lukas exchanged glances with Trevor at the helm. Trevor raised his eyebrows, shrugged, and turned back to his console. Lukas took over the main screen to do his work. Trevor chimed in from time to time.

Lionel opened up a private channel to Devin. "You think the convoy will come out of jump at that point in twenty-seven hours."

"Twenty-six hours, forty-two minutes." Devin put a counter on his screen. "And twelve seconds."

"So exact. And why this system? Why not stay on their original course?"

"They were diverted, because their scout ship reported that they saw *Pollux* and at least two capital ships lying in wait for them."

"Two capital ships? What type?"

Lionel explained the explanations that Hernandez had messaged she would pass on to Lord Bracebridge.

"You knew this was going to happen? You ordered Hernandez to do this?"

"She did it herself."

"That's friendly of her."

"She's a friendly girl."

Lionel raised his eyebrows at Devin's tone, then shook his head. "And the scans?"

"She had enough ambiguity on her screens that she can get away with classifying the tankers as capital ships. Her plan was to lie about the forces facing them, and have the convoy turn back. She suggested Merhack as an alternate, because we could lie in wait for the convoy here and ambush it."

"Ambush it?"

"Yes."

"That's a great idea, Tribune!"

"Isn't it?"

"Yes, except…"

"Except what?"

Lionel held his hands out wide and ticked things off on his fingers. "We don't actually have two capital ships. We have zero capital ships, one frigate, and some corvettes and some other light ships. We'll get slaughtered."

"You told me the *Pollux* could take on a battleship."

"I lied."

"You did?"

"I was trying to make you feel better. Only crazy, insane people take on a battleship with a frigate."

"A hundred-year-old battle ship with a modern frigate, with newer, better weapons."

"Yes, hundred-year-old weapons. But lots of them. Quantity has a quality all its own."

"You're very philosophical today."

"It's because you're very suicidal today. Brings out the theorist in me."

"Sir!" Lukas interrupted. "Course is on the screen."

Three lines ran from the jump limit. Two headed for the same destination, decelerating all the way. One kinked slightly as it passed by a rocky planet, the other beelined straight in. Both indicated a pause for fueling, then departed on a standard course, accelerating all the way to the jump limit. The third course crossed half of the system under power, then flipped and decelerated, coming to rest next to a different gas giant for fueling. It had a much shorter hop to the jump limit.

"Explain these to me," Devin said.

"This course—" Lukas highlighted the system-crossing course. "Minimizes time in-system. Accel into the gravity well, flip, accel out."

"Wait." Lionel held up a hand. "They're not a naval squadron. It's a bunch of freighters. Half of them won't have a full crew complement. They won't do that elaborate a maneuver. Skip that one."

Undeterred, Lukas highlighted the kinked course. "If that's the case, Prefect, then they won't want to do this one either—it has a close pass gravity assist maneuver. That leaves this one."

Lukas highlighted the straight-line course. "This is the simplest, most obvious solution, come out of jump and head for the nearest gas giant. Throw everyone into the atmosphere and hang out until the freighters suck their tanks full. Top up the warships first on a high orbit in case they have to maneuver, then top them up again before you head out. This is the course that I would recommend to a rookie convoy commander."

"Very well." Devin nodded. "Tribune Lionel. Get Santana and the others on comms. I need to disperse some Marines."

The *Valhalla*, four corvettes, five freighters, four miscellaneous gunboats, and the *Heart's Desire* had been loitering in the system, waiting for Devin. He put out a call to all the naval commanders, including Dirk.

"Our plan is to seize all the ships in the convoy and redirect them to our own use. Brigadier, you will break your groups into as many boarding parties as you can. Arm them for ship security operations. Stuff the corvettes and the gunships first. I want each of them to have at least four different boarding parties. I know—" Devin held up his hand as the message lights flickered on from the corvettes. "Life support is an issue. I understand corvettes can't carry double crews forever. These Marines will only be on board twenty-four hours, probably less. My staff is sending a list of asteroids, rocky moons, comets, whatever they can find. You warships, take your Marines, ground on the moons. In twenty-five hours and—" Devin checked his comm. "Forty-two minutes, Convoy Core-Verge thirteen will enter this system and proceed on the course indicated. At the signal, you will drop and commence seizing the freighters in the convoy, deploying one party per ship, size dependent on the ship."

Devin ignored more lights requesting questions. "You will inform the crew that they are guests of the provisional government of the Empire, and that if they pilot the ships to a port we specify, then they will be released there, with such pay and benefits as they are owed. If they aren't willing to do that, they will be our prisoners and will be transported to confinement on the *Valhalla*. Anyone who doesn't accept an immediate boarding, fire into them. One shot should be more than enough to convince the freighter crews to surrender. If it isn't, well, you're Marines, you know what to do. Questions so far?"

"Tribune," Santana said. "What will the convoy escort be doing while this is happening?"

"*Pollux* and her consorts will be engaging and neutralizing the escort at that time."

"Consorts? Who will those be?"

"Your ship, for one. And our two trusty tankers."

"We are armed for self-defense only. We can't beat anything bigger than a corvette. While I'm willing to do a death-or-glory charge for the Empire's defense, I don't see that we'll have much impact on the escort listed on your plan. There's a battleship there, according to this report."

"The *Canopus*. An old battleship. And you have my permission to break off whenever you feel your ship is in imminent danger of destruction. It's not even necessary for you to come in range of her guns."

"Tribune, they'll laugh at us."

"They won't laugh. You and the tankers have military-class electronic warfare suites. We'll use a deception. One of the tankers will be squawking a Suffren class cruiser beacon, the other an Admiral class pocket battleship, and you'll be a... Lionel, what will he be?"

"Sound class fighter carrier," Lionel said. "Roughly same displacement and size. I suggest ISS *Bogue*."

Santana shook his head. "Once we get closer, they'll see right through that. Even at a distance, if they have good optics or they can get a good radar mapping on us, they won't believe it."

"They don't have to believe it forever. Just long enough for our corvettes and the gunships to get in close and get crews on the freighters. We've got ten small ships, give them two hours and they can each get two or three boarding parties out there. That means thirty or more of those freighters will be running in all directions."

"They do have some escorts. They can run down the escaping ships."

"They won't be able to, they'll be busy. And too far away to intervene."

"With respect, Tribune, what will they be busy doing? What will occupy them so much that they'll send fleet elements away from a convoy?"

Devin smiled and tapped his comm. The main display of the meeting changed from the bridge of the *Pollux* to a new one labeled '*Heart's Desire*.' Everybody in the conference saw Devin's smiling face replaced by Dirk's frowning one.

"Lord Duke Friedel, so glad you could join us." Devin smirked. "Let me explain your task in our upcoming operation."

Chapter 43

"You want us to do what?" Ana asked. "Attack an entire Imperial convoy and its escort?"

"No, no, no," Dirk said. "Not attack a convoy." He'd been in his quarters during the meeting with Devin, and he'd come out into the lounge to explain things. "Not attack it, no."

"Good, 'cause that would be stupid. Yes, Private?" Ana looked to Scruggs, who was waving to him. He'd spent the last shift talking with her and dissecting her actions protecting the truck and organizing the defense of the barges from the bandits. He was impressed that she'd accomplished so much without direction. Impressed enough that he'd decided that she wasn't junior crew anymore, and didn't have to do the majority of the cleaning and cooking. Of course, that meant that somebody else had to pitch in to pick up her extra shifts.

"It's your turn on the kitchen rota, Centurion," Scruggs said. "If you still want to take it."

"So it is." Ana stood. "And I do. That was an outstanding job back there, and you deserve your reward. And it will give me time to plan my next test for you."

"You do that, Centurion. Whatever it is," Scruggs said. "I'm ready for it."

Ana paused and looked at her. She was the same small woman who had joined the crew so long ago, but she didn't act the same. More confident, less worried. Older. *I'll bet she is ready for it, after all.*

"Ever thought about being an officer, Scruggs?"

Scruggs shrugged. "Being in charge is hard work, Centurion."

"The hardest," Ana agreed. "Everyone, dinner will be ready in five minutes."

"About time," Gavin muttered. "You should have been in here earlier setting up."

"You're right, I should have." Ana plodded to the microwave. "And I apologize for the delay. I'm moving slowly right now."

"Do you need more time in the med pod, Centurion?" Scruggs asked. "And I can take your turn—"

"No, and no." Ana fed trays into the microwave. "The last thing I need is more time in the med pod. I need activity, need to move around. Too much time lying, and you stiffen up. Fixing dinner is just the trick."

"Fixing? You mean heating trays?" Dena said.

"You don't have to eat them if you don't want to."

"They're disgusting."

"Yes. Your point?"

Dena sighed. "Give me a red one."

"Red ones are the best," Scruggs said. "Too bad Cleon and Clara weren't here." The twins had been sent to the *Pollux* as aspirant officers. RC had been sent to the *Valhalla*, officially because there was more room, unofficially because everybody worried that the Tribune would stab him to death when he remembered he was there.

"Why is that?" Dena asked.

"Well, then they'd be junior. Junior crew gets the dirty jobs."

"Dirty jobs?" Dena grinned. "What type of jobs?"

"Well," Scruggs said. "They could do chores and things. Help us out."

"They're not trained spacers, Baby Marine. They don't know ship things."

"I could find them something to do," Scruggs said. "Cleon for sure. He's good with his hands."

Dena hid her guffaw behind her hand. The others exchanged grins or looked at the floor. Lee took a moment to suppress a giggle.

"What?" Scruggs said. "He helped fix the truck and move those planks."

"He did. He did." Lee nodded. "But back to the matter at hand. Pilot, if we're not going to be attacking this convoy, why are we heading out to the jump limit?"

"And heading out slowly," Gavin pointed to the screen in the galley. "Quarter-G? Not that I mind reduced gravity, but what's the point?"

"We're not going to fight this convoy," Dirk said.

"No?"

"We're going to let them jump in and discover us. The convoy commander will dispatch ships to catch us, and take us in for questioning."

Ana slammed the microwave buttons. "Is this the new Imperial mind control I've been reading about? Make them dispatch escorts. Why would they do any of that? First, why would they dispatch ships at all? They've got a convoy to run. Second, even if they care, why would they bother to take us in for questioning? At this point, if they don't ignore us, we're pretty much committed to Tribune Devin's rebellion. This will be a Core convoy, they'll figure out that we're not their friends pretty quickly. Why not blow us to space dust and call it a day?"

"They will pursue us, because the person they see on the radio will be somebody worth pursuing."

"Who?"

"Me," Dirk said. "I'll show myself, and I'll make sure I'm irritating."

"Be yourself, in other words." Ana slid one set of trays out and dumped them on the table, then fired the second ones in. "That is a good plan. The list of people who want to shoot you for being yourself is long. In fact, I'm on it. Given the choice, I could see myself diverting my ship to shoot you up. Well done."

"Skipper." Gavin shoved his food with his fork. "That's a great plan. I agree with the centurion here, that any Core-based convoy commander might want to send out a few ships to shoot you."

"You don't have to sound so happy about it," Dirk said.

"I'm not, exactly." Gavin lifted his fork. "Isn't this supposed to be red mush? This is more like red glue."

"Tastes the same," Ana said.

"Right." Gavin dropped his fork. "But, Skipper, given that a lot of people want to shoot you and all, how do we keep them from shooting us at the same time? We're in the same ship after all."

"Good point. But I have a plan to stop that from happening." Dirk spooned some red mush into his mouth and swallowed. "It doesn't taste like glue. More like that silicone hatch sealant we use."

Dena pushed her tray away. "Leaving aside how you know what hatch sealant tastes like. What's your plan?"

Scruggs had already eaten her tray. She pointed at Dena's. "You going to finish that?"

"Help yourself," Dena said. "Dirk? Plan?"

"Who's worth more alive than dead right now?"

"Not me," Dena said. "Nobody cares about me. Lee's tight with the Empress, but if these are Core people, sounds like killing her won't make the Empress any angrier with them than she already is. And lots of Imperials already want Gavin dead."

"And Confeds and Nats." Scruggs scraped some food from Dena's tray onto hers and put it down for a grateful Rocky to lap up. "Lots of people want Gavin dead."

Dena nodded. "Nobody cares about the old man, and you're in the Navy in theory, and Navy people die all the time. Nobody gets upset about that."

"I'd be upset," Dirk said.

"Nobody important, I should have said." Dena watched Scruggs spoon up the red glue. "And isn't there a price on Scruggs's head, dead or alive?"

Dirk nodded. "New update from the Core about Scruggs's warrant."

"Cancelled?"

"Increased." Dirk pointed at Scruggs. "The new Chancellor wants to talk to her. New bounty on her head, quarter-million credits. Bring in for questioning." Dirk grinned. "Nobody will blow this ship up while they have the chance of catching her."

"You want us to do what?" Monti looked at Hernandez across the bridge.

"Look, even your buddy Bron said I'm good on the sensors." Hernandez tapped her screen. "I'm just asking for a little leeway in my interpretations, and a delay in sending updates to the flag."

Monti turned to Hooper. "You think she's good on the sensors?"

"She doesn't suck." Hooper pointed to her own screen. "She was in Naval Intelligence after all, or Internal Security, and we've got enough problems keeping this ship from shaking apart. Why not let her do sensors? Our sensors suck anyways. We wouldn't see an enemy unless we banged into them."

Monti pointed at Hernandez. "Bron, I thought you hated her."

"I do. And she's lying. But she's the most competent sensor operator on board."

"Better than you? Better than me?"

"Franky, we have a ship to run. We're barely going to keep it together as it is. We don't have enough trained officers."

"I could ask the flag for some help."

"First, that would kill your career."

"I don't want a Navy career."

"And second, Admiral Bracebridge might shoot you. He's already managed to get his aide dumped out an airlock."

"That wasn't judicial, it was an accident."

"Pretty strange accident."

Monti turned to glare at Hernandez. "She's lying about something."

"She's lying about everything." Hooper shrugged. "So what. But consider this. The only way you could stop her doing what she says she wants to do is not have her on sensors. Or double-check her all the time, which you won't have time to do if the tabbo hits the fan."

Monti cursed quietly. "Something is going on here."

"Something bigger than us." Hooper glanced down as a light flashed on her screen. "*Hydrogen Queen* calling. There's a slot for us in thirty minutes. What should we do, Captain?"

Monti cursed again. *I don't trust her. She's up to no good. Just make sure she doesn't get us blown up.* "Take the slot. Fuel up. Then set a course for the jump limit, per the admiral's course."

Maneuvering jets fired, and the *Collingwood* aligned to intercept the tanker. Monti glared at Hernandez in silence.

Hernandez gave the cross-chest salute. "The Empire."

"Bite me," Monti said. "And get us to that tanker."

Chapter 44

"Turn us around," Lee said over the intercom. "Again."

"Stupid Tribune, stupid Empire, stupid rebellion," Gavin answered. An alarm bonged, and five seconds later, the *Heart's Desire* flipped, then the main drive fired.

"How long now?" Dirk asked. He, Lee, and a napping Scruggs were in the control room. The Tribune's oh-so-precise estimate had expired thirty-five hours ago. Devin had made one call for all the ships to remain silent and keep position until otherwise instructed. Dirk had been ordered to keep on a racetrack course back and forth, shuttling between two moons, both with ice deposits to give some sort of cover for his weird behavior.

"Too long." Lee yawned. "Eight more hours at one-quarter-G. Boring, but I'm glad we're not in those corvettes."

"The Marines will be defecating in their suits by now," Dirk said. "Imagine the smell."

Lee sniffed, then wrinkled her nose. "I don't have to. I live it. Have you skipped your shower again?"

Dirk ignored the gibe. He didn't shower as often as he should. "The plan was to keep them suited up until they could board. That will probably backfire now, so to speak."

"Who'd be a Marine?" Lee asked.

"Brave, patriotic and hard-working Imperial Citizens, that's who." Ana said, pulling himself into the control room. His breathing was labored. He still spent an hour in the med pod each shift.

"Yeah, yeah," Dirk said. "Wait, Centurion, you were in the Army, not the Marines."

"True." Ana belted himself in and brought up a weapons and sensor console. "I was. But I did try to join the Imperial Marines at one point."

"Really?" Dirk raised his eyebrows. "How'd that go?"

"Didn't make it. Failed the IQ test."

"Sorry to hear that," Dirk said.

"My second choice was the Imperial Navy," Ana said. "Failed that test too."

"Oh. Wow. I didn't know that. Which test?"

"Intelligence again."

"You failed the Navy's Intelligence test?"

"And the Marines both. They said I was too smart to be a Marine, and way too smart to be in the Navy."

Dirk glared at Ana. Scruggs, who had woken up, laughed. "You walked into that one, Pilot." Then she pointed. "Radar receiver just flashed. Something's out there."

Lee ran through her screens. "Jump light. Jump signatures. Many jump signatures."

"Put your game face on, Private," Ana said. "Showtime."

"Emergence," Silaski, the *Collingwood's* helmsman, said. The jump light flashed on her display, and stars replaced it. The ship shuddered and slewed sideways, then corrected. She waited. Nobody answered. "Emergence," she said again. Still silence. She turned in her seat and looked at Hernandez, seated next to her. Hernandez tapped her earpiece, then her helmet just in front of her mouth. Silaski stared for a moment. "Stupid helmets. I hate being buttoned up when we come out of jump. This is dumb. I hate this ship. I hate the Empire. I hate the officers." She tapped her collar and tapped a stud until her radio setting glowed green. "Emergence, Captain."

"I know." Monti's voice came through her radio. "Your speakers were off, not your microphone. I don't care if you hate me. Just do your job. Are we where we are supposed to be?"

Silaski's face burned red. "Um, I'll check, Captain." She turned to her board. Now, how to cross-check her location. There was a way to use the telescope. She'd watched a tutorial. Maybe reload the tutorial...

"Beacon," Hernandez announced. "Imperial freighter *Heart's Desire*. Inbound from Papillon, general cargo. Captain Dirk Friedel commanding."

"—well, use one of the other thrusters, then." Monti was arguing with Weeks in engineering. "We can't have them unbalanced at a critical moment. Say again, Hernandez?"

"That freighter on the screen, it's the *Heart's Desire*. Last commander was Dirk Friedel. He's with the rebel Devin now."

"The rebel Devin, what an interesting way of describing him." Monti checked her screen. "He's turning away."

"We should pursue," Hernandez said.

"We should not give advice to captains, Lieutenant Hernandez," Monti said.

Hooper suppressed a giggle. "Not this captain anyways."

"Shut up, Bron."

"I thought you said no nicknames on the bridge?"

"Shut up. Hernandez?"

"Yes, Acting Temporary Captain Temporarily Activated Lieutenant Monti?"

"Shut—oh, to Hades with it. Silaski, get us an intercept course for the *Heart's Desire* and chase her down."

"Um." Silaski bit her lip.

"Hades. Bron?"

"On it." Hooper brought up the navigation screen. "Stand by for vectors."

"Acting Captain Temporary Lieutenant Monti?"

"Hernandez, give it up. Call me whatever. What do you want?"

Hernadez highlighted the main screen. "Should we contact *Moncton* and *Trail* to join in the pursuit?"

"No, they've got their own sectors to sweep. We'll run this one down ourselves."

"Understood. Thank you, Captain. Good call." She busied herself with her sensor board.

Monti glared, then opened a private channel to Hooper.

"I'll have a course in a few minutes, Franky," Hooper said. "Have to crunch the numbers from the telescope."

"Hernandez thanked me."

"Creepy. Very. What's she lying about now?"

"Everything. As usual."

"Doesn't help."

"Why not?"

"We know what she says is a lie." Monti shook her head. "But that doesn't help us find the truth."

Devin's bedside console bonged, waking him. "Yes?"

"They're here!" Lionel's voice answered.

"Where?"

"Where you expected. Just almost two days late."

"That Admiral Bracebridge is more incompetent than I thought."

"Blame the flaws in your plan on the enemy. Well done."

"Who takes three days to muster a convoy to jump?"

"The core squadrons of the Imperial Navy, that's who. No rush, but could you come up to the bridge? We could benefit from your unique and fresh command perspective."

"I'll need a few minutes, but I'll be there."

Devin called Imin and explained his needs. Imin helped him suit up, then disappeared on the ordered errands. *Pollux* was in an unpowered orbit, so Devin had to pull himself up on the bridge.

"Report," he said after settling in his chair.

Villa, the navigator, jerked her head sideways. "Midshipman. Brief the Tribune."

Rudnar, the trainee midshipman, swiveled to see Villa. Her eyes widened and she shook her head no. Villa nodded back emphatically. Rudnar's eyes widened further.

Devin concealed a grin. "I'm waiting, Midshipman."

Rudnar gulped, then sat straight and faced her camera. "Sir. Tribune. Sir. Elements of Convoy Core-Verge Thirteen have jumped in-system. We've identified seventeen ships so far, including the battleship *Canopus*, and an unidentified cruiser, class uncertain, designated Enemy-Capital-1 and 2. An initial wave of three corvettes and a destroyer arrived ahead of the main body." She highlighted dots on her screens. "The corvettes are well in advance of the convoy in a broadly dispersed wedge formation, apparently sweeping for hostiles. The convoy itself, now... nineteen ships, has very poor spacing. The *Canopus* and the enemy cruiser are leading the convoy by an unusually large margin."

"How confident are you of your identification?" Devin asked.

"High confidence on the capital ships sir. The *Canopus's* physical dimensions check out on the telescope, and its electronic emissions match the signature we have in our database."

Lionel grunted. "That doesn't help. Our database signatures are years old."

"No sir. I mean, yes sir. But no." Sweat broke out on Rudnar's face. "But according to the database, the *Canopus* signature update is only a few weeks old, as are the corvettes. The signatures for the destroyer and the cruisers are much older. That's probably why the computer can't positively identify them."

"When did we update sensor signatures?" Lionel asked. "More importantly, who updated them? Did you do that, Rudnar?"

Rudnar shook her head. "I don't know sir."

"You don't know if you updated them? Surely you—"

"Sir," Lukas, the sensor operator, interrupted. "Rudnar lacks the authority to do that. Only a command officer can update sensor signatures."

"Well, I didn't do it." Lionel looked to Devin. "Tribune?"

"Um, Dirk had sent some information in, and I reviewed it, and it seemed correct, and well…"

"You took it on yourself to update the sensor database, and didn't inform us?"

"Of course not. I would never do such a thing."

"I see." Lionel crossed his arms. "Then who updated the signatures?"

Devin looked down. "I, um, told Imin to take care of it. And to not bother me with the details."

"Your steward has command access to the ship's computers?"

"I'm not saying that." *Did he give Imin his command codes?* He didn't remember doing that. But all that paperwork. He'd thumbed a lot of reports.

Lionel tapped the private channel button on his console. Devin ignored it. Lionel waited, arms crossed.

Lukas coughed. "A few more points sirs?"

Lionel tapped the channel request off. "I'm sure you'll brief me more fully later, Tribune. For now, we have a battle to plan. Lukas?"

"Sir. The destroyer is badly out of position, far, far behind one of the trailing corvettes. We think a mis-jump. Or incredibly bad navigation. And there's a lot of freighters out there. We're up to fifty-five, and the formation doesn't look complete yet. The Tribune's estimation may be low. And we've got a base course for the convoy."

"Already? They just got here."

"Sir, the warships are powering in at full speed, all of them. Except for that destroyer, they've all crossed the jump limit. And the freighters are maneuvering as well—as soon as they clear their jump emergence, they've all set a least time course for Merhack-1J, our estimated re-fueling point. Except for one corvette that is maneuvering to intercept decoy-1."

"Meaning the *Heart's Desire*. Summarize the situation for the fleet, Lukas."

"Status change," Rudnar broke in. "Enemy warships are changing vectors. Stand by for new course display."

Everyone shut up while Rudnar fiddled with her screen. Devin opened his mouth, but Lionel held up a hand and pointed to his console. Devin brought up the shared display. On one screen, Rudnar was having the nav computer calculate the new course. On the other, Lukas had split his screen and was mirroring her calculations. Rudnar was as fast as the more experienced Lukas. They would have to wait.

The bridge was silent for forty-three seconds before the first of Rudnar's courses displayed on the main board. Lukas looked up at the main board, glanced over his shoulder at Lionel and Devin, nodded, and returned to his board.

"Course calculations complete." Rudnar shook her head. "All the corvettes are now pursuing decoy-1. The big ships have changed vectors, but I'm not sure exactly what they are doing..."

"Sir." Lukas added circles around the two capital ships on the display. "The *Canopus* and Cruiser one are maneuvering to bracket decoy-1. They're trying to get clear shots if she changes course. The corvettes are straight out closing. If Captain Friedel maneuvers to get away from the corvettes, the capital ships will get him. If he keeps running the corvettes will overhaul him."

"What about the convoy?" Devin asked.

"Continuing on course to fuel sir. They'll pass right by our hidden units."

"Outstanding." Lionel nodded. "Right according to your plan."

"Yes, things seem to be working for once," Devin said. He bit his lip. "They can't be that stupid, can they? Leave the convoy unprotected?"

"That's what they're doing."

"Just what we wanted." Devin shook his head. "Worrisome. What are we missing?"

Chapter 45

"That's not Dirk Friedel," Hooper said. "I looked him up in the database."

"You sure?" Monti asked. As the *Collingwood* sped after them, a balding older man on the fleeing *Heart's Desire* challenged them to identify themselves.

"Yup, I've seen his picture."

"It's not him," Hernandez said. "I've met him."

The whole bridge crew turned to Hernandez.

Monti shut off the audio. "The Butcher of New Madrid? You've met him? In person?"

"We had dinner. A group of us. On Tribune Devin's ship."

"The rebel Tribune? You had dinner with the leader of the rebellion?"

"He wasn't called that then. He was just a Tribune. The rebel thing is new."

"What's it like eating with a traitor?"

Hernandez shrugged. "He wasn't then. But Dirk Friedel was there, and that isn't him. That's one of his crew, though. An older Army guy that was with him."

Hernandez shrugged again. Monti and Hooper exchanged glances. "But this is his ship—what's he doing—"

"That's him." Hooper pointed. The screen had changed. Now Dirk Friedel sat on one side, and a young red-haired woman in uniform sat next to him. "That's him. He matches the picture."

Monti looked at Hernandez. "Well? Is that Friedel? The Butcher of New Madrid?"

"Yes, yes, that's him." Hernandez nodded.

"And the others? The woman?"

Hernandez shook her head. "One of his crew. Nobody important."

"Well, keep pursuing, but the admiral will want to know. Bron, call the flag, and tell them—"

"Jove's knees, Jove's knees," Silaski yelled, then focused the screen on the redheaded woman on the left. "It's her."

"What? Her who?" Monti asked.

"It's Sandra Caroline Ruger-Gascoigne."

"Who's that?"

"She's this fabulously wealthy heiress who ran away from home to be a space pirate. She's run away to the Verge and she's on this ship with that Dirk guy. She steals from the rich and gives to the poor."

"She what?"

"Don't you watch *Galactic Edition*? Susy the newsy? Her news vids."

"Um. No." Monti shook her head. "Susy the newsy? *Galactic Edition*?"

"Yes." Silaski nodded. "It talks all about the most fabulous people at the Imperial Senate. I mean, she's not a senator, Sandra isn't, but her family is really rich. They own shipyards, and orbital mines, and like... herds of tabbos. All sorts of stuff."

"Her parents are rich?"

"Her uncle. She ran away. She's the heir to his shipyard, they say. He was friends with the Emperor, and the Chancellor. They were always in the news. They donate money to the charities and give money to schools. Susy is always interviewing the people who get their money. She's a star!"

"Who is? Susy?"

"No, Sandra."

"Which Sandra?"

"Her!" Silaski pointed. "Sandra. On the screen. She's on that ship. That's what Susy said!"

Monti remembered Silaski's news program now. "Well, we're supposed to destroy any rebel ships we find."

"But she's not a rebel! I mean, not a real rebel." Silaski's mouth dropped open. "You can't shoot her. I mean, yeah, there's an Imperial warrant out for her. But Susy says that's just a ploy, to get people to stop her. The Emperor wants to award her a star cluster, but she's run away, so the only way to stop her is to arrest her, and bring her back to—"

"Much as I want to hear what Susy the newsy says," Monti said. "I think—"

Hernandez flashed details of an Imperial warrant on the screen, next to Scruggs. "There's a reward for her capture. A big one. Alive."

Monti sighed. "Of course there is."

Hooper zoomed in on the details. "Yep. Sandra Caroline Ruger-Gascoigne. Wanted for questioning. Alive. Reward, Holy don't-shoot-me, two hundred fifty thousand credits. Often seen in company of the rogue naval officer Durriken Friedel and his nefarious crew."

"Nefarious?" Monti asked.

"Says so right here, Franky. Nefarious."

"We can't shoot her! She's famous!" Silaski said. "And nefarious. Anyways, the Emperor wants to talk to her."

Hooper glared at her. "Spaceman first—"

"Shut up, Spaceman," Monti said. "And never mind, Bron. Hernandez?"

"What?" Hernandez glared at her.

Monti grunted. "Why did I ever want a command slot?"

Hooper shook her head. "Personality flaw, most probably."

"Hernandez, why do you know so much about this Gascoigne person? That warrant, that's an odd piece of information to have at your fingertips."

"Maybe I watch Newsy-Susy."

"I doubt it." Hooper shook her head. "Secure weapons but continue pursuit. I'm going to bump this upstairs. See what the admiral wants us to do."

"Do you think he watches Susy the Newsy?" Hooper asked.

"Every day." Monti typed her message. "And twice on Sundays."

"It's sheer stupidity," Lionel said, looking at the courses on the screen. "They're dumber than a herd of tabbos during rainy season."

"They can't possibly be that dumb." Devin shook his head. "Not and run a starship. Or a convoy. It's got to be a trap."

"Look at the way that convoy is deployed. Warships in the wrong place. No trailing escort. The tankers are out of position, and their station keeping is a mess. That's stupid."

"You're the first person to tell me that freighter captains never follow orders."

"They'd follow your orders. You're the Mad Dog of the Verge. They'd be afraid you'd kill them. Ah-ha." Lionel snapped his fingers. "That's it."

"What's it?"

"They're not afraid of this commander. No matter what they do, they don't think he'll stab them to death."

"A little stabbing is good for the heart." Devin shook his head. "Well, my heart, not theirs. Bridge staff?" All heads turned. "Hands up who thinks our enemies are stupid."

All the officers except the two midshipmen raised their hands.

"Very well." Devin nodded. "Who says it's an incredibly subtle fiendish trap laid by highly experienced naval officers designed to trick us?"

Only Calroy, the junior midshipman, raised his hand.

"Thank you, Mr. Calroy. Ms. Rudnar, you haven't raised your hand?"

"Um." Rudnar colored. "I didn't think you wanted our opinion sir."

"You're part of the bridge staff, and yes, I do. Stupidity or cunning plan?"

Rudnar raised a hand. "Stupidity sir. They're as thick as a herd of tabbos."

"Calroy, you're the only one to disagree. Explain."

"Sir." Calroy paused. "Tribune. You're a member of the nobility, same as me. Imperial nobles like ourselves come from a long and distinguished line. We have history and years of training behind us. That type of education and intelligence doesn't just go away. It must be a cunning plan, one that's too subtle for these others to see."

"Riiigggghhtttt." Devin nodded. "Right."

"Midshipmen!" Lionel ordered. "Both of you. Immediately calculate a course for *Pollux* to the jump limit. Direct routing. Maximum speed. Send it to both the Tribune and myself."

Devin turned to Lionel and raised his eyebrows. Lionel pointed down at his screen then held up a hand, counting on his fingers.

Devin waited. Rudnar's course appeared in three seconds. She'd been running a continuous plot since they got into the system and had been updating it. They sat in silence for over a minute, then Calroy's course appeared.

Lionel examined it for a moment. "Calroy?"

"Sir?"

"This course has us slicing through the core of an outer gas giant at an appreciable fraction of light speed. Do you think we would survive that?"

"Ah, no sir," Calroy said.

Lionel waited. Nothing. "Calroy?"

"Sir?"

"Do it again. Right now. No planet busting this time."

Calroy busied himself at his console. Lionel popped Rudnar's course up on the screen. "Rudnar?"

"Sir?"

"Are you, or any of your family, members of the nobility by chance?"

"No sir. Not going back ten generations, at least."

"Thank you, Rudnar. Carry on." Lionel turned to Devin. "Well, Tribune? I think we've seen a good example of what the Imperial nobility is like these days."

Devin shook his head. "Shouldn't we at least pretend it could be a trap? Some of the Core nobility must be good at something?"

"No doubt, Tribune. No doubt." Lionel steepled his hands. "Could you provide me with some sort of list to study? A list of competencies?"

"Perhaps we should wait for more information."

"Like a transmission from one of the ships?"

"Perhaps."

"Tribune." Lionel lowered his voice. "It's one thing to hide sending a message when you're the only ship in a system, it's another when you've got an entire flotilla running along behind you, watching your every move. I don't think your spy will be contacting you right now. And you've got all the information you're going to get. You need to decide now."

Devin sighed. "Comms?"

Carrol, the comms officer, snapped to attention. "Tribune?"

"Messages to the fleet boarding elements," Devin said. "Execute, execute, execute."

"Something's happening back there," Hernandez said. "The freighters are changing vectors."

"Something good, I hope," Monti said. "Nothing good up here." The *Collingwood* was now the focal point of the pursuit of the *Heart's Desire*. A hemisphere of warships was converging on the renegade freighter. They were already over-reaching their quarry, but the heavy ships continued to accelerate. "If they keep on this course, the flagship will blow past that freighter so fast, there won't be an engagement window."

"Some of the freighters are dropping accel and coasting. Others have made some wild course changes."

"What's on sensors?" Monti asked.

"Nothing that we can see." Hernandez put up an outline of the *Collingwood* on the main screen. Different colored spheres surrounded the ship, with focused cones pointing ahead. "Which isn't saying much. Our sensors are crap. Especially our stern ones."

"Lieutenant, if our sensors are crap, how can we see that the freighters are stopping?" Silaski asked.

"Beacons," Hernandez popped up the info on the screen. "For Imperial ships, we can decode their beacons. And the beacons show current heading and speed as reported by the ship's own computers." Hernandez looked at Silaski. "You don't know about beacons?"

"No ma'am."

"Did you bribe you way past every test?"

"No." Silaski turned to her screen. "Not *every* test."

Monti watched for a moment. Silaski was bringing up another tutorial, this one on beacon information. "Well, nothing we can do about it. We're so deep in the gravity well here—"

"Message from the *Hydrogen North* on the all ships channel."

"What—"

Hooper cut the transmission in. The voice of Captain Llewling, the Naval Reserve captain in charge of the *Hydrogen North*, came over the channel. "Understood. We are cutting acceleration and awaiting your inspection party. We are unarmed, and will not resist. "

The channel fuzzed. Someone was transmitting, but too far away for their speech to be clear. Llewling's voice came back. "Understood. We will accept parole conditions, provided they guarantee life and safety of the crew. Standing by for your inspection parties."

"They're being boarded?" Monti asked. "By who? Where are the other ships?"

Hernandez shrugged. "Can't tell."

Monti drummed her fingers on her console. *The convoy is too far back to protect from whatever is happening, and the admiral is an ass.* She sniffed disaster in the air. Best to make sure she wasn't blamed. "Inform the flag. They have better sensors than we do."

Hooper widened the display on the screen, showing the *Collingwood* and her consorts chasing the *Heart's Desire*, deep in Merhack's gravity well. The freighters formed a cluster on the jump limit. Less than half still showed acceleration vectors. Most were drifting with no thrust. Whatever was happening out there, they had no hope of interfering.

"But not better tactical judgment."

Chapter 46

"No battle plan survives contact with the enemy," Devin said. "Except for this one."

"This one is doing much better than we ever planned." Lionel highlighted the warships on the display. "Nothing is in position to hit the boarding parties except that destroyer. And it's not moving."

"Sensor failure?"

"Or a complete unwillingness to get involved."

"How many of the freighters did we get?"

Lionel put the list on the screen. "I don't have a final count yet. We've only boarded twenty three so far. The rest are drifting or ambling along. Quarter-G. Lukas, how many evaded?"

"Four jumped out before boarding commenced sir," Lukas said. "They were all outside the jump limit, took one look at what was happening, then panic-jumped. Jove knows which systems they'll eventually reach. Two more over here—" Lukas highlighted two freighters who were near, but not outside, the jump limit. "They're moving at one-quarter-G, and we don't have anybody near enough to catch them if they increase accel. If they figure that out, they can power away and we won't be able to get them, not unless we dedicate one of the escorts."

"Stick to the plan, Tribune," Lionel said. "Let them go if they want. No need to get fancy."

"I will." Devin nodded. "What's Dirk's status?"

The bridge quieted. Nobody spoke.

Devin looked around. "As bad as that?"

"Well." Lionel took a slow breath. "Admiral Bracebridge, who we now can confirm is in charge, with his insanely reckless and mindless pursuit of the *Heart's Desire* drew his entire squadron out of position. They've got so much velocity, there's no way they can stop us mopping up the whole convoy. They can't get back in time."

"But?" Devin asked.

"They're going to squash the *Heart's Desire* like one of your strawberries after a herd of tabbos runs over it." Lionel pointed. "Nothing we can do. They'll overfly her no matter what she does. Soon, if they keep up that insane acceleration profile."

"Let Dirk surrender, then," Devin said. "Won't be the first time he's been in an Imperial prison cell. We'll get him and his people out afterward in an exchange. Some of these freighter people are bound to want to go coreward."

"Yes. But we can read some of their message traffic. And..."

"And what?"

"They're not recognizing them as a Naval Auxiliary. Admiral Bracebridge has said he's going to space them as pirates. If he doesn't blow them up first."

"Durriken Friedel is an Imperial Naval officer. So is Praetorian Michaelson. And even that annoying Army fellow is an Imperial Auxiliary soldier. Plus, there is a huge warrant out for that redheaded young lady, Lee's friend, Scruggs." Devin frowned. "Wouldn't want to be that spy fellow, though. They can shoot him no problem."

"Admiral says he doesn't care. The word of a rebel doesn't count for anything."

"What about the word of an Imperial noble?"

"Tribune. We can't—"

"We can and we will. Set course to pursue."

"Tribune, I don't—"

"Rudnar?"

The midshipman sat up straight and her face colored. "Sir?"

"Set a pursuit course for that armada. We are going to support the *Heart's Desire*. I'm going to my cabin to speak to Imin. I have a matter to attend to. Do it now, and don't tell me you can't calculate the course. I know you have one laid in already. Execute it."

Devin strode out of the control room. He ignored Lionel calling the *Valhalla* as he left. That wouldn't end well.

"We're all going to die," Ana announced, tapping his console.

"You don't have to sound so happy about it," Lee said. "And are you sure?"

"Of course I'm sure," Ana said. "If your numbers are right. Which I'm sure they are. Never said Praetorians are bad at math. And even these crappy sensors show every warship behind us gaining. There's nowhere to hide ahead, and they could see us trying anyways. Death awaits us."

"You still sound too happy."

"Not at dying," Ana said. "I mean, there are days, but that's not it. I've always known something like this would happen. In fact, I'm surprised that it took this long. But I am excited."

"Excited about a violent death by decompression?" Dirk asked. "Or the burning to death first in the explosions?"

"The training potential," Ana said. "What a great learning opportunity this is!"

"Death as a learning opportunity?" Dirk shook his head. "Not very cost effective, is it."

"We are not dead yet," Ana said.

"That would be the way to bet," Dirk said.

"Agreed. But it hasn't happened yet." Ana flicked the intercom. "Everybody come to the lounge. We need to talk about imminent death." He unbuckled and pulled himself out of the seat. "Let's go, Private. Coming, Navy, Praetorian?"

"Somebody has to drive the ship," Dirk said.

"Put it on auto. We're doomed. Nothing you can do makes any difference, right?"

Dirk looked at his screens, shrugged, and unbuckled. "I hate it when you're right."

The crew collected in the lounge. Ana made a detour to his room and brought back a bottle of his Amiens brandy and poured everyone a healthy glass. Then he put up the courses on the lounge screens, and with Lee's and Dirk's help, explained the issues.

"To summarize." He took a slug of brandy. "No escape. We're outclassed in terms of speed, firepower, armor, and everything else. We'll be blown to spacedust shortly. Questions?"

The room was silent, until Dena said, "What happens now?"

"Now?" Ana poured himself another drink and drank it in a gulp. "I could use a nap. I think I'll go to bed. You should too, Nature Girl."

"Much as I want to go out in style," Dena said. "Being with you at this moment would be a poor second choice—"

"Not sleeping with me, you young idiot. I mean sleeping-sleeping. I'm still done in from the shooting. Now for the rest of you, what we have here," Ana said, "is a classical dilemma. And you know who fixes dilemmas? Officers, that's who. Not me."

"You mean Dirk?" Dena asked.

"He's a poor example of an officer," Ana said. "I was thinking more of asking Scruggs here for a solution." Ana gestured to Scruggs. "Making hard decisions under stress is an important milestone in a young officer's career. And she'll be an officer someday, so this is a good test for her. Excellent training." Ana drank down his glass. "That's good stuff."

"But, Centurion, what do you want me to do?" Scruggs said.

Ana shook his head. *Time to see what she's made of.* "That's not how it works. Time to step up. You've had fun. This runaway thing, waif of the spaceways and all that. Time's up. You need to decide what to do. This rebellion thing, all this other stuff. If you're officer material, you'll figure out a way to do this."

"But I don't want the responsibility—"

"I know." Ana held up his hand. "I know. That's why you ran away. Too bad. Responsibility caught up with you. I think that you can figure a way out of this. Get chopping, Sandra."

Dena blinked. "Who the heck is Sandra?"

"That's her name," Dirk said. "We never use it, though."

"Right, I forgot." Dena turned to Ana. "Why call her Sandra, why now?"

"Because before she was Scruggs, now she has to be Sandra." Ana smiled. "If this is going to work."

"Baby Marine, what's he talking about?" Dena asked.

"Taking charge," Dirk said. "Stepping up. I know what he means."

"I certainly don't," Dena said.

"Ana was in the Army, long time ago. Gavin's not from here. Neither are you, Dena, not really. Lee works for the Empress, which is not a great thing right now. Me, well, everybody knows about me."

"And nobody cares about you, Navy," Ana said.

"Certainly not some Core-appointed fake-admiral," Dirk said. "I'm just another snooty noble to him. Killing nobles would only cheer him up. But there might be somebody here, somebody whose family is from the Core, who he might be interested in talking to. And not want to kill. Any thoughts on this, Ms. Sandra Caroline Ruger-Gascoigne?"

Scruggs sat still. Rocky wandered over and she scratched his head. "I don't want to do this. One of you should take care of it."

Ana shook his head. "We can't. Up to you this time."

Scruggs continued to scratch Rocky. He wagged his tail. "What do you think, boy?"

Rocky wagged his tail again and barked. Something was going on, something dangerous from the way the others smelled. But the pack was together. Wasn't that good enough?

"Rocky says yes." Dirk nodded. "What's it going to be?"

"Fine." Scruggs stood. "But we'll do it my way. Centurion?"

"Yes?"

"I may have to make some unpopular decisions. If I asked you to, could you shoot the crew? The whole crew."

Ana jumped up. "Let me get my guns. Oh boy." He rubbed his hands then pulled himself down to the hatch. "It's like Saturnalia. And my birthday." He stopped at the hatch. "Two birthdays. At the same time."

"*Heart's Desire* has cut acceleration," Silaski said.

"Are you sure?" Monti asked.

"You don't believe me, Captain?"

"Given your record so far, no." Monti played with her screen. "He has cut accel. That's not going to help him escape the admiral. Thanks for the notification, Silaski. But I'm going to keep double-checking you."

"Okay, fair enough." Silaski thought for a moment. "What would I need to do for you to trust me?"

"What?"

"I mean, I know that I'm not the best helmsman." Silaski shrugged. "I did, I did that payment thing, you know, rather than passing the courses. I didn't think I'd need to. But now I realize that if the paperwork says I can do stuff, I should really be able to do some of it."

"Wait, what," Monti said. "You suddenly want to become a competent helmsman and navigator?"

"Yes."

"Why? For the glory of the Empire?"

"I don't want to die." Silaski shrugged again. "You two, you three officers, you're good at your jobs. All three of you can navigate, and run sensors, and, well, do everything I'm trying to do. When I do something wrong, you already know, and you can fix it. What's going to happen to me when I get on some ship where the navigator person is an idiot? I'll crash us into a moon or something, and they won't bother to correct me. Or even know they are supposed to. The more I know, the more I can figure out who to trust."

"So it's self-interest?"

"Yes."

"Good. I was worried for a moment that you were developing a conscientious approach to your job. I see it's straight egotism."

"Mostly." Silaski shrugged again. "It is embarrassing that you two are always correcting me, though."

"Encouragement through social shaming." Monti shook her head. "Fine, I'll take it."

Silaski's board bonged. "Status change." She put a display on the screen. "*Heart's Desire* is now decelerating relative to the admiral's pursuing squadron. Looks like she's stopped running and is closing instead."

Monti reached to check Silaski's sensors, then consciously drew her fingers away. "Very well, helm." She rested her chin on her hands. "That's strange. What's his plan?"

"Not his plan." Hernandez tapped her ear. "*Heart's Desire* is broadcasting a surrender on an all ships frequency."

"The admiral might still destroy him." Monti shook her head. "I hope he has the guts to do it himself, and not get us to do it."

"Not him, the admiral won't be destroying him. He'll be destroying a her."

"...Ruger-Gascoigne out." Devin tilted his head. Carrol at comm was playing the *Heart's Desire's* message for the whole bridge.

"Message repeats," Scruggs's voice continued. "I have captured the ship in the name of the Empress, and seized the traitor Dirk Friedel, and various and sundry members of the rebellion onboard. The ship is secure and under my control. I am decelerating and will rendezvous with the nearest fleet elements to hand over my captives. Sandra Caroline Ruger-Gascoigne out."

Devin slumped back into his headrest. Three-G was hard to move in, but not impossible. Given the geometry of the running *Heart's Desire*, the chasing squadron, and Devin's instruction to come zero-zero to the flagship, five- or even six-G wouldn't get them there much quicker. They could certainly overhaul the squadron, but they couldn't race by them.

"Interesting message," Lionel said. "I'll bet it was pre-recorded."

"Why do you say that?" Devin asked.

"Who uses 'sundry' in a sentence when they're stressed?"

"Everyone, if they got proper schooling."

"Let's see where your schooling has got you." Lionel ticked items off on his fingers. "One, you're in rebellion against the largest empire in this part of space, two, you've been cut off from all your family and friends and home and money, and three, you're charging a battleship with a frigate."

"And its escorts. Don't forget them," Devin said. "Glorious, isn't it?"

"You should have paid more attention in school."

"Probably. Too late now." Devin's console bonged. "And a message from Brigadier Santana. Brigadier, how may I help you?"

"Just asking for a status report, Tribune." The brigadier's voice came clearly over the radio.

"Your voice is suspiciously clear for somebody who is supposed to be on an assault carrier fleeing the system. You should be some great distance behind me, at this point."

"We have been following closely behind, Tribune."

"I don't remember ordering that."

"There's been a lot going on. I'm sure it slipped your mind."

Devin expanded his screen view. There was the *Valhalla* running along behind him. He hadn't noticed the extra blip, focused as he was on the drama ahead. A glance around the bridge revealed guilty-looking officers. None of them had lied to him, they'd only left out a few things.

"Prefect?" He had to push the words out though his compressed chest.

"Tribune?"

"Cut thrust to one-quarter-G. I need to go to my cabin, and I need Imin with me. We have some things to deal with."

Lionel gave the necessary orders and the weight on his chest disappeared. Devin got up and waddled to the control room door.

"How long at this thrust, Tribune?"

"How long do you need to sneak Santana onboard with however many Marines you'd planned on stuffing the ship with?"

"Seventeen minutes if he launches now." Lionel waved at Lieutenant Carrol. She nodded, then brought up a private channel and chattered into it.

"Should be enough time." Devin saluted the bridge. "The Empire."

Devin returned to the bridge twenty-three minutes later. He acknowledged the two new Marines belted into the thrust hammock at the entrance door, and greeted Brigadier Santana, seated at one of the spare bridge consoles. Imin followed him in and sat at a spare console.

"Tribune?" Lionel blinked. "I thought you were out of formal robes?"

"Imin whipped these up for me." Devin seated himself. "How do they look?"

"They look fine to me. Like formal robes should."

"Imin made them out of spare table cloths."

"Table cloths?" Lionel tilted his head. "I never would have guessed. You can sew, Imin?"

Imin looked up. "Oh, yes sir. Took a course on it, years ago."

"Don't you need a sewing machine or something like that?"

"Have one sir. Keep it in the pantry, next to the coding machine."

"Of course you do." Lionel shook his head. "Of course you do. In the pantry, next to the coding machine. Orders, Tribune?"

"Put the status up on the screen." Devin peered at the display. "Just to confirm. Can we catch the *Canopus* before she overruns the *Heart's Desire*?"

Lionel shook his head. "No."

"With our weapons, can we destroy *Canopus* before then?"

"Not before then, no."

"Can we damage her—"

"Tribune." Lionel shook his head. "I'll go up against her if you ask. I think we have a chance of winning a one-on-one with her, but even if we do, there are other ships in-system. Including a cruiser. The answer for any question that involves *Canopus* and the other escorts is 'not-really, but I'm willing to try."

"Very well. The convoy?"

"It's ours. We've got almost every ship. They're all heading for the jump limit now. They'll hit the rendezvous. All the opposing naval ships are out of position. They can't stop it."

"How much fighting?"

"Almost none. Shots fired on two ships. Twenty-three of the captured ships halted and took instructions so well, the Marines assigned to them decided they didn't need a guard."

"Very well. So, mission accomplished, we can head out of here with a job well done, except for the possible destruction of the *Heart's Desire*."

"Ms. Ruger-Gascoigne has sent a message—"

"I heard it. It should help. It might now. Very well, record a message."

"Sir?"

"Order all the naval ships in-system to rendezvous. Ours and theirs. Find the nearest point we can all get to at the same time, somewhere we can dock or transfer with shuttles, or whatever. I want all the captains of all warships to be together for a discussion."

Villa, the navigator, bent to her screen. Rudnar did as well. Both typed furiously.

Lionel glanced back to Devin. "On what ship will this discussion be held, Tribune?"

"On the *Canopus*, of course. The *Pollux* is a wonderful ship, but too small for this. We'll all meet there."

"You're going to surrender yourself to your enemies?"

"Of course not."

"But you're going onto their ship."

"Yes."

"For a meeting?"

"Yes, with all the captains." Devin adjusted his robes. "So we can discuss the current situation in the Empire."

"Bracebridge will have you shot," Lionel said.

"Perhaps." Devin shrugged. "But I have my duty."

"Sirs?" Villa interrupted. "I, that is, we, Rudnar and I. We have courses for the fleet rendezvous. On the screen."

"Excellent. Well done both of you." Devin beamed. "What time will this rendezvous be?"

The two officers conferred, then put a time hack up on the screen. "Late second shift sir."

Devin nodded. "But not third. Imin, what do you think?"

Imin was looking at the screen. "Too late for lunch, Tribune. Too early for dinner."

"Ah? Then..."

"Canapes, Tribune?"

"Canapes." Devin nodded. "Outstanding. Send these orders. And, Imin?"

"Sir?"

"Bring the good wine. The very best." Devin nodded again. "The very, very best."

Chapter 47

"I cannot believe this is happening." Monti adjusted her uniform.

"Which part?" Hooper smoothed her own. "The entire rebel fleet is sailing up under our guns, or that the admiral can't figure out how to get everybody on board his own ship?"

The logistics were complicated. *Hydrogen Pride* had to blast in-system at full speed. Devin's group—the *Pollux* and the *Valhalla*—followed the warships pursuing the *Heart's Desire* at a sedate speed. Bracebridge's warships had pivoted and fired against their previous course, dropping velocity as fast as they could. All the crews hated that. The *Heart's Desire*, even though ahead of the warships, had less velocity to drop. She loafed along until the various fleets converged on her.

"I told you he wasn't hired for his naval experience. Good thing that Captain Mahony figured things out." Captain Mahony had brought the *Hydrogen Pride* in close and launched her pinnaces to collect all the attendees. "What is she doing here?" Monti pointed. Hernandez was climbing into the airlock, with Weeks behind her. Silaski followed.

Hernandez closed the hatch. "I remind you that we're not part of your crew, Monti. We've only been helping out temporarily. We're on Internal Security business."

"Is that so? I thought it was Naval Intelligence business?"

"Both."

"You've forgotten, haven't you?"

Weeks coughed. "At the admiral's request, we're coming to help identify the crew of the *Heart's Desire*, Dirk's ship. We know them all by sight."

Admiral Bracebridge initially screamed threats over the radio. Then his long-suffering naval aide pointed out that, given their current vector and the spatial geometry involved, they couldn't bring the *Pollux* and *Valhalla* to battle unless the two rebel ships let them. The willingness of them to come under his guns, plus the ability to re-concentrate his squadron before engaging was too good to miss. And Captain Mahony's willingness to bring her shuttles into play meant that he could keep *Pollux* within range of *Canopus's* weapons, but out of range of her weapons.

"The admiral asked that?"

"His aide did. After I reminded him."

Hooper blinked twice. Then she turned to Monti. "She's lying again. I'm sure of it."

The ship shook as the *Hydrogen Queen's* shuttle docked with them.

"But they're such elaborate lies." Monti shook her head. "Gotta give her credit for creativity." She smoothed her dress uniform. "Into the lion's den, everybody."

Devin waited until the hatch light lit hard seal, then nod-ded to Imin. The *Pollux's* shuttle was roomy, but with him, Lionel, Imin, four stewards, some of his bridge officers, in-cluding Rudnar, Santana, and four Marines, they rubbed shoulders.

Imin held his ear, listening to his radio.

"Any time, Imin." Devin gestured.

Imin nodded, once, twice. "Understood. Out." He stepped in front of Devin and straightened his uniform. "I oiled the scabbard, Tribune. Should come out like corn through a tabbo."

"Stop fussing. Who were you talking to?"

"Tara. She and I arranged to have all the shuttles arrive at the same time. *Canopus's* boat deck didn't know what to do, they're so discombobulated already. We just need to wait about another forty seconds."

"Tara? Tara Mahony? Captain Tara Mahony?"

"Uh, yes sir. That's her."

"You call her Tara?"

"Know her a long time, Tribune."

"But do you—Imin, are you blushing?"

"No sir."

Devin turned. "Santana, is he blushing?"

"I wouldn't know sir." Santana ignored Imin's red face. "In the case of your steward, I find it's best to mind my own business. Otherwise, he might kill me with a fork."

Imin held the lock door shut while waiting for the signal. Everybody ignored his muttered 'don't need a fork to kill a

Marine' until he got a bong in his ear and swung the door open.

They lined up to exit. Devin glanced back. "Imin, what do your people have there?"

"Chafing dishes sir?"

"Chafing dishes?"

"Best way to keep the soup warm sir."

Devin strode through the lock, his sword swinging, robe swishing, every inch the Imperial Tribune. A squad of Marines waited inside, pointing their gauss rifles. A group of naval officers stood behind them.

"I am Devin, the Lord Lyon," he announced. "Imperial Tribune, Governor of the Verge Sector. Here to see Admiral Bracebridge. Where is he?"

"Sir," the sergeant at the head of the squad said. "By orders of the admiral, you have been stripped of your titles and are under arrest."

"Don't be silly, Sergeant..." Devin craned his head to see his name tape. "Sergeant Paksi. First, you can't strip the powers of an Imperial Tribune. Only the Senate can do that. Second, the admiral is a military official, not civilian. He can't arrest anyone."

"Um. He's the governor of the Verge Sector. That's a civilian appointment."

"No he's not. Not yet. I'm the governor. Until the Emperor relieves me. Or sends a replacement who is duly sworn in, which he hasn't, yet. And he can only arrest me with an Imperial warrant. Do you have an Imperial warrant with my name on it?"

"I have my orders sir."

"From who, Sergeant Paksi?" Brigadier Santana stepped from behind Devin and extended his hand. "Show me these orders."

"Brigadier Santana!" Paksi drew his weapon to his chest. "Sir, I didn't know you were here."

"No problem." Santana smiled. "I see you got your stripe, finally. Congratulations."

"Thank you sir."

Santana turned to the group. "Paksi was with me at St. Barts. He was one of the last ones to get out. Got me out. Marines. Attention."

The Marines with Santana braced. Santana saluted, a full, formal, cross-chest salute. "Sergeant Paksi. Thank you for your service. On my behalf, and all of those you saved." The Marines with him mirrored the salute. "The Empire!"

Paksi flushed, shoved his rifle at the next trooper, then returned the salute. "You shouldn't salute me, General. It's not protocol."

"It should be. Show me your orders, please."

"They were verbal orders sir."

"From who?"

Paksi pointed over his shoulder. "The lieutenant over there sir."

"Well, I countermand them."

"But..." Paksi "You can't countermand them sir."

"I'm a Brigadier General. Of course I can. Those orders are canceled."

'Um. Lieutenant?" The sergeant looked over his shoulder. "Sir, they say—"

"I heard them." The lieutenant behind Paksi wore a custom skinsuit, with a tailored uniform over the top, a uniform that could only have been tailored in the Core. His name tape said 'Heru.' "My instructions supersede theirs."

"No, they do not," Santana said. "I outrank you."

"You're a Marine!"

"Very perceptive, Lieutenant," Santana said. "Glad to know you're good at something. Your service record notwithstanding."

"My service record?" Heru looked confused.

Santana tapped his chest. He, all the Marines, Imin, the naval officers, everyone, were wearing their formal uniforms. The crew of the *Pollux* had been busting pirates and fighting other empires for years, and the Brigadier had brought his combat troops along on operations with them. They all had five or six rows of bright colored decorations on their formal uniforms. Of the Marines holding guns over them, only Paksi approached the number of decorations. The lieutenant had only one row.

"If I understand naval awards correctly, which of course I do, you have the capital system defense medal, one deployment medal, and a good conduct medal." Santana leaned closer. "Third-class good-conduct medal."

"These are the admiral's orders." Heru said. "Sergeant! Arrest these people."

"Um. I'm confused, Lieutenant. You say the admiral said to arrest them, but the Brigadier said not to, and the Tribune here—"

"Arrest them," Heru yelled.

Devin held up his hand. "Everyone, be still. Bring me to the admiral, and we can sort this out. My business is with him, and not with you, and—"

A second lock to their left suddenly banged, and the lights shifted to green as it swung open.

"Expecting more guests, Lieutenant?" Santana asked.

"Sergeant!" Heru yelled louder. "Arrest them now!"

"Sir, I, whoa. Weapons up!" Paksi grabbed his gauss rifle from the trooper next to him. The squad swung their weapons up to point at Devin's party, then back to the opening airlock, then back again. Paksi cursed, then called out names to split their aim. Scruggs marched out of the second airlock with Rocky trotting by her side. Dirk, Ana, Dena, Gavin, and Lee exited in a loose group behind her.

"Hold up!" Paksi's squad pointed gauss rifles at Scruggs. "Drop your weapon!"

"Why?" Scruggs gestured to the group. "I need it to control these criminals. Hey, are you taking custody of them, then? I'll need a receipt."

"Drop your weapon!" Paksi yelled. "Now."

"Drop it?" Scruggs shook her head and held up her shotgun stock first. "This is a custom-made boarding shotgun. Walnut grip. Titanium barrel, nickel-plated. I'm not dropping it on a steel deck. Besides, I'm on your side. I'm here to deliver these criminals to you for justice. Right, Rocky?"

Rocky barked and wagged his tail. Something exciting was going on!

"Regardless of whose side you're on, only officers and Marines on duty can be armed."

"Oh." Scruggs looked over at Devin. "Hello, Tribune Devin."

Devin nodded. "Ms. Ruger-Gascoigne."

"Call me Scruggs. What are you doing here, Tribune?"

"Waiting for these Marines to shoot me."

"Really?" Scruggs looked back to Paksi. "I can do that, if you want, Sergeant. I'm pretty angry with the Tribune. Last time I saw him, he had me arrested, kidnapped and sent to the Core as a prisoner."

"If by that you mean saved your life in a med pod, and then sent you on a luxurious cruise, then well, yes, call it a kidnapping. Pretty cushy one, at that. And by the way." Devin's eyes narrowed. "What did you eat? I got the bill from that trip. It was stupendous."

"Me?" Scruggs shrugged. "Nothing expensive. Basic and trays. I like trays."

"Trays?" Devin said. "Like food trays?"

"Yes."

"I got this bill—"

"Oh, that." Scruggs shrugged again. "That's all the shopping I did. Clothes."

"You bought clothes? You spent all that on clothes?"

"Ma'am. Ms. Scruggs," Paksi interrupted. "You can't have a weapon here. You have to give it to the Marines."

"Even if I'm willing to shoot the Tribune for you?"

"I have no orders to shoot the Tribune ma'am."

"Not even a little bit? I can shoot him in the leg, would that be okay?"

"Ma'am." Paksi shook his head. "You can't have a weapon. Give it to one of the Marines."

"Fine. But you're responsible if any of my prisoners escape." Scruggs gripped her shotgun by the barrel, stepped sideways and handed it across.

To Santana.

The gauss rifles wavered away from Scruggs, then pointed at Santana. He pointed the shotgun at the ceiling and racked a round into it. "Very nice weapon, thank you, Ms. Ruger-Gascoigne."

"Thanks." Scruggs nodded. "And call me Scruggs."

"Why did you do that?" Paksi said.

"You said only the Marines can have guns. He's a Marine."

"He's not—" Paksi shook his head. "I mean… I don't know what I mean. Lieutenant?"

"No guns! Arrest them!"

"I remind you, Sergeant," Santana said. "That I have countermanded those orders."

The lieutenant's face flushed. "And I remind you, that you are Marine officers. And shipboard Marines take orders from the Navy."

Dirk raised his hand. "I'm a naval officer. A sub-commander. That means you can take orders from me!"

"Prove it!" Lieutenant Heru snarled. "Identify yourself."

Dirk cocked his head. "Don't have to. I'm famous. The Butcher of New Madrid! Everybody knows me, knows what

I look like. Knows I was arrested. And knows I'm still a sub-commander!"

Paksi looked closely at Dirk's face, then looked relieved. He shouldered his gauss rifle. "Thank Jove—I mean, your orders sir?"

"Imin." Dirk pointed. "Are those chafing dishes?"

"Yes sir." Imin nodded. "Indeed they are."

"For soup?"

"Three kinds sir. A cold watermelon soup. Pepper seafood chowder, and a spicy ragout of land-boar."

"Outstanding." Dirk rubbed his hands. "My orders? Let's have lunch."

Monti, Hooper, and their crew marched in a moment later from another airlock. Groups of Marines and sailors stood chatting. Hernandez and Weeks greeted Scruggs first, then Devin and his party. Devin smiled as he talked with Hernandez. Weeks hugged Scruggs then moved to chat with Dirk. The Marines all mingled in groups. Imin and his crew had handed out small bowls of soup, cunningly shaped with a spout so you could drink from them without using a spoon. Santana chatted with Ana and let him try the shotgun. Lee stood next to Devin.

The naval lieutenant had disappeared.

"This is awesome." Hooper licked her lips. Imin's people had shoved bowls of soup in their hands as they arrived. "How come we can't eat like this on the *Collingwood*?"

Monti slurped up hers. "Because we're a corvette, we don't have a cook, or a kitchen, or supplies."

"Is this mint?"

"Don't know. What happens next?"

"The beef thing—what's a ragout anyways?"

"Don't know." Hooper shrugged. "Hey, Marine person?" Paksi stood next to them. "What's going on?"

"What?" Paksi shrugged. "The admiral wants the Tribune here stripped of his titles, the lieutenant wants him shot, they both want all of those crews arrested, but we have no warrants, at least none that mean anything, I've got generals and sub-commanders and Tribunes and governors issuing conflicting orders."

"What's the charges?" Monti asked. "For the Tribune, I mean."

"Fomenting rebellion," Paksi said.

Monti turned in a circle, watching the thirty people in the boat bay. "Fomenting rebellion? Looks to me like the only thing they're fomenting is lunch."

"Same to me," Paksi said.

"So what happens now?"

"Lieutenant ran off to the bridge. I'm sure he's talking with the admiral's staff now."

"And after he talks to him?"

Paksi shrugged. "Not sure. Admiral will say arrest them. Tribune will say he can't. Admiral will say shoot them. Brigadier will say no."

"What are you going to do then?"

"Do?" Paksi shrugged again. "Do? I think I'll get me some of that soup, that's what I'll do."

Chapter 48

"He can't just shoot you," Santana said. "The Marines won't stand for it."

Devin supped on his soup and shrugged. The landing bay had evolved to a festive atmosphere. Many of the Marines had served with Santana before. The Core officers were jealous of all the awards and experience Devin's crew had. The crew of the *Heart's Desire* were minor celebrities. Many crews watched Susy the Newsy, and everybody loved Imin's soup. "He could. I'm totally exposed here."

"Marines won't let him. They're confused, but they won't shoot you. Or me."

"You sure of that?"

"Bet my life on it."

"You have." Devin handed his bowl to a steward. "Everybody been fed?"

"Steward Imin says he'd like five more minutes, Tribune."

Devin surveyed the boat deck. As Imin had predicted to him earlier, the combination of a formal uniforms and extra-special snacks had reduced tension. Seeing their commanders chatting with a fully togate Tribune slurping their lunch had confused *Canopus's* Marines. And confused Marines fell back on two behaviors. Wait for orders or kill everyone in sight. With no obvious threat other than their own senior officers, all of *Canopus's* Marines and all the boat bay crew had joined the lines for soup and crackers.

After all, they reasoned, they could always kill everyone later.

Devin made chitchat. Imin checked his comm and mouthed the word 'bridge.'

"Attention!" Devin yelled. The bay quieted. "Finish your meals, please, and return to your duties. I have given Admiral Bracebridge time to appear, but he has slunk away to the bridge. I shall go see him. Sub-commander Friedel, you are with me."

"I'm coming too." Scruggs pointed at the *Heart's Desire* crew. "Somebody owes me a lot of money."

Devin nodded. "Very well."

Paksi and the rest of *Canopus's* crew hurried to drink the last of their soup. "We'll escort you sirs."

"Better that you stay here, and guard the boat bay, Sergeant. In fact, you're ordered to stay here."

"Thank you sir." Paksi took the cup one of the other Marines gave to him. "But I think, oh...."

After Imin and his stewards handed over the last cups, they reached under the chafing table and pulled out gauss carbines. Shorter than the regular rifles, but just as deadly. Lionel and the rest of *Pollux's* officers armed themselves, then herded *Canopus's* crew into a corner.

"Sorry, Paksi," Santana said. "But you're out of it now. Whatever happens in the next few minutes isn't your fault."

"Seizing a ship by force is treason," Paksi said.

Devin handed his soup bowl to a steward, then held up his hands. "Not sure how we're going to seize the ship. Neither the sub-commander nor I am armed. But thank you for your confidence."

Lionel stepped up to Devin and whispered, "Please take some Marines. Take Imin. Take me."

"No." Devin shook his head. "This is about leadership. My leadership. I'll deal with this upstart myself. If I can't talk a single bridge crew around, what am I worth?"

"A core bridge crew!"

"I'm a noble. I'm the Tribune Devin. They'll listen to me."

"And if they don't?"

"I have Dirk. He'll help."

"By seducing their women?"

"He's a noble too. And Ms. Gascoigne will be with me. She's famous."

"I still think—"

"Keep thinking, but I need you here. Use the Marines and the officers. Take control of the ship, like we planned."

Lionel cursed but issued his orders. The Marines cancelled each other out. Marines didn't want to fight Marines, and with Santana there to defuse things, they were already shouldering weapons and waiting to see what happened. *Pollux's* officers performed the same function—he dispersed them through the ship to talk the other naval officers around. Their experience, earnestness, and chests full of medals made them hard to argue with.

Villa already had the captain and crew of that corvette, *Collingwood*, nodding at her explanations. Hernandez and Weeks could take care of any Internal Security people.

The various naval and Marine crew in the bay didn't have a full idea of what was going on, but they knew there was some sort of problem. And whatever else they knew about Tribune Devin, they knew he had a reputation for solving problems.

Devin led up the stairs, Dirk following, Scruggs behind them. Rocky wagged his tail and trotted along.

"Tribune!" Devin turned.

The *Collingwood's* captain, Monti, was waving. "I got a comm. I'm supposed to be at an all-captain's meeting on the bridge." She looked down. "The admiral is angry with me being late."

Devin laughed. "Well, we'll explain why together. Come along, then."

Monti clambered up behind him. The procession traipsed up the stairs to the bridge level and marched forward. It took several minutes to navigate the corridors and hatches—battleships, even old ones, were big—and reach the bridge corridor.

"Where is everybody?" Dirk gestured to the empty corridors.

"Imin contacted everybody he knew on the ship. Santana did as well. We didn't ask for any promises, just to stay out of sight. Let their seniors sort this out."

"Not much of a seizing the ship for the Empire," Dirk said.

"These are Imperial Marines and sailors," Devin said. "Following properly given orders. The fact that the person at the top is not fit to give them is not their fault."

"What happened to 'kill everyone and let Jove sort them out'?" Dirk asked.

"Jove is not here right now." Devin stopped. "There will be no violence."

"You can't capture a ship without violence," Dirk said.

"We'll find out." Devin proceeded in the silence.

Scruggs walked behind the Tribune's party. She couldn't see over Devin and Dirk, so she side-stepped, holding her shotgun. The *Collingwood's* captain bumped into her.

"Sorry," Monti said and introduced herself. Scruggs did the same.

"I know all about you," Monti said. "One of my crew watches Susy the Newsy."

"Susy?" Scruggs rolled her eyes. "She's a horrible gossip."

"Whatever. Why are you here? On the way to the bridge, I mean?"

"We're here to watch the Tribune take command of this ship," Scruggs said.

"Seize command, you mean. A rebel."

"Nope." Scruggs shook her head. "The Tribune is an honorable man. He hasn't heard from his sister, the Empress, in months. I hear nobody has seen the Emperor either. Is that true?"

Monti shrugged. "I didn't exactly talk to him myself on a regular basis, before. Could be true, though."

"Well, the Tribune is here to fix that," Scruggs said.

"That's it? That's your rebellion? The Tribune's sister is mad at him, and the Emperor's busy, so you revolt? That's a stupid reason for treason."

"It's not that," Scruggs said. "The Empire is falling apart. You can't see it in the Core, but you can in the Verge. Not enough ships to suppress piracy. Incompetent Imperial Advisors. Old ships that break down and aren't replaced. The Confeds and the Nats are backing rebellions on a dozen planets. Trade is down. And the only Imperial officials are venal non-entities. Incompetent venal non-entities."

"Wow." Monti grinned. "Lots of big words. But that doesn't mean a thing. Look, I'm just along for the ride here. I'm an Imperial officer. Well, Imperial Naval Volunteer Reserve officer, but I support the Empire."

"Do you?" Scruggs waved her hand. "You support all this mess?"

"We do as we're told. That's how the Empire works."

"Does it?" Scruggs said. "Work, I mean? You know what an idiot that admiral is. I heard he got the entire crew of a destroyer killed by accident."

"It's not a question of following him," Hooper said. "It's following the rules. Other people fix things like that. We drive the ships, they hire the admirals."

"And fire them," Scruggs added.

"Think he's going to get fired?"

"That's why the Tribune's here. To fire him."

"What if he doesn't want to get fired?"

Scruggs tapped her shotgun. "Then he'll need help."

"You're horribly outnumbered."

"We are."

"And also, I hate to admit, very brave."

"Well," Scruggs looked at Monti. "There's different types of bravery. There's defending what you promised to defend, even if it kills you. Deciding that you're wrong and correcting it is a whole other type of bravery."

Two of *Canopus's* Marines guarded the bridge entrance doors, standing at parade rest.

"Sir?" the right hand one asked.

"I am Devin, the Lord Lyon. I will speak with Admiral Lord Bracebridge. I am unarmed."

The Marine pointed behind Devin. "And these folks sir?"

"Witnesses," Devin said.

The Marine thought that over, then turned to the bridge comm and muttered into it. The other glanced down. "Is that a sword sir?"

"Yes." Devin nodded. "My senatorial sword. That is my nefarious plan. Board one of the Empire's most powerful warships, subdue the armed crew and take control of it with just a sword. A daring plan, don't you think?"

"Sir."

"I thought so too." Devin pointed at his robes. "And imagine what I could do if I wore pants."

Both Marines laughed. The second one nodded at Scruggs. "The young lady has a shotgun sir."

"She does. She's not under my authority. She says she needs to drop off some prisoners or something. I haven't sorted that one out yet. If you want her shotgun, you have to ask her."

"No." Scruggs shook her head and stepped out from the group. "You can't have it. Not until I deliver these prisoners."

The Marine gave her a look. She gave it back. They exchanged looks for a while. Then he shrugged. "Brigadier commed us. Not my issue." The two Marines saluted, then pushed the bridge open control.

Devin stepped over the hatch coaming . The bridge was packed. Every station was full. He'd never been on a battleship before, and it was bigger than he expected. He stopped and surveyed the room as his crew crowded in behind him. The watchers might have thought he was being regal. In reality, he didn't know what the admiral looked like.

None of the assembled officers were familiar. And since they'd all served in the core squadrons, near the Capitol, they all wore gorgeous custom uniforms that obscured their rank markings. Devin couldn't even pick out who were the senior officers.

"Lord Bracebridge?" Devin tracked from face to face. *Jove's knees, shouldn't the commander of a fleet look the part?* That's the first thing I'll do. Institute some proper uniform discipline on these pretty birds.

A short, peevish, grumpy-looking man stood from one the consoles. "Why aren't you dead? Why isn't he in jail! Seize him. He's charged with treason!"

"I am taking this ship in the name of the Empress," Devin said. "You are dismissed." He glared at Bracebridge across the bridge. "Don't make me—"

"Make you do what?" Bracebridge folded his arms. "Do your job? Your job was to stay in the Verge and fight pirates, not attack the Verge like the rebel you are. Not destroy the Empire."

"I have not destroyed any empire," Devin said. "In fact, I've been careful to not even damage the Empire. I've limited my destruction on ships and crews to the bare minimum. Jove's knees, I even came here alone, well, without Marines, and unarmed." Devin raised his voice and addressed the others. "I appeal to you all. Soldiers and sailors of the Empire. We stand at a crossroads. The Chancellor has unlawfully seized power. It is necessary to remove this usurper—"

"Hands up or I shoot!" Bracebridge pointed a pistol at Devin.

Devin wrinkled his brow. "Where were you hiding that?"

"Sash." Bracebridge pointed at the swath of fabric tied at his waist.

"Well." Devin nodded. "I'll speak to my steward. Next time, I want a sash."

"Nobody cares what you want, Tribune." Bracebridge pointed the pistol at Devin. "I'm here. I'm in charge. The Chancellor appointed me, yes. But what of it?"

"The citizens of the Empire deserve better."

"The citizens? The citizens?" Bracebridge whooped. "You're a noble, a Tribune. What do you care? Do you think any of these officers here cares what the citizens think? It's bad enough that we have to have Marine or naval officers who aren't of the noble class, but we even have to let all these stupid colonials have real jobs. Look there, at that corvette captain, from the backwoods of New Melbourne, or somewhere.

We can barely understand them. They're rustic idiots. They're not fit to rule."

"That is not—"

"And are you really any different?" Bracebridge asked. "You and your sister. Nobles as well. You own a planet. Your sister gave you a frigate to get you away from her. Oh, I've heard all about you, Tribune Devin. Your sanctimonious snootiness, your 'special meals' that not one in a hundred ships has. You baby your crew, you fill them with talk of the Empire all the time, but do you really mean anything? What have you ever given up? You travel the galaxy in gold-plated luxury, with a crew as your personal servants, you play act as if you're some tin-plated god. You're a poser and a coward, Tribune."

Devin blinked. "I'm here unarmed. I think that's brave."

"That's not brave. That's just foolhardy. You think you're so special, I won't kill you. Well, I will. You and all your troops and your friends here. The Chancellor sent me."

"You can't do that."

"I can. You'll die as easily as all those poor, stupid, trusting Marines you've dragged here."

"I will restore the Emperor—"

"You brainless twit!" Bracebridge yelled. "Do you think any of these brainless, useless, worthless low-class twits care who the Emperor is? Have any of them asked who he is? As long as they get along in their stupid little lives, do any of them care?"

Devin stopped. He opened his mouth, then shut it. *Well, maybe if he...*

BLAM

The shotgun boomed. Bracebridge bounced back across the bridge, blood spattering the wall and the two officers behind him. His nearly headless corpse slammed into the wall, then slid down.

"I care who is Emperor." Scruggs stepped forward, shotgun smoking. "I care."

Chapter 49

"There was no need to shoot him!" Devin raged at Scruggs. The Marines had come running onto the bridge, secured the scene, and wisely bumped the problem upstairs. Imin, Santana and Lionel had arrived minutes after their comm call.

"Every need," Scruggs said, wiping blood off Devin's robes. "Imin, the Tribune got splattered."

"We could have come to an agreement," Devin yelled.

"Not likely." Dirk wiped blood off his face. "Imin, when you're done with the Tribune, I could use a towel, or something."

"I've sent some folks for it sir."

Devin wiped his hands. "I cannot be seen to have taken command by violence—"

Santana held up his hand. "Yes, you can. It was necessary. You needed a fleet. Now you have one."

Imin stepped up and dabbed at Devin's robes. Devin raged for a few minutes, cursing Scruggs, Bracebridge, shooting, the universe, and robes. Imin tried, but finally, he gave up. "I'm sorry, Tribune. But your robes are ruined. Again."

"Never mind the robes. What am I going to do with her?" Devin pointed a silent Scruggs. "Why, why did you do that?"

Scruggs nodded. "It needed doing."

"Why kill him?"

"You started a war. People get killed in wars."

Devin gaped. The others hid smiles. Devin recovered. "I'm putting you under arrest."

"No, you're not," Scruggs said.

"What do you mean?"

"Your people won't allow it. I just saved your life. And maybe theirs. And probably the Empire. We need a new Emperor. I can't do it. They can't. Only you can be the Emperor. So we're not going to let you die."

"But, but—"

"Excuse me sir," Imin patted Devin's arm. "I have something to say."

Everybody on the bridge quieted. Imin didn't speak without reason. Devin blinked. "Go ahead, Imin."

"Tribune. Prefect. Brigadier. All of you here." Imin waved around the bridge. "There is one thing we have to keep in mind. Ms. Scruggs?"

"Yes?" Scruggs tilted her head up.

Imin walked back to where Scruggs had stood at the back of the bridge and paced off the distance from her to the bloodstain where the admiral had been. "That was an excellent shot." Imin grinned at her. "A really excellent shot."

"And with that out of the way, let me be the first to congratulate you on your promotion, Admiral Mahony," Devin said. "I'm sure you'll serve the Empire well."

"I plan to, Tribune, I plan to." Former Captain and now Rear Admiral Tara Mahony, Imperial Navy Reserve, answered. Her smile filled the viewscreen of the battleship *Canopus*.

"And don't worry, after we get these ships settled, we'll be along to pick you up, and form a task force. I have plans."

"I'm sure you do. With your permission, Tribune, this convoy has a long way to go. And if we're to make the jump windows your staff navigator has proposed, I'll have to get these ships moving. We have two gravity assists, and very tight jump spacing."

Devin looked down from the screen at the seemingly enormous span of bridge in front of him. The *Canopus* was so huge, there were thirty-two consoles on this bridge. He didn't even know the names of all the bridge officers.

He did know the name of the owner of the red-faced acting lieutenant at the secondary navigation console. "Well, if Acting Lieutenant Rudnar has given you too difficult a course, you have my permission to thrash a few ship masters."

"No need, Tribune. It's difficult, but it will save us a few days' transit. And most important, it saves us nearly nine percent fuel on the usual course. There isn't a freighter captain alive who won't take himself through six-Gs if he saves fuel in the long run."

"Faster service for his customers?"

"More profit." Mahony nodded. "Fuel cost comes right out of operating profit. Less fuel, more money for the captain."

"Of course. Money trumps logic. *Pollux*—sorry, *Canopus* out."

Devin cut the connection and brooded as he examined the bridge. They were heading to the jump limit, and he had lots of paperwork to do. Promotions, demotions, executions. And an extraordinary amount of documentation to review from Raka Flintheart and Francis Rail at Verge Development, asking for more tax concessions. He'd have to win this war quickly or bankrupt the Empire. He thumbed his agreement on laws regarding corporate tax structure. *I don't understand all of this, but I need the money. Need to get somebody who knows this involved in it. I wonder if Ms. Gascoigne could do it?*

Not sure what to do next, he brought up a private connection to Lionel. "Status, Prefect?"

"The fleet is at jump stations," Lionel said. "All personnel transfers completed. The captains report ready."

"I'm worried about the others. The other captains."

"Villa will be fine on *Pollux*. The crew know her and trust her."

"I meant the other captains on the other ships. Especially the…what's his name on the light cruiser here."

"Him." Lionel nodded. "What's his name? I've got Trevor and Lukas over there to watch him. And some of Imin's friends. I'm waiting for a report."

"If he doesn't cut it?"

Lionel shrugged. "Maybe we'll put that corvette captain in his place. Monti? She seemed to know what she's about."

"Put a Naval Volunteer Reserve Officer in charge of a light cruiser?"

"Or put her in charge of the destroyer and move the destroyer captain over."

"What about putting Llewling there…"

"He's a reserve captain. Experienced ship-handler, but no real combat training. He's better running all the support ships—"

He and Lionel talked moving captains for a while. Nothing was going to happen right away. They were taking their new 'fleet,' really a flotilla, for maneuvers to see how things worked out.

"There's bound to be changes," Lionel said. "We'll know more once we start making mistakes."

Devin grimaced. "Like I did. I should have come on board guns blazing. Then we'd have taken the ship. We'd still have that corvette. "One of the remaining corvettes had quietly slipped away during a jump test. Probably to go warn the Capital.

"Well," Lionel said. "You were trying to run a rebellion without killing good people."

"What do you mean?"

"Up until now, you've killed bad people. Criminals. Pirates. Officers who disobeyed your orders. Now that you've got this started, it's a real rebellion. We need to win, quickly. You can't soft foot around."

"My methods so far have been a mistake, haven't they?"

"Yes." Lionel turned from across the bridge and stared at him. "That was nearly a fatal mistake. Don't make another one. We can't afford it."

The *Heart's Desire's* quarter-G acceleration was light enough that when Scruggs bounced Rocky's ball off the bulkhead, Rocky jumped after it and bounced off the ceiling to catch it.

"That is one happy dog," Dena said. Rocky woofed his reply around the ball clutched firmly in his mouth.

"Glad somebody's happy."

"What's with you?"

"I feel bad."

"Because you shot that admiral?"

"No. All the others who got shot. There was no need for that. I should have waited." Scruggs's shooting of the admiral had secured the bridge. But there had been other incidents. Scruggs had been involved in a few.

"No, you shouldn't have. The Tribune was supposed to talk his way out of that. It didn't work. You did what you had to do. And your shooting the admiral meant that you'd won before you started."

"I guess so." Scruggs sighed. "The centurion is proud of me. He says always start a fight on your own terms. Not theirs."

"That's what you did." Dena tugged the ball in Rocky's mouth. Rocky fake-growled. "Where is everybody?"

"Centurion is back in the med pod. He's worse than he looks."

"The cancer's back?"

"It never left. Gavin's doing something engineering-y down back. Dirk and Lee are talking to the Tribune. Lee wants to go see the Empress."

"Isn't the Empress a prisoner? And won't the Chancellor guy kill her when he hears about this battle?"

"Devin and Dirk think he won't hear it for a while. Lee wants to sneak into the Core sector and meet up with some Praetorians. She thinks they'll come to her side when they know what's going on with the Empire."

"Wouldn't they already know? And wouldn't they have already done something about it if they cared?"

Scruggs threw Rocky's ball down the corridor. Rocky bounded after it. "You'll have to ask Lee."

Dena pursed her lips. "I'll bet we could find some good parties in the Core sector. With you being a wealthy heiress and all."

"Is that all you think of? Parties?"

"Nope." Dena shook her head. "I think about men a lot too. But seriously, Scruggs, I was supposed to rot married to some old rancher dude on a backwater planet while my sisters stole my best clothes. Now I'm with a bunch of desperados. We have our own ship and we're out to save the Empire. How much more exiting can it be?"

"And how do we do that exactly?"

Dena shrugged. "No idea. But Dirk and the Tribune and all those serious people, they can figure it out. Like the old man said, that's officers' jobs."

"About that. Guess what." Scruggs rummaged in her skin suit pockets. "Look at this." She handed Dena a paper.

"Well, well, well. What have we here." Dena grinned. "If it isn't the consequence of your own actions." She read the document out loud "Confidence, faith. Here we go. Second lieutenant in the Imperial Naval Volunteer Reserve? You volunteered for the Navy?"

"Was voluntold. I think Dirk made the Tribune do it."

"Well! You're an officer now. Am I supposed to call you ma'am or something?"

"Yes."

"Well, you can kiss my hairy buttocks ma'am." Dena laughed.

The intercom bonged. Lee's voice came through. "We finished downloading the courses we need from the *Canopus*. We're off to see the Empress."

"Outstanding," Scruggs said.

"Would the newly minted second lieutenant like to come to the bridge to observe the jump sequence?"

"No."

"That wasn't a suggestion," Lee said. "Pilot Dirk is a naval commander, so he'll be handling your naval education. He requires your attention so he can teach you a few things."

Dena laughed. "Well, listen to that. Him getting all teachery. When you get up there, remind him, there was this thing we used to do, where we—"

"On my way." Scruggs mashed the intercom off. "Never mind, Dena." She marched off.

Rocky watched her, his ball gripped in his mouth. He turned to Dena hopefully.

"Sure, Rocky, give it here." Rocky dropped the ball and Dena tossed it down the corridor. "Guess what, Rocky!"

Rocky wagged his tail.

"We're going to the Core. The real Core. The big cheese. The whole shebang. The heart of the Empire. Never thought I'd get there."

Rocky's tail thrashed even more. His tail thumped on the bulkhead, but he kept his eye on the ball. Dena tossed it, and Rocky jumped and caught it in midair, then dropped it at her feet.

Dena looked down. "Well, there you go, Rocky. Adventure awaits!"

Rocky barked once. He liked adventures.

50

Books by Andrew Moriarty

Adventures of a Jump Space Accountant
Trans Galactic Insurance
Orbital Claims Adjustor
Third Moon Chemicals
A Corporate Coup
The Jump Ship
The Military Advisors
Revolt in the Palace
Decline and Fall of the Galactic Empire
Imperial Deserter
Imperial Smuggler
Imperial Mercenary
Imperial Hijacker
Imperial Privateer
Imperial Raider

J oin my mailing list and get a free ebook

Thanks for reading. I hope you enjoyed it. Word-of-mouth reviews are critical to independent authors. Please consider leaving a review on Amazon or Goodreads or wherever you purchased this book.

If you'd like to be notified of future releases, please join my mailing list. I send a few updates a year, and if you subscribe you get a free ebook copy of *Sigma Draconis IV*, a short novella in the Jake Stewart universe. You can also follow me on Amazon, or follow me on BookBub, or even follow me on Goodreads or Facebook!

Andrew Moriarty

52

ABOUT THE AUTHOR

Andrew Moriarty has been reading science fiction his whole life, and he always wondered about the stories he read. How did they ever pay the mortgage for that spaceship? Why doesn't it ever need to be refueled? What would happen if it broke, but the parts were backordered for weeks? And why doesn't anybody ever have to charge sales tax? Despairing on finding the answers to these questions, he decided to write a book about how spaceships would function in the real world. Ships need fuel, fuel costs money, and the accountants run everything.

He was born in Canada, and has lived in Toronto, Vancouver, Los Angeles, Germany, Park City, and Maastricht. Previously he worked as a telephone newspaper subscriptions salesman, a pizza delivery driver, a wedding disc jockey, and a technology trainer. Unfortunately, he also spent a great deal of time in the IT industry, designing networks and configuring routers and switches. Along the way, he picked up an ex-spy with a predilection for French Champagne, and a whippet with a murderous possessiveness for tennis balls. They live together in Brooklyn.

Please buy his books. Tennis balls are expensive.

9 781956 556261